I0771278

BRIZ AND BAYLA

THE BRONZE AGE BOUNTY HUNTERS

Also by Jeramy Goble

Fantasy:

Coven Queen

<u>Wrathlore</u>
Eulogy for the Dawn (Coming 2020)

Science-fiction/space opera:

<u>The Akallian Tales Trilogy:</u>
Souls of Astraeus
Games of Astraeus
Fates of Astraeus

Noachian
Books

North Carolina

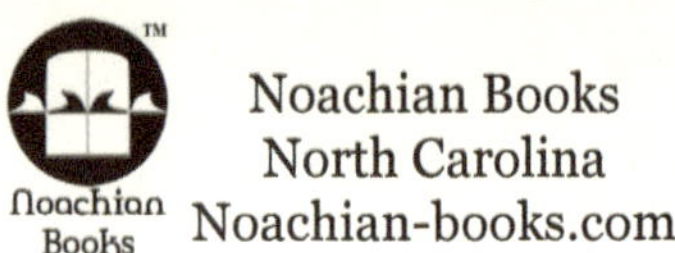

Noachian Books
North Carolina
Noachian-books.com

Noachian Books and the portrayal of a flooded Martian silhouette, with stone tablet insets, are trademarks of Noachian Books

Printed in the United States of America

jeramygoble.com
facebook.com/JeramyGoble
twitter.com/JeramyGoble
Cover art by Pedro Krüger Garcia
Book & jacket design by Jeramy Goble

Publisher's Cataloging-in-Publication Data

Names: Goble, Jeramy, author.
Title: Briz and Bayla : the Bronze Age bounty hunters / Jeramy Goble.
Description: Maggie Valley, NC : Noachian Books, 2018. | Series: Moving targets, bk. 1.
Identifiers: ISBN 978-0-9898841-9-8 (hardcover) | ISBN 978-0-9990435-4-7 (paperback) | ISBN 978-0-9990435-3-0 (ebook)
Subjects: LCSH: Egypt--Civilization--To 332 B.C.--Fiction. | Magic, Egyptian--Fiction. | Bounty hunters--Fiction. | Revenge--Fiction. | Fantasy fiction. | Historical fiction. | BISAC: FICTION / Fantasy / Action & Adventure. | FICTION / Fantasy / Historical. | FICTION / Historical / Ancient. | FICTION / Occult & Supernatural. | GSAFD: Fantasy fiction. | Historical fiction. | Occult fiction.
Classification: LCC PS3607.O26 B75 2018 (print) | LCC PS3607.O26 (ebook) | DDC 813/.6--dc23.
First Edition

10 9 8 7 6 5 4 3 2 1

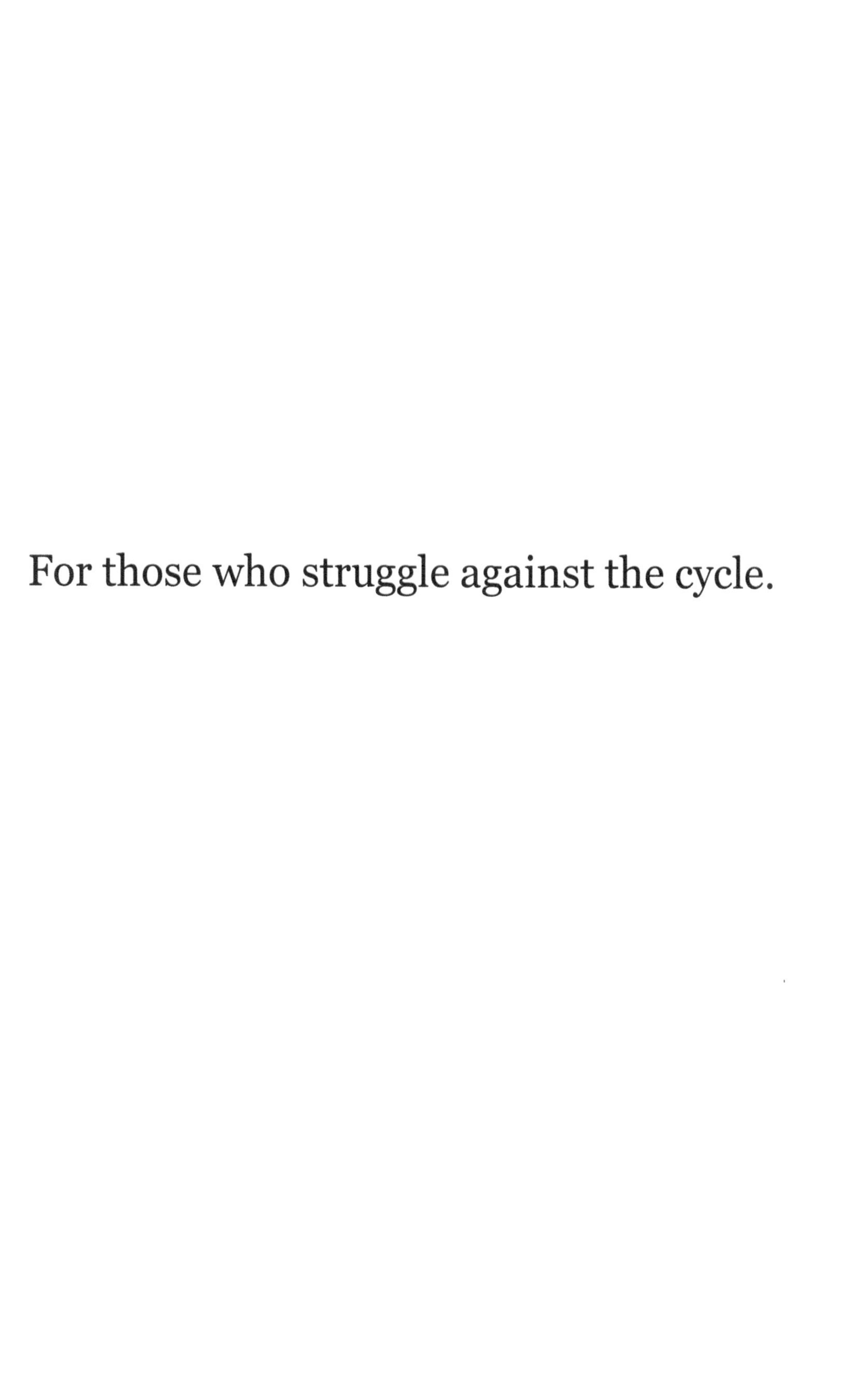

For those who struggle against the cycle.

38th Year of Mentuhotep II

Chapter One - The Double Stinger

Briz

Bounties for these scorpion beasts don't come up very often, and that's fine with me. A scorpiron's outer scales are as hard as rock and resist even the newest bronze blades. Their tails pack as much punch as the fattest man's legs but whip about like the thinnest woman's arms. And then there's the stinger and venom. Lethal. But life is lethal after all. And until the world takes me down, I'll take my chances if the pay is right.

I knelt behind a tree and peered around at the nest long enough for the patrol to circle their large home four times. The tree was the closest object of cover before a long, flat expanse leading to the nest. A thick sandstorm was rolling in and all my squinting made it hard to maintain a clear line of sight on the patrol. It took them a while to complete the circuit, and while I was glad to have the storm for cover, I worried the patrol would pass before I felt good about making my final approach.

As I monitored them, I used the time to dip into a pouch and scrub myself in a slurry I made from local sand

and scorpiron urine. It took me days to collect that mess. And even through the wind of the storm the smell found a way to sting my nose.

Ugh. At least you scorps pay well, I thought.

After the patrol passed a fourth time, I waited for their torchlight to disappear around the side and sprinted out.

The light from the nearest fire helped me keep my bearings. I stayed low to the ground but slowed to a jog as I neared the fire. Before its light could spoil my approach, I cut off diagonally for a darker edge of the nest. The wet sand on my skin—cool at first—started to dry and itch.

In one movement I flipped my bow over my shoulder and came back with my club—a memento I took from my last scorpiron bounty. It's a huge femur type of bone. Almost twice as long as a human femur, I'd say. I've collected horns, tails, scales, and skulls from other jobs, but my scorpiron leg bone is the only one that's been of practical use to me. It serves as a pretty decent club. I get it dipped in bronze every so often to protect it from chipping and splintering, and the metal adds a bit of weight from just above my hands up to the business end of the thing. It makes a mess when it smacks into something, but it's effective.

I pinched one eye closed to keep it accustomed to the darkness—so I could see better once I was away from the fire. I snuggled up to the outside of the edge of the nest even more and knelt down on a knee. While closing my other eye to help it catch up, I listened.

The wind whistled and the sand scratched at my eyes and filtered through the brush. Occasionally, the closest fire would pop and crackle. *No sounds of the scorpirons yet.* Even with cloth around my mouth, my skin crawled as my teeth slid along on the grit and persistent sand that found its way in.

I opened my eyes and blinked quickly before setting off along the edge of the nest again. By design, paths into and out of the nests were infrequent and not easily noticeable—to try and deter would-be attackers from doing exactly what I was trying to do. I had no other choice but to follow the edge of the nest until I found an opening, but I crept along in the same direction as the patrol to maximize the time I had.

From the previous scorpiron bounties I've taken, I learned that as a species, all these humanoid, scorpion things construct and refine their nests with similar designs. The younger warriors, without families, live and work towards the outside of the nest. What I would call officers and leaders live and work in the next ring of the nest, with the females and young being protected and living in the center. From all I could gather, my target would be located in one of the interior rings. Again, I had no desire to deal with, or kill anyone but my bounty. There's no money in extra killing.

I traced around the edge of the nest longer than I wanted to—so much so that I caught up to the faintest hints of the patrol's torchlight. But just as I saw them, I came across a trail cutting into the bushes. While waiting for the patrol to move on, I closed my eyes again and focused on every sound I could identify before entering the nest. The wind continued to howl, but there wasn't a fire nearby. This time, I was able to make out faint sounds of hissing and clicking, and the odd hint of broken, human-sounding syllables. There wasn't anything I could understand, but I didn't care. All I knew is that I wanted to steer clear of those noises.

But some new sounds found me anyway.

The conversational clicks and light hissing of the patrol grew louder. With a violent twist of my neck I turned and saw the patrol's light returning.

They must be changing it up! I panicked internally. *Reversing direction?*

I had nowhere to go. It was too late to run back out to the cover of the trees, and the nest's entryway was too exposed. *They might see me when they walk by.* I wasn't sure how far down the initial path I would have to go before finding somewhere to hide.

I've got to take them, I decided.

With a gentle tip-toe I stepped just inside the nest's entrance, spun to face out, and crouched around the corner.

My heart raced as I held my club over my shoulders. The chatty snips and pops grew louder. I prepared to make a lethal lunge.

Hints of stirring shadows slid into view just ahead of me. They grew longer and darker as the scorps' contrasting torchlight approached with them.

Maybe they won't turn. Maybe they won't look.

The first of the two scorps stepped in front of the entryway. I wiggled my club as the second scorp stepped into view—both of them staring straight ahead. I pushed up on the balls of my feet as they both took another step, and then another. With another step they almost passed the entryway. The focus of my vision blurred from a quick pulse of adrenaline as my anticipation couldn't decide whether to attack or be relieved.

Just one more stride, and they'll pass me.

Inches from passing the entryway, the scorp closest to me turned to look into the nest.

Did it see me?

I couldn't risk it.

I launched up from the ground and came off my feet as I brought my poised club down on top of the closest scorp's head. I didn't want to give either of them time to squeal, hiss, or pop a warning to the rest of the nest. But I didn't want to kill them either. Scorps let off a nasty stench when they die, which would be just as much an alarm as their sounds. I just needed them unconscious.

The first scorp crumbled to its knees and slumped onto its side. The second one sucked in a massive breath and ripped out a reverse hiss of crackling rips. But it started out soft and didn't last even a second. I smashed it in one side of its face and sent it stumbling before following up with a return slam on its other side. It too crashed over onto its chest like a rotten tree.

After taking a second to stare at them, I froze and stifled my panting to listen while scanning the darkness.

No new sounds.

I looked back at the scorps and sighed.

You better not be dead.

After taking a second to drag them out of view of the entryway, I squeezed my club and entered the nest.

The shapes and scale of my surroundings grew more defined as the nest's paths became increasingly protected from the sandstorm. My eyes adjusted as much as they were going to and made the most of the bit of moonlight persisting through the storm overhead. My confidence grew as I crept deeper into the nest. The wide paths that accommodated the bipedal scorpirons resembled well-beaten game trails and allowed me to move quickly and confidently.

This latest scorpiron I'm after is—what I call—a gatherer. Gatherers seem to be part of the elite in a particular nest. I've seen them lead raiding parties, hunting parties, or any other effort meant to bring resources into the nest. Whenever I've tracked them in the past, these gatherers hiss and click orders at the others. The one I've got a new bounty for led an attack through a village that robbed its citizens of most of their food, and a large portion of its men. The scorpirons are malicious, merciless, and devastating. They've never been known to assemble in groups larger than their specific nest, but if it ever came to that, no major city would stand a chance.

Like the outside of the nest, entries to sections other than new corridors were few and far between, but I had to remain vigilant and not accidentally step into an area of restless warriors rather than the next branch of a path. There were no fires internal to the nest for obvious reasons, so I relied completely on sound—of which, I heard none.

I kept walking and listening.

No sound.

I passed by a break in the path and peered around and through the edges of the brush. Light played and reflected off numerous bits of different scorpiron scales. My adrenaline spiked and shocked my nerves. I ducked away from the opening in the path almost as quickly as I leaned in. I took a gentle but giant step past the opening and continued on.

My thoughts returned to the patrol.

Are they awake?

Did I kill them?

Are they up and alerting the others?

My paranoia tried to swell, but my experience kept it in check. I hunched over and took steps as deep as I could without scraping gravel or rustling against the brush. As I progressed, the high, short chirps of their sleeping young registered in my ears, signifying the nearby center of the nest. I was in the thick of the ring of the nest where my target should be. I slowed and looked for the next opening.

When I finally came upon one, I held back even more. The light improved and I didn't have to pass through the threshold as much as before. While looking in, I inspected the tails of the scorpirons in the room and tried to spot a double stinger. My bounty was apparently the only one in his nest with a rare, double stinger at the end of his tail, and should make it easy to pick him out.

No double stingers in here.

I continued along the trail of the nest's interior rings. An empty space came next, followed by another room with another group of scorpirons. Normal tails and stingers, *again.* The sound of the families at the center of the nest grew louder. Doubt started to trickle into my mind. I had been in the nest longer than planned and my odds of being caught before killing this thing were rapidly increasing.

Not long before the patrol gets discovered, or wakes up!

I ducked into the next entryway.

My first thought was disappointment as the light shone on only one sleeping scorpiron, but as I traced the figure down from its head to its tail, my skin tingled with excitement.

Two stingers!

I took a quick, steadying breath.

Time to get to work.

Before continuing further into the room, I stepped back and reviewed the path to confirm my exit. I had no idea how the paths would fork or merge if I continued forward, so I decided I'd leave the way I came after making the kill. I ran the layout through my head.

One entryway with sleeping scorps. An empty room. Another room with scorps, and then the exit.

I inched in where my bounty slept and scanned the room. The weight of my bone club felt good. I squeezed it and crept closer and pulled out my dagger as a backup. There was more of a chance of stunning it or killing it with a solid slam from my bronzed bone than there was a first attempt at stabbing it. Its tough scales practically guaranteed it.

I slipped over closer and listened. The sound of the chirping offspring was still all I heard. My scorp's eyes were shut. Its tail with double stingers was still. I lifted my mallet and raised my arm quietly, ready to unleash all I could into its face.

As I reached the top of my preparatory stretch the muffled whoosh and whistle of the wind was overtaken by a deafening blanket of hissing.

The nest is awake! Now!

My arm plummeted down towards the target.

The scorp's body jerked, whipping one of its huge pincers up to block my attack. I swung my dagger around to try and stab it in the head, but was countered by its other arm as it scrambled to stand. The dagger flipped out of my hand. As it finished standing, I spun to match it and came around with the full force of my mallet, cracking it in the side of the face. It stumbled back a step but returned swiftly with a kick to my gut. I tensed my belly just in time and absorbed some of the violent crunch, though less than I'd hoped. As the kick landed, I dropped my club and grabbed the scorp's leg before shoving the beast back in a chaotic stumble. I reached down for my club but was bashed in the side of the head by something that flashed into view just before it struck. My vision went dark, but I was still conscious.

I crashed onto my side and rolled into a wall of thorny vines and prickly bark that poked my skin. Sand whipped up into my mouth and grated my face. I raced to brush away the sand as the chirping of the offspring stopped. In its place was only hissing, clicks and pops.

More are coming. Gotta get out of here!

I scrambled to my feet and shook some focus and clarity back into my head. The double stinger beast rushed at me. With no dagger or club, I locked my fists together and swung at one of its hooking arms. I smacked it out of the way and dodged its other arm before finally landing a solid jab to its face. If I was going to have any chance with my bare hands, it would be by landing hits to its face—the smallest, but most vulnerable area.

My first jab landed hard. It squealed and hissed as it shuffled back but I didn't give it time to regroup. I shot forward and landed two more jabs—a left and right. It swung around with its tail and caught me in the upper arm. It hurt as bad as a slice from a jagged blade but the movement from the blow swung us both around—shoving me closer to my club.

I jumped over a low swipe of its tail and lunged in for a left jab and then an uppercut. The uppercut landed squarely, to the point the scorp couldn't even squeal as it teetered backwards. I seized the opportunity and leapt forward to bend down for my club. But just before my taut fingers touched the handle, a massive blow smacked the back of my head. It wasn't a direct hit. It glanced off as I was bending down. It was enough, though. I tumbled over my club, rolled, and landed on my back with hazy eyes. My vision returned quickly, but a slab of dread crushed my soul.

Looking up from the ground, I saw that four warriors had entered. Two held spears and stayed close to the chamber's threshold. Two others, bulkier, were closer to me. My target with the double stinger stood up and tapped itself with its arms and tail to rattle off sand from our scuffle.

I squinted then stretched my eyelids, searching in the dark for any light reflecting off my bronzed club. It was behind the two scorps closest to me.

My dagger? Couldn't see it.

My bounty clicked and popped some new sounds.

The guards at the door responded but I didn't know what they were saying. They must have known I was coming, or had been listening to me infiltrate the nest for a while. They hadn't killed me yet, so that was good.

One of the two closest scorps walked towards me, clicking and hissing to the others. Again, I was still alive, so I wasn't too worried. Besides, before I really had time to panic, the approaching scorp fell down on all fours and bashed me in the head with one of its claws.

All of that fighting, my fading mind thought.

For free.

* * *

My awareness of life returned and my eyes opened to dawn's bruised blue sky far above me. My head throbbed while registering the increasing light. I was no longer in the nest and before I could identify exactly where I was, smoke drifted into view above me, robbing my sight of the sky. The smell of burning brush overcame me. I rolled onto my side.

The nest was in flames, abandoned and set alight by its previous occupants after I, an outsider, infiltrated it. A caravan of scorp families, workers, and warriors trailed off in search of a new home—up and over a dune in the distance. A few of the warriors who had stayed back clicked, popped, and hissed—no doubt discussing what to do with me.

I tried to move but my hands were shackled behind me. I wasn't surprised. I strained against my bonds. They were sturdy. I went to roll around to get up to my feet, but I was shackled at the ankles, too. A squeaking and creaking distracted me.

A few other scorps returned from around the burning nest, pulling a cart by a few hefty lengths of rope with a cage on top of it. They rolled it up close to me and joined the other guards. As one of the scorpirons gestured at an unfamiliar man to get back into the cage, a different scorp pulled out my club and brandished it angrily at me through pops and hisses.

"Oh. Was that a cousin?" I asked.

The scorpiron sprinted at me and lifted my club, but one of the others popped an order at him. He slid to a halt. The remaining stragglers approached me, picked me up, and tossed me into the cage.

Well, I guess it's time for plan B.

Chapter Two - The Prayer Comes First

Bayla

I couldn't look up.

Well, I *could* have, but my rolling stomach convinced me otherwise. Instead, I stayed my nausea by trying to stare a hole through the box in my lap. As our priest, Didymus, addressed the entire village, I withdrew into my mind and listed the box's contents to distract my nerves.

A fist's worth of stones of various size, I thought.

A clump of soil that sustains our crops.

"By the grace of King Minos," Didymus declared, "we gather once more to honor our beloved Ariadne!"

Petals, stems, and thorns.

"Today we will be blessed with a most rare treat," Didymus continued. "Rather than having demonstrations from graduates in only one ranking, we will get to see displays from a graduate of both rank one, *and* a graduate of rank two in the Arts of Ariadne. All on the same day!"

A palm's worth of the Aegean's grace.

"Yes! It just so happens," Didymus added as he held

his hand out towards my family, "that Bayla here has just recently finished her rank one studies, and her older sister Cilana, has just finished rank two!"

The village burst into applause and chipped at my focus. I tried to think louder.

Six figs with which to share or—

The priest's voice punched my attention as the clapping ceased.

"Bayla!"

My head flipped up and my stomach turned. I swallowed and kept it calm.

"Please, take your place and show us what you have learned!"

My surrounding kin—immediate and extended—fell silent. I looked back down to my box of materials, and as I considered the possibility of panicking, I shivered. A waterfall of calm poured over me instead. I found nothing else more thrilling than practicing the Arts of Ariadne.

It's time.

My mother patted my back while I confirmed my resolve. Not wanting her to think I was hesitant, I looked at her and smiled. My father reached out for the container made of wood and bronze and held it while I stood up. Cilana leaned in and grabbed my wrist.

"Don't forget," she whispered quickly. "The prayer comes *before* the ingredient and target."

"I know!" I shot back with an annoyed whisper of my own.

She squeezed my wrist and smiled a different type of smile than the kind we usually exchanged. Instead of a smile born from winning an argument, or generated when one of our parents scolded the other, this was a softer smile. The accompanying gaze of her eyes wasn't squinted in arrogant satisfaction. Instead, her beautiful chestnut brown eyes were opened wide with what I thought might have been a sisterly pride. She then winked and removed any doubt.

I reached down to retrieve the box from my father and turned to face the waiting village. But rather than focus on the deep rows of kin and neighbors, I held my sight firm on the wooden pedestal in the middle of the square. My steps were quick but deliberate. I just wanted to make it to the pedestal without tripping over myself and spilling my materials everywhere. While keeping my eyes diverted to my box, I reached the center of the square without incident.

After setting the box down I sucked in a huge breath—slowly, with the hope of hiding my insecurities. I let it out quickly under the sound of my feet spinning towards the priest.

"I'm ready," I said firmly.

"Excellent!" Didymus bellowed. "Good luck to you, dear Bayla! We look forward to seeing your knowledge in action!"

The priest turned and stood on the balls of his feet to gesture at someone towards the back of the gathering. After a few waves of his arm he turned back and spun to address the gathering once more.

"Let the demonstration commence!"

The priest turned to me with a toothy smile and patted my head as if I were half my eighteen years. I glared at him. His smile fell and he cleared his throat. Combined with being annoyed from being patted, my passion for magic outweighed any remaining nervousness and helped me bring my eyes up confidently to the front line of onlookers. While slowly turning in place, I scanned the crowd for any hints of my first test.

Once Didymus crossed back over the demonstration

boundary—marked off with closely-spaced stones—the exhibition officially started. Since I hadn't been met with any immediate threat yet, I took advantage of the available time.

I slapped my hands and held them together before closing my eyes only long enough to bring my hands to my lips.

"Petra me frouta. Ischyri alla porodis," I whispered. As my breath tickled the sides of my fingers, the words echoed in my mind.

Stone with fruit. Strong but porous.

A muffled rustling rushed up from behind the crowd. My eyes popped open and I felt myself slowly grin like a crack in weakened ice.

With a few quick dips of my fingertips into two of the box's small compartments, I pulled out a small stone and a chunk of fig. I slapped my hands together again. As I rolled them in my hands the stone pulverized the fig into a chunky jelly. With a quick toss, I flung the clump of rock and crushed fig to the sky, leaving my hands completely clean. The combined ingredients flew up over my head and just before falling back down, they fused and flashed, shooting a dome off opaque protection over me.

The spectators involuntarily parted at various points as sprinting attackers tore out towards me.

Just in time.

I crouched down and prepared to defend myself while whipping my head around to identify all attackers. As they broke free into the demonstration square, each one lurched, jumped, and sprinted for me. One by one they clashed with my protective enchantment. And one by one they bounced off, slid across, or crashed back into the abrasive gravel.

A restrained chorus of polite chuckling popped up

throughout the crowd.

Despite consisting of friends, family, and more senior students, the group of attackers had to test the quality and strength of my protective dome. I've had to help test others before, and even helped test Cilana during her rank one demonstration. And though I felt bad for stunning them, it wasn't enough to prevent me from looking at Cilana and winking at her. But the second of arrogance cost me.

"Bayla!" Cilana shouted.

One of the boys had come to his feet and started banging at the enchantment.

Each blow weakened it as the sound of the strikes shifted from dull and wobbly to crisp and snappy. The others quickly recovered, stood, and joined in trying to bring it down.

My eyes shot back and forth between my ingredients and the walls of the dome.

What do I do now?

Back to the ingredients.

To the dome.

The ingredients.

I shot a hand in and grabbed another rock and fig. While rolling the fig and stone in one hand, I plucked out a spent wood coal with the other, to harness the memory of the fire that charred it. The recently recited spell I was going to use with the fig and stone was still active. I only needed to speak the words to call upon the power of fire.

"Meioste afti ti mageia me ti fotia sas," I rushed to say.

Reduce this magic with your fire.

As the spent coal in my hand roared back to life, I spun around and considered each of the assailants.

Whose weapon do I want?

I stopped to face young Cineas whose simple but elegant sword caught my eye.

"Is that from Crete?" I asked in a veiled challenge.

Cineas stopped hacking at the dome to consider my question but then swung his sword over his head to prepare for another hit on the dome. As his arm fell, I threw the flaming coal at the area of the dome Cineas stood in front of, weakening it enough for him to strike and stumble through. Only one of the other attackers noticed in time to try and race around to enter through the weakened spot, but I had already prepared to shore it up. While Cineas stumbled past me and fell to the ground, I threw the extra chunk of stone and fig at the dome to reinforce it. I then spun around and snatched up Cineas' sword.

As I tossed the sword from hand to hand, he rolled onto his back.

"Thank you," I said in playful condescension. Disarmed and dejected, he slumped back onto his elbows.

Before I could wound his pride further, the continued banging of the others reclaimed my attention. I flicked the sword between my hands a final time and appealed to Boreas.

"Megali Voreia. Pote den tha borousa na ekmetallefto tous etesians sas, alla epitrepste mou na deixei ti dynami tous se olous ekeinous edo."

Great Boreas. I could never harness your etesian winds, but let me show their strength to all those here.

My hands dipped into the box of ingredients once more. I picked out a coal, a rock, and a fig and walked backwards to an edge of the dome. I crunched the rock and fig together and threw the coal over my shoulder. Once the dome had been weakened again, I stepped back to exit it before immediately tossing the reinforcement ingredients.

I bent my knees and stretched out my arms. Before my thrashing assessors could register that I had emerged from the protective membrane, I strained and flexed as I fought to contain just a fraction of the freely available wind about the village. My arms whipped and shook as I focused on the power of the wind.

Slamming the mass of invisible power down on one side of the dome, the edge carved into the ground and spun the whole thing under itself before scooping up the others. I flipped my arms around and pushed them apart to widen the dome, rendering a hunk of earth and those who sought to test me, helpless—rolling around like a pile of grapes in a bowl.

With my embarrassed foes temporarily suspended, I smiled up at them and meandered over to my ingredients. But before I could collect my box in triumph, a frantic yelp ripped up from the rear of the crowd.

"Stop! Stop!" The male voice shrieked. "Stop the demonstration!"

Didymus shot into the demonstration square, his face contorted in concern. He looked over to me and waved both palms at me. Though I felt a tinge of disappointment, I reluctantly walked over to the dome and waved a quick dash of wind to tip it over and gently spill my friends onto the ground.

The panicked man broke through the crowd and rushed over to Didymus, breathless. It was Hybrias—a man from the northern end of the village. He doubled over but quickly stood up. My father and a few of others rushed in to confer with our scared friend. They didn't speak long and I couldn't hear what was said, but father soon raced back towards me.

"Bayla, come," he said, scooping me towards mother

and Cilana with his arm. As other neighbors and kin heard the news, father shared it with us.

"Ships have been spotted in the waters north of the island," he said calmly, though his eyes spoke differently. "We need to prepare in case they plan to land here, understood?"

"Yes, papa," Cilana replied.

While father stepped away to speak with another neighbor rushing by, mother leaned in and pulled me and Cilana closer.

"What perfect timing to have learned your lessons, hmm?" She said with a lush warmth. Her accompanying smile was the only thing I knew that could destroy even the most entrenched doubts, fears, and uncertainties.

"I'm sure they'll pass us by," she added. "But if not, we will be ready."

There had been increasing news of raids on villages throughout the Aegean and our village had recently bolstered defenses as a precaution. The threat up until then had only been hypothetical—unfortunate stories of things that happened to *other* people in *other* places. But as the gathering of friends and family scattered throughout the square like frightened bugs exposed to sunlight, my thoughts started down a path of violent imagination.

Papa raced back over with my box of ingredients.

"Here. We need to get back to our home," he said, scanning a hectic stare across the village. But after looking down to me, Cilana, and mama, his voice steadied. His eyes relaxed.

"Don't worry, my beauties," he said, looking to all three of us. "We have the strength. We have the knowledge. Now come. Let's go."

We jogged calmly out of the square but picked up

speed with each stride. When we returned home, we each flew into a flurry of activity. Father disappeared into his and mother's room and returned with a flat bundle of cloth draped across his arms. He let it slide down before catching it in his palms. After placing it carefully on our kitchen table, he flipped back folds of the fabric revealing our family's two swords. He placed his hands on the blades.

"Agapimeni Ariadni," he whispered in prayer. "Evlogiste afta ta spathia. Prostatepste tin oikogeneia mas."

Beloved Ariadne. Bless these swords. Protect our family.

When father said Ariadne's name, the swords glowed and crackled with an emerald-tinted magic. He finished his prayer and the light on the blades receded, having imbued them with one of the most advanced arts of the third and highest rank. Father handed a sword to my mother and peered out the kitchen window.

"Bayla, help your sister," mama said. "Get a collection of ingredients together in case we need them."

"Yes, mother," I replied quickly. "I still have most of what I brought with me to the demonstration."

"That's right!" Cilana said. "Let's go see what I have, Bayla. I've been collecting things for some time."

"Listen, children," father said as he pulled away from the window. "If something should happen... If anyone attempts to do us and our village harm, your mother and I will defend you," he added, holding up his sword. "You both however must use all of your powers to keep yourselves safe. Use your best reflection spells. Your deflection spells. Do what you can to shield us, but only after you have protected yourselves. Do you understand?"

"Yes, fath—" I started.

"But I've started learning rank three," Cilana

interrupted urgently. "I can help!"

"No!" He blasted back. "Your mother and I are most able to attack and defend in a fight. You both must be dedicated to protection for all four of us. I need you two to understand this."

Cilana nodded but her chin dipped quickly to her chest in disappointment.

I reached over and squeezed her arm, like she had done to me in the square. She tilted her head up just enough to look at me, and smiled.

"Now, go," mother said. "Gather your ingredients."

Cilana and I both scurried off to our room. While I flipped and poked my fingers through figurines and the few jars of ingredients I hadn't pulled from before the demonstration, Cilana scooped her arm out from under her bed, sliding out pots and baskets.

"Ha," she laughed gently to herself. "I'm running out of room."

She looked up at me, her flash of humor dropping from her lips.

"I hope we can keep them safe," she said.

I pulled my hand away from my shelf, rattling the small toys and containers as I brushed up against them.

"You could protect us all," I said as I knelt beside her. "All on your own."

She floated a hand over and patted my knee before looking under the bed again. Once we found everything in our room that we thought may be of use, we brought it all into the kitchen and shoved them together on the table. I retrieved my demonstration box from inside the door where father had set it and brought it over as well. With the weapons enchanted and our ingredients collected, we sat down at the table and looked at each other with similar side glances of apprehension.

"We've had lookouts for months," father whispered. "For exactly this type of concern. If someone comes, we will have warning."

My eyes blurred as I retreated into my mind. But they focused again when I looked over father's shoulder and through the kitchen window.

"The sun is setting," I said. "When do you think they will come?"

"Oh, there may be no one coming," mother rushed to say. "It was just a report of ships. They've probably sailed right by."

"Ah!" Father blurted. "I have an idea. Let's practice your languages while we wait to hear that the ships have passed. Cilana," he said, turning to her. "We'll start with you since the demonstration was cut short before you could participate."

Cilana stood up.

"No, no," he said. "No papyrus today. From memory," he directed.

Mama gasped in playful shock as she tilted a candle to light another.

While my father and Cilana debated which language to practice, I folded my arms and laid my head down. My vision settled on the swords before drifting to mother's candles, and then to our boxes, pots, and piles of ingredients. My eyes grew heavy. The last thing I saw before falling asleep was Cilana's eyes pinched closed as she tried to remember a word's pronunciation.

* * *

My mind woke, but my eyes hadn't yet. In the split second of time before tensing any of my muscles, I involuntarily rolled and jostled.

My eyes sprung open. Cilana was shaking me.

"Bayla!" She shouted.

The next one was a whisper.

"Bayla!"

I blinked with the speed of a hummingbird's wings and sat up.

"What?" I asked. "Is it my turn?"

Cilana couldn't answer. A scream out in the village stole her focus.

"Oh, no, no!" I whined. "Mama? Papa? Is it them?"

Our parents flanked the door, one on each side.

Mama snapped and pointed at the table.

"Say your spells!" She said through a weighted rasp. "Get some material ready!"

More screams ripped through the village. Voices shouted locations and the movements of the attackers.

"There's a group up by the well!" Someone yelled.

Horrific crashes of blades and meaty smacks tore out into the night.

They grew louder as they grew nearer.

My thoughts constricted. Fear tugged on the thousands of thoughts in my mind, leaving only one for me to use.

Say a prayer. Say a spell!

Papa raised his sword.

"I love you girls," mama said.

A flickering amber light flared to life through the window. It saturated the room. Shadows flew across the walls as figures outside ran past. My chin started to shake.

Say something, I thought. *Say something now!*

"Syndeste afto to derma kai to xylo. Prostatepste tin oikogeneia mou."

Fuse this hide and wood. Protect my family.

I slammed my hands onto the table and snatched up strips of hide and a pile of twigs. I clapped them together and instantly pulled my hands apart from top to bottom. As my hands separated, a shield for each of my parents stretched into place in front of them.

Our door rattled in a thunderous crash. Cilana reached for the table, picked up a handful of wilted vines, and spoke her spell.

"Anapnefste ti zoi se afta ta fylla, Hegemone. Prostatepste kai enischyste tin porta mas."

Breathe life into these leaves, Hegemone. Protect and reinforce our door.

The door cracked and rocked again. The third blow brought it down, but Cilana threw her clump of leaves and vines in time. The mixture of vegetation flew through the air, growing exponentially before latching onto the entryway, sealing it. In place of a door, there was now a wall of vines, roots, and flowers just as thick, and possibly stronger than the door.

"Get behind us!" Papa yelled.

An odd sound ruptured outside. The temporary barrier bulged and throbbed in creeping fire before sizzling into bits of ash. A cluster of hooded figures rushed through the door.

Father swung his arm in a circle behind the free-standing shield. Three swords flashed into place in front of the shield and struck out at the group. Papa stepped to the side and engaged another attacker.

Mama stepped back and held her sword behind her as it grew in bright energy. But just before she could lash out from behind her own shield, a ball of sizzling light shot through the entryway and struck the shields. The massive orb crashed and spilled out, slamming my parents to the ground. With mama and papa knocked down, Cilana flew forward.

"Bayla!" She shouted as she dipped down for my mother's sword. "Give me a guard!"

My eyes raced around the room.

Papa's not moving.

Mama's crumbled in the corner.

My brave, amazing sister's taking up the fight.

I flung my hand to the ingredients on the table and grabbed a rock. I brought it to my lips, kissed it, and threw it towards Cilana to coat her in a film of stone.

But the rock just sailed over her shoulder and smacked the wall.

In my panic, I had forgotten to say the prayer first.

A crude and neglected blade of eternal blackness ripped into my soul as Cilana rushed into the fight.

She's expecting protection.

I've given her none.

A smooth and refined blade ripped into Cilana's neck.

"Cilana!" I shrieked.

I reached for the table, desperate to grab something, anything. But before I could, something bashed me in the face. And a second hit slammed into my own neck. I crashed to the ground as a sensation of a stinging and cold wetness spread across my skin. Before my vision faded, I watched countless feet flood through the room—feet wearing peculiar shoes of thin hide. The smattering of clay and the cracking of crates rattled my ears, but along with my vision, my hearing dwindled to nothing.

The sound of a collapsing home next door must have stirred me awake soon after. I instinctively propped myself up and rolled to my side. I put my hand into a small puddle of my own blood that had partly dried.

Cilana. My beautiful sister. Gone. Mother and father—collapsed into each other. Dead. Their enchanted weapons were nowhere to be found.

The despair of seeing my family forced an attempted scream, but I choked and gagged. Dry heaving and crying again, the sight of my dead family blurred in my tears. I scratched towards my sister as the neighboring home's fire jumped and took hold onto ours. The floor of our home that had supported my family's feet through the years was now a foreign expanse leading only to corpses. The corpses of my parents. My sister's corpse.

Closer to Cilana I crawled, but a sharp throb to my neck made me stop. Only then did I remember I had been struck in the face and sliced in the neck. As I looked back to confirm how much blood I had lost, I reached up to my neck and gently felt around with the backs of my fingers. My blood had started to dry and flake. I pulled my hand away and only had hints of wetness as I kept crawling.

"Cilana!" I wailed. "Cilana!"

I looked over at mother and father.

"Mama! Papa?"

Only the fire spreading through our home spoke.

I scanned the room and tried to determine how much time I had. Our few valuables and bronze statues were gone, and the nearby furniture added fuel to the fire. A few rugs, linens, and wooden shelves caught quickly. I had to get out, but I needed to touch Cilana first. I needed to confirm with my own hands that my sister was gone.

I scrambled along on my elbows and insides of my legs, in quicker, longer gaits. My vision blurred again as I felt myself begin to gag.

Without knowing with certainty where my hand would land, I reached forward.

I choked out a tear-smothered sob as I landed on her arm. It was cool, even in the approaching fire's heat—like my grandmother's when I touched hers when she passed. I wiped my eyes. I had to see Cilana with clarity.

Her chest was still. Her eyes and mouth were frozen open.

The corner of our roof collapsed onto my parents' bodies. I instinctively covered my head, but almost immediately turned to look back.

"Mama! Papa!"

My eyes went blurry again. The fire spread and crept towards me. I turned back and reached for Cilana and shuffled up to her face.

I kissed her forehead.

"I'm sorry! I'm so sorry, Cilana!" I shrieked through tears.

The smoke coated my throat.

"I'm sorry!"

The fire inched closer. The heat was beginning to sting.

"I love you Cilana!"

I reached for the necklace I had made for her and ripped it from her neck. After scrambling and clawing up to my knees and then my feet, I stumbled and tripped out of the house and into the street.

I rolled over onto my back and shuffled away from my crackling home, the heat too much to bear. I watched in horror as the fire consumed all that I had ever known as good and loving. I heard nothing but the fire eating at the context of my life. There were no more wails or screams. No sounds of fighting. All I heard at that moment, was fire. It rolled through the village, chewing and coughing itself onto home after home.

Against the increasing heat of the claustrophobic flames, I felt a cool kiss on my neck followed by a gentle throb. I reached up and brushed the backs of my fingers against my wound again. When I pulled my hand back, it was wet with fresh blood. I had agitated the injury, the severity of which I still had not been able to determine. The fire had become too hungry too quickly. I had to get out of the village.

As I stood up, the last stubborn bits of our home's timber and clay crackled and crashed to the ground. They clinked together like massive clay pots rubbing up against each other. The trapped heat inside our home blasted out as the debris settled and bit me with blistering pain. I stumbled backwards and fell, but shuffled back to my feet just as quickly. I squeezed Cilana's necklace and shot out towards the safety of darkness at the end of our village's fiery corridors.

My mind emptied as I sprinted. All I focused on was the smudged promise of escape through my wet eyes. My hands sliced through the air. My legs bent and whipped along faster than I think they ever had. Finally, I broke through the edge of our village, past flames and out of the heat, refreshed by the wind generated by my desperate sprint.

The wind used to usher in calm and quiet through the streets of Skarkos. It would tickle my skin with remnants of ages past and ignite a wonder for the world around me. But now, instead of hints of salt from the Aegean, it escorted endless echoes of the screams of the dead. The smells of olives and tulips were supplanted by those of burnt wood, straw, and clay. What used to be a place to where my people belonged—a place of safety and love—was now only a pile of death and debris. After racing through the leftovers on the edge of my village's former vibrancy, I fell to my knees, exhausted. With my back to the village, my chest heaved and my soul hollowed out as the raging fires mocked me.

I could feel it mocking me. I could hear it mocking me. The fire didn't care how it came to be or why, but only that it existed and was thriving on the fuel of my family. My people. My village.

But I found a way to face it. I realized the fire, too, would die. The fire wouldn't last forever. I turned to face it, to let it know that I would be there when it burned itself out.

Wait. Would anyone else outlast it?

Forgetting about fatigue, I popped back up and started looking for movement. *I couldn't have been the only one to make it out.* I looked further down the edge of the village.

No signs of survivors.

I started jogging, peering and hoping for someone, something.

"Hello!" I shouted.

I tried to run back in a few times, but the blaze was too widespread. Too hot.

"Can anyone hear me?" I screamed.

A new crash of timber and clay roared to my attention on my right. Someone careened out just ahead of the collapsing debris and fell into the dirt. I raced over.

They were burned. Horribly. I wanted to grab onto them and hold them, but their burns were too devastating. The olive skin of our people was now a volcanic black on this person. I couldn't recognize them. Their left arm was gone, with a wet and red hole in the top left of their torso. They didn't have long. I sat as close to them as I could without touching them.

"Help! Someone help us!" I shouted towards the fire.

I looked back to my dying kin.

"Shh, shh," I said, at a loss for anything else to say. "Let me go find something to wrap—"

"No!" The person rasped. "Stay with me," they begged, grasping at me weakly with their right hand. "Stay."

I turned into my shoulder, ashamed from being helpless. My chin quivered, but I turned back to them. A portion of their face was darkened but not burned. I reached out and stroked their cheek.

"Okay," I said. "I'll be here. I'll be right here."

Their focus drifted off of my face and I tried to hide that I too had to look away. I couldn't watch them die. Instead, I wanted to watch the fire die.

Chapter Three - In the Cage with Khetikare

Briz

The wagon and cage creaked with just enough irregularity to pick at my nerves and keep me awake. I was exhausted more than anything, but still wasn't too worried about my fate. The fact that I was riding with another guy helped me maintain the hope that I was being kept alive for a reason. We'd probably be sold off as fighters or laborers eventually, but until then, I just needed to keep an eye out for an opportunity to seize.

We'd been riding for two days with a few stops, but no water. Well, no water for me or the other guy. The sun was its relentless self and while we weren't expending any energy sitting in the cage, I was thirsty and my head hurt. And though I had no reason or need to try and talk to my fellow captive, boredom got the better of me.

"You're not tied up," I said.

The man didn't look at me. He didn't even offer to look over as I spoke, keeping his eyes on the receding dunes behind us. I wasn't sure if he understood me, but if he could, he was ignoring me. I took a moment to really study him. His skin was as dark as mine and his clothes appeared to be local. He had a broad face with high cheekbones which also looked familiar. If he wasn't from near Kerma, I'm sure he was at least Nubian.

I continued to stare at him while leaning over slightly and craned my neck into his periphery. I hoped to make him feel awkward enough to induce a reply, but all I got was more uncomfortable.

"All right," I relented.

I sat back, flexed my aching rear, and stretched my back to force some relief into my sore bones. My shoulders stung too from my arms being bound behind me for so long. I extended them as much as I could and rolled my shackled wrists inside the itchy bronze.

"They make me do things for them," the stranger offered.

I looked over in mild surprise as he continued.

"They can't do a lot with their hands because they're so close to their claws, so they make me hitch the wagons, tie up other prisoners... Things they can't do easily or quickly."

"How long have you been with them?" I asked.

The stranger who still hadn't looked at me turned slightly to look at one of the cage's slats. I watched as he ran his finger down numerous banks of cuts in the wood.

"Four hundred and seven days," he replied.

"Four hundred?" I repeated in shock.

He finally turned and drilled a heavy stare into me.

"And seven," he corrected.

Over a year, I thought. *Trapped in a box of wood, reeds, and rope.* My eyes drifted to the floor of the rocking cage, trying to imagine what that was like. Day in and day out of oppressive sun, little water, and who knows what for food. *How could he have lasted so long?*

"I was out hunting when I came across them setting up their last nest," he resumed. "Well, it was the one they had before the one they just burned. I didn't think they heard me. I fell back and kept my distance, trying to hide from them. They were clicking and hissing, and by the time I considered that they were communicating with some scorpirons closer to me, I got bashed in the head. I woke up similar to how you did. Been their prisoner ever since."

I didn't need to ask my next question.

"I've tried to escape twice. Haven't tried in a while, though. The beatings are pretty rough. It's been harder and harder to retain enough strength to even consider trying again. But I will, some day. I have to get back to my wife and son. I must. Maybe together we can do something."

The sun was bright, and I squinted as he spoke, which, on top of being dehydrated, made it challenging to focus on what he was saying. But I caught it all.

The wagon continued rolling slowly along, connected to long ropes and dragged behind a half-dozen marching scorpirons. The scorpirons are a good deal larger and stronger than men and they didn't seem bothered by the work.

An escorting scorpiron jogged up from the rear and slapped the side of our cage a few times. It pointed a pincer at us and hammered at the air furiously, clicking and hissing the whole time. A few scorpirons ahead of our cage hissed back at the annoyed one.

After its last flurry of hissing, the moody scorp spat out a few syllables that I thought I understood.

"Shto... tal...," the creature said.

Stop talk? I considered.

"They want us to be quiet," the stranger confirmed.

I made no immediate attempt to speak again, and waited for the annoyed guard to fall back. It didn't take him long, but I still didn't resume talking. Instead, I leaned over slightly to try and get the attention of my cellmate silently. He looked up.

I licked my lips and feigned an exaggerated swallow. He shook his head and shrugged. I guessed he had no clue when we would get some water, either. I could only nod and think. Through a mind thickened by dehydration and fatigue, I tried to take advantage of the available time.

In addition to the notion of being sold, I also thought they might keep me for manual labor like they had my fellow captive. And then, of course, there was the possibility of my fate being something more final. But the fact that I had been caught inside the nest more than likely tipped them off that I was a hunter. And if they thought I was a hunter or assassin, or if their communications with other scorpirons was advanced enough to trade knowledge about threats, then I thought it was as a safe bet they were hoping to trade or sell me to another nest that was looking for me.

And if selling me was going to bring food, resources, or some other valuables to the nest, then they would want to keep me alive for as long as possible. That allowed me to postpone my panic over water. It also freed me to consider how I could press my luck before being sold. I probably had more leeway than my new friend. If he was simple slave labor as he suggested, they could just kill him if he got out of line and replace him with someone else. But this stranger was still too new to me. I wouldn't share any details of my circumstances, work, or bounties, until it served a purpose, for me.

The ride was quiet between me and the other guy for a long while thanks to the insistence of our captors. Even though the scorpiron that chastised us fell back into line, we didn't try to talk again. It just wasn't worth the hassle. The scorps didn't communicate all that much, either. Most of the sound came from the rickety cage.

Our caravan eventually slowed down, with what looked to be about an hour left before sunset. I thought we were stopping to relieve ourselves or set up camp, but as I shifted in the cage, I was able to look past a donkey burdened with bags and spotted a water station. Just as I noticed what it was, a scorpiron slapped the tied door at the back of the cage and hissed, beckoning us with its pincer.

I looked at my cellmate. His face drooped from an expectation of routine. While the scorp opened the cage and clicked impatiently, my fellow human leaned over and unlocked my shackles.

"Go ahead," he said.

I pulled my arms around and fanned out my legs. It hurt to do so, but felt wonderful at the same time.

"What are we doing?" I asked as I crept over to step out.

"When we're on the road, we'll usually stop around dusk to rest and sleep for a bit," he replied. "And then we'll pick back up before dawn.

I stepped out and down from the cage. A scorp hissed at me as I landed next to him. I took a few steps and stumbled before bending and catching myself on the knees. I hadn't been able to stand in a while and had to bend back up slowly. It hurt.

The scorp shoved me with the meatiest part of his pincher and gestured at the nearby well with his other. I turned and snarled at him for shoving me, but inside I was screaming with joy.

Don't drink it too fast, I warned myself.

Before turning back towards the well, I saw my friend begin to follow. They didn't shove *him*.

"What's your name?" I finally dared to ask. A few scorpirons growled a series of clicks, but none approached.

"Khetikare," he replied.

"Okay. Khetikare," I said. "I'm Briz. Going to gesture at the well over here, as if I'm just talking about the water. Can they understand us?"

"If they can, I don't know. I haven't been talking to myself all that much," Khetikare answered.

"Right," I said, as I stopped and stretched my back.

I had hunted a few and knew their behavior, but like Khetikare, didn't know much about their comprehension.

Khetikare walked past me. I stretched while my friend fell gently to his knees. As his knees dug into the sand, he leaned over and rolled a few substantial stones off the well's wooden top. I joined him at the edge of the well's low walls and pushed off a few more. I slid the top off and looked down to the pleasant surprise of seeing my rippling reflection about five feet down.

"Hmm, I wasn't expecting much," I said. "Go ahead. You first."

Khetikare nodded gratefully before picking up a small wooden cup attached to a length of rope. He lowered it down and came back up with a drink.

"Going to talk in quick, soft bursts so they don't get too suspicious," I said.

Khetikare looked at me as he drank.

"Is their priority setting up a new nest?" I asked.

Khetikare swallowed and took the cup away from his mouth as if examining how much was left.

"Normally, I'd say yes," he replied. "If the nest was destroyed by fire or weather, yes."

I knew what he was getting at.

"But I don't know what their plans are for you," he added, before lowering the cup for a refill.

I looked around. There were half a dozen scorpirons within a reasonable distance, and while two seemed to be hissing in conversation, none of them seemed concerned about us.

"It looks like we've been heading northwest away from the river. Do you recognize the area at all?"

Khetikare finished his cup and handed it and the rope to me. As I lowered it for my first drink in days, I yelled a mental reminder at myself.

Don't drink too much or too fast!

My friend leaned up on his knees and propped up slowly before standing erect. He twisted and stretched and looked around. Finally, he shielded his eyes and looked in the direction of the setting sun.

"I think that's right. It took forever to lose sight of the Nile to our right and behind us, so, northwest seems right."

I brought the cup up to my mouth for my first drink. My heart raced with dehydration-enhanced anticipation.

You'll be able to drink more. Slow at first. Sip.

The sip of water crashed into my mouth like a wave on a forgotten beach. It stung a stab of tingly cold that I had to make sure I didn't react to. I swallowed it quickly to lessen the shock, which only led to shock of a new kind. I felt the water plummet down my throat and through my innards. Again, a slight hint of pain overwhelmed me, which then quickly settled into a numbed relief. I took another quick sip and swallowed. My skin started to itch as my stomach turned.

Stop for a second. Wait for it to pass.

"If we're headed northwest," I considered. "Then it's possible they're taking me to the nest where I took a previous bounty."

Khetikare rubbed under his eyes.

"How long ago was that?" He wondered.

I thought about taking another sip, but I forced myself to wait.

"Hmm, about two years now I'd say."

"I wouldn't think that nest would still be in the same place," Khetikare offered.

"What makes you say that?"

"Well," he added, "like I was saying, the weather... sandstorms, fire... they get wiped out fairly often. But then, I'm only going off what I've experienced with this group of scorps."

I made a point to make it obvious I was considering

his thoughts before giving into another desperate drink. I took in a bigger gulp. A lesser wave of sensation washed over my mouth. When I swallowed, the feeling of water coating my insides didn't feel as noticeable and didn't seem to sink as low. My nausea stayed the same.

"They don't seem to be as rampant as they used to be," I said. "The number of available beast bounties seem to be going down, and the number of bounties on humans seem to be going up."

Khetikare's head jerked around as he stared at me. His eyebrows raised with concern.

"You hunt humans, too?"

"No, no," I replied quickly. "Too much trouble," I added. "As long as I can keep finding the bounties on things like these scorps, and as long as the money is good, I won't need to."

Khetikare's face relaxed and I finished my cup. The sensation was negligible and felt somewhat normal. My annoying nausea was still present, though, but was tolerable. Khetikare continued while I drank.

"I remember before I got caught, hearing more and more about other settlements that had run-ins with scorps, boars, titanodons, and all manner of things. But I also heard about a growing number of expeditions being announced by the king to try and eradicate a lot of them."

I swallowed. Not from drinking water, but from worry. If I was to survive this encounter, I didn't like the sound of having my livelihood threatened.

"Well, that would explain the decreased bounties," I said in a huff. "I thought it might have just been a slow period."

Khetikare tilted his head at me.

"I don't talk with others all that much," I said before tossing the cup back over to Khetikare.

As he caught the cup a smaller scorpiron approached us slowly. It was similar in proportions to the others, but its pincers and stinger were slightly smaller than the others. It let out a soft, sustained hiss as it grew closer. The other nearby scorpirons turned to pay attention.

"She's getting water for them," Khetikare advised.

I stepped away slowly from the well. Khetikare followed suit. After a few extra steps, I got shoved from behind.

Though stunned in surprise myself, the female was startled by the commotion and turned to hiss. I spun to see what shoved me. It was a scorp. It waved one arm at me before waving both.

"Do you know what it wants?" I asked Khetikare.

I looked over. He shook his head and shrugged.

A few of the other scorps scampered down the dune. One came up behind Khetikare and shoved him towards me.

The female let out a low series of clicks while the others and those that shoved us erupted in a series of skipping and bouncing hisses, almost like they were amused.

One shoved me again. Then Khetikare got pushed. With each slam we came closer to each other.

"I think they're wanting us to fight," I said through a sigh.

"What?" Khetikare blurted.

"No, don't worry," I moaned. "I'm not going to hurt you. I just don't know what they'll do when I don't play along."

Khetikare got shoved again.

"Here, just come over and punch me," I said.

"No," he said. "I won't fight eith—"

"No, really," I insisted. "Just land some smacks to my face so they don't do anything to you."

"But what about you?" He asked.

"Just hit me," I said.

I got slammed forward again.

"Hit me!"

Khetikare balled up a fist and raised it slowly.

"Go ahead. Go," I said.

He pulled it back and swung it into my jaw.

Though his punch landed solidly, there wasn't a lot of weight behind it. But it was enough to send the scorps hissing and clicking. Their delight soon died down. One of them poked at my shoulder.

"Punch me again."

"Briz, I just d—"

"The quicker they realize I'm not going to fight the sooner this show will be over. Hit me again."

Khetikare punched me again. Like the first one, it was aimed well, but that was all.

The female emitted another rolling ripple of sounds that seemed disapproving in some way. She pulled away from the well and climbed the hill of sand before disappearing over the dune. One of the males rushed me and knocked me over with the broad and flat part of his claws. He stepped over and swiped me with his tail before kicking me. His arms raised up and swung down into my side like a punishing pendulum.

"No! Stop! Please!" I heard Khetikare shout as he sprang towards us.

A scorp shoved him to the ground. Khetikare slid

onto the ground in front of me and as he flipped over and shuffled back, another slam landed in my ribs.

As I waited for the next hit a shrill and piercing squeal rang out behind me. I pressed down on my wrists to lift my head up enough to look back. On top of the adjacent dune stood the silhouette of a scorp. One of the biggest I'd seen before. The scorps that had been roughing me up clicked a series of soft clicks and backed away.

The massive scorp fell to all fours and walked down like its much smaller cousins might, but even on all fours, its height was almost as much as one of the others. It crept over next to me and slowly stood back up on two feet.

The other scorps inched back even more.

The big guy whipped an arm at the ones that must have been his subordinates, hissing and clicking furiously. He then turned his sights on me, twisting his head slowly. Its mouth parts scissored and twitched as it stared. After locking eyes with me for a few seconds, he shot over towards the others and motioned at Khetikare.

He clambered up to his feet and shuffled over. While he helped me up, the grunts that tried to have us fight got scolded further by the big one.

"Well," Khetikare whispered as he reached down to pull me up. "I wasn't expecting that."

I growled and grabbed my side.

"Yes," I grunted. "He probably had a good reason," I said, nodding at the big scorp. "Or for me, a really bad one."

Chapter Four - A Host of Trials

Bayla

I woke up well past sunrise in the exhausted ball I curled into the night before. My stomach throbbed with nausea. The grieving soreness in my throat mixed with scratchy and smoky dryness. I peeled my tongue off the roof of my mouth to try and help it, but it just made it worse. As I started to open my eyes, I paused.

Maybe it was a dream. Maybe it didn't happen.

If I could have kept my eyes shut for the rest of my life to fool myself into thinking the attack was just a nightmare, I would have. But I knew better.

With a quivering jaw, I forced my eyes open. A huff of sorrow heaved through my nose.

My eyes cracked open slowly and the mounds of my burnt village crashed into view.

I wailed into the ground, the loose soil at my mouth shooting away. My pain morphed into hiccups and gasps.

Oh no, oh no, I thought. *Is he still there? Is the man still here? Maybe he lived and got up... Wandered off somehow.*

I lifted my head and looked over. No. The body was still there, still in the same position as he was when he left the world.

My body writhed in sorrow like a stunned worm on a hot stone. While crying through a fresh wave of sorrow, I found relief in closing my eyes again. Relief in the darkness. Relief in denial.

But my aching muscles grew tired of my continued crying. I shook into silence and opened my eyes back to the horror in front of me.

Everything... I thought. *Consumed by the fire. Burned. Destroyed. Ashes. I'm... I'm so thirsty.*

My eyes drifted over to the poor man next to me and sent my mind hurtling back towards thoughts of death.

I need to get back home! I need to bury them!

My dry tongue licked my chapped lips.

But I'm so thirsty!

I argued with myself while staring at the dead man as if he were half of my conscience.

Not burying them is not even a question, you ungrateful brat, I admonished internally. *Get up and go see to them!*

There was a moment of hesitation as a part of my brain tried to postpone their burial, but I stomped the thought out of my head and stood up.

My stomach rolled and growled as I walked, but I pushed the nuisances to the bottom of my thoughts as I begged Ariadne to welcome my family. To love them. To bring them peace. I thanked Ariadne for being spared. Indeed, I recited prayers silently, thankful for my life. Thankful for surviving the terror inflicted on our village. I rambled and repeated prayers, trying to distract myself from what I would find when I returned to the remains of my home. I had to say something. To think something. I don't even know if I really *felt* any of the prayers. But still, I prayed as I approached.

Ariadne, please be with me now. With the strength of your serpents to encourage me, please see my courage restored. Together with your father, Minos, my King, guide me. Please bless me with the will and stamina to tend to my family. Help me lay them to rest in such a way that pleases you. I come to you now, forever and always, as your child.

My footsteps were quick and confident though I looked mostly at the ground. I couldn't bring myself to look at my poor village any more than I had to. Though the majority of the village was rubble, I knew the layout of our streets and path as well as I knew my own body. And I was thankful for that familiarity as I walked.

Though a night's sleep made returning to the bodies of my family seem surreal, I found an unexpected fortitude in contemplating the logistics of what I needed to do once I returned.

Our family's burial tomb is about a ten-minute walk from where our home stood.

My poor grand papa and grand mama. I'm sure they had no expectation of being joined so soon by any of us.

If I can get Cilana and my parents on a board of some kind, I could probably pull them to the tomb.

As long as I could get them onto something, I can take my time and take breaks. I can bring them to our family's final resting place.

I can do that. I can do this.

As I realized I had no further immediate thoughts to continue distracting myself with, I rounded the last bend near the ruins of our home.

When my eyes fell onto the mangled sight of our home for the first time since I ran from it, I was slammed in the stomach by an overpowering nausea. I instantly leaned over and vomited the bit of fluid I had left.

My breathing became irregular and a knot formed in my stomach. For all my praying and procrastination, my efforts to bolster my courage had failed. My sharp snorts of breath grew too hard. I had to open my mouth. My eyes blurred and I cried once more. My lower torso burned in exacerbated pain. I wanted to fall to the ground and curl up and cry until I died, but I stayed erect. I made myself stay standing. My family deserved it.

Just stay here. Cry or vomit all you need to, but stay here. Do not fall. Do not leave. Look forward.

I couldn't see my family from where I stood, which is the only reason I think I was able to stand my ground. My chest heaved as I bawled heavy, deep bellows. The annoying hints of tickling tears I felt streaming down my face soon numbed my cheeks as they increased. I could only stand, cry, and stare.

I finally told myself to get it out. I allowed myself to cry without judgment. Rather than continuing to tell myself to do this or that, I began to reflect on memories of chasing my sister around the trunks of the olive trees. The voice of my mother trumpeting out from the kitchen window. My father setting me on his lap just before telling one of his fantastic stories. As I remembered, I found strength. My crying slowed. My chest relaxed. I rubbed my aching head before swiping down to wipe my eyes. I forced a hard swallow and walked closer to our home.

You're going to see their bodies soon. Be ready.

I wasn't.

After stepping over the bits of debris that had fallen where our front entry had been, I felt like vomiting again. I looked up to where I knew their bodies would be. I had to get it over with.

I choked out a fresh burst of crying but stifled it when I saw them.

"Mama! Papa!" I cried under my cupped hands.

I walked over slowly, gently sliding away piles of debris with the side of my foot. I heard myself start to cry again, but I kept going.

At last I was within reach of their bodies, mother and father still crumpled onto each other where they fell. I spoke to them once again through tears, with the hope that somewhere they might hear me, and somehow, may even speak to me.

"Cilana!"

Her corpse was still at the base of where the table stood.

I sniffed and huffed another series of sobs but looked around. A few long strides away was a broken wooden chair from the kitchen. It was partially crushed after sustaining a blow from part of a collapsed wall, but unburned. I crept through the rubble towards it and examined it. One of its legs had been snapped off, but the back was intact. I pushed it over and kicked at the remaining legs and seat until they broke off. I brought the back over to my family.

The task before me—something I could focus on, something I could make forward progress on—was clearing a spot next to my parents. I put one end of the chair's back on the ground, leaned over, and shoveled bits of the rubble away. I did it again. I repeated the process seven times. Taking note of the amount of times I needed to scrape the floor with the back of a chair to make room to prepare to move the bodies of my parents was apparently important to me.

Seven times.

Once the floor was clear I placed the back of the chair next to my parents—as close to them as I could. I slowly lowered myself to my knees, and teetered over. My body was overcome with a sharp, cold blanket of fear. I was going to have to touch my burned parents. I was going to have to transfer their charred bodies to this piece of chair.

I couldn't touch them. I wouldn't!

But I had to.

I sat back on the heels of my feet, pushing the piece of the chair over slowly. Once it was as close to my father's body as I could get it, I fought back another wave of dark agony and reached out.

I reached out for my mother to try and move her off of my father. Her shoulder was closest. My breath shook again with sharp sips of air weighted in despair. I made contact with her skin, and just as I registered how slick and smooth her charred skin was, the area crinkled and gave way to the bone below which also partially crumbled to ash.

I screamed and launched myself back involuntarily. Into a jumbled pile of debris I thrust myself, needing to get away from my destroyed family—more than I had ever needed anything. Fixated on the collapsed portion of my mother's shoulder, I was tortured with a series of horrific questions.

Did my parents know they were dying?
Did they feel the fire?
Could Cilana feel her skin roasting?
Were their last thoughts of pain and torment?
Were they afraid?
Did Cilana realize I had failed her? Did she know I had forgotten to say the spell first?

I buried my face in my hands as I wailed. Louder and louder my screams and cries grew, wanting to try and drown out my thoughts of what my family might have endured. I looked up and over to my mother again. Back to my hands. I stayed buried, sheltered, and ashamed in my hands for a length of time in which I lost myself.

But at some point, the fear over what my family experienced, and my pain in losing them, was overcome. At some point, the hate seeped in. What began as small hints of anger seeped into the cracks of my loss, froze it, and then expanded. The anger punched out and broke off parts of my pain, which made room for more hate. The hate poured in furiously, froze me colder, and took more room in my heart.

I looked up at my parents. Rather than heaving with tears, I seethed with hate.

I looked over to my sister, as if to test my new resolve. My hate not only held its ground, but took a step forward.

They killed my sister!

I looked back to my parents.

They killed my parents! I will not let this go unanswered! I will not let these monsters escape! I will have their blood!

I shoved the debris out from around me and crawled back over to my parents.

I looked at my mother's collapsed shoulder once again, but rather than crumbling myself, into a mess of emotion, I went straight to thinking of how I could get my parents buried.

Their bodies won't stand up to the road to the tomb. They're too fragile. Too delicate.

I raised my head to the sky.

Will you permit me to bury them, Ariadne? I want to do right by them, in the manner in which I have been raised, but I do not want to cause harm to them. I do not want to scar them forever in the afterlife.

I looked back down and listened for an answer. I

listened, and reached out to the world, and waited to feel Ariadne's answer. My heart eased, and my skin rippled with relief. I would bury them.

My hate, fully in charge of my soul at the moment, fed my anger and fury as I set forth with my task. I scowled and sneered as I shoved the piece of chair out of the way. I grunted and cursed at the broken slats of our home's floor as if they were intentionally getting in my mission's way.

I continued pulling up an area of the ruined floor next to my parents, revealing the ground below. It had been spared exposure to the fire.

After jumping down into the hole I'd created, I spent the next few hours, and the energy I would've used transporting my family to our tomb, digging out a grave instead. I quickly learned how therapeutic digging a grave could be, especially as it provided me with ample time to plan the demise of those who killed my family.

At last, the grave was complete. It looked large enough for my parents and my sister.

With the grave ready, I slowly picked up my parents, mother first, father second. Though there were bits of flesh and bone that collapsed at my touch, I was able to push past it. I was done with tears. I had none left anyway. My hate drove me, and I was glad for it.

Slowly, but lovingly, I lifted their torsos. And where parts of them separated—arms or sometimes legs—I picked them up separately and placed them gently into the grave. It was almost finished.

With my parents placed in the grave, I returned to my piece of chair. And rather than using it to transport anyone to our family's tomb, I instead used it to transport my sister's body to the makeshift grave. Not as burned or disfigured as my parents, my sister's body was intact and heaviest. While I hesitated and considered taking her to the tomb, I decided, after beseeching Ariadne, that it would be best she be buried with my parents. I placed her on the slab of wood, and gently pulled her over to the hole in the floor. As I encircled Cilana with my arms, under hers, I slid her off the floor and down into the grave to join my parents. It would be the last time I ever touched them. In this life.

As soon as my family was tended to, I crawled over the rubble of our entryway and the shriveled remnants of Cilana's barrier. I plopped onto the ground and stared blankly down the path. Blurry piles of charred debris mixed with memories of life and joy. I reached up and tapped the slice on my neck and examined my fingers.

Dry.

I don't know how long I sat there, but time passed in a hazy void bereft of plans or cares. At some point, a dull weight wore on my head and pulled me out of my focus on nothingness. My lips felt slick in taut dehydration. My heart raced and my breathing was shallow. I needed water. I wanted a drink so terribly, and my stomach hurt with hollow hunger. I decided my best chances of securing anything to drink or eat would be to search the ruins of our village while working my way to the well.

After clambering to my feet, I stepped gingerly over an especially jagged pile of debris and kept to what had been a fairly wide corridor that seemed to be my best chance of reaching the well. I frequently wiped my eyes and face from my tears and smoke, but I paused occasionally to make sure my bearings didn't drift.

While continuing towards the well, I came upon an intact wooden box that had tumbled out from a home and into the middle of the path. It was a mundane box and was sealed only with a sliding latch. Hoping for food, I leaned down and slid the lever and flipped the top. Inside, I found some clothing, a blanket, and below those, a pair of axes. I eyed the weapons admiringly and pulled them out.

With one in each hand, I tossed and caught them a few times. Their weight felt good. Their bronze blades looked well cared for, and they looked solidly made. They must have been made by one of our warriors or by a seasoned hunter.

I slid my fingers along the handle as I felt a building lump in my throat. I wondered if I knew their maker. I wondered if their owner had tried to get to them during the attack. I didn't know, but the focus of rage and vengeance in me grew that much more.

After sliding them under my belt, I continued on and spotted a pile of debris that used to be a house that stood in front of the well. I got nervous as I approached.

The destroyed home smoked and smoldered and even in the humidity and heat of our burned village, I felt myself sweating while my hands turned clammy. I inched closer and could finally peer around the pile of rubble.

My heart sank and I screamed with hateful frustration. I couldn't make out the well. It was covered by piles of charred brick that had collapsed onto it from the nearby granary. I walked towards it, regardless.

When I got as close as I could to where the well should have been, I stared at the jumble of brick. Despite knowing I was going to search for it, I pondered the likelihood of it actually still having drinkable water. I answered myself by digging.

I slumped to my knees to grab and sling chunks of brick. I swept some bits away with my arm, but had to heave or roll the bigger ones. Every so often, I would look up at my newly-acquired axes and picture myself wielding, flourishing, throwing, or hacking with them. Each stab of wood into the ground was a pretend slice into the faces of the murderers. With just enough stamina to continue until I discovered the state of the well, I picked up the next brick and was flooded with hope and excitement. A piece of timber had landed over the top of the well and seemingly blocked anything from falling in.

I tried to push the piece of timber but it easily resisted me. I looked down the length of it and saw that it was quite long and covered by the majority of the collapsed brick.

After standing up and racing down the length of it, I kicked away as much of the brick as I could. I then shot back up to where the well was, fell on my butt and strained with my elbows against the ground to try and shove the piece of timber out of the way. I gritted my teeth and grunted. It initially put up a fight, but I felt it start to give way. My elbows felt like they were being sliced open, but the gravel helped me. The piece of wood fought back, but I waited it out. The momentum of sliding along the gravel defeated it, and I was finally able to shove it forward the distance of my stretched legs.

A sigh of exhausted breath puffed out. I spun around onto my stomach and stuck my head in the well. The rope that I hoped was still attached to the bucket had also been freed. I grabbed and pulled.

There was some weight to it, so naturally I imagined it being filled with mud or rocks. I reached and pulled, pulled and reached. And it finally came into sight. The bucket rose up towards me, and along with it, my reflection. It rippled in the reflection of the wobbly water inside.

I laughed and gasped in exhausted relief as I finished pulling it up. Once I had it, I plopped it down beside me, dunked my hand in, and pulled up some water before letting it escape through my fingers.

It's clear!

I leaned over and tipped the bucket towards me and drank as much as I could, as quickly as I could. I drank and drank, careful not to lose too much through the sides of my mouth. Instead of feeling like just a day since I last had water, it felt like weeks. Once I'd had my fill, I sat back up and laughed again, my mind confused on how to react to such a good thing amid such horror. I would survive the next few days, at least, and that was time I could spend looking for the murderers.

I shared a few more laughs of shock with no one but my emboldened hatred. After another few gulps, I lowered the bucket to refill it and brought it back up before looking for some skins to take some with me. I found a few and filled them up before finishing off the bucket.

My exhausted laughs didn't last. They gave out and gave in to sobbing once more as if my laughter knew I was fooling myself. I couldn't hide. Even with my thirst quenched, the smoldering timbers around me shoved me back into reality. As if offended from the afterlife, the nearby dead with their shriveled skin demanded my tears. My head fell from the weight of my sorrow, making my chin bounce and dig into my chest as I cried.

How dare I laugh?

How dare I laugh with so many of my kin cooked to death around me?

How dare I laugh while my parents and sister rest in the ground mere yards from me?

My breathing slowed and my mind drifted back to nothingness. Revenge was no longer a consideration. There was none to talk to. No tasks to take care of. Nothing to accomplish. Past, present, and future blended together in a blank definition devoid of hope, home, or ambition. But as my head bobbed with smoother and deeper breathing, my vision shifted slightly. The axes I had found captured my thoughts once again. I reached behind and pulled them out from my belt.

Chapter Five - Luxuries

Bayla

My mind spun into a frenzy of thought after being hollow and hopeless. The pain in my throat—lingering from before my rage took over—disappeared.

I scraped my eyes against my sleeves and shoved up to my feet. I ran back down the path and leapt over piles of rubble to return to our home's ruins. With an axe in each hand, the added weight helped whip my arms back and forth as I jumped and ran. They felt great. They felt natural, like an extension of myself.

When I encountered piles I couldn't jump over, I fell to all fours and crawled. After a few more bounds, I was back at the crumbled but mostly-unburned kitchen area. While carefully stepping around the final piles of hot debris and smoking cinders, I scanned the kitchen. Though I knew the raiders had stolen my parents' magically imbued weapons, I hoped to find certain other items undisturbed.

I tossed and kicked the rubble. I threw and slung everything that was in my way. Strewn about the ground were blackened pots and singed platters. Broken bricks and clay fragments sparkled brightly after the extreme heat. But there was a small chest where mother kept some of her weaving implements. And it was where father stored my papyrus.

Papyrus. A luxury on our island. Father had traded for it at some point during his travels. Mine was only one of two in the house. The other was Cilana's. The papyri were beyond special to me and my sister. They were where we documented our lessons—the lessons towards our rankings in the Arts of Ariadne our parents taught us.

A lot of good it did me. A lot of good I was to Cilana.

I reached down into the chest and flung mother's weaving materials out of the way and crunched down onto the papyrus with a claw of anger. I squinted at the rolled-up document with contempt.

All these years of defensive training, finishing rank one in magic, and I forgot to say the spell first. Lost my sister. I might as well have killed her myself. My family.

I whipped my head around looking for a hot ember to destroy the papyrus with, but as soon as I had the thought, I looked back at it, and loosened my grip. A new blanket of shame fell over me.

"No, no, I'm sorry," I said to no one. Well, maybe I was speaking to the papyrus. Or to my family. Or the magic, the village, the history. Maybe I was saying it to all of them.

I looked back to my family's grave. I crawled, stepped, and clambered back over to it before kneeling next to it. After reaching for a rock and a piece of wood, I rolled the papyrus out and weighed it down.

My chin quivered and my eyes started to water, but I kept it together. The scratches and scrawls of my and my father's writing dared me to lose my composure, but I didn't. The past year of talking, listening, learning, and testing my lessons with father flashed through my mind, again, daring me to lose control. But I didn't. Shared experiences, now only known only to me, raced through my mind.

The image of me and my father sitting at the table, with only the light of a single candle keeping us company as he explained a spell to me.

My mother walking by us the same night, laughing affectionately at us, correcting my father's mistaken pronunciation of a spell.

My sister sitting on the front step, watching the moon and listening with a smile to the same lesson she had learned just a year before me.

The papyrus below me reflected the same priorities the rest of the village had, in all its disciplines through the previous generations. First, I learned the fundamentals of fortification. When I first heard these referred to, I thought mother and father were speaking of violent skills, or at least skills pertaining to structural defense, but that wasn't it at all. My first experiences with magic involved acts, practices, and prayers to help encourage crop growth or protect food and plants from decay. My first lessons also included the beginnings of how to protect the natural elements of a structure, as well as minor lessons in healing, whether from sickness or wounds.

The next section covered what are still my favorite topics. Wards, guards and shields. Forms of magic I could not only use to protect myself, but protect those around me. While I would have to study for years to perfect them and strengthen them, I was first taught how to summon and call upon energies.

After the base teachings surrounding fortification and wards came my latest entries on the parchment. I had most recently learned lessons of deflection and reflection. Much like our martial arts, father—and mother especially—

taught me how to deflect those energies of harmful intent, or with more focus and energy, reflect that negative power back at its origination.

Tears welled up solidly but I kept them there. I kept them at bay. It felt too good to remember the loving nights spent learning with my family in the candlelight. My tears would not fall. Not until I let them.

The papyrus blurred slightly from my tears' persistence, but I could still make out the symbols and scripts created by me and my parents as I learned. I traced the symbols with my fingers. I recited portions of the scripts aloud that I had committed to memory. Once I had memorized them, and my parents confirmed I had, I committed them to the papyrus.

As I reached the end of my entries, I let my tears fall. In silence, I couldn't identify anything that was of any immediate use.

I had no knowledge or spell that would return those I loved to life, if such a magic even existed. I hadn't yet learned anything that could have protected our home from such a devastating fire. And even with the magic I knew, I still failed to execute it properly.

I didn't say the prayer first.

She even reminded me during the demonstration.

Oh, Cilana. I'm so sorry for failing you.

For all that I had been taught, whether farming, fighting, or magic, I was still surrounded by nothing but death and destruction.

I looked at my new axes for inspiration. They rekindled my rage and ironically calmed me. My shoulders fell. My eyes dried up. I breathed slowly through my nose.

I had no magic to help me enact my revenge, but I had my axes. Between the axes and...

My memories stepped back in.

Mother walking by. Father sitting at the table with me. My sister on the steps smiling at what she had already learned.

She had started learning magic before me.

She was a rank two!

She had her own papyrus!

I spun and scanned the debris.

Where were her notes? Where did she keep hers? Where did father keep it?

I continued spinning in the small, cleared out space of our jumbled floor.

And then I remembered and jerked to a stop.

The steps!

It wasn't the outside front steps, but rather, the small set of five steps leading up to my and Cilana's room. Sitting across five tiers of steps were five boards. I crawled over and kicked debris. As I made it to the stairs, I kicked off the lowest step. The area below the step was hard to make out. Between the shade from the sides of the stairs and the fire's char, the hope in my heart bottomed out.

I shoved my hand down into the abyss, and hit dirt. And with stretched and curled fingers, like mimicking a hopping spider, I tapped around on the dirt.

Rocks.

Straw.

A clump of charred material gave way only slightly as I felt around. I reached further back towards the second, third, and fourth step. My skin itched and tingled with worry that it was gone.

The fire must've gotten to it.

But then I felt a flattened material with a moderate texture. The edges felt like a checker pattern, but then smoothed out towards the center. My eyes shot open in surprise as I grabbed it and pulled it out.

Cilana's papyrus!

"I found it!" I screamed. I held it up in the direction of my family's grave. I waved it around as fresh tears of joy spilled over my eyelids.

I grabbed my axes and Cilana's notes and darted over piles and memories and sat down on the remnants of our front stoop—where my sister sat at night.

I scooted my legs up close to me and started reading over Cilana's writing. I first tried to make out the labels of topics. Just like mine, hers started with fortification, wards, and deflection and reflection.

My heart thumped a few hard beats.

What comes next?

I skimmed for the topics.

The next one after deflection and reflection, what I assume I would have started learning next, was communication. I read the notes my sister had taken— the symbols and text, but I couldn't focus. My eyes darted back and forth as I considered what might be encompassed in such a large topic. I could have tried to read the notes for clues, but I was having too much fun anticipating the possibilities.

Besides, as my parents taught me, there is very little about the magic of our people that is straightforward. Whether it is the symbols, speech, or language of our magic, it can't always be taken literally, and makes very little sense to those untrained on how to interpret what is written or said. Other than the topic heading, I would need to study the document for some time before I understood it completely. I was also fully aware that anything attempted from these sections I hadn't yet learned could be extremely dangerous, and would likely result in something unintended.

I'll look into that one later.

The next section covered enchantments.

Enchantments!

It was exactly the type of thing I was hoping to find. I still had no idea if I could make sense of Cilana's notes, separate from my own studies, but I had to try.

I traced over the symbols and uttered the parts I recognized out loud. I skimmed and floated my finger down the papyrus. Puzzled by the advanced lessons I hadn't seen before, my face flinched and jerked as I encountered the complex tasks. But as I looked further down, something scribbled off to the side, almost as an afterthought, caught my eye.

Items can be enchanted to be an instrument of any spell from rank one. Use the appropriate spell and ingredients, but the caster's blood is also required. Add it to the mix to contain the energy of the spell within the item. Make the item to be enchanted the target of the spell.

I pulled the papyrus away. My head tilted in astonishment. I had to read it again.

I continued staring at it but looked at my axes and then back to the papyrus. My face relaxed. I breathed heavily as a hint of excitement flooded my veins. My eyes widened and I launched myself back over to the ruins of the kitchen. As I gently picked at and shifted clay, stone, and wood, I plucked out the bits of remaining ingredients I could find—left over from what Cilana and I had gathered.

After scanning the floor to confirm I had most everything I needed for every spell I knew, I saw that I was missing one ingredient.

Blood.

My excited eyes relaxed as the realization filled me with dread. I looked at a palm and wiggled my thumb.

Without another hesitation, I brought up an axe and sliced a shallow but long cut across the meatiest part of my palm. I hissed from the slice but quickly refocused. I crawled and loomed over my collected ingredients while I confirmed a few drops of blood fell onto each bit of material. My eyes widened again in anticipation. I wrapped my hand quickly and spoke the spell of my first attempt.

"Pollaplasiaste to yliko se afto to stoicheio. Afxiste to se megethos kata dyo fores."

Multiply the material of this item. Increase its size by a factor of two.

I swiped up the first pile of ingredients and clapped my hands before shoving my open palms at my axes. The axes popped in a vibrant flash of green light. I jumped back a bit and stared at them.

Did I do it?

I picked up the axes and examined them slowly. They felt the same. They looked the same. They hadn't changed in size, despite my spell.

Did I enchant them?

My eyes fell off the axes as I scanned the room. I stopped on a small clay pot laying on its side. A large chunk had been broken off its rim.

Okay, I thought. *So, if I were doing this spell directly, I would say the prayer, which I've done, and then direct the energy of the spell and ingredients at the object. But how do I do it with the axes?*

I waved them at the pot.

Nothing.

I stuck my arms out and pointed the axes at the pot.

Nothing.

I don't understand.

I leaned back over to Cilana's papyrus to see if I had missed something.

No. Nothing else seems to be related. Do I need to throw them at the pot like I would the ingredients? Well that wouldn't be very useful.

I stared at them, wondering how else I could possibly get the spell's energy from the axes to the pot.

What if I hold them up and...

Smack!

I tapped the axes together. A wave of rippling wind shot out from them just as if I had done it with my own hands. The energy washed over the pot. As it rippled across its surface, the pot swelled in size.

"Ha ha! Yes!" I shouted.

As if wanting to call my sister over to show her, I yelled her name.

"Cilana!"

My eyes floated around the room to find another object to test on.

Smack!

I struck the axes together again and faced them towards a large brick. Again, the energy of the spell shot through the room and struck the brick. It popped into a form twice its original size. I squealed in delight.

"I can't believe it! It works!"

I tested it on another brick.

Smack!

A piece of wood.

Smack!

One by one I said my spells. One by one I infused my axes with my ingredients. One by one I tested each spell on more pots and rocks and bricks and wood. Amid the rubble of our home and among the ruins of our village, I walked and tested. Most of the time I walked along giggling in awe, but spent a great deal of time crying as I experimented.

I hope you all can see this.

By the time I finished enchanting my axes with everything I knew, I was beyond exhausted. It hit me hard when my exhilaration wore off. I was already completely spent from the previous night's attack, so while I waited for the day's hottest heat to pass, I tried to find something to eat.

Most of our village's food—at least where I suspected it could be found amongst the rubble—had long turned to ash. I found bits and bites here and there, but the lack of food was just another reason to hurry up and get moving. I spent the bulk of midday searching as much of the debris as I could, but as the sun started to descend, I decided to leave.

I wanted to find out who destroyed my village, and I wanted them to answer for it, but at the same time, I didn't want to leave. Though the only remnants of my people were ash and destruction, the idea of abandoning even the leftovers of my village's life tore at everything that was me, my soul, and my heart. I had only ever lived *there*. And I almost died there. It's where my parents and sister were buried. By me.

But I mentally swam through my tears and gnawed away at my anxiety. I would not let my fear of leaving stop me from finding these people. They would not escape me or my justice. I didn't care how long it took, what I needed to do, how I needed to do it, but those people would die.

I reluctantly returned to the village perimeter, turning my back on all I had ever known as home. Ruin, death, and questions were behind me. Answers and revenge were before me. And so, too, were the tracks of the raiders.

The tracks were fairly narrow and changed little as they approached from the north and exited our village to the southeast. In the center of the tracks, there looked to be some number of wheeled carts with footprints for three people wide, on each side of the carts. I of course couldn't determine the size of the group. But at least I knew which way they were going, and that's all I needed.

I swallowed and choked down my shivering urge to cry again. I couldn't allow it anymore. I had to focus and move. I had to move forward. I had to follow these tracks to the killers of my family.

One foot in front of the other.

Don't look back.

I didn't give in, but it cost me. I burst out crying once more.

Forward.

As I cried, I stepped forward. I moved forward. Through my tears I saw the tracks and footprints glide beneath my own feet as I followed them.

One step closer to revenge.

I never did look back. Having allowed myself the privilege of crying, I made the deal with myself that I wouldn't set my eyes on anything behind me. But with each step that I took away from my village, the guilt from abandoning my home conjured up a haunting spirit that I swear I heard chastising me for leaving. In the last few crackles of the charred embers of my village, it was as if something were amplified, threatening me for surviving. My conscience looked back, but *I* didn't. My conscience could look back and engage with my guilt all it wanted, but I had control of my feet, and I moved them forward. I had control of my eyes, too, and I focused them forward. Though everything else in my body wanted to turn around and run back to the graves of my family again and scream how sorry I was for surviving, I didn't. I couldn't. I wouldn't.

Each step was a challenge. Every step I took was a dash of salt in the wound of my awareness that I was far from home, and that home was now nothing but ash. Each step and stomp, though, came with slightly drier eyes. Slightly lessened guilt. A more silent conscience.

It got to the point where I was falling asleep and

getting woken up by tripping or outright falling. I'd slide on gravel and kick stones the wrong way and hurt my foot. I'd almost pass out, step too wide, or slide down in an uncontrolled split. Other times a leg would give out and I'd crash down on a knee.

My stomach was hollow and it spun and wrapped around itself to remind me. My head hurt with a groggy pain and my thoughts drowned in a sea of confusion. At times I didn't know why I kept going. Very often I would forget who I was, or where I was. The awareness of what happened to my village evaporated from my thoughts like the first drops of rain on hot stone.

Eventually, I was sleeping more than I was watching where I was going. The darkness and sleep outnumbered the wakefulness. The jarring jolts of falling and stumbling stopped bursting out of my bouts of unconsciousness. But in what was almost my last sliver of consciousness before completely passing out, I saw the silhouette of a small village ahead of me.

I remember thinking, *I need to go down there. I need to get down there.*

I couldn't remember why at the time. My mind shifted about slowly like meandering clouds.

A wave of dizziness unexpectedly sent me swaying, but I blinked heavily and stretched my eyelids. I just *had* to get to the village.

I stumbled along only able to register how much impact my knees were weathering as I walked. I must have been clopping along like a donkey.

Clop, clop, clop. Ouch, ouch, ouch.

My state was such that I was aware of the pain, but couldn't think about changing my posture or pace to walk better. Something else propelled me.

I remember catching a glimpse of the Aegean to the

side of the village as I approached.

I smiled.

The sea made me happy. Its sight and smells. It was fresh and alive. I decided to veer off around the side of the village towards the beach.

I must have looked silly, clopping along like a drunk with a ridiculous grin on my face. But those thoughts were definitely not in my mind at the time. No, I was only thinking about the pretty water.

Something changed as I walked. Something became more pleasant. The frequency of *ouch, ouch, ouch* in my mind decreased. Something must have felt better to my knees.

That's it, I thought. I switched from walking on uneven rocks and packed earth to lush fields of grass. And I grew warmer. I lost the occasional cover of trees as I approached the beach.

After surviving the walk around the outer edges of the village I stopped on top of a hill. Looking down through the village I could see a path leading to the water.

I don't remember why I stopped. I didn't have a coherent motive for stopping, but I can remember being absolutely fascinated by whatever those things were down at the water's edge. They ended up being two beautiful boats docked at the village piers. I had enough sense to make my way to them.

The walk down to the docks grew even easier. The slope down was slight, and the grass wasn't very thick. And I don't know if it was because I was getting a second, third, or fourth wind, but I found just enough energy to think to myself that I was either dehydrated, hungry, hot, or all three. Regardless, I knew that I had to make an effort to think.

I looked down at my feet. They offered me no

assistance, but I was mainly just letting my head relax for a moment. As I strained to begin the process of thinking about what I was doing, I looked back up to the village. I smiled again. Not because I recognized it immediately, or because I knew where I was, but only that it looked similar to Skarkos. I was still home, to some degree, and that was the extent that I cared about that at the time. I turned back to the docks and resumed my strange but less painful gait towards them.

I couldn't understand why there were massive centipedes sitting in the water, and why they had sticks in their backs and blankets attached to them. I stopped again, this time, close enough to hit them if I threw a rock. I stood, puzzled as to what was going on with the centipedes.

You're so stupid, was all I could think at first, but then I justified my self-admonishment.

Those aren't centipedes.

A mental fog tried to settle in my brain again.

I saw a man whipping and flinging his arms around, pulling and stretching them.

Is he going to wrestle the centipedes? What's going on?

And then, a stubborn pinch of clarity blessed my brain. I rubbed my head and rolled my eyes at myself.

"Those are ships, and those men are rowers," I said in silly chastisement to myself.

They can sail the seas, I thought, but I hadn't quite pieced reality back together yet.

They can sail. They can sail the seas. They can travel...

And with absolutely no warning, my brain crashed down onto my memories which in turn refreshed my awareness. *I was traveling to try and find the killers of my family. I was tracking them in the direction that led me to this village*, apparently.

I couldn't tell right then if I was still on track or if I had wandered and gotten lost, so I started to shout out questions while I was coherent enough to ask them.

"Where am I?"

The few men I could see from my vantage point didn't speak. No one even looked in my direction as I yelled more questions.

"Who are you? Where are you going?"

I squeezed and flexed my eyes once again. *Is it a perception issue? Do I think they are closer than they are?*

"Hello? Pardon me! Excuse me!"

I saw a man carrying things onto one of the boats look over at me as he saw out his task. He disappeared behind cargo and equipment on the boat but quickly returned.

"Can you help me?" I cried again, hoping someone would answer.

This time, I saw a few more men lean up and look.

I rubbed my face. The pressure of my hand seemed to linger for many seconds after. My skin craved additional stimulation to keep itself awake, just as my mind craved sleep.

A small boulder nearby caught my eye. I hunched over and shambled over to it as if preparing to scoop down and pick up a small child running towards me. Instead, I swooped down and collapsed onto the weathered stone. I leaned over and caught my head in my hands before closing my eyes. As I settled Ton my seat, one of the men approached.

"Is everything all right?" He asked from nearby. My sleep deprived state wouldn't allow me to look at him just yet. His voice was rough and deep, though his question bounced along with what sounded like genuine concern.

I slowly pulled my head out of my hands and opened

my eyes. A few curious villagers up from the beach had stepped out in curiosity.

Is everything all right? I repeated to myself. I had no idea how to respond.

Seeing what looked to be a loving mother and dutiful adolescent son up the hill concussed my chest with a clear, living nightmare of my circumstances.

I looked up to the concerned sailor.

"My... village was burned," I managed to say, my throat crumbling from exhaustion and mourning. "My family..."

The man shifted his feet and looked back to his boat before turning back towards me. I swallowed repeatedly in hopes of getting rid of the sorrowful knot in my throat, but it wasn't helping. Maybe I could talk it away.

"I need to—" I started.

The sound of people approaching caught my attention. I looked up in time to see the sailor finish waving the mother and boy down from the village.

"I need to find those who raided my village," I finished as the mother and son approached.

"Someone has destroyed this girl's village," the sailor said to the woman.

"What?" She asked with sharp shock. "Where are you from?"

At that moment I could not recall the name of my village.

"I need to find them. I need to track them or find them or kill them!" I said with a delirious bite.

The mother recoiled and pulled her son closer.

"I don't think you're in much of a condition to pursue anyone," the sailor replied.

The sailor and mother exchanged concerned glances.

"You should rest, young lady," the mother said. "If

you wish to come with me, I will ask about finding you a place to rest and regain your strength."

"No, no," I said, shaking my head. "I need to find the ones that destroyed my village. Please. I just need to rest here a moment."

The woman reached for her son's shoulder and shuffled him around her, steering him back to the village. She shared a look of pitiful worry for me with the sailor before turning back to the village herself.

The sailor turned to look at his ship again but looked back.

"I wish you health and luck in finding those responsible, but I must leave," he said, turning back towards the sea.

"What village is this?" I asked despite his attempt to leave. "How long have you been docked here?"

Having already taken a few steps away, the sailor stopped and partially turned back.

The sailor stared at me silently, trying to decide, I'm sure, whether to answer or continue on.

"Milopotas. This is Milopotas. My men and I are traders. We arrived mid-morning today after a few previous stops. We set out from Manika eight days ago, on our way to Alashiya."

Milopotas. Milopotas. I had to close my eyes to focus, but I finally placed it. After a few additional seconds of concentration, I realized I was extremely familiar with the name. A wave of comfort washed over me as I found some relief in knowing where I was. I uncovered another note of calm after remembering my thought process that led me to where I was. I had made the decision to head to our island's port most likely to be used by the marauders as they left the island.

I strained to look around and behind the sailor and study the docks.

"Is there anyone else here right now?"

"No, and we'll probably be one of the last for the summer. The storms at sea are getting into the height of their harshest period. Speaking of which, I really need to get back to preparing for—"

"Please, wait," I said, as I somehow found energy to jump to my feet. "Was there anyone else here when you arrived?"

The man sighed.

My burgeoning quest for vengeance was at a crossroads. My energy was long spent and I knew I was doing some kind of harm to myself by robbing my body of rest, water, and nutrition. But it just wasn't my priority at that moment. I looked at the sailor with a weathered face wrinkled and contorted in a desperate need for information. My need to pursue those responsible for my village's atrocity far outweighed any selfish needs, and only making progress on the former would allow me to consider the latter. The sailor must have recognized that.

"There was a Persian boat that set out shortly after we arrived. And according to them, there were some Egyptians and Phoenicians that left last night."

I opened my mouth, preparing another question, but he anticipated it.

"I don't know how many of which, or what they were doing, trading, or what. Someone in the village may know."

I looked up the beach. The mother and boy were nowhere to be found.

"Now, please, I really must get back to my ship," he said.

I leapt a few steps towards him.

"Please, wait, let me go with you!"

"Don't be silly," he snapped with a scoff. "The seas are treacherous enough for a boat full of rowers, much less for a young woman!"

I stepped closer, waiting to sneak in a response.

"No," he continued. "It will be months before we get back anywhere near close to Ios. Surviving the journey isn't a guarantee for me, my men, and surely wouldn't be guaranteed for you!"

"I understand the dangers. I'm willing to risk it," I replied.

He raised a hand and tried to interrupt.

"I won't be a hindrance," I added. "I promise. I'll stay out of the way of the boat's operation and will find ways to help, if you won't let me man an oar."

"You don't understand," the sailor replied. "Having *anything* unnecessary on any ship presents a danger to it and the people that are *supposed* to be on it. Don't you see?"

He threw his arms up at me as he turned to his boat again. He fortified his position as he walked.

"And there's not even a guarantee that we'd be sailing in the same direction. The seas are vast, miss. Almost as vast as your delusions."

I followed after him as my insistence helped spike my coherence and wakefulness.

"You said the other boats were Persian, Egyptian and Phoenician, right?"

"Yes," he said in a grumpy huff.

"And you're heading towards Alashiya?" I asked to confirm.

"Mm hmm," he replied. He suddenly stopped walking and turned to me to shove a finger in my face.

"Don't be so daft!" He shouted, before forcing himself into a whisper. "Just because those other boats were manned by people who originate in the east, and just because we're heading east, does not mean—"

"But there's a chance! There's a chance we can catch up with them! Most boats and traders end up at the same ports, right?"

Whatever points I was trying to make were not having much of an impact as he resumed his march and stomped back to the docks.

"Absolutely not!" He growled. "And as I already said, I will not have an unnecessary passenger endangering my goods, or my men! Now get away!"

"I will pay you! I can pay!"

The sailor stopped again, and put his hands on his hips as he dropped his head. I stopped as well, letting him come to his decision without additional prodding, confident that a promise of pay would help secure my passage.

"How much?" He asked softly. I only just made his question out.

I panicked. I only had one statue reclaimed from my village. It wouldn't be enough to persuade him.

"I... I salvaged what I could from the village as I searched for survivors and food. I buried all of the valuables I found close to the village. I couldn't take it all with me, of course, but I brought this with me."

I pulled the golden statue of Ariadne from my bag and rubbed the inset turquoise stones with my thumb. The shifting of his shadow out of the corner of my eye told me that he turned back towards me.

He must be intrigued.

"I will tell you where to find the rest when we arrive at the next port, for when you pass back this way."

"You won't be wanting to come back with us?"

A bit of relief trickled through my veins since he didn't automatically refuse again.

"If I don't find them at the next port, I'll gather whatever info I can, and perhaps, continue on with you.

If I don't find them by the time we get to Alashiya, or if I do indeed realize my vengeance, then perhaps I will come back. But I suspect I'll find very little reason to return to a destroyed village."

Distant movement caught my attention. A small group of men had stepped away from the docks.

"Captain Nereus?" One of them shouted. "We're about all set here!"

Captain? I thought. *Of course!*

He offered them a quick wave in acknowledgment but continued looking at me. He stepped closer and squinted a gritty glare of cynicism and experience at me.

"And how do you intend on inflicting your revenge upon this mysterious band of murderous bandits you're attempting to locate?"

I swallowed, but my resolve refilled.

"I haven't yet defined the specifics, and still have information to gather, but..."

I reached behind me and slipped my axes out from my belt as I continued. The blades glowed brightly as I stirred them, their warmth rekindling my passionate hate. Nereus' eyes bulged wide.

"I will be ready," I said.

In the moments of silence that followed, I saw Nereus' eyes dart nervously back and forth between me and the axes. A spike of worry surged through my veins. I slipped the axes back behind me and changed subjects.

"But yes, I can give you this statue now, and I will tell you where the rest is later."

Before he could speak again, I handed him the statue. Though in truth there were no other valuables to eventually lead him to, I was the most nervous I had been during our conversation as I hoped the single statue was enough to entice him.

He rubbed his eyes and stared at the statue.

"Listen," he started. "One statue and a girl's promise of a buried treasure is not going to win my men over."

Oh, no! He's going to refuse!

I argued with myself on whether to say something else, or stay silent. I had to bite my tongue to prevent saying a jumble of worthlessness. But I finally let my tongue go when I thought I had something that would seal the deal.

"We can keep this between ourselves, if you wish."

Nereus slowly turned to look at his men, but eventually turned back with a mischievous grin.

Chapter Six - Benches and Plazas

Bayla

"So, listen. Let me do the talking," Nereus told me as we approached the boat. "I'm going to tell my men that the village has paid to send you to Alashiya to tend to your father who has just died."

Nereus stopped abruptly.

"I mean no offense to you or your village to lie like this, but a death in the family is one of the few things I can hopefully get the men to accept easily. Do you understand?"

"Why must you convince them?" I wondered. "Aren't these oarsmen slaves?"

Nereus scowled at me with what resembled a mixture of confusion and contempt. "What? No. These men are free. They are proud seafarers who trade for their homes and villages back on the mainland."

I swallowed and nodded. "I apologize. I didn't realize."

Nereus seemed to forgive me with a quick smirk and a hop of his eyebrows. He started back towards the boat.

"And this statue... I'll just say it's what the village paid us to see you to Alashiya. All right?"

"Yes," I whispered quickly.

Some of the men on the ship stopped in their tracks or put down their cargo to stare at us as we approached. The ship these trading men called home for a large portion of the year was a sleek instrument of the sea. Its top deck was flat and largely clear of obstruction, save a single main mast. The majority of the deck was dedicated to well-organized stacks and bundles of spice, fabric, and grain. Protruding out from one side of the ship were, as I counted them, twenty-two oars stowed along the length of the ship, with a matching number on the other side.

Nereus and I stepped onto the docks. Our footsteps beat on the wooden planks and summoned the attention of even more men. Streams of scantily-clad bastions of strength streamed up from the lower deck. Some stepped out onto the dock to greet their captain.

"Gather 'round men," Nereus began before shouting a repetition. "Gather 'round!"

The top deck grew crowded with oarsmen filling in every space possible between the stacks and piles of cargo. As I looked back to Nereus, I noticed countless gazes lighting on me like buzzards to decaying meat. Between expressions of lust dripping down from my face to my chest, to my legs, and glares of contempt and distrust due to the anticipated news Nereus had to share, I started to feel cold and itchy. It made me want to cover up with something.

"This here young lady's father has died, men, and she needs our help," Nereus began.

I stood frozen, but my eyes scanned to survey their reactions. *No appreciable change.* Inside, I sighed with a hint of relief.

"She was originally sent here from Alashiya to help her aunt after her uncle passed, but now, she has lost her own father and needs to get back home."

"We mean to sail with a woman, captain?" A man on deck shouted.

"Yes," Nereus responded immediately. His voice boomed with confident authority as he bolstered his orders with heaping helpings of guilt and honor. "Yes," he repeated. "We will help this young woman who has already lost an uncle get home to attend to the father she has just lost."

Some of the disgusting and hateful stares lessened in intensity. Others, did not.

"As thanks and payment, the village here has offered us this statue of gold and gems," Nereus continued, lifting it up for all to see. "I will sell this where we can get a good price for it and split it amongst us."

The crew ruffled with mumbles and groans of approval.

"What do you say men? A little extra coin just for sailing the lady to Alashiya?"

The majority of the crew that I could see from my point of view responded with claps, nods and even stronger, approving grunts. Like ripping a piece of cloth from a gift, my anxiety was ripped away with a refreshing quickness. Nereus had done it.

As the mens' reaction died down, a few voices burst out from the ship.

"What good is coin to us at the bottom of the sea, captain?"

Nereus laughed quickly.

"I made no mention of the bottom of the sea. To what are you referring?" Nereus asked. "I could guess, but I don't like to assume. Please, share your concerns with us."

Only the gentle lapping of the waves at the dock pylons could be heard in response.

"Oh, don't be shy. Out with it!" Nereus ordered. "We

don't have time for this."

The man with the complaint stepped forward, out from the main throng on the ship's top deck.

"I'm sorry for saying so, miss, especially with your recent loss, but, captain... Having a woman on board is just asking for trouble. If not from the gods, or the sea, at least possibly from the temptation she would encourage."

Some of the men grumbled and gestured in agreement. Not as many as those who responded in agreement with Nereus, but enough that it had to be addressed. Nereus looked over to me, and then back to the men.

"Temptation she would encourage?" Nereus questioned. "What do you mean by that?"

"Well, sir, she's a woman. She would be the only one on board. Some of the men may not be able to help themselves."

Nereus looked up to the sky and smiled before slowly lowering his head.

"You said something very important just then," he replied. "About the men not being able to help themselves."

Nereus allowed for a pregnant pause to see if the man could come to Nereus' point on his own.

"The men damned well be able to help themselves. You are free, proud, strong, and successful men. You have a will and brain of your own, and each one of you *can* help yourselves."

Nereus looked at me, his face rigid with clarity.

"And don't hear me wrong, men. I'm not under the impression any of you would act in a dishonorable way."

Nereus' voice grew louder. His syllables clipped quicker with increasing annoyance.

"I'm simply replying to this man's suggestion, and refuse to believe that just by virtue of being alive, and being a woman, that any of you would lose control of your minds and bodies and do something that I would make you regret!"

"And as far as your insinuation that the sea or the gods may take umbrage to our passenger, let me remind you of our beloved Amphitrite, daughter of he whom I am named after, and wife to Poseidon. Perhaps you should pray to the gods for *their* opinion of women on the sea!"

An awkward silence followed. It allowed me an uncomfortable moment to reflect internally on how thankful I was for Nereus' comments, but I managed to somehow feel guilty for being the reason the man was being chastised. I maintained as neutral a disposition as I could while staring at Nereus and considering his words. His stance and stare hadn't changed since he completed his reprimand, but he eventually had more to add.

"Does anyone have anything else to say?" He prompted.

There was no reply.

"All right. I obviously expect respect and courtesy to be shown to our guest while she is with us, and I'm sure she'll find ways to make herself useful as we sail. Now finish securing our cargo and prepare to depart."

The ship and dock burst into a flurry of activity with men tossing the last few bundles of goods from the docks to the ship. Others on board slid and stacked wooden crates. Once tasks on the docks were complete, the men ran across the modest gangplank spanning the short distance between the docks and the ship.

I took a step closer to Nereus.

"I will of course do anything and everything asked of me," I offered softly. "But, what types of things might that involve?"

"Oh, nothing too drastic or foreign to you. Probably fetching water, food, cleaning, scrubbing the decks, mending cloth, those types of things. And maybe we'll have you take turns with an oar and give the men a break from time to time."

The perfectly-timed and repeated clonk of dull wooden thumps rippled through the air as men prepared their oars. The single, main sail was untied and rigged for hoisting.

Internally, I was intimidated by the prospect of handling an oar, and wasn't looking forward at all to scrubbing decks, but I just looked ahead to the ship as the men scurried along, preparing it for departure. I had no desire to risk my chances of pursuing those who destroyed my village. When I saw movement out of the corner of my eye, I looked over to Nereus.

He winked and grinned. I smiled back, half playfully ignorant, half legitimate.

"What?" I asked.

"I was only serious about the cleaning and the scrubbing. We won't need you to handle an oar."

I smiled and laughed only through whispered huffs. I turned back to the ship.

"Ah, you're afraid I'd do it better than the men," I said, looking back to Nereus. "I understand."

Nereus' grin crept out even wider.

* * *

We set out from Milopotas no more than an hour after Nereus introduced me to his men, if you could call it an introduction. After stepping on deck, Nereus immediately pointed to a bench towards the rear of the ship.

"You're to sit there until we clear the island's rocks," he directed.

I said nothing as I complied, wanting to begin my passage the same way I hoped my entire journey on the ship would go—quietly.

The majority of men scurried below while a small contingent remained up top to tend to the main sail and final securing of cargo. The seat beneath me vibrated and pulsed as I felt the men below releasing their oars. As I craned my neck to try and see what was happening, I heard most of the oars splash into the water with a controlled restraint. Within a few minutes, the ship had cleared the docks such that the oars from both sides could be swung out completely. Once the men could fully extend their oars, the distance between the ship and the docks quickly increased. We pulled away from Milopotas, the island, and my entire life up until that point.

The instructions I had been given just minutes before completely left me. I stood up and walked to the rail as if second-guessing my actions. Despite no longer having a home or family, something inside scratched at my will, and tugged on my courage's sleeve.

You have no business leaving this island, a doubt inside said. *What chances do you think you actually have in exacting your revenge against a group of raiders, much less locate them?*

I gripped the rail and looked up to the receding Milopotas.

If you had any sense you would jump over this rail and swim back as quickly as you could.

I looked down to the water which wasn't very far away. I could have jumped and been fine and swam back to the docks easily enough. But the oars stole my attention. Their rhythmic swings back and forth in conjunction with the rhythmic chants down below shushed my doubts. Their sounds and sight pulled me back to my mission. Their trance-like patterns lulled me back to a confident hope fueled by my hate and anger. I let go of the rail.

"What did I tell you?" Nereus barked. "I *just* got

finished telling you to stay seated until I told you otherwise."

He leaned in as he continued. He spoke more deliberately, and softly.

"If this type of distraction is what I can expect while you sail with us, then perhaps I should set you back out on those docks."

I was already scampering back towards the bench before he finished speaking.

"No, no," I offered swiftly. "I apologize. I just thought we had cleared the docks. I didn't intentionally disobey."

"I said rocks. Not docks," Nereus scolded. He shook his head and sighed before turning to the rail. He waved at me to look while scanning the island's coastline.

"Do you see those three boulder formations over there?" He asked. "The tallest of the three I'm looking at is on the left. Do you see it?"

"Yes," I answered.

"Once we pass those, we'll be clear of the rocks and then you can walk around as you like. That's when we will begin making our best speed to the next port. Just let us focus on getting out of here safely. If I have to ask again, I'll throw you over. You will not endanger this ship or my men."

I had not meant to anger him or jeopardize my passage, but his frustration was understood. I sat and waited for the rock formations to pass—not because I had a burning desire to get up again or go exploring the top deck of the ship, but just so that I knew without a doubt that I would not anger anyone again so soon.

I forced a few deep breaths. I tried to find a calm that could help me really register the implications of what I was doing. With the steady drone of the mens' chants below and the slapping of the oars in the water, I found my focus. I found the focus that helped remind me of why I was leaving, and what I intended to do. From that point on, I would be able to dedicate myself entirely to planning on how to carry out my revenge. I could consider all manners of hypotheticals and prepare for contingencies. Whether it was how to go about discovering relevant information, tracking the raiders, or the actual hunting and killing of the murderers, I would have plenty of time to think and plan.

As the rock formations approached to my side, I kept my seat and considered our next port. I would of course ask Nereus for details when he was available, but pondered where we would go next.

We were headed east with an eventual destination of Alashiya. And as we had discussed previously, there's a fairly decent chance—regardless of my eventual prey's identity—that they would also be heading east. It made sense to me that if this was a band of raiders or pirates, that they would make targets out of the same major ports that we would be visiting.

But I almost instantly refuted myself.

If they're only interested in raiding port cities, then why would they have come inland to my village and apparently spared Milopotas? I should've spoken with some of the villagers in Milopotas before we left!

I had missed the opportunity to speak with anyone in Milopotas, and turning back was obviously not an option, so the urge to leap from my seat shot to the top of my mind. I wanted to ask Nereus what he thought about my revelation.

Wait, wait! Are we past the rocks?

I leaned over and strained to look to the coastline. I sighed and scratched my head.

So sleepy, I thought.

With the first real break in conversation or need for action, my eyes instantly felt a hundred times heavier. My head thickened into a worthless slop. *So tired. I need to ask Nereus what he... thinks... about...*

Darkness.

* * *

My eyes opened to a wall of wood only a few inches from my face. Some of my fingertips slipped down the nearest rough board, its coarseness instantly irritating me. My face was sunken into a jumbled pile of cloth. I blinked what felt like a hundred times before I had any meaningful thought.

It's dark out here. Where'd my bench go? I hope we've passed the rocks. Wait, where am I?

My inner voice screamed louder with confusion.

Wait. Am I inside? Where am I?

I was prone and on my side. I violently flipped over to the other side in barely-conscious hysterics. My elbow slammed into the floor. I quickly made out the faint hints of a darkened cabin I hadn't seen before. A man sat with his back to me at a small table at the other end.

Where am I? I've been captured! I've been sold!

I shoved up to my knees and pressed my back against the wall, kicking and scratching all the way up. The man turned in his chair.

"Ah!" The strange man said. "You've come around!"

I scrambled and clawed with my palms as I slid around the edges of the floor, making for the door halfway between me and the stranger. He stood up.

"Wait. Whoa, wait!"

I pushed away from the wall, onto my knees, and leapt up. I darted for the door. But the man caught me.

"What are you doing?" The man asked with a laugh. "Where are you going?"

He wrapped his arms around my torso, attempting to lock my arms in place. I kicked and wriggled and flailed.

87

"No!" I shouted. "Get off of me!"

"Will you just wait a—"

I cut him off by slamming my head back into his chin.

He weathered my hit with a grunt and squeezed tighter. Holding me slightly off to his side, he started to drag me out the door.

Where is he taking me? I had a second to think. *I wanted to leave this room anyway!*

He kicked the door open and the sun slapped me in the face. As I squinted to try and adjust to the light, I saw a crowd of surprised men turn towards me. As I continued being dragged, we passed a bench.

Oh, wait. Oh no. The men. My bench!

The man continued dragging me, inching me closer to the rail. As I was picked up and thrown over the side, I remembered everything I should have remembered a few moments too late.

That was Nereus!

I smacked onto the water before tumbling under. The cool salt water flooded my nose. I paddled and kicked and even before breaking back up to the surface, I could hear dozens of men laughing. I felt more stupid than I ever had before.

When I made it to the surface my humiliation increased as I watched dozens of men lean over the rail to laugh at me. The ship was docked and its oars were stowed. Some men offloading bags of grain continued walking across the gangplank while laughing. Over to my side, a whole other group of men leaned over the edge of the dock to laugh. Nereus justifiably took his time crossing over from the ship to the docks, but once he finally had, tossed down a length of rope to me. I climbed up and collapsed onto the dock. Nereus stepped back with an unabashed smile and crossed his arms. He waited for me to catch my breath.

"I would've thrown you overboard a day or two ago and been rid of you, but you were still breathing every time we checked!"

I found a way to crawl out from my humiliation and look up at him. His smile could not have been bigger.

"I don't know what to say. I feel like a fool," I said. I grabbed a handful of soaked hair, annoyingly stuck to my face and whipped it to the side.

"Ahhh," he said in a forgiving huff. "You were exhausted. We hadn't even cleared those rocks before you slid off the bench onto the deck. You've been asleep in the corner of my cabin ever since! You were the ideal passenger!"

I squinted and took in my surroundings. We were at a new port. Up from the beach was a valley that widened quickly with a village about the size of Milopotas spread across either side.

"How long ago was that?" I asked.

"Two and a half days ago," Nereus answered.

My head fell slightly as my eyes glazed over in disbelief. The legs of the men loading and unloading cargo blended together in a blurry curtain.

"Two and a half days," I said in disbelief.

"Mm hmm," Nereus said. "You'd occasionally grumble in your sleep or roll over, but I figured I'd let you sleep."

"Is this our first stop? Where are we?"

"Well, it's *your* first stop. This is Ialysos," he said. "It's too late to set back out so we'll stay in port here tonight. It should give you some time to see what you can find out."

The sun was hanging on just above the horizon and caught me right in the eye again.

"I meant to ask you before," I started. "If the people I'm after are just some random raiders, why would they have ridden so far inland to attack my village but leave Milopotas alone?"

Nereus continued staring at me but let his smile fall. His eyes drifted away as he considered my question.

Before he could reply, a commotion of disorganized footsteps and angry shouts seeped out from the village. As I stood up to see what was happening, Nereus held up his hands towards his men on the docks. With their captain's silent instruction, they set their crates down. The crowd of approaching men carried clubs and bows. A few had swords.

"Um, Nereus?" I asked in a quick panic. "What's going on?"

He didn't answer. He kept his eyes on the mob. As his eyebrows lifted, he shook his head.

"You there!" A man towards the front of the group shouted. "Stay where you are!"

The dock rumbled with the wooden clatter of some of Nereus' men running back to the ship.

"No, no, men. Be still. Stay put!" He shouted.

As the group of angry villagers stepped onto the dock, Nereus turned back towards them and slowly raised his palms.

"Hello, there," he offered softly.

The small group of men with bows stayed on land at an angle from us, just before the docks. They nocked and drew arrows before aiming them in our direction.

"Who are you and what is your business?" One of the group interrogated.

Nereus' hands remained frozen in place as he replied calmly.

"I am Nereus, and this is my crew. We are traders from the mainland."

The villagers peered at Nereus with suspicion as

various others from the mob strained to gauge the demeanor of the rest of the crew, and then me.

"What about her? Is she a member of your crew?" The group leader spit.

"No," Nereus answered calmly. "She is our guest and will disembark when we reach Alashiya."

The same inquisitive villager continued to stare at me. His face wrinkled and twisted as he looked me up and down multiple times.

"Why is she wet?"

Nereus' mouth dropped open, preparing to provide an answer that he hadn't yet conceived.

I forced a nervous laugh.

"Oh, captain Nereus, you don't have to worry about causing offense," I said. "You see," I added, speaking to the villagers this time, "I slipped off the gangplank. The captain here had just helped me out of the water."

Some of the villagers towards the back chuckled. Even more of Nereus' crew behind me laughed.

The face of the man at the front of the mob relaxed.

"I don't remember you, or this ship," he said with a lessening doubt. "Have you been here to Ialysos before?"

Nereus lowered his hands and looked side to side.

"Um, yes. We have," he said. He held one hand back up quickly as if asking for the villagers' indulgence and waved over one of his men. "We have a record of our last visit, I believe."

Nereus' man moved slowly towards a box while keeping a suspicious eye on the villagers. He too held his hands partially in the air. He slowly lifted off the crate's lid making sure the villagers could see its contents. On top was a papyrus, which the man picked up and offered to Nereus.

"Thank you," Nereus offered the sailor. "Yes, here we are. Um, we were last here, seven months ago. It was on our return from Alashiya. It looks like the primary business was grain and spices in exchange for some cloth and bronze."

Nereus looked up to the villagers.

"We conducted the transaction with a man by the name of Stelios," he concluded.

"Stelios?" The man echoed back. He looked around at his group as they whispered amongst themselves.

"Well, that would explain why I don't know you. Stelios died five months ago. Amyntas here replaced him."

A man from a row back stepped forward.

"Amyntas, it's a pleasure. As previously stated, I am Nereus, captain of the crew and ship behind me. This girl over here... Her name is Bayla."

The villager who had been doing most of the speaking stepped out and waved his arms at the archers. As they lowered their bows, he turned and approached Nereus with an outstretched hand.

"Welcome to Ialysos, Nereus. I am Tomiki."

Nereus grabbed and shook his hand with enthusiasm. A smile found a way to creep out as well.

"I was afraid my reputation had proceeded me," Nereus said with a chuckle. "Or that maybe I had forgotten a payment or a crate of goods."

"No, no," Tomiki said with a small laugh of his own. His momentary amiability quickly crumbled back into a cold distance. "No," he continued. "I'm afraid our village was attacked night before last."

I took a few steps closer to the villagers. My eagerness to let my questions fly must have appeared odd. Nereus looked at me quickly to stay any interruption.

"We haven't been able to determine with certainty who they were, but we have suspicions," Tomiki added. "We formed a small band of men from the village to repel any future attacks."

Nereus placed his hands on his hips and nodded as tensions continued to calm.

"You say you were attacked?" Nereus sought to clarify.

Tomiki nodded.

"Were other villages raided?" Nereus asked. "Any idea what they were targeting?"

Tomiki looked around to his men before turning back to Nereus.

"The sun's just about gone. Why don't a few of my men and a few of yours stay with your ship and cargo. You are welcome to follow us into the village for some food. Perhaps we can share experiences and news, and get a clearer idea of who is behind these attacks."

Nereus looked quickly to me, but then looked at his senior men. With no apparent disagreement, Nereus obliged.

"That's a great idea," Nereus said.

"And you, miss, Bayla, I believe it was..." Tomiki continued. "We might even be able to find you some dry clothes."

I almost rolled my eyes at myself. If it weren't for concern that I'd give Tomiki the impression I was rolling my eyes at him, I would have. Instead, I extended my appreciation.

"That is awfully kind of you," I said. "Thank you."

"Of course," Tomiki replied. "Please, follow me."

Nereus and I followed the men as the majority of the ship's crew fell in behind us. The initial walk to the village was quiet, allowing my concentration and eyes to wander to the cliffs. While they were colored by the dwindling rays of pink and orange, a blissful wind strolled through and rustled the tops of the trees surrounding the village. As the limbs waved and licked at the outermost buildings, it appeared as if the village was a pillow and the trees were fluffing it in preparation for their slumber.

Tomiki had drifted towards the front of the group but fell back when the village center neared, letting his men pass. He waited for us to approach.

"If you would, friends, head towards that covered area across the courtyard there," Tomiki requested. "Men, please see to some wine for our guests."

As most of the men dispersed, Tomiki led us through a courtyard and garden towards an old but charming plaza. At the center was a series of shallow steps leading up to a bird bath stained with mildew and clumps of moss at the base.

"Nereus, if you and your men would care to rest a moment, I'll ask my wife to help Bayla here with some clothes."

Nereus was at a loss for words in response to Tomiki's generosity and extended his hand in gratitude.

"Oh, Tomiki," I tried, feeling guilty for imposing. "There's no need, actually," I said before laughing at myself. "I will dry. There's a good bit of wind and it is still quite warm."

"No, no, it's no trouble," he insisted. "We can loan you something while your clothes are washed and dried overnight. Please, come with me."

I shook my head with a smile, giving in as I realized he would not allow a rejection.

"You're too kind," I said.

He smiled and waved me over as he headed for his home.

We passed across the stone plaza and after a small, grass path, entered through a doorway into a warmly lit home. I felt my will buckle slightly as my insides felt as if they crumbled as well. It reminded me of home. Small stone braziers on columns about two-thirds my height were perfectly situated in the main room we entered. The rambunctious flames danced and splashed the room with thick swaths of gold. The white plaster of the inside glowed yellow as if they were on fire themselves, teased by the enigmatic mystery of ancient fire.

"Kuria?" Tomiki asked, announcing our entry. "I have a guest with me."

I had only taken a few steps inside when I noticed an enchanting rug on the ground. It was worn well, but mended and darned exquisitely. It was obviously made for practical, rather than decorative purposes. Regardless, I realized I was dripping and stepped back out. As I did, a woman emerged from another room. She was holding a small loaf of bread.

"Ah!" Tomiki said as he lit up. He stepped over quickly and kissed her cheek.

Kuria's head tilted slightly as her face wrinkled.

"Uh, yes," Tomiki resumed. "This woman is traveling with the men that just arrived—the ones we went to investigate. It's all right. They're just traders. They've been here before."

Kuria looked to her husband, then back to me.

"You're *traveling* with them?" Kuria asked.

"Yes, well," I stuttered. "My village arranged for me to sail with them to Alashiya so that I can tend to my mother who has passed."

The moment I said that, a cold splash of hysteria rubbed my nose in my mistake. Tomiki shot his head around to look at me.

"Your *mother*?" He challenged. "I thought it was your father that died?"

As he stepped over to a window to check the disposition of Nereus and his men in the plaza, I attempted a hasty correction.

"Yes, of course. I just misspoke. I'm going to help my mother tend to laying my father to rest."

My answer didn't completely assuage him. He continued to peer and evaluate the situation in the plaza. After apparently seeing nothing to alarm him, he relaxed and pulled away from the window.

Tomiki looked over to Kuria.

"And," she started to ask, shaking her head in amusement, "why are you wet?"

Her question blew on the coals of my embarrassment.

"I slipped off the gangplank as I was getting off the ship."

Kuria couldn't totally hide a grin, and thankfully only nodded.

"I see," she finally said. "I think I can get you into something dry. Follow me."

I did as instructed, without comment or question. While I was thankful and grateful for their hospitality, I wanted to push past my humiliation as quickly as possible. I stepped through the room in little hops to minimize getting the floor wet and passed Tomiki as I followed Kuria.

We walked quickly through a quaint kitchen with bowls of fruit and vegetables on a counter, and even larger bowls of water. A bundle of herbs sat on another counter with a few handfuls of wildflowers adjacent to them. As we exited the kitchen, we turned and entered what I imagined was where the couple slept. I stayed at the room's threshold, waiting for further word from Kuria. I wanted to make as little fuss and cause as little offense as possible while we were here. As she approached the corner of the room and lifted the lid off a chest, she looked back at me.

"Well, come on over," she said gently.

She bent down and started sorting through a few small stacks of clothes and quickly pulled something out.

"Here you are," she said as she placed the garment in my hands. She then walked over and lit a few candles on a shelf before closing the wooden shutters of the room's single window.

"Go ahead and get into that and just bring out your wet clothes," she said, already making her way out of the room. "We'll wait for you out here," she added. She then pulled on a rope and released a heavy curtain to block the room's entryway.

"Thank you so much for this," I said. She smiled as the curtain fell into place.

I started undressing the moment the curtain fell, almost rushing. I couldn't really think of a reason I wanted or needed to rush, but something just told me not to take long. I slipped my axes out and laid them down. I shoved my skirt down and stepped and stomped out of it as I lifted my shirt over my head. The next and last item to come off was a tunic which I quickly tossed down at my feet. Curious as to exactly what she had given me to wear, I gently picked and pulled at the stack of clothes. To my relief, she had given me an undershirt, as well as a dress. The clothes were a heavy but soft linen. I dropped them over my head and wriggled into them. They settled into place and felt as comfortable as a stranger's clothes could. After reaching down and picking up my wet bundle of clothes like an unruly head of cabbage, I scurried out of the room.

I walked back through the kitchen and caught Kuria's eye first.

"Ah, that fits you perfectly!" She said, genuinely pleased. "Ah, and your axes! Beauty and brawn! Here, let me take the wet ones."

She marched over and took them from me before gliding over to a large basket next to the home's main entry way.

"I'll wash these out and set them out to dry before bed."

"Oh, no, please, at least let me wash—" I attempted.

"Nm mm," Kuria grunted. "You have plenty to think about and plan for and will have plenty to do once you reach Alashiya. Let me to do this small thing for you."

I felt my eyebrows slope in as her and Tomiki's generosity humbled me. I looked over at Tomiki who met me with a sloping smile.

"Thank you, both, so very much," I said again.

"Thank you, dear," Tomiki whispered quickly to his wife before turning back to me. "Shall we go check on your friends?" He asked. "Let's go see if they've brought out the wine!"

I nodded and offered a small bow of my head. Tomiki kissed his wife on the cheek once more and started off for the door.

"Come out and join us if you like!" He said to Kuria as he exited. I waved and smiled at her and turned to follow.

The wine had indeed made its first appearance. A few men already had cups, and a decanter was being passed around to some of the others. A few of the other wives from nearby homes brought out bread, fruit, and cheese.

"Tomiki," Nereus bellowed. "This is all really not necessary. Please. We have provisions on the ship and can replenish—"

"Ah, no!" Tomiki interrupted. "No, no! We may have had a scare the other night, but that won't stop us from practicing our usual hospitality!"

One of Nereus' senior men laughed in surprise.

"You go to all this trouble for every ship of traders that pulls up to the docks?"

Tomiki snagged a cup of wine from a woman looking for someone to offer it to before nodding in appreciation.

"Ha! No, we don't, but I figured this was the least we could do since we met you on the docks with swords and arrows ready to fly into your skulls!"

The plaza boomed with laughter from trader and villager alike.

"Well, it's very much appreciated," Nereus said. "Especially so soon after your people were attacked. Might I ask what you feel like sharing about it?"

Tomiki's next sip of wine coincided perfectly with the ending of Nereus' question. He took his drink, swallowed, and maintained a silent stare on Nereus.

"Of course," Tomiki finally responded. "After you tell me why you're *really* here."

The assorted conversations throughout the plaza died. Some of Tomiki's men stood with a rigid posture of elevated awareness.

Nereus scanned the area slowly but made no movements of his own. I could tell the rest of our evening would be greatly influenced by what transpired over the next few seconds.

"What?" Nereus asked carefully. "We told you. We're on our way to Alashiya."

"No," Tomiki said bitterly to Nereus. "Not you. *Her.*"

Tomiki, sitting on the lowest step leading up to the small bird bath, leaned over and looked past Nereus, to me. As he did, the eyes of the men and women from the village, as well as Nereus' men, slid towards me. A shock of cold anxiety pinched my skin.

Nereus stammered as he turned to me, but said nothing. His eyebrows twitched as he offered me the slightest of shoulder shrugs.

"You're not traveling to aide in the affairs of a deceased family member, are you?" Tomiki questioned confidently.

I swallowed.

What do I do?

The truth?

Insist on the lie?

"No," I decided to reply. There was no reason for me to keep my intentions secret from the villagers any longer.

"I didn't want to get into it when we first arrived, especially considering how we were received," I said.

"Well, now you all know why you were received that way," Tomiki said. "So, why don't you fill us in on why you are really traveling with these men. Are you with them willingly?"

Nereus turned back to Tomiki. His brow collapsed some as he scowled, preparing to take umbrage with the implication.

"Yes, yes," I rushed to say. "I am not a prisoner or anything like that. I'll explain why I'm here."

Tomiki slowly stood up and placed his hands on his hips.

"As I said, we just thought it best to wait to see how our arrival unfolded before getting into too many details."

"By details," Tomiki replied, "you mean, the truth?"

"Yes," I answered.

"And what is that?" Tomiki pressed.

Nereus huffed a breath of annoyed surprise. I assumed it was for the benefit of his crew, as if he were learning of my true intentions for the first time.

"I am indeed traveling east with these men, as a passenger. That is true," I replied.

Tomiki fortified his stare and said nothing.

"But I am not sailing to meet family. I am searching."

Tomiki's face of impatience morphed into one of confusion.

"Searching?" He asked.

"I have no family on Alashiya. Both my mother, father, as well as my sister, and my entire village, were slaughtered by a group of raiders. I am sailing with these men as they make their way to Alashiya in hopes of finding those responsible."

Tomiki's face relaxed. He blinked and scratched his face before turning to Nereus.

"Are you and your men… going to… kill these raiders?"

Nereus started to respond but I answered for him.

"No, *I* am going to kill them."

Tomiki snapped back to me with widened eyes before erupting in laughter. The majority of his fellow villagers—as well as some of Nereus' men—joined in.

My vision flooded with red. In a quick and fluid motion, I reached behind me and grabbed the handle of one of my axes. I shot up to my feet and whipped my arm over my head, flinging the axe across the length of the plaza and striking a massive wooden column at the approximate height of a man's chest. The glow of the axe blades, stimulated by my actions, subsided soon after.

I looked at the doubtful village leader as the others stood around him looking embarrassed. They had attempted to react to my movements, but I was too quick. The plaza fell silent.

Still doubtful? I wondered.

He licked his lips.

"Mmm," he mumbled quickly. Still looking at where my axe landed, he extended an arm towards me. "Well, maybe you are!"

Kuria, who had emerged from their home just as I threw my axe, stepped over to the wooden column. After looking at it for a few seconds, she reached up and heaved on it to dislodge it. She then approached me with a combined look of respect and annoyance. She slowly handed me my axe.

"Thank you," I said softly. She stared at me for a moment and joined Tomiki.

"If I can get good information, and find them," I said, speaking louder. "I will kill them."

Tomiki smiled and outstretched his arms to everyone in the plaza, urging they resume their relaxation.

"I apologize for doubting you!" He said with a playful charm.

Most of the men who had stood, preparing for action, sat back down. Cups were refilled, and decanters resumed their journey through the plaza. I sat back down as well.

"After we found out that your demeanor on the docks was out of worry and defense, I was going to tell you what my true intentions were," I said. "I just didn't know the opportunity would present itself so quickly."

I offered Tomiki a smile of my own.

"Fair enough," he said. "I knew something was going on when you accidentally said in the house that you were traveling to tend to your mother."

I heard Nereus chuckle. I looked over to see him roll his eyes.

"Well, then," Tomiki continued. "We may have been visited by the same group, Bayla. And let me say, I'm terribly sorry to hear about your village. With the mercy of the gods, we fortunately did not experience a tragedy to that degree."

I nodded as I tried to choke down a building lump of emotion, and luckily, Nereus spoke next.

"What exactly happened here, Tomiki?"

Tomiki breathed in deeply as he seemed to be

recollecting, and motioned for a refill of his wine. The sun had slid well below the horizon. The light from the plaza's stone braziers had taken over the sun's lighting duties, casting shifting silhouettes onto the fire-teased stones on the ground. The breeze picked up, as if emboldened by the sun's disappearance. In concert with the wind came a choreographed cool of false reassurance, and with it, a worn, salty scent of the ancient sea. The island's trees and flowers added pinches of sweet and savory accents, but strained to make an impression.

"It was very confusing and hectic," Tomiki began. "News of a previous raid on the southern tip of the island had spread to every village, so we took measures to be prepared. We arranged for sentries to walk the perimeter of the village, and another team to walk the streets. We took turns, rotating out every four hours."

"There were plenty of us that were fit and ready," Amyntas added. "We felt confident. We even created an alarm to alert the village and get the men together if we came across anything."

"And we did," Tomiki continued. "We heard of another attack, and rumors of strange ships being spotted. We assumed they were still nearby, and were possibly still on the island. We continued our patrols and lit additional fires at night."

"That's when it happened," Kuria resumed. "This was a few nights ago. With a rumble and crash of sticks on metal, Tomiki and I awoke to screaming, shouting, alarms banging... It was terribly frightening."

"I'd been going to bed dressed so that I could race up and out for exactly this reason," Tomiki said. "I jumped up, shot out into the plaza here where those not on patrol agreed to meet whenever the alarm sounded. One of our sentries on patrol," Tomiki said, turning to Amyntas, "your brother, right, Amyntas? Raced through the village and told us they had spotted a group of unknown size approaching from the southeast. In less than a minute, we gathered our weapons and raced out to meet them."

"Did they know they had been seen? These strangers?" Nereus leaned over with wide eyes. I imagine his life on the sea had made him hungry for land excitement.

"I'm not sure if they saw our patrols or heard our alarms," Tomiki considered. "But they either hadn't, or must not have cared, because when our group broke out from the village interior, we saw that they had already engaged our patrol."

"But that's when they started to care," Amyntas said, following with a hearty laughter. "There were only about ten of them or so. When they saw our group of forty men, they immediately turned and ran."

"How well could you see them?" I asked. "What did they look like?"

Before I finished my questions, Amyntas and Tomiki both were already shaking their heads.

"Most of them were hooded," Tomiki said. "And I don't think we had a chance to really examine the few that weren't. Like Amyntas said, they started running the moment they saw our main group."

"Anything special about their clothing? Did you see what they wore on their feet?" I wondered.

Tomiki just shrugged and shook his head again.

The conversation paused while the night's patrol walked through the plaza and lit additional braziers. The only remaining sign of the sun was the faint line of plum sky far at the horizon's edge. Though the occasional gusts of wind presented a challenge, the patrol finally moved on once the extra fires took hold.

"So, why did they run?" Nereus asked, curious. "I just don't understand why they gave up so quickly."

Tomiki started nodding, apparently reciprocating Nereus' curiosity.

"I don't know for sure," he said. "But I think the men we ran into were a scouting group."

"Ah," I said, understanding. "They weren't expecting a fight? Or were supposed to avoid one?"

Amyntas nodded at me. "Right. That's what we believe."

"We gave chase as soon as they started running," Tomiki resumed. "But we never caught them. We kept up for a while, but our men eventually gave out a few at a time until we lost them completely."

"Did you find anything? Anything special about their tracks?" I asked.

"No," Amyntas answered quickly. "But here comes the most interesting bit of the whole night. We all tired and had to stop pursuing them, but a few of us had stopped on the final ridge that overlooks the northeastern coast—the direction they were running. We watched them run down the hill, to the beach, and from what we could tell, they started swimming out to a ship."

My eyes widened with intrigue.

"A ship? How could you—"

Tomiki anticipated my question.

"We could see its silhouette against the light on the horizon, and it was extremely close to shore."

Nereus rubbed his chin as his eyes—and no doubt, his mind—raced with intrigue.

"That would make sense that the men you encountered were scouts, then," he said. "Could you make anything out about the ship? Any size or shape from the silhouette?"

Tomiki looked to Amyntas before turning back to Nereus, and then me.

"I can't say for certain, but it looked like it could have been Phoenician, or maybe Hittite," Tomiki said. "It was a bit larger than your ship."

"Hmm," Nereus hummed, pondering. "And there were some Phoenicians at Milopotas recently."

The dark of night had settled in around the village. The wind had ceased for the most part, save a few strong gusts which sprang up unexpectedly.

"Hmm... The Phoenicians," Tomiki pondered. "Well... It appears, young Bayla, that you may be closer to identifying your raiders."

"If it is the Phoenicians," Amyntas suggested, "then you'll need to make some really good speed if you mean to catch up with them. And that's assuming they'll be making for Alashiya. That's where you said you're headed next?"

Nereus nodded before sipping his wine.

"Yes, that's a solid stretch of open sea," Amyntas added. "That's just more of an opportunity to increase the lead they have on you."

"Well, that's where we're headed," I said, determined. "And there's one thing we have to our advantage that you haven't considered."

I felt everyone turn to me as they patiently waited for me to elaborate.

"They don't know they're being hunted."

"True enough, young Bayla, true enough," Tomiki said.

"We'll need to set out fairly quickly if we want to have a chance of catching up with them at Alashiya," Nereus said.

"Right, of course," Tomiki obliged. "Did you want to conduct our transactions tonight, or perhaps on your way back?"

Nereus took a moment to look around and check in with his men silently. He then looked at me. I could only assume he was trying to consider how to proceed as to not threaten his chances of collecting on the buried valuables I had told him about.

"Now, I want my men to hear me out on this," Nereus began, "but we might make our best possible time if we offloaded most of our cargo and left some of our men behind to not only look after our cargo, but assist the village in the event someone returns to try and carry out their original plans for an attack."

Only crickets and the distant lapping of the largest waves could be heard.

"Captain Nereus," one of his crew began. "I don't think that is—"

"I understand your concern," Nereus interrupted. "But if we mean to see the task of getting Bayla to Alashiya through, and to help her locate these raiders, then sailing faster will see those tasks completed sooner."

Tomiki shifted uneasily.

"Captain, I must say that I completely understand your crewman's concern. I personally wouldn't feel comfortable with any amount of your cargo being left behind for any amount of time."

"I appreciate your candor, Tomiki. But with some of my men staying, I am confident our goods would go unmolested."

Tomiki turned to glean what he could from Amyntas' face. He then turned towards Nereus' men.

"Well, as a show of good faith and to build a little

trust," Tomiki said. "I would suggest some of my men accompany you to Alashiya in the event they can assist in some way."

"But I'm leaving men, as well as cargo, behind to make travel—" Nereus started.

"Right, I know," Tomiki said. "...to keep weight down. But we wouldn't trade one for one. Just a few of our men to help if and when needed."

I turned to Tomiki.

"What do you mean, help?" I asked.

Tomiki tilted his head. "Surely, you realize that one person alone will need help if they hope to—"

"I don't want to have anyone put in danger on my behalf, Tomiki," I politely interrupted. "I intend to see this through on my—"

Tomiki turned to Nereus with a question.

"What are your thoughts on her going about this alone?"

I scoffed at the conversation.

"I'm not expecting or asking for help, Tomiki. Having a large mob prowl about will only increase the chance of having the raiders alerted to my intentions. Let me assure you that I have enough sense to investigate and plan before I act. If I find at any point that I need help, I'll solicit it, then."

Nereus rubbed his chin. "Yes, this is her fight. We're just helping her find it," he said.

"Well, I just think there could be a middle ground," Tomiki said in response. "A few people to scout, investigate. That kind of thing."

"I truly do appreciate the consideration," I said. "But I would prefer to keep my efforts small and quiet, and adapt if and when it's needed."

"Tomiki," Nereus started to add. "She still doesn't know exactly who she's looking for. She might have a clue to chase, but she doesn't know definitively. This could possibly lead into something larger, sure, but what if my whole crew were to take up arms against this shadowed band of raiders, just to end up with everyone killed? And then what happens to these mens' families? What if these raiders kill my men and then seek out our homes and villages back on the mainland? I think we should honor Bayla's wishes and follow her lead."

Tomiki leaned back, looking up to the sky, before pacing a small circle. After exchanging glances with me and Nereus, he shared his final thoughts on the matter. Initially, he spoke to Nereus, but then addressed all of Nereus' men throughout the plaza.

"I agree," he began. "Without more information, it wouldn't be wise to over-complicate the effort. Let me just leave it at this, Nereus: You are more than welcome to leave some of your men here, along with some of your cargo. And given the possibility that those responsible for raiding Bayla's village may have also been those that were active on our island, we do have a keen interest in helping solve the mystery of their identity. As I had said previously, we would like to have a few of our men accompany you in the event more information is learned, or to assist in any potential confrontations, if that is acceptable."

After looking around at his crew for any noticeable objections, Nereus nodded.

"All right, then," Tomiki said. "How many men were you thinking of leaving behind?"

Nereus scanned the faces of his crew, pointing occasionally and silently mouthing a count. He then rubbed his chin and came out with a number. "I think I'll leave fifteen men behind," he said.

"And you'd still have all the oarsmen you'd need?" Tomiki asked.

Nereus nodded. "How many of your men were you thinking of sending with us?"

Tomiki ran his hands through his hair. "Five? Ten? Like you said, now that I think about it. It's hard to say without knowing who we're looking for, or how many."

"Right," Nereus replied.

"So, I'll say five men," Tomiki said. "Amyntas, will you select five men that can be of the most benefit should something happen?"

"Of course," Amyntas obliged.

Tomiki turned to me. He started to speak but sighed. He then approached slowly and lightly grasped my shoulder.

"I have no doubt that you can and will see anything done that you want to in this life," he said. His mouth moved deliberately. His voice was warm and comforting like my father's. "That includes your vengeance. The display with your axe proves you seem to be capable of exacting your wrath upon those who took your family from you," he continued. "I want to help make sure no other family or village suffers what yours has—what ours almost did. I support you. You just don't deserve the burden of trying to pursue this on your own. If my men can help, either by protecting you, fighting with you, or helping search for information, I will make sure they do."

Tomiki's sincerity humbled me more than I already had been. I immediately felt like I had to clear my throat as I felt my eyes water. The unexpected, reinforced support and confidence seeped under the foundation of my emotions and began to erode it. I had to look down as he finished speaking, if not to hide my tears, to shore up my heart's wall.

Nereus approached. "If you want to follow me to the ship," he said to Tomiki, "we can conduct our business. And then I'll be able to decide what cargo I'm leaving behind."

"Of course," Tomiki responded.

Chapter Seven - Claws, Talons, and Shackles

Briz

While the big scorp scolded the others for roughing me up, I patted my sides and checked for cuts.

"You might as well get some more water while you can," I said through gritted teeth.

"Are you all right?" Khetikare asked instead. "Those looked like pretty rough hits."

I was sore, but I didn't know how bad it was. I shrugged. I mostly just wanted to get back into the wagon.

Just before repeating my suggestion for Khetikare to get more water, the boss scorpiron swung around and marched back towards us.

"Looks like we'll be moving again," Khetikare said.

Good. The wagon.

The leader, or whoever this huge guy was, walked up and stopped in front of Khetikare. He twirled and pointed his pincer at Khetikare before gesturing at me.

"Yes, I guess he wants you to shackle me again," I assumed.

Khetikare held his hands up at the scorp.

"Yes, okay. Okay," he said. "I need to get them."

He pointed over at the wagon and the shackles draped over the back.

The scorp let out a soft, but long hiss. I guess that was some kind of answer. Khetikare walked over to the wagon. I just stared at the scorp, waiting to be bound again.

While Khetikare approached the back of the wagon, I found myself dwelling on the big beast's face. The small appendages around its mouth slid and curled as they had before.

"What are you looking at?" I asked it.

It hissed at me.

Khetikare came back over with an accompanying noise. I thought it was his footsteps, but after looking at them, the sound fell out of rhythm with his gait.

"What is that?" I whispered.

The scorpiron hissed again. Louder this time.

The quick whip of sound grew louder. It was familiar but I couldn't immediately place it.

"Khetikare? Do you hear that?"

I spun around. My eyes locked on the top of the dune. I turned more and looked to the assembly of lesser scorps but kept turning. Khetikare, halfway back from the wagon scanned the area as well. Even the big scorp was looking around. The others had stopped their hissing, clicking, and popping. I made a complete circle and shot my eyes back to the top of the dune. The sound snapped at the air from behind it, and painfully punched my ears as the makers of the mystery sound appeared.

An immense flock of zarafteryx soared over the dune before diving down, sending me and Khetikare to our stomachs, and the scorps down to all fours. Resembling much larger giraffes—their distant relatives—but with wings, the zarafteryx dotted the surrounding area in sun-choking shadows. The scorps flew into a panic and raced away in a dispersed panic. The big scorp scampered over and slapped at my back with a pincer, hissing at Khetikare and shoving us back toward the wagon.

"No, wait!" I shouted. I helped Khetikare up.

I caught a quick glimpse of a zarafteryx over the leader's shoulder.

"Move!" I yelled.

I pushed Khetikare out of the way and then shoved the leader.

With just enough time to dive back to the ground, a zarafteryx swooped down over all of us. Its massive talons were stretched out, ready to puncture and snatch one of us up. But it missed.

I flipped over and dug in before stumbling to my feet. I ran to the side of the wagon and pulled out my club. A scorp ran up to me, hissing and clicking. I pointed to my club and then up to the sky.

"I'm trying to help, you stupid scorp!" I shouted. Another dive from the zarafteryx made us duck. When we stood back up, the scorp tried to smack my club out of my hand. But the leader put him in his place. The lesser scorp looked over and backed away before scurrying off.

"Khetikare!" I yelled. "Get over here and get under the wagon."

My friend ran over and slid next to me.

"I'm sure this won't last long," I said. "They'll probably move on if they catch a few scorps."

"Great," Khetikare said, short of breath. "Hopefully they won't catch *us*."

I couldn't help but fling a smile and pat him on the back.

"Get under the wagon," I repeated. "Stay there until they clear out. I'm just going to make sure they steer clear from you and me."

Khetikare crawled under. I looked out across the sands and watched as what must have been around fifty zarafteryx swoop and attack. I had never seen such a number of them before, much less seen so many in an attack.

Zarafteryx are twice as large as their far more docile, and flightless cousins. Their necks are proportionately extended like their smaller relatives, with their wingspan twice that of their neck. Their mouths and teeth weren't a danger but their elongated, keratin talons in place of hooves, were.

I stayed low and close to the wagon and watched the fight unfold, while a few scorps on the edge of our caravan seemed to have outrun the main attack. Together with me and Khetikare, the majority of the scorps were stuck in a wide basin surrounded by high dunes. Some scorps jumped out of the way of an attack on two feet, while others plopped down to all fours to duck under the flying threat.

Out in front of me, towards the other side of the fight, a zarafteryx flew down at a scorpiron. The attack caught my eye just as the would-be target scorpiron leapt forward onto his front legs and swung his tail around at its highest reach. The scorp swung wide of the retractable talons of the zarafteryx and bashed it in its side, sending the flying beast rolling onto the ground. The scorpiron chased after as it rolled. Its tail stretched back as it raced, poising the stinger for a lethal shot of venom. The scorp leapt at the zarafteryx just as it rolled to a stop and brought its stinger down. But it missed, puncturing nothing but dirt.

Having caught sight of the pursuing scorp, the zarafteryx added an extra roll to dodge the stinger. It pushed itself up with the help of its grand wings and powerful neck before charging. The scorp stood up, stretched out its arms, and opened its claws. Galloping at a full sprint, the zarafteryx charged for the scorp but instead kicked into the air, slammed its wings back and brought its rear talons up and aimed for the scorp's face. The scorp stepped out of the way and clamped down on the zarafteryx. I didn't see what part had been caught, but it tumbled past, uncontrolled, before escaping sluggishly into the air.

Closer to us, another scorp had been singled out by four or five zarafteryx. While scraping the ground on all fours, it whipped around in a frenzy dodging swoops and dives from the gigantic predators. With each attack from the air, the scorp lashed out with its claws to cut and slice.

I felt a tap to my leg.

"Do we just wait for this to be over?" Khetikare asked.

I looked down. His head was just barely sticking out from under the wagon. His eyes flickered and floated up at the commotion in the sky.

"Yes, I guess so," I replied, turning my eyes back to the battle. "I'm hoping the zarafteryx can clear out enough of the scorps that we can make a run for it."

"And if they don't?"

I turned my head to say something, but a deafening screech turned me back. A zarafteryx plummeted for us, talons out.

"Get back!" I shouted.

I stepped out from the wagon a few paces. The animal scooped towards us. Its alternating neighs and squawks poked at my ears, leaving them ringing with hollow whistles.

With a few wide sidesteps, I circled farther from the wagon. I pulled my club as far back as I could and whipped it around, landing a solid crack on its lower leg.

That sounded like an ankle or a bone of some kind, I thought.

The zarafteryx tore out with a painful screech. Its pain reminded me of my own, sending me wincing and grabbing my side as the beast shot up and circled around. I checked my surroundings for any new threats and focused back on the returning zaraf.

It plunged sharply and landed before tearing off towards me. It lowered its head. My plan was to dodge it again and try to hit it square in the head as it approached, but it never came to that. It ground its feet into the sand and slid to a stop, but pivoted, striking me with the full force of one of its enormous wings. As the creature brought its wing around, it turned it sideways to cut through the air with minimum resistance. Just before it hit me, it flipped the wing up, crashing its ferocious structure of bone, webbing, and fur into me.

I crossed my arms in front of me just in time, holding my club tight against the length of my body. The wing slammed into me and threw me back. I turned as I was hit, spilling to the ground, and rolled harshly on my side for what felt like dozens of times.

It's going to trample me, I managed to think. When I felt myself slowing, I squinted my eyes open, blinking through the dust and tumbling.

Where is it?

I looked up and frantically searched the desert floor.

Where is it?

I grunted and jumped to my feet when I spotted it charging again. I tore off to meet it.

We raced towards each other. A splinter of light bounced off the bronze of my mallet and caught me in the eye. I squeezed it. The impending clash sent a thrilling jolt through me.

The zarafteryx lunged at me. With a single, shallow beat of its massive wings it jumped and threw itself at me, poising its lethal talons to rip at my flesh.

At the last second, I summoned every bit of energy I

had to get a few extra steps in and jumped. With a violent whip, the zarafteryx hooked its front legs around, ready to impale me with its talons, but I tucked my legs in as I jumped and sailed right over them.

I grabbed my mallet with both hands and as I jumped, swung it around and battered the beast with a punishing blow on its cheekbone.

As we passed, my legs loosened some and caught on a wing. I crashed, but rolled into a kneeling position. The huge animal stumbled diagonally before falling onto its side. I ran over to finish the fight.

I crept up from behind, giving its rear legs and wings a wide berth before moving along the length of its long neck. Its chest rose and fell rapidly as I grew closer. I could hear it breathing.

Must just be stunned.

I squeezed my club, ready to dash over and land a killing blow to its head.

But with a violent shove into the ground with one of its wings, it rolled over, sending its massive legs and the other wing down towards me. I slung myself back to dodge it, but it wasn't enough. Just enough of its talons snagged me and sent me stumbling. But I caught myself. I ran back over just as it started to stand.

Its jumble of legs, long neck, and gangling wings scrambled to help it stand. I ran back up, launched myself off one of its feet and crashed my mallet down on its wing, close to where it meets the body. The zarafteryx jerked in pain, slinging me off to the ground. It finished standing and brought a leg up. Its talons folded out as it prepared to stomp and stab me.

Its foot sunk down and clamped just around my leg.

It missed!

I leaned up and sunk my teeth into the lowest bit of

foot flesh I could reach, sending it jerking and screeching with piercing fury. The monster's neck whipped back and flew back down. I reached for my club, but my fingertips slipped off it.

Its neck flew down towards me, ready to pound me into the ground. I felt its talons crimp tighter around me. I couldn't move.

Just as I expected the crushing blow, a dark blur ran into view, shoving the zarafteryx off me. The blur walked ahead in pursuit and I quickly made it out as the scorp leader.

The zarafteryx stumbled back, but the scorp was already running towards it. The zaraf turned and took off, but it was slow and clumsy. Blood on its wing from where I struck it shined in the sun. The scorp had too much speed and jumped. It latched onto the back of the zaraf and weighed it down, back towards the ground.

Before I saw them hit, another zaraf soared into view. I caught it just in time out of the corner of my eye and fell flat to dodge it. My shirt flapped on my back as the energy from its raw power rippled over. I spun over to track it. But since it didn't hit me, it had flown too low and slammed into the wagon before it could recover.

The wagon tumbled over, sending Khetikare up and over with it. I watched as he flipped up and behind where the wagon landed.

"Khetikare!"

I clawed at the ground, shot up, and ran over before grabbing onto a wheel and sliding around.

My lungs emptied out. A bone was sticking out near the top of Khetikare's leg and his face looked like it had caught the full brunt of a talon. I knelt down next to him.

"Hey, hey," I said, trying to softly smear my words over his pain. "Hold on. Let me get this wagon tipped back over so I can get you back underneath it."

I stood up and slammed a shoulder along with my hands into the wagon. It rocked and creaked.

"Just a few more hits..."

Slam!

"...and I can get some momentum and push it over," I said to Khetikare.

But before I could heave into it a third time, a dense hiss came from behind. My head jerked around.

It was the scorp leader. Part of one of his claws had been ripped off.

He hissed again. A rapid series of percussive clicks followed. He waved his good claw at the wagon and stepped towards us.

"Please," I said. "He's hurt. Bad," I added, motioning at Khetikare. "I'm just trying to keep him safe."

The scorp walked even closer and looked down at Khetikare. His head tilted some, seemingly registering his wounds.

It looked back up to me before lunging at the wagon. With a hardy blow, the scorp slammed into it. The wagon resisted a little at the apex of its roll, so I jumped over and added my own weight. The extra help worked. The wagon smacked back down onto all four wheels.

I leaned down for Khetikare, but the scorp hissed and smacked my arm with its good claw.

"What?" I asked, turning back in confusion.

It rattled off a bunch of popping noises and gestured at the cart.

"Okay!" I barked. "I'm just pulling him under the wagon."

I reached down again.

Some kind of combination growl and hiss came next. The scorp leaned down to meet my eyes. It slowly extended its arm at the wagon.

I couldn't figure out exactly what he wanted or why, but I tried making some kind of compromise.

"Me," I said, pointing at myself.

"Him," pointing to Khetikare.

And then I pointed up at the cage in the back.

The scorp continued to stare at me but finally nodded and slowly backed away.

I sighed some form of relief and reached down a third time for Khetikare.

"Okay, my friend. He wants us *in* the stupid wagon for some reason. I'm going to reach under your good leg here, all right? Real slow now. Here we go."

I slid my arms under him and through his legs as gently but quickly as I could. I strained and wiggled a bit as I got my feet underneath me and lifted him up. He should have screamed out in pain.

But he didn't.

I brought him around to the back of the wagon and leaned over to get him in as far as I could before letting go. Once the broken bone in his thigh cleared the back, I let go.

The scorpiron hissed at me. I looked over and was met with another impatient wave of his arm.

"He's in!"

The scorp flailed again.

"All right, I'm getting in!"

I couldn't help but turn slowly in a bit of defiance, but I finally stepped back up.

The scorp walked over and smacked the gate shut and gestured at the rope.

"You're seriously making me lock myself back in?" I said in disbelief. "I was helping you fight!"

It smacked the gate and motioned again at the rope.

I blew out a huff of hate and started tying the gate

closed.

"I hope you all get turned to zaraf food out there," I said.

It hissed and gestured again. This time, it was at a set of shackles.

I held the scorp's gaze with a squint soaked in disbelief before swiping the shackles in disgust. I shook my head before clamping one down on one wrist, and then the other. My feet came next.

The scorp leaned in, touching the wagon's cage with its head as it examined the shackles. It then pulled back and smacked on the door.

"You sure are a brilliant bug," I blurted. "It's tied!"

It didn't look at me or acknowledge the insult that it probably didn't understand. It just turned and darted back into the fight.

Khetikare groaned.

"Hey! Khetikare!" I rasped excitedly. "Can you hear me? Hey."

I slid closer, pulling myself over with bound feet and hands.

The area around his thigh wound shone wet with blood. His face was sliced bad with folds of flesh resting in a jagged mess.

With no warning, a light flashed, blinding my sight and soaking my mind as if sneaking a glimpse of the sun. But I wasn't looking into the sky. I was looking down at Khetikare.

"Khe—" I started.

Another flash of light.

I brought my arms up and wiped my sweaty face with my forearm.

"Khetikare?"

My eyes flashed again. Another slap of sun to my eyes

and mind.

My memories had taken over.

* * *

I sprinted and slid through the entryway of our smoking home after slinging the gazelle I had returned with onto the ground outside our home.

"Khensa?" I whimpered.

I fell to my knees and crawled over, slipping my hand under my wife's head. She choked on a bubble of blood before gargling and coughing. A spray of red splattered on me.

"Where is..." she fought to ask. "Where... is... Asata?"

I hadn't seen her outside and spun to scan inside our home.

"I don't know," I said. "I'll find her. Don't worry. We'll find her. Who did this? Who did this my love?"

But Khensa's head rolled to the side and went heavy.

"Khensa?" I cried. "Khensa?"

I titled her head back towards me and tried to find life in her eyes.

"Khensa!"

The air punched out of my lungs.

"No! Khensa! No, no, no, no, no!"

My chest heaved, rose, and fell through its maximum capacity, but I still felt like I was suffocating.

"Asata?" I whispered.

My tears fell on my wife's cheek as I gently placed her head on the ground. I looked up and scanned the room again.

"Asata!"

I stumbled back from my wife's body and tore outside. After whipping my head back and forth to confirm I didn't see her, I ran around to the rear of our small hut. Something dark stuck out against the white sand. I ran up to it and quickly saw an arrow sticking out.

It was Asata. She had an arrow in her back and had fallen down on her face as if trying to run away.

My mind blanked as my memories shuffled again.

* * *

The bow and arrow had been in my hands for hours—arrow nocked and ready. Days of tracking those that killed my wife and daughter had paid off. As I stared into their camp from a distance, I waited for night to fall. Darkness eventually came and at the height of the noise from their campfire and drunken conversation, I walked over.

I remember there being nothing in my heart or mind that resembled doubt as I approached them. There was no worry or concern. There was no hesitation. Fear wasn't a factor. I marched towards them only with a lust to kill.

Having the element of surprise, I stopped walking just long enough to steady my first arrow and fire it. It sailed true and landed left of center of one of the men's backs. He fell forward off a rock.

The second of three men spun where he sat, peering out into the darkness. As he noticed me, he reached for something, but he didn't make it far. I shot another arrow through his cheek.

The third and final man had made it to his feet by that time and rushed for me.

I never stopped moving forward. I rushed towards him, ducking and slamming into his stomach before standing and throwing him over my shoulder. He landed on the ground with a solid thud. After letting out a quick shout of pain, I plunged down towards him with a dagger to the throat. It sunk quickly, down to the bottom of my fist. I jerked it away and out with a violent yank.

After examining all three to confirm they were dead, I walked over to their camp and ate their food in silence.

* * *

The silence lingered. It allowed my mind to pull away from my memory and snap me back into the present. Khensa had left me for a second time. My daughter, lost, a second time. In place of their bodies rested Khetikare. He too had passed. The weight of my thoughts and rekindling of my grief wore on me. I let my head fall.

I had to sniff. My eyes blurred but I didn't wipe them. My nose dripped, and I didn't care. But the silence remained, even back in reality. I looked up and saw dozens of scorp shadows scurrying towards the horizon. The shadows of the flying creatures swooped and strafed them.

I was alone.

Chapter Eight - New Studies

Bayla

With a small group of their own men in tow, both Nereus and Tomiki marched out of the plaza towards the docks. While the majority of men went to the docks, the others returned to their homes for the night, leaving me with the other women. After the initial conversation of shared concerns over the potential for an enemy to still be near the island, the chatter shifted to admiring jokes at the mens' expense. They were the same types of conversations my mother, aunts, sister, and other women in the village used to have. I found myself having little to say in these strange womens' company because I was *unable* to say anything. Despite having only met them hours before, they felt as familiar to me as the smell of my own mother's hair.

Nereus and Tomiki returned with their men fairly quickly, adhering to their earlier agreement—that to have any chance of catching up with the Phoenicians, we would need to leave as quickly as possible. After a quick confirmation of which of Tomiki's men would be joining us, we were ushered swiftly into homes around the plaza to sleep however much we could. Dawn would come early.

And early it was when I woke up to being shaken. I jerked violently to life, dreamily remembering being woken by Cilana.

"Come Bayla, they're almost ready," Kuria said. Her voice much softer than her hand that shook me.

I felt as though I had only been asleep for mere minutes and my eyes felt closed though they were open. My head tingled and throbbed as though someone had squeezed it before releasing it to unravel to its normal size. I had only had a few sips of wine a few hours earlier. This was just a lack of sleep. And though I was tired, it was nothing like my sleep-deprived state when we left Milopotas.

Kuria continued shaking me as I stirred, rolled, and stretched my eyelids. She shook me until I looked directly at her, at which point she left me alone and started flitting around the home. Ducking over as if trying to hide from prying eyes, she moved around her own home making long strides as if she was preparing to flee an attacker. For a moment I thought the raiders may have indeed returned, but no, she quickly returned to my spot on the floor.

"The men from the village that are going with you have already left for the docks," she said. "You must get going. They want to leave very soon."

I bit my tongue. I wanted to complain that it was too early and that I was too tired, but as I rubbed my eyes, an epiphany smacked me in my mind.

"Where's Tomiki?" I asked.

I saw Kuria's face when I asked. Her eyes strained and her lips rolled in as if she was biting the insides of her lips and straining to maintain her composure.

"Kuria, he's not going is—"

"Of course he is," she snipped. She flickered back and forth through the house like a leaf being fought over by the different directions of the wind. She grabbed a small blanket here, and a few apples there. She then rushed back over to me. I saw the features of her face in the room's fire light, mixed into a pinch of pink from the earliest beginnings of dawn outside. Her cheeks were wet.

"Yes, of course he is," she repeated. I first thought she was angry at me for being the reason Tomiki had cause to leave, but then decided she was probably upset with him for deciding to go. But I don't know for sure. To her credit, she held in any specific complaints. Regardless, I felt like shouting out my apologies. At that moment I wanted to run out and tell Tomiki and his men to get off the boat. I wanted to tell Nereus to forget about our arrangement. I didn't want anyone to risk themselves in any way for me. But before I could call off my intended vengeance, Kuria reached for my hand and pulled me up. She jerked me close to her.

"You find out who killed your family. Find out who destroyed your village. But do not let anyone rush into anything. Do not let my husband, the others, and surely don't let yourself, rush into a fight. Do what you need to do to make sure you can win. Do you hear me? My husband better come back to me safely, and soon."

I wanted to crumble. My lip and chin quivered and I was flooded with reinforced doubts. But again, before I could say anything, Kuria plopped the bundle of goods in my arms and shoved me out the door.

As I came to a stop after practically sliding out on my heels, I turned back in time to see Kuria stumble back into her home. I sidestepped a few paces and saw her head fall into her folded arms on their table. I wanted to speak. I wanted to shout. I wanted to finally utter my desire to stop my pursuit and let everyone go on with their lives. I wanted to drop the bundle of food and blankets Kuria had given me and run to the water. I wanted to start swimming. Back home.

But home was gone.

Instead, I turned around and faced the docks.

Nereus stepped out from behind a home.

"Come on, Bayla. We're ready," he shouted as he waved me over. "Good news. Tomiki's coming with us."

I forced a grin and nodded. As he turned towards the docks, I looked over my shoulder at Kuria, still buried in her arms at the table.

"Thank you," I said.

I spun around and marched to the docks. On my way, I passed an open area covered by massive segments of fabric sewed together. It covered a wide and deep space between two homes. A large portion of Nereus' cargo had been placed there.

The docks were close by. I stepped on and was immediately in the middle of a flurry of activity lit by lanterns and torches. As I turned and ducked to dodge the busy men, Tomiki approached.

"We just finished getting the crates off to a staging area back there," he said. "The men staying behind will get it moved to a more suitable spot. Other than that, I believe we're ready to go."

"Tomiki," I started. "I didn't realize you were planning on going."

Tomiki looked at me. His face wrinkled as if I had told a joke he didn't understand.

"Well, of course I am," he said, with joyful lilt in his voice.

Of course he is.

"I couldn't ask any of our people to potentially risk their lives and leave it to them while I am able and healthy," he explained. "No, I'm glad to help. And like I said... I want to make sure no one threatens *our* island again.”

“Kuria is quite upset, from what I could tell,” I said.

Tomiki nodded quickly while watching the men make their final preparations.

“I know,” he said. “I know.”

“But if she *absolutely* didn’t want me to go,” he said, turning to me and offering a wink, “she would have told me. And if she had, I would have stayed.”

I dipped my head, and slowly raised it.

He winked again and slapped me on the back. “Let’s go get on board, hmm?”

“Sure.”

We walked down the docks and neared the ship. The few men still not on board grabbed the last crates to be rearranged, the sorted supplies, and ran across the gangplank. Tomiki and I boarded as well at which point Tomiki tapped me once more on my shoulder and waved over his other men that were going. As we began discussing our plans, Nereus walked up.

Without saying a word, Nereus pointed to my bench— the same one I had fallen asleep on when we left Milopotas. I rolled my eyes at him.

“Mm hmm,” he grunted. “Sit.”

As instructed, I shuffled over slowly to my bench. Men raced and shot by carrying boxes, heaving bags, or ran down to the lower decks. Just before sitting down, the solid thuds of the oars sliding out and into position rumbled the ship. The men untied and unfurled the sail, and hoisted it up.

Leaving Ialysos was much more stimulating than leaving Milopotas, but that might have been because I was completely awake for this departure. As the sky over the sea’s horizon started to pour more light into the world, the commotion of the ship and our departure went from shadows on shadows to shadows on the ship, and then visible men on the ship.

"It's still pretty dark," bellowed Nereus. "Going to need some help navigating the shoals I saw when we came in, Tomiki."

"Of course my friend, of course," Tomiki said. As he answered, he walked towards the bow of the ship. "Just continue shoving out north by northeast and after approximately five miles, we can turn towards Alashiya."

"Hear that men?" Nereus asked.

The entire crew shouted their acknowledgment, which was echoed by the men below. As the light slowly ruled more and more of the sky, I saw the safety of Ialysos drifting away. Together with the motion of the sea, I could feel the ship's rhythm lurch, first deep, and then shallow, with the thrust and the rebound of the oars.

When we cleared the shoals, I watched the ship begin to turn. Remembering my instructions from our last departure, I waited to do anything until we had reached open waters. Intrigued by how the ship was turning, I ran to one side quickly and looked down.

The oarsmen were swinging the full length of their oars' reach, back and forth. I could hear at least two different callers shouting orders. One gave orders to row their maximum length possible which made me wonder what the other oarsmen were doing. I sprinted to the other side and looked down.

I felt my mouth pop open.

"Ahh!" I said quietly to myself. "This side isn't extending as far as the others. That's how they're turning."

I smiled. I loved learning. For a moment I felt as though I were a seasoned sailor capable of navigating the world's oceans by myself. But instead of shouting out orders or calling out commands I didn't yet know, I simply watched as the ship straightened out. I felt the noticeable rhythm of the back and forth of the rowing return.

The ship was a machine, made up of indomitable materials, and practical design. The sleek vessel was being expertly maneuvered by numerous, human pieces, synchronized and executing their movements, flawlessly. For a moment, I thought that in a different world at a different time, *I could be a trader. I could be a sailor. I could get used to life on the seas.* Being on the water offered a vast peace that I had never felt before. And not only was the sea vast visually, but so too were its destinations and possibilities. And maybe its potential for forgiveness was vast as well.

As the ship rocked me back and forth in an ironic lull, I wondered if it would forgive or forget the vices or injustices carried out by those that sailed it. *Would it forgive those who plan violence on others? Would it forgive those that use it to find those they mean to kill? Would I be allowed to use it to lend to my quest for vengeance?*

I could go anywhere in the world I wanted to go, or I could if I had my own ship. I could get to anywhere that I needed to go, to carry out whatever action I needed to. And maybe because the sea was so vast, it didn't have the capacity to remember one's actions. Maybe sailing the seas was like starting fresh in life with each new port. Perhaps that regardless of what I did on land, the sea would welcome me back and let me plan a fresh route of fate.

I leaned on the rail and pondered romantic philosophies for over an hour. I then ran to the other side as the sun rose and found a whole other slew of questions to ask the horizon. From sunrise to midday I moved around the ship. Port railing. Starboard railing. Bow. Aft. I sat and memorized the look of the sea from every point on the ship. The singular smell of the water made up of foamy salt and decaying sea-life, first intoxicated me with exotic hints of bits of the world that had floated, sunk, risen, and flowed, for eons. But even the majesty of the sea's smell grew familiar. By mid-afternoon of our first day at sea, I found myself searching for diversions other than the sea.

I sat on my bench for a while, voluntarily. With my mind off the sea I was able to focus on the movements of the few crew on the top deck tending to the rigging, but also the ones rearranging and organizing the cargo that remained on board. Once the activity in front of me quickly became predictable and tiresome, I focused once more on the steady chanting of the oarsmen down below. I slid off my bench and found a gap in the top decking I could see them through. The chanting mesmerized me. It was primal and powerful. Coupled with the men's movements I could see beneath me, I grew enraptured. My heart beat faster. I was fascinated. Such strength. Such force. *These men are moving this massive ship all on their own.*

The next day grew tiresome for me far faster than the first. After initially scaring myself into a panic after not being able to see land just after dawn, I quickly settled into a similar pattern of exploring the ship as I had the day before. But even so, I found myself sitting on my bench before the sun had reached the top of the sky.

It was then that I started bothering the men for conversation. I knew I was bothering them, but I couldn't help it. I needed to talk about *something* with *someone* to get *something* new into my head. In an effort to minimize how much of an annoyance I must have been, I started by asking various members of the crew questions about sailing. *Why is that called the mast? How do you know how big the sail has to be?* I also changed up who I spoke to so I wouldn't bother a single person too much and risk them spreading word about how irritating I was. I didn't want to be avoided, and I didn't want to avoid them. But as with everything else up to that point on the sea, I bored myself with my own questions.

I then turned to my papyri.

I mostly just stared at them for the longest time. I rolled them out onto my lap and stared at them, letting my eyes glaze over. Occasionally I would focus my eyes and recite pieces of the lessons to myself softly. At first, I was self-conscious about it, but I realized I wasn't speaking loud enough to be heard over the bits of chatter on the top deck, or the rowing chants below, but especially not over the slushy crashes of the growing waves against the side of the ship. I looked up as an especially raucous one distracted me and crested just over the rail. In an unplanned jerk, I jumped to dodge the bit of water that spilled over, accidentally letting go of the top papyrus on my lap. As soon as it was free of my arm, a gust of wind shoved it away from me and launched it into the air towards the rail. I shot my arm out, already closing my fist before my arm had fully extended. I was too slow.

But thankfully, Tomiki had approached. He reached out and grabbed it with perfect timing.

"Oh, thank you, thank you, thank you!" I blabbered as I looked up at him from my bench. I instinctively reached out to him. He smiled at me and handed me the papyrus.

"Of course, of course," he said, sitting down next to me. "That's papyrus, right? Oh, my! You have two?"

He leaned back and away from me as his eyebrows raised slowly.

"We only have one piece between all of us at our village," he continued. "How did someone like you come to have two?"

"Someone like me?" I asked.

"Well, yes, I just know how expensive they are," he

added.

I didn't know how to respond and rather than feeling tears build up immediately, I only felt weighed down by my memories. All I could manage was to continue looking at the papyri while fiddling with one of the corners.

"Anyway, I've only ever seen ours and maybe one or two others that have passed through with traders," Tomiki continued. He then chuckled. "It was probably Nereus that brought them through!"

"Right, I know they're terribly hard to come by," I found the strength to say. "My father arranged to get them for me and my sister to document our studies of magic."

Tomiki tilted his chin in towards his chest.

"You know magic?" He asked.

"Yes," I said, confident. "My village is known for it. We've passed it along for, well, for as long as there have been people on my island, I guess."

Tomiki's head straightened up mostly, but he maintained a smirk of what appeared to be curiosity.

"So, what are these then?" He sought to confirm. "What are these symbols here?"

He leaned over them and squinted at the details. As he inspected them, another wave, bigger in every way, slammed into the side of the ship. The ship crested and rolled with a nauseating ebb and flow. We turned and looked when Nereus shouted out to his men.

"Mind those waves, now! Get a few extra spotters for the lower decks," he shouted.

"Be careful," Tomiki warned, turning back. "You'll lose them again!"

I felt myself start to laugh, but the choppy waters distracted me. Tomiki leaned in further.

"So, you can read these?" He asked. "What do these say? Are these your prayers, or, what are they called…

spells?"

"Yes," I replied kindly. "These symbols here are what the spell does, with the words to recite here, and if needed, the materials over here."

"What are these symbols running along the border here?"

Tomiki leaned over more and slid a few fingertips under one of the papyrus edges.

"I'm sorry, may I?" He requested politely.

I nodded and slid it towards him.

Tomiki held the papyrus up and examined it. "Did you draw these?" He asked.

"Yes. That one was my sister's," I said. "She and father worked on the decoration along the edges. My father and I worked on mine. The symbols on the edges honor the blessed Ariadne, and her mighty father Minos."

"Ah, yes!" Tomiki exclaimed. "Of course! I know what these are now. We also honor Ariadne. Here are symbols for her labyrinths and serpents," he said, his finger falling down the edges of the papyrus. "And here are her other gifts. This must be the bull? Oh, and lions. And there's a dove!"

"So, here's a row of weapons," Tomiki continued. "A bank of shields. A basket of, what is that? Bread? Vegetables? Vegetables next to weapons and shields? That's odd."

He continued reading.

"Now, here's a series of blank spaces next to the food and weapons... separated by marks."

I looked at the lessons above, and flipped the papyrus over to examine the back. I then picked mine up for comparison.

"Her lessons were a lot like mine, you see," I said, sliding the papyri next to each other. "Each of my lessons began with describing what the particular magical topic affected."

His eyes darted back and forth as he compared our documents.

"The beginnings of mine were much more straight forward though," I explained. "Mine began with single symbols, like grain, the symbol for protection, or the symbol for magic being deflected."

He looked back at Cilana's papyrus.

"Why are there so many different symbols at the beginning of this lesson of hers? Why the blank spaces? Was she supposed to fill something in? Was she supposed to choose—"

I accidentally interrupted, excited by his enthusiasm.

"It's something like that. I believe it's saying that the practitioner is supposed to choose from any number of items they wish to enchant. These enchantment methods could be applied to numerous things."

"Hmm!" He mumbled with interest. He read on.

"All right, so, once you pick an item, what do you do?" He asked, as we both hovered over the papyrus.

"Umm," I delayed, looking back to my papyrus. "After addressing what item I'm intending to manipulate, father had me list and gather whatever materials I would need. In my ward and protection lessons, I was to obtain a segment of a healthy item, a ripe item, or something that represents my target."

"Okay, so," he said, after flipping back to Cilana's papyrus. "The next line under each enchantment result must be what materials are needed. Here's a symbol of red droplets with dashes leading to, what is that, a flexing arm? And next to the arm is a small tree followed by a larger tree."

"I imagine that means blood is required to make something stronger? Something harder? Larger?" I proposed.

Considering the spells and discussing Cilana's advanced lessons filled me with an excitement close to how I felt when I studied with papa. It felt warm. It felt good. It felt like blessed innocence and naiveté. My heart almost felt like it had substance to it again. Almost like my family was still alive.

"How much blood? Whose blood? Any blood? Human blood? Mule blood?" He wondered humorously, perpetuating our intrigue.

The next line had what looked to be a serpent cut in two. The dashes leading away from the serpent went to a knife or a short sword with a symbol of serpent fangs on top of it. Next to the blade with fangs was an axe with the same added imagery.

"Look at this," I said, pointing. "I wonder if this means I can somehow make an object poisonous. Perhaps I can imbue things with poison?"

Tomiki continued looking while holding his chin.

"Okay, here's some kind of bird," I continued. "It looks to be falling, no, um, diving? It has a drawing of a feather just above it. There are other symbols next to the bird... This looks to be an animal pelt, I believe. It's a spotted hide, and is drawn above some kind of cat. I guess this is supposed to tell me that I would need a hide, and show me what type of animal to obtain it from."

"Ah, right," Tomiki added. "And next to the cat and its hide is a lean creature with antlers, with a set of antlers above the creature they would come from?"

The skies had grown dark, and the sea was becoming more agitated. I let my eyes drift to the turbulent waters out of increasing concern, but eventually remembered Tomiki's question.

But, as I sat and considered the antlers, I couldn't

determine an obvious meaning for them. I wasn't sure if I would need a feather, hide, and antlers together, to accomplish the desired effect, or if I would need just one of them. And even then, I don't know what the desired effect was.

I heard a muffled voice shout a command below.

"Loosen the grips a bit men, and wait for the waves to break," the spotter said.

"Let's see," I resumed. "Off to the side of the feather, hide, and antlers, separated by a series of dashes like entries above... It looks to be a pair of human legs in the act of running. Does one need all three of those items to make a person faster? Can we make other things faster? Move quicker? That will definitely require testing. Oh! Maybe that can be applied to warriors. Help them move faster in battle, possibly?"

But even with all the questions we posed, it was still the easiest portion of the papyrus to evaluate. The section that came next would be the most trying.

Following the topics and the materials required, came the section where the incantations were written. But they weren't simple text. They were made of symbols. Meant to protect the magic from falling into unfriendly hands, the spells were taught and recited in our ancestral tongue, only verbally. The written symbols were only hints and reminders of the text.

I looked at the symbols for the spells Cilana and I had learned on both papyri. As suspected, they matched. The symbols that represented the spells for the lessons I *hadn't* been taught yet were there on Cilana's papyrus, but I had never heard them spoken, or been taught how these symbols should be read to achieve the desired effect.

I fell back slightly in disappointment and intimidation.

"Hmm," Tomiki said with a chuckle. "I don't know

what to make of all those."

I smiled and started to respond but was startled by a frantic announcement from Nereus.

"A rogue wave, men! Grab hold! Grab hold!"

The main sail rippled and whipped with its concussive slap of massive fabric. The interruption was followed by the ship's violent roll to starboard. I tried to ask Tomiki what to do but a rupture of thunder cracked overhead and silenced me further. The smothering blanket of thick clouds overhead stretched and tore, unleashing a punishing wall of water.

The ship rolled to the port side and then back again to starboard.

"Get inside!" Tomiki shouted. He grabbed the corner of the cabin wall behind us as the rolling of the ship slung him into it.

"Nereus!" He shouted as he stumbled away, trying to navigate through the rocking of the deck.

"Where?" I shouted, wondering if I should go below with the oarsmen or into Nereus' cabin. But he didn't hear me.

I rolled up my papyri and stuck them down my shirt. The ship rolled and threw me into the nearby railing which caught me in the stomach like a massive fist. I gasped for breath as the angle of the deck tipped me to within feet of the sea. In a flash of cold through my veins, I was stunned into fright but was slung backwards onto the deck as the ship rolled again.

Rather than trying to decide on whether to go below or into Nereus' cabin, I just wanted away from the water. I wanted protection as quickly possible. I flipped over onto my stomach and in-between the merciless rolling of the ship, I scratched my way into Nereus' cabin.

I shoved my palm into the door, slung it open, and

pulled on it to drag myself in. I kicked with the sides of my feet and made it inside before kicking the door closed behind me.

As I tried to flip onto my back, the ship rolled. It kept rolling. It kept rolling and overturned. As I fell face-first into the ceiling-turned-floor, I heard dozens of oarsmen screech out in cries of terror and chaos.

We've lost control! We're upside down!

As if I wasn't aware, my mind had to make sure. As the sound of the storm grew softer, the sound of the sea's power increased. Crouched on all fours, I could only stare down at the ceiling while the upturned ship rocked back and forth.

Though there were no windows in the simple, square room of wood, the sea had already found plenty of ways in. Popped out knots and poorly-sealed boards betrayed me. I had to get out.

I looked at the door and hesitated.

If I open it now, the water will pour in that much faster.

Well, you need to get out sooner rather than later. You're going to end up in the sea anyway. Get out and find something to hold onto while you can!

I crawled and splashed over to the door and pulled it open with what felt like just the faint hint of my hand. The pressure of the sea shoved it open. The water shot in and washed me to the back of the room.

Even through the wetness and temperature of the water, I felt myself shiver with the fear that I might not make it out. There were only inches of air left. There were no structures or anything secured in the room that I could use to help me move. I could only swim, stand and plant my feet, weather the next roll, and keep making for the door. When the last dips and peeks of sky disappeared, I finally reached the door frame and pushed my way through.

Like emerging from a womb of horror, I swam out through the cabin door and glided under water. The top deck was already completely submerged. Its plummeting shadows darkened the water beneath me as the ship sank.

Air, air, air, was all I could think. *Keep your head up! Get a hold of something!*

The sea slung me to and fro, rolling me into a wave, before covering me up with another. As soon as I felt any inclination that my face was clear, I sipped in a rapid breath and opened my eyes.

Most of my teases of vision were swarming with sea. Grays and blues and greens. White foam. Smears of water as waves crashed over me. But there was the occasional piece of debris.

Oars.

Cargo.

Men.

They shouted and screamed, but I could never make out if anything was actually being communicated. There was no coordination or command. It was well past that now. Those who hadn't already drowned only screamed in fear and panic.

At some point I managed to grab an oar that I had rolled into. It didn't do me any good. As I tried to wrap my arms around it and hold onto it, it just sank and bobbed below me.

More smears of sea.

Get air!

Your face is clear. Get a gulp of air!

The natural inertia of the water threw me sideways.

Hold your breath!

Your face is clear! What can you see?

Men flapping their arms.

My ears filled with crispy white noise of water and fear.

I soared and plummeted in the palm of the raging ocean. My hands slapped the top of the water in one instant, and dragged in the thickness below the next. Each trough and crest was a sadistic tease of my impending death. Between hacking and gargling the persistent gulps of water that tried to drown me, I stole a breath. Just enough to keep me alive. Just enough of a breath to sustain my fear that it would be my last.

When I found slivers of time to focus my eyes, I saw the rippling and rupturing sea, the malignant sky, and receding dark splotches I couldn't identify. After more surges and rolls than I could count, I brushed up against one of the dark blotches.

More parts of the ship.

I reached out. I smacked my fingertips on it, but the water swept it away. With the gift of an extra second above water, I looked out across the board I had missed and saw small specs scattered around.

The crew!

An especially violent ebb flipped me forward and tossed me almost completely out of the water. As I pitched forward and crashed back into the water, the salty froth rushed up my nose, but somehow, the poke of something in my back found a way to steal attention from the fear that I would drown.

My axes!

The hateful wave rolled again and I used it to turn over and thrash violently. When I broke the surface, I choked in as big a breath as I could and grabbed for my axes.

I fell sideways and trapped a piece of wood between my legs. Though I was still floating on the surface, I held my breath to focus and smacked my axes at the board.

The magical force splashed water out of the way as it shot towards the wood and struck it. It swelled to the size of a decent raft, knocking my legs away as it grew. I sliced and whirled my arms through the water and scrambled onto it. After holding onto one of the edges just long enough to let me use my axes again, I smacked them to envelop myself and my raft in a dome. I let go of my breath and raced to gasp and catch up. I stood up on the deck of my little floating boat and scanned the sea for any other debris.

As soon as I would see something, I smacked my axes at it and grew it. Nearby crew swam over and crawled onto boards and crates. When each one seemed full or floated out of range of nearby crew, I'd wrap each makeshift boat in its own dome of safety. I couldn't tell how many men had made it to one, or who specifically. But I made a raft out of everything I could until the violent waves pulled me away or shoved everything else out of sight.

Oh, Ariadne, I begged. I tied my axes around me and clung to the inside of my dome of protection. The sharp rips of the sea and eruptions of thunder were muffled just enough for my thoughts to break through my stubborn layer of fear.

Please let Tomiki be on one of those rafts.
Please get Tomiki back to Kuria.
Please get them home.

Chapter Nine - Shifting Sands

Bayla

I didn't die.

My eyes almost opened, but my doubts made them wait.

Maybe I did die. Mama? Papa? Cilana? Are you there?

Whatever I was laying on was hard. As I waited for a response from my family, I curled my fingers and bent a leg up to my side.

It's crumbling beneath me! Why is it so coarse? So painful, but it's giving way! I'm falling! I'm sinking!

My eyes opened, and I immediately regretted it. The sun had risen above the horizon and stirred me awake with its full potential. The searing heat and punishing brightness overcame my hazy panic. With my head still on the ground I looked down.

Sand. It's just sand slithering with the tip of a receding wave.

The small cracks I dug out with my fingers while grasping for consciousness quickly dried out. Now exposed, the wetter, darker sand slowly grew paler under the thirsty heat of the sun.

I had to shut my eyes. It was too much, too fast.

So tired. So thirsty. Again.

But the scratchy sand irritated my eyes back open. Though I felt twenty times heavier than usual, I started to peel myself off the sand. After rolling onto my rear and swaying over myself into a sitting position, I lethargically loomed over my legs.

I swatted the annoying clumps of sand off my leg and lifted my head. Slowly. I didn't want to see anything but a thriving village. I wanted to see green, trees, palms, buildings, smoke from fires cooking food, and people running out to bring me water. I wanted to see Tomiki, Nereus, and the crew.

But no, just sand. Dunes, heat, and sky.

I started to shake with anger. I looked to the barren horizon and realized any hope for survival disappeared when my eyes opened last.

There is nothing out there, over there, or here.

Every nerve in my body vibrated with accumulating anger. I had just survived a destroyed village, a shipwreck, and now here I was on a lifeless beach. I balled up my fist, whipped it in front of me and slammed it down into the sand. I beat the ground as hard as I could. Over and over I punched it, slammed it, attacked it. The coarse and packed sand felt like chips of stone to my skin, but I didn't care. I wanted to expend and waste all my energy. I punched the sand and began to scream. At first, I shouted all of the air out of my lungs through deep, rapid bursts of primal hate at my surroundings and circumstances. But that didn't make me feel better. I took deeper breaths and constricted my throat. I pushed harder and pierced the area with sharper daggers of sound. More and more breaths I took, to scream longer and louder and higher.

"Why?" I occasionally screamed in-between my extended shrieks of fury.

"Why?"

I had survived the murder of my family. The murder of my village. The burning of my village. The days of walking. The shipwreck.

"Why?" I yelled again.

I waited for tears, but they never came.

Nothing happened. There was nothing in sight. No one came. I could only look up to the dunes and think at that moment how I didn't care that I was alive. I didn't care that someone killed my family. I didn't care about vengeance. I was sickened by the idea of having to keep going after all this.

But then I punched the sand again. Again, and again, and again. Not from resenting being alive, but from even contemplating that I didn't care about avenging my family.

I leaned over, swung my feet beneath me, and stood up.

To get a feel for the condition of my condition and energy, I stood up slowly, staring at the ground as I rose. My heart pulsed a bit faster and harder as I stood, and my head pounded at itself. But I was surprised. I didn't feel as poorly as I did when I walked to Milopotas. I turned around towards the sea and remembered washing up on the shore. I remembered thinking to myself that I just needed to crawl up the beach enough to be safe from the tides before passing out from exhaustion. I remembered how I had gotten there. After turning back to face the dunes, I remembered what I was meant to do.

The beach didn't have anything on it that I could use. With the realization that nothing, *and no one,* else from the ship had washed up at this spot, a jolt of terror pierced my veins.

My axes?

I flung a hand behind me. My chin quivered in relief when I felt my axes still tied to me.

Cilana's necklace?

A quick slap to my chest found it still around my neck.

My papyri?

I plunged my other hand down my shirt, grasping and reaching. I bent and twisted to feel to my sides and around towards my back. I spun and searched the sand.

They were gone.

The records of my and Cilana's lessons with our father, were gone. My chance to continue trying to learn Cilana's advanced lessons. Gone. The last tangible link I had to my father, mother, my sister, our home. Gone.

I wanted to fall. I wanted to fall back down to the sand and beat my fists flat into piles of bloody pulp in anger. And if not fall to the ground, I wanted to fall to hades, fall to blackness, fall to nothing. I stared at the ground, waiting. Waiting to fall.

Fall!

Fall!

Fall!

But I didn't. I couldn't. I wouldn't. I forced my head to disobey the defeat completely consuming me at that moment and look up. No, I would not fall. I looked up to the dunes and stepped towards them.

* * *

I took that first step, and then another step, and then quickly lost count. I didn't know how long fate—or what I had convinced myself was fate—would help keep the heat and exhaustion out of my mind. But while my renewed ambition of vengeance gave me new strength to continue on, I focused on just one step. One step at a time.

Slogging up that first dune was a hearty check to my reality. While it didn't completely defeat my will, it knocked my already-limited expectations back a bit. Each meaningful step up the dune took three regular steps. I would step up, sink into the sand a bit, bring my other foot around, and as I did, I would slide back down the dune a step's worth. I kept looking to the summit of the first dune and planned to take a break, excited to scan the area from its height.

My feet felt lighter as I approached the top of the dune. The thickness of the sand seemed to loosen up and the difficulty of the climb seemed to ease. I knew I was probably just being fooled by my anticipation of reaching the top, but I didn't care. With only a few more sandy steps, I made it.

There was no reward. There was nothing. Just more sand. A slope down leading to a new slope up. More dunes. Hundreds, thousands, millions of steps awaited me. It might as well have been an eternity of walking in the hot sand with no visible destination ahead of me.

Is this Alashiya? I asked myself. *It can't be this vast. Or can it? Does it even have deserts?*

I looked behind me and back out across the sea. An equally intimidating expanse of water that I couldn't drink stared back at me and dared me to continue on through the desert. But I didn't turn away immediately. Tracing along the beach as far as I could from my elevated vantage point, I wondered how far it went. If I were to go back down and follow the coast, I might come across a village. A town. Whether or not this was Alashiya, I assumed that there must eventually be someone or something on the coast.

But what if I washed up on an uninhabited island?

What if there are coastal villages, but they're too far away?

I turned back to the desert and lifted my hands to cover my eyes. My vision flexed between various strengths of squinting as I slowly scanned the horizon. Perhaps there would be smoke, structures, movement of people or animals. Maybe some kind of...

Blue!

A thin sliver of reflective blue crept up from the far reaches of the sand. I massaged my eyelids and shaded them again before forcing multiple blinks. I focused back on the distant blue.

Is that water? If it is, is it just the coastline that has meandered back around to that point? Or is it fresh water?

Fresh. Water.

My chest felt heavy and I heard myself breathing though I hadn't trudged through the sand in many minutes.

So hot.

I turned back towards the sea and leaned over with my hands on my knees.

Trace the coast? Flatter land at the beach. Easier to walk.

Might come across a village. Might not.

Still leaning over, I peered back into the depths of the desert.

If I still see the hint of blue on the horizon when I stand up, I'll head inland.

I stood and turned slowly to once again face the desert. It was still there. The faint tease of something blue. But something kept me from taking that next step immediately.

Is that just coastline? More saltwater?

I closed my eyes to rest them if just for a second.

When I opened them again I strained to focus without straining them to blurriness, and to try and keep my eyelashes from obstructing my eyesight too much. From all that I could tell, there was land and sand behind the slit of blue.

A chance for freshwater versus a coastline that may never have any signs of life.

I decided.

My throat attempted a pitiful, dry swallow as I took my first step down the other side of the dune. The steps were easier in that I was going downhill, but I still had to fight with my footing in the shifting sand.

Fear colluded with the heat to make me doubt my decision, but not enough to make me change my mind. When I had decided, I decided. I knew I had to split my journey into segments, especially without knowing how long the trek would take, or if I would reach the blotch on the horizon that I hoped was water. It had to be one dune at a time. One ascent at a time, then one descent at a time.

I was able to keep the ever-present bully of the sun just enough out of my mind to allow me to proceed. Though I continued to hear myself strain and labor to breathe as I traversed the dunes, I reserved most of my focus for my individual goals of separate dunes. Each dune summit, I stopped to take in all that I could to the horizon in all directions. The sea grew smaller and the disk of blue remained. It wasn't growing as quickly as I would have liked, but I pressed on after each little break to confirm I was heading in the right direction.

The amount of time that passed between making the decision to travel inland and when I started to worry seemed like a meaningful amount, but I don't know for sure. I just knew that after more dunes than I wanted to count that I found myself walking slower, walking up at a wider diagonal to make the climbs easier, and taking longer at the tops of dunes.

Soon after the worry planted itself in my mind and started to sprout roots of hungry paranoia, I knew I had to distract myself. My first attempts at taking my mind off the heat consisted of counting steps, counting dunes, and measuring the amount of sea I could fit in-between my fingers held up in front of my face at each dune's summit.

But that quickly started having the opposite effect.

Less ocean.

Farther away from the coast and flatter beach.

More steps, more dunes.

I soon transitioned to reciting what I could remember from my and Cilana's papyri. That worked. That helped. My mind emptied some, and I was able to focus on remembering something dear to me rather than the expanse of desert that I was walking deeper into. I didn't remember as much of Cilana's, so I started with speaking bits and pieces of her advanced lessons. Speaking out loud also helped take my mind off of how hard it was to breathe.

"Incantations. I remember papa saying to Cilana recently that you didn't always need to have ingredients for certain spells. Maybe he was talking about incantations?"

Up came the top of another dune. The ocean was still back there when I turned to check. Down the other side I stomped.

When I really had to dig into the sand or focus on an especially-troublesome ascent, I took my thoughts internally.

I don't remember any of the materials or spells for those incantations.

I suddenly stopped thinking and stopped talking, though I kept walking. Cilana flashed into my mind's eye, and for a moment, nothing I felt or sensed was greater than how badly I missed my sister. I reached up and clutched her necklace. I squeezed it as hard as I could. My hand began to hurt.

Maybe?

Finally, I stopped walking as well and closed my eyes.

Cilana? Are you there? Can you see me or feel me holding your necklace?

I spoke out loud to her.

"Parakalo miliste mou, agapimeni adelfi. An me akoute kai an milate, epitrepste mou na akouso i na aisthantho xana ti foni sas."

Please speak to me, beloved sister. If you can hear me, and if you can speak, let me hear or feel your voice again.

All that I knew at the moment was silence, and Cilana's stone in my hand.

It was all that I knew, and all that I felt.

Nothing happened.

I hung my head and sighed, still holding the stone.

"What about enchantments, hmm?"

I reached back for my axes and resumed my hike up and down and through the sand.

"What did the papyrus have for that again?"

Ah, yes, I thought, nodding to myself as I remembered. *Choose an item to be selected. There were a bunch of symbols. Food, and weapons, I think.*

"Okay. I've enchanted my axes already with my rank one spells," I stated to no one but myself and the dunes. "But..."

What else could I enchant them with?

I flipped one of the axes and spun it end over end before catching it.

"There's a whole lot of nothing to—"

Wait. There's a whole lot of sand! But what can I do to my axes with sand?

I looked down as I wondered, and gently flung the axe into the slope of the dune I was on. I stared at it and repeated myself out loud.

"What good is a bunch of sand to an axe?"

I stared for a few more seconds but reached down and pulled it out before taking the last few steps up to the top of my latest dune. With my axes hanging down to my sides, I scanned the horizon once again.

The sea was now noticeably smaller. I woke up on the beach just after sunup, and the sun was now a bit past midday. I couldn't tell how many dunes I had crossed, but I estimated that I had been walking for about six hours. And while the size of the water I was heading for didn't seem to change as I walked towards it, its shade of blue did seem clearer, and more vibrant.

My breathing caught my attention for the first time in a while, which shattered the facade I had wrapped around everything else. My head clouded over with the most pain I'd felt since beginning to walk. My feet and legs stung with fatigue. With each breath my lungs felt like they were expanding against the coals of a roaring fire. And rather than taking the energy to tie my axes back to me immediately, I tossed them both into the sand and rubbed my face.

Completely surrounded by sand and can't use it for anything, I thought. While still rubbing my eyes, I considered what from my magic lessons I could begin reciting next.

Wait!

There has to be water under there somewhere!

I ran over and swiped my axes out of the sand and filled my mind with the spell I knew to manipulate the wind. With a quick glance at my axes and after turning in the wind the direction was blowing, I slammed my axes together towards the tip of the dune ahead.

A gigantic curl of air blasted from my axes and shoved a mass of sand into the breeze.

I gasped into a smile.

I can dig for water!

I smacked them against each other again. Again and again. With each powerful blast, the walls of sand flew out. But just as I got into a repetitive rhythm, the ground beneath me started to move.

Uh oh.

The sand slid and shifted and poured down into the adjacent valley, taking me with it. I had moved too much sand, too quickly, and had no control over the resulting slide. I lost my footing and fell over, digging my hands into the sand and keeping myself stable for a few moments. But it wasn't enough. I rolled and tumbled down.

After crashing and swirling in the sand, the world finally settled beneath me, or I finally settled onto it. My head throbbed along with my body and my throat felt like there was a pile of sand in it. I coughed and choked, but each quick breath in-between only sucked in that much more sand because my face was still on the ground. I cursed and shoved myself up. Once I was sitting up, I coughed freely and cursed myself again for my clumsiness. With no immediate end to my coughing in sight, I brushed myself off, smacking my clothes, chest, and hair. My eyes were closed the whole time, but I eventually opened them. Still hacking, I looked back up the dune I had rolled and tumbled down. The indentations I had made in the sand from rolling down were already smoothing over with the sandy breeze. I started to feel a bit better knowing my stupid mistake would soon be erased.

"Hey, miss," someone said.

A chomp of fearful surprise bit at my heart. My body jerked around to identify the speaker. The sound of another human—the first I had heard in days—scrambled my emotion and spiked my adrenaline. The drastic shift and crash in my nerves made me immediately feel like crying, but I was too focused on taking in what I saw.

I hadn't seen it as I rolled down the dune, but back behind where I had landed was a wooden cart. Inside were what looked to be two men with no one else around that I could see. In and around the area were some destroyed crates, a fire pit mostly covered up with sand, and behind the men, what looked to be a well. My eyes locked on the well, making me temporarily blind to all else.

"Hey, can you hear me?" One of the men asked.

I was panting, for a host of reasons—my fall, being startled by the men, and being surprised by the sight of the well.

I rolled around on my rear and stretched out my legs to test how I felt before trying to stand up, but I kept my eyes on the wooden cart. I brought my legs back around and slowly came to my feet.

The men in the cart were laying on their sides as they spoke, and made no effort to move that I could see. I took my time and took in the whole area in greater detail. The surrounding dunes, the small valley we were in, the abandoned campsite, the cart, and the covered well. That was it.

"There's no one else here," the man said.

Before I took a step towards the wagon, I looked at my hands to confirm I was still holding my axes.

I squinted my eyes. From the distance I was at, I could tell that the man speaking was a dark-skinned man, but saw nothing in his clothes or the debris around the cart to give me any information as to where he was from. He spoke to me in my own language, though, which filled me with a wave of hope that I may not be too far away from my home, or at least my island where my home used to be.

My breath was still labored, but I felt my chest begin

to loosen. For the first time since this stranger surprised me, I felt how weak my legs were, how parched I was, and how much I wanted to sleep. Before I approached the cart, I just stood, rubbed my eyes, and slapped more of the sand off of me.

When I finally looked back towards the cart, I saw one of the men had moved and leaned into the side of the cart's wooden slats.

"Hey, can you get me some water?" He asked.

Feeling slightly safe with the man being in the cart, I stepped towards it slowly. I kept my eyes trained on it, while occasionally scanning the nearby area for any surprises. The man stared at me as I approached, weighted and weary, it seemed, with thirst and oppression from the heat.

"Please," he asked as I grew closer. "That water in there is fresh."

I hadn't said anything to him yet. I didn't have anything to say, yet. I had no idea where I was, who he was, and why he had apparently been someone's prisoner. And in an effort to get more information, I would need to eventually speak with him. And in order for that to happen, he needed to be alive.

After closing to within a dozen or so feet from the cart, and being able to see the debris more closely, I examined the area for any new information I could glean.

There was the small fire pit, covered up by a natural, still wave of sand blown in by the wind and not by a person that I could tell. So, he must have been here for a few days. I saw a few water skins and spears, crates of food, and not much else other than the ropes attached to the cage that must have either been severed, or abandoned. I stepped closer to the cart and looked in for my first real close glimpse of the men.

The air crunched out of my lungs.

The man who had been speaking was still pressed up against the edge of the cart's slatted walls, and behind him in an opposite corner was the body of a man who I previously thought was alive as well. But he was not. His dark skin was partially bleached and shriveled. A part of the side of his face was cut, punctured, sliced, and beginning to rot.

I stumbled back out of sheer reflex.

"I couldn't do anything for him," the living man said. As he spoke, he lifted his arms up, revealing his wrists bound with shackles. I looked to see if his ankles were bound as well. They were.

My short breath, momentarily exacerbated by the sickening sight of the dead man, slowed.

"There's a water skin over there," the man said. "The well…"

I swallowed and half fell, half stumbled down to pick up the water skin and headed for the well behind the cart. Every so often, I would turn to make sure the man was staying put, or that nothing else in the area was approaching.

Upon reaching the edge of the well, I dropped the bladder and fell to my knees and pushed the lid off.

Ripping reflections!

I shoved myself over and was already heaving the rope up before I registered dropping the cup down. Water spilled and hit the sides of the well as I raised it recklessly. With a final jerk of the rope, I flung the cup up, caught it, and guzzled it down.

It was the most delicious thing I had ever tasted. It was fresh, clean, and clear. At one point, I gagged in-between gulps, but I think that was from the speed at which I was inadvertently trying to choke myself. I splashed some on my face and stared at mirrored miracle.

"Are you going to get me some or not?" The man

snipped bitterly.

I popped up to my feet, agitated by his attitude.

"Will you wait a second? I can keep walking, you know," I snapped back.

He huffed and rolled onto his back.

I stared at him for a bit before kneeling back down to the well's edge, taking my time with each movement. After pondering my reflection again in the water, for absolutely no reason at all but to make the stranger wait longer, I reached back for the water skin and filled it. Before standing, I looked back and saw the man still on his back. I got up and walked back over.

I crept up to the cage from an angle so I could confirm his wrists were still bound. As I brought the water skin up, he rolled back over and shoved his hands between two slats as much as he could. I pushed just enough of the skin between the slats so he could grab it. He snatched it from me, brought it up, and worked to catch every drop of his fast pour.

"It looks like it's been a few days," I said before pulling my hand away.

He had to catch his breath. He rolled onto his back again and gasped from the exhaustion of quenching his thirst.

"It has," he said through quick breaths. "It has."

Despite the slats of the cage between us, I was able to examine the man and his dead, cellmate—I guess he was—with extraordinary detail. But even so, neither men's clothes revealed anything that I could identify.

"What is this place?" I asked.

The man rolled his head to me and looked at me with a blank stare. Using his shoulders and bound wrists, he shuffled backwards and propped himself up against the side of the cage. His face wrinkled into one of confusion.

"You don't know where you are?" He asked.

I stared back, with a head tilted in impatience.

"This is Egypt," He said.

My eyebrows dipped and my head rocked back. I stared at the man as I felt my face shift through numerous states of confusion. I scanned the area with blurry eyes, but then I focused them as the evidence for his assertion made more and more sense to me. The expansive desert, the dunes, the sand, the heat.

"Egypt?" I repeated in astonishment.

"Yes," he started. "Where are you from?"

I couldn't immediately answer. Though I knew what had happened, I flooded my mind once again with all that had transpired to make sure I truly knew. I replied, but mostly to myself.

"We were headed for Alashiya," I said, as I slumped down to the side of the cage. The partial shade from being next to the cart registered a slight relief, but not enough to distract me.

"We were on a ship," I continued. "We set out from Rhodes, looking for someone. There was a terrible storm that overturned us. I floated for what felt like forever and washed up on the beach. I've been walking ever since."

"Alashiya?" The man asked. "Isn't that," he added, pausing, "Cyprus?"

My confusion over what he was referring to, stirred me out of my foggy recollections. I pushed away from the wheel and stood back up to look at him.

"Cyprus?" I asked.

He let his head relax as he looked away.

"I've heard it called both," he said. "Doesn't matter. But I thought you looked Cretan. Is that where you're from? Crete?"

"No," I said, shaking my head. "I'm from the island

of Ios."

The man held a long blink before a few quicker ones.

"I don't know where that is," he said.

"Just north of Crete," I replied.

"Mmm," he grunted. "Who were you looking for?"

Instead of answering, I reached in for the skin. Once I had it back, I took a few drinks of water and started back towards the well for a refill.

"Why don't you tell me why you're in that cage, first?" I prompted.

"Uhh," he said through a sigh that was fueled by what sounded like embarrassment.

When I reached the well I turned to face him as I dunked the skin.

"I got captured—" he started.

"Oh, really?" I interrupted, extending my hand towards the cage he was in.

"I was going to say," he said as his head dropped in frustration, "that I was captured by the bounty I was hunting."

"Bounty?" I asked, unfamiliar with the term.

"Mmm, a bounty, a target, the target of a hunt," he said.

I swigged a gulp of water and tilted my head.

"What do you mean? How can you get captured by something you're hunting?"

He reciprocated my look of confusion.

"Huh?" He said. "I'm not talking about boars or dogs for food. In this case, I'm talking about scorpirons. I'm talking about money."

"Scorpions?" I asked, thinking I'd misheard.

"No. Scor*pir*ons. They're really large creatures that stand upright, and have a lot of the features of the smaller scorpions," he answered.

"And you hunt these things for money?" I sought to clarify.

"What? Yes," the man said, snapping at me. "Don't villages pay people to take care of particular pests where you come from?"

"No, we take care of them ourselves," I answered, almost laughing.

He scoffed and collapsed back into the slats of the cage after straightening up some in aggravation.

"I don't think you know what kind of creatures I'm talking about here," he said, dismissive.

"Apparently not," I said, somewhat offended by his implications. "It's these pests that threw you in a cage?"

"Yes," he growled.

"And you hunt these pests for money?"

"Yes," he growled again.

"So, you're a hunter," I clarified.

"Yes," he said with another growl. "But they're not just pests. These scorpirons are intelligent, and fierce."

"Fierce!" I said with a lilt of doubt.

He sighed.

"When they attack caravans or villages, they're virtually silent, scampering along quickly and quietly," he said. "And once the slaughter begins, their prey has very little chance. You see—each scorpiron has two pincers, a massive tail, a stinger, and can stand on two legs—a few feet higher than the average man. They leave nothing but carnage in their wake, and leave more questions than answers on how their victims might have properly defended themselves if given any kind of warning."

I stuck with referring to them as pests.

"And these pests are called bounties?"

The man shot up straight and leaned forward.

"A job to kill something someone pays you to kill, as

well as the target itself, is called a bounty. I am a bounty hunter. This particular bounty was for a scorpiron. I was trying to kill a specific one. I got caught and thrown in here. We were traveling along when they got attacked by a flock of zarafteryx who chased them off, and I got left here."

"Hmm," I mumbled. "Zarafteryx? I've heard of those. Never seen one though."

"Can you just let me out?" He asked. "And I'll be on my way."

I didn't appreciate his condescension, and as I processed this profession he apparently had, I didn't give him the satisfaction of reacting to it. And I surely didn't entertain his request for freedom immediately.

"Hmm, we just don't have a need to hire people to kill where I come from," I said. "Maybe that's because we don't have things like giant scorpions, or, what did you call them, *scorpirons*, on my island."

"That's wonderful," he said. "Look, what is your name?"

"Bayla," I answered.

"Great. Will you—," he tried.

"What's your name?" I returned.

"Briz," he said quickly. "Will you let me out?"

"What else do you hunt?" I wondered.

He deflated and sighed.

"Whatever pays," he huffed.

"So, Briz, if someone comes to you and offers you payment to kill, you'll kill?"

"Yes," he said.

"You'll kill anything?" I asked.

"Will... you... just... let me out?" He repeated softly. He looked me in the eye before erupting in anger. "I can't get out of these," he said, flinging his bound wrists and ankles in my direction. "Just let me out and if you can free my ankles, I'll shuffle out of here and out of your life."

"So, you're a killer. You'll kill anything?" I pressed. "Will you kill other people?"

"I don't hunt humans, lady."

"What?" I challenged immediately. "Too hard for you?"

The man sniffed out a laugh.

"No," he replied. "Too easy. Too much drama. Too little reward."

"Too easy? But didn't you get captured by these scorpiron things?"

He closed his eyes and stretched his face before leaning back against the cage slats.

"Setbacks are part of the job, Boola," he said before opening his eyes again.

"Bayla," I corrected.

He closed his eyes again and nodded in silly circles before continuing.

"Right. Anyway, setbacks are part of it. I get captured. I get free. Sometimes I get something to eat or hear some information before I escape. In that sense, getting caught is sometimes a bonus. Either way, I seem to have been fairly successful so far."

"Mmm, but too little reward? I can't believe there's more money in killing one of these guys as there is another person."

"Sure there is," he countered quickly. "Whole villages will pool their resources together to take out a herd of beasts or a mob of raiders. People are usually wanted dead by only a few people with little means. It's not worth it."

"Hmm," I said. "And here you are, tied up in a box in the desert," I said.

"I had a few plans and getting caught was one of those." His voice was soft, but stabbed sharply.

"And if I continue walking," I said, confident with my position in the argument, "your plan will be at the mercy of the sun."

Briz rolled a bit from side to side and eventually settled before burrowing a stare into me. He then smiled wide.

"You won't leave me here."

I scoffed at him.

"You have absolutely no way of knowing that."

He was laughing before I finished speaking.

"You wouldn't. You're just not the type," he said, settling into small snorts of laughter.

I looked at him and tried to empty all emotion out of my face as I walked closer to him.

I brought the water skin up to him. He leaned towards me. I pulled it back through and smiled.

"Good luck to you," I whispered.

I stomped off at a quick march towards the well.

"Wait, wait," he said with a reserved urgency. "All right, okay," he added. "I shouldn't have said that."

I leaned over and filled the water skin again.

"I only meant that you're nicer than me," he added.

As he continued with his slightly veiled begging, I took the time to drink more water.

"You wouldn't do what probably most of the rest of the world would do. You're not the type to leave me here."

I dipped down and topped off the water skin, and continued my march, away from the cart, never looking back to Briz.

"You're not a killer," he said, his voice fading off with an increased realization that I may not turn around. "You're too nice to hurt people."

His last statement punctured my resolve. I stopped walking and kept my back to him while in that moment,

I questioned everything I was and everything I thought I wanted to be. My mind, heart and soul had gone in and out of all variations of hate and malice over the past few weeks. I had seen glimpses of a potential event where I destroyed those who killed my family flash through my mind, as well as images of my innocence and naivety crumbling into a corner of self-imposed isolation in some village where I would live out my days in peace, silence, and regret.

When he described me and decided who and what I was, and what I wasn't, I forced myself to step out of my immediate awareness. With my entire existence, past, present, and what I thought might be my future, I truly made the final call on who I was, and what my intentions were. I shivered as a torment of emotion rolled within me and crashed upon the rocks of my fate. I turned and faced the cage once again. Briz was sitting up, silent. Waiting.

I walked back towards him and his cage.

He was frozen where he sat, expressionless, no doubt unsure of what type of response to expect.

"I just..." he began to say gently, "thought you were nice."

I leaned in, close enough to spit on him, which I definitely felt like doing. I dug a stare into him, taking every opportunity to scan every speck of his eyes.

"I *was*," I whispered, strangling all hints of warmth out of my voice as possible.

As I looked at Briz, he didn't blink. He didn't slink or shrink away, but his eyes jerked around gently as my words sank in.

While I let my statement simmer in his mind, I walked around to the door of the cage and began untying the bundle of rope holding it shut. Briz watched me carefully and said nothing.

"A group of raiders burned my village and killed

everyone in it, including my mother, father, and sister," I said, as I untied the rope. "I bought my way onto a ship to try and hunt them down."

The last knot in the rope loosened as I tugged and stretched it. I swung the door open and stepped away.

Briz looked at me and made no effort to move.

"Who were they?" He asked.

I took in a huge breath and shoved it out, exhausted by just the idea of having to explain it to him.

"I don't know exactly," I said in a rush to move on.

"So, you were rushing out for your vengeance, without really knowing who you were searching for?"

"I have some ideas. There were a few possibilities that some people in a few different ports thought it could be, and we thought we would be able to catch up to them in Alashiya, but I never made it there, obviously, so whoever it was is probably long gone and scattered throughout the world by now."

Briz looked away as I spoke and squinted at the horizon, seemingly unimpressed with my reaction to his concern.

"Look, I appreciate you asking," I said, anxious to get away from the conversation, "it's just that I've pretty much lost all opportunity to find some new clues as to who it was, okay?"

"Yes, I understand," he said dismissively. "But you said there were a few possibilities. Tell me—"

"Briz!" I interrupted. "They're gone! I've lost them. I've been swimming and walking for days. They're long gone!"

"My business is searching and hunting," he insisted. "You can find anything or anyone if you really want to. Who... were... the... possibilities?"

My first inclination was to just tell him to forget it,

but as I stood there, looking in on him bound and at my mercy, I had a sense he might really be interested, though to what end or for what motive I wasn't sure. After another exasperated sigh, I threw my hands up as I blurted the worthless information.

"There were a few groups that had been through various ports recently. Egyptians, Phoenicians, Persians..."

Briz looked away.

"Hmm," he said. "They all have traders going back and forth. Were you there when they attacked? Did you see anything? Did they leave anything behind?"

His questions surprised me and caused my chest to spasm with the desire to burst out in tears.

"Yes, I was there," I said softly, looking over to a dune. "They attacked and swarmed the village really fast. They traded some spells with my family before hitting me. I went down, but before I did, I got a good look at them. They wore an odd sandal I had never seen before and were wrapped in long, flowing fabric of brown and black. Their heads were wrapped, too. The fabric covered their bodies, legs, and arms, but I could see their hands and the skin around their eyes, and from what I saw, they could have been from anywhere in the world."

"Dark-skinned? Light?" Briz asked.

"All kinds," I said.

Briz held my eyes for a moment but looked away, nodding.

"Look," he said. "If you Targets to come with me while I—"

"No. I'm not going to go with you while you hunt your... bounties. No," I said.

Briz's head dipped as he paused for a moment.

"I was just trying to say that if you want to come with me, I'll do what I can to... help you get back on track."

My first thought was one wanting to accept his offer, followed by a dozen about how I didn't need him. I could get to a town on my own. I could ask questions and get back on track, on my own. But I didn't respond right away.

"It wouldn't take me long to finish my job," he said. "If you'll free me up here, we can pick up the trail easy enough, and then finish up. Then, we can get to work on your job."

"I don't do *jobs*, Briz, okay?" I yelled.

Briz rocked to the side and looked away, apparently embarrassed by his word choice.

"I have one thing I need to do. I need to avenge my family," I continued. "Nothing else, and not for payment. I just want justice for my family."

"Bayla," he rushed to respond. "A village hired me to exterminate the scorpiron responsible for staging the attack on their village."

"Right, I understand—" I attempted.

"These scorpirons raid villages. Steal resources. Kill people."

"Yes," I attempted again, "but I'm not going to accept payment and take this as some kind of lifetime occupation."

"Well, what if someone like me had been hired to go after the people that attacked your village, huh? Your family might still be alive, and you might not be lost in a desert a continent away, trying to do something you have no idea how to do!"

I grabbed the cage door and slammed it shut. Without being tied closed, it hit the cage and smacked back. I grabbed it and slammed it shut again. When it slammed against the cage and flew back again, I got a hold of it and slammed it over, and over, and over, before grabbing onto it with both arms and burying my head in the insides of my elbows, already sobbing in despair.

"Bayla, Bayla," Briz scrambled to say. "I'm so—"

"No!" I screamed as I pushed away from the cage angrily. "No!" I turned towards the well and did all I could to stifle my pain. With each gasp for air and every second of blurred vision, I grew angrier at myself. I quickly remembered the conversation I'd had with myself just minutes before. I had made the decision to kill those responsible, and to have the best chance at that, I needed Briz's help. I took as deep a breath as I could and spun back to Briz before stomping back to the cart.

Briz looked down and leaned against the cage on his side as I walked back. I had ripped the door partially away from the cage and when I got back within arm's reach, I pulled the hanging door back open. Briz looked up with eyes drooping under a weighted brow.

"I'm sorry for that," he offered.

I looked over my shoulder and searched for tracks leading out of the valley.

"Come on," I said. "Those tracks will be gone soon."

He looked down at his shackled ankles and back to me as he started scooting towards the door, taking a moment to look at his departed friend.

"Oh," I muttered before scanning the ground. After spotting a large rock near the fire pit, I retrieved it and brought it back to Briz. "Stretch the shackles over this," I said. While he did so, I kicked the sand and looked around for another rock to use as a hammer. "Okay," I said after finding one. "Let me try to break this chain."

I started to beat the links, gently at first with low taps to get a feel for it, but quickly increased the height from which I struck, and started hitting as hard as I could.

"I don't think that's going to do it," Briz interjected between bashes.

I stopped and tossed away the rock, unsure of what to try next.

"What about your, uh, axes?" He asked.

We exchanged an awkward glance. I guess he was wondering why someone he previously labeled as nice was walking around with two axes. I took the opportunity to pull them out and flip them in my hands. I had never used them to hurt anyone, or hurt anyone at all, but he didn't know that.

"I don't know what these shackles are made of," I said, "but I'll try."

Briz pulled the chain taut and leaned back.

I raised up my axe and swung it down with as much violent force as I could muster. It hit solidly with a metallic thud and I immediately inspected the axe head which appeared to be in good shape. Briz leaned up to look at the chain.

"Looks like it took a good chip out of it," he said, before leaning back again.

I swung again and registered another good hit.

"Pull the chain tight!" I yelled.

I hit it again, and then a fourth time. The chain snapped apart.

"Ah!" Briz coughed out in excitement. As he started to twirl his feet and repeatedly fan and close his legs as he stretched, he groaned again in relief.

"That feels better!" He said, smiling down at his legs. After a few more bends and wiggles of his legs, he stretched the chain of his wrist shackles over the rock.

I didn't move.

He looked up and tilted his neck while shaking his wrists at me.

"Oh, come on," he whined. "If we come up on those

scorpirons while my hands are still bound…"

"We'll worry about that later," I said. "For now, your legs will do."

Chapter Ten - Sound and Silence

Briz

I had been in more embarrassing situations in my life, but being captured by a bounty, only to be partially freed by this girl wasn't too far off. I was glad that I had my legs back at least. While we filled up a few water skins, well, while *she* filled them up, I got to stretch my legs and knees. I was able to swap between sitting and laying down in the cage over the past few days, so it wasn't too bad, but standing helped. It wouldn't be too long though before I was tired of walking. After filling up the water, Bayla graced me with a bladder to hold and tied an extra to me before starting our trek.

"Let me know when you want that other one," she told me.

"Or, you could just... break these, too," I said, holding my wrists up.

"If our positions were swapped, would you cut me loose?" She asked.

She had a valid point, but agreeing wouldn't help me.

"Yes, of course," I lied. "Especially if there's the very

real possibility of an upcoming fight."

"Well, I never said I wasn't going to cut you loose. I'm just not going to right *now*," she said. "Just get us to where these scorpirons are and we'll go from there."

"Great," I said with as little energy as I could. But then something caught my eye that injected me with a bit more energy.

"Hey," I blurted. "Will you grab my club over there? It's towards the front of the cart."

Bayla went back to the wagon and walked around, looking for it. She stopped and kicked something. A hunk of fabric came flying out from the side. I couldn't help but smile when I saw her freeze.

"Is that..." she started, "a bone?"

I snickered.

* * *

She did have good instincts when it came to the condition of the tracks, though. The ones closest to where I got left behind were already smoothed over a good bit from the blowing sand, but we had set out in enough time to meet up with tracks with better definition. For the longest time, it was a lot of boring walking, but was a fairly easy path weaving in and out of valleys between the dunes.

"So what else can you tell me about these scorpirons, hmm?" She wondered. "If I have to help with these things, I want to know what kind of fight to expect."

I was really glad that she asked. An idiot blindly willing to help is far more dangerous to have around than someone with sense, even if they're stubborn.

"Mm hmm, they're pretty tough," I said. "But it's not just the physical challenge these scorpirons present. They're smart, too. They strategize. They use the terrain to their advantage. They build sprawling, confusing nests. They might as well be labyrinths. They anticipate and exhibit patience. A fight with one of them is more than just dodging and ducking. A snap from one of their pincers, and *whoops*, there goes an arm. There's absolutely no room for error. I'd probably be long dead if bounties for these things came up more often."

"They don't?" Bayla asked.

I shook my head.

"No. A lot of times there's no one left alive to even issue the bounty, much less enough resources to cover the cost."

"So, do you just wait for big payouts, or what?"

"Oh, no way. I couldn't survive if I did that. For the past ten months I've been forced to take a bunch of small bounties that barely kept me interested. There was a herd of titanodons I had to take care of a while back. They've got a massive single tooth flanked by rows of smaller teeth. Those were dangerous, but not challenging. They only really become bothersome when they clash with villages over water sources or if they're encountered out in the bush. This herd kept running people off from their water and gored a few villagers before someone sent for me. Others aren't dangerous or exciting at all. I'm more or less a zookeeper for some of these things. The cynohippus bounty. There's a perfect example. No one was being harmed or killed by the dog-like horses, but they were snuggling up to farmers and slowing down their harvesting process. They're as sweet as either half of their name implies, so again, just a nuisance."

We shuffled in silence while Bayla came up with another question.

"Are the scorpirons the most dangerous things you've had to fight before?"

"They're definitely up there, I'd say. I don't stand a chance against a nest, or even just a few on my own. I have to stalk the nest and the area where they live for weeks.

I need to watch, and learn their habits. And when they travel, I need to figure out what size groups they travel in, anything I can use to my benefit. I have no desire to fight a whole nest. I need to give myself every opportunity to achieve an element of surprise, attack, make my kill, collect proof of death, and escape. Their patrols are easy to monitor during the day, and I can do so from an inconspicuous distance. Their dark scales stick out against the bleached sand and faded vegetation. And their natural armor will occasionally reflect a nice flash of light, some spots shinier than others. At night, their fires and torches help create similar circumstances. The light and dancing shadows keep me apprised as to their movements. Where the challenge comes in, day or night, is trying to monitor movement even just a few feet into the trees and bushes because it's so thick."

"And even with all that planning, things can still go poorly, apparently," she said.

I wanted to shoot back a retort but didn't. She rattled off another batch of queries.

"Are they in other regions? Or just in Egypt? Where exactly in Egypt are we anyway?"

I had to think for a second after laughing at her barrage of questions.

"Uhh, well let's see," I started. "This all started down near Kerma. After they caught me, we rode northwest for a long while. I don't think we ever left Egypt."

"Do you know where they were going?"

"I'm not sure, but since they kept me alive, they were probably going to sell me off to someone that wanted me dead. Probably another nest of scorpirons."

"Heh," Bayla chuckled.

"What?" I asked, already agitated by whatever she was about to say.

"I just think it's funny. The bounty hunter being bounty hunted," she said, smirking at me over her shoulder.

"Sure, it's hilarious," I said, drawing my syllables out slowly.

I heard her sniffing through more muffled laughter.

"Anyway," I resumed. "The zarafteryx that chased after them drove them east—the way we're headed. So that's good."

"Why's that?" Bayla asked.

"Because we're getting closer to Memphis. Food. Water. Things to break shackles."

Bayla looked at me again over her shoulder, this time with a sneer.

"All right," I said. "My turn for some questions."

She turned and looked at me with raised eyebrows. I wasn't expecting any answers but figured I'd try.

"I saw the sand whipping around like mad before you rolled down, and I've caught your axes glowing a bit from time to time. What's that all about?"

She sighed and stopped.

"Let's get some sleep and pick back up in the morning, okay?" She said.

"Heh. Not even going to answer one of mine?"

She whipped her head around.

"I will, I will. All right? I just want to get some kind of camp set up. Not a lot of light left."

"Fine, fine," I said.

It didn't take long to set up the little place that could barely be called a camp. A few rolls of cloth, and water. There wasn't anything to make a flame with, and nothing to eat. As the sun set, we fantasized about food, crops, and farming techniques to sustain our hungry dreams. The moon gave us some decent company as Bayla slowly found her way to answering my earlier question.

"Right, so only after a child spends time in the fields, next to their families, can their studies expand to other subjects. For years, they must learn to cultivate, nurture, and harvest crops for their village. They must learn to take care of others. The survival of the village is paramount. In times of peace, farming is the absolute most important aspect of what a child learns in Skarkos."

"But peace is not always guaranteed," I said.

"No, it isn't," she agreed. "Once the young in the village have developed their agricultural skills well into their adolescence, are they then taught martial skills. Again, the focus is on thinking of the village as a whole. Our martial arts are based in defense, deflection, and transference of energy. After approximately five years of martial education, a select few from the village are chosen to begin their magical training. After they can prepare food for the village, and defend the village, can some then be trusted to call upon the energies of our village."

"Hmm, so anyone can study? Anyone can learn? It isn't really like that in Egypt," I said.

"Well, the children chosen to study magic are selected by a rotating council of our village elders. The criteria or qualities the elders look for are not a secret and the village as a whole goes out of its way to instill the desired qualities in all children. The characteristics most sought after are selflessness, empathy, and compassion. And while all children have the ability to throw tantrums or act out, it is quite easy to see who would be the best candidates for harnessing the magic of our village by virtue of humility and respect."

"Ah," I said. My rattling wrist chains distracted me as I reached for a water skin.

"There are of course advanced studies unrelated to magic that other children are more suited for," she continued. "Most other children are trained as farmers or warriors. As for my family, my sister and I were selected to be trained in magic, as my parents were before us. It was never promised, and it was something never expected by my parents for me and my sister. We still had to show a natural inclination towards it."

"That sounds nice," I said, as my focus started to drift. "I was hoping to continue some traditions with my family."

"Hmm?" Bayla pressed. "What do you mean?"

"Never mind," I said quickly before turning away and laying down.

She didn't challenge me, and I was glad for it. I was afraid she wouldn't be able to resist trying to pry it out of me. But nothing else was said until I fell asleep.

* * *

When we woke up the next morning, it was as if we were hungover with regret from all that we had spoken about. That's how I felt, anyway. Bayla woke up first and tapped my foot. Nothing was said immediately. We rolled up the cloth and sipped some water before setting back out.

The walk was uncomfortable, as far as conversation went. The odd amount of sharing the day before stood in stark contrast to the sparse bits of talking related to direction and tracking. There wasn't any detectable animosity or distrust. To me, it just felt like two lifetimes of darkness and loss that didn't want to go into any more detail than they already had. We just kept walking.

"Briz!" Bayla finally whispered. She crouched down and waved me up to the tip of a dune she had reached before me.

It was a village. One of the biggest I've seen outside of Memphis. Homes and other buildings sprawled across the desert floor with tall cliffs surrounding it on two sides. Plumes of smoke spun up into the air at various points.

"Did the zarafteryx drive them towards this village?" Bayla wondered.

"I don't know," I said. "Maybe."

"I hope the village was ready for the fight," Bayla said. Her voice was cold, as if she thought differently.

A jumble of screeching pierced the air far in front of us.

"Briz," she said. "They scorps are still in the village!"

I scoured the area and ran over to an outcropping. After stretching my wrist shackles and chains across the tip of a boulder I looked back to Bayla. She looked to the village, then back at me, and didn't move.

"Come on!" I shouted. "Break 'em!"

She still didn't move. She turned to the village again and kept staring.

"Bayla!" I screamed.

She jerked out of her hesitation and ran over, raising her axes up over her head as she approached. I stretched my wrists as wide as I could. As she landed her blows on the chain, my wrists reverberated with a violent thud. I still wasn't free. As I strained to keep the chains taut, she hit them a third and fourth time. The metal snapped and my arms flew up. I rolled my shoulders and stretched my neck. After spinning my arms around a few times, I reached back for my club. As I squeezed my fingers around the solid bone, I turned to face Bayla.

"Let's go," I said.

We shot off from the boulders, sprinting for the village.

"Let's stay towards the outskirts at first so we can move easily," I said, using the jolts of exhaled breath while running to speak. "We can sprint out to the perimeter if we need to. I have no idea how many are in here."

"Are we going to help the village or are you just

looking for your bounty?" Bayla asked.

As we ran up on an outlying fence, I leaned down and peered over.

"What do you mean, *we*?" I asked.

"I'm not going to go slaughtering these things, but I can help protect you and the village," She said.

"Oh, right. Your magic," I said, feigning relief. "Well, I'm hunting for a scorpiron with two stingers, but I have to start somewhere."

"Fine," she said. "I'll follow you and help where I can."

I rolled my eyes and shot off around the fence, into the village.

The streets were a mess. Items were strewn out into the dirt and voices rang out from all over the village. Some sounded like shouts of pain while others gave orders or directed people to what I assumed was the location of scorpirons throughout the village. A woman sprinted out from a nearby home screaming a man's name.

"Hey, hey!" I shouted at her, trying to get her attention. She didn't stop or turn. I chased after her. When I caught up to her I grabbed her arm. She spun around with a whipping arm.

"Whoa, hey, I'm trying to help," I said after ducking. "How many are there?"

The woman just shook and screamed in my face.

"Hey!" I tried again. "How many?"

The woman continued to try and wriggle free, but after bending in Bayla's direction, she froze and stared at her. I shook the woman's shoulders again.

"Hey! Talk to me!" I barked.

The woman swallowed and looked at me with eyes shocked wide.

"Scorpirons," she said. Her voice seemed to be fueled only by fright.

"I know," I tried to say calmly. "Listen. How many? What happened?"

"They've been stealing our livestock and crops for months," the villager continued. "We wanted to stop them once and for all. We had a hunting party of zarafteryx drive them to the village so we could take care of them once and for all."

"Okay," I said. "You need to go back in somewhere and stay put. Do you know how many there are?"

She shook her head.

"The zarafteryx drove the nest towards the village but they overpowered us. Most of our fighters ran out of the city to get them away from our homes and families, but there are still some running free through the town!"

"All right," I said while shoving her towards the side of the path. "Get inside and—"

Before I could finish, a scorpiron rounded a corner. It hissed and ducked down before standing rigid, flexing, and whipped its tail around at me. I shoved the villager back towards a building and flung myself backwards just in time to miss the beast's tail. The momentum of the scorp's tail forced it to turn away from me as it missed, allowing me to take advantage.

I jumped towards it and brought my club up over my head before slamming it right where its shoulder met its neck, causing it to bend over and stumble to the side.

"Bayla!" I roared as I spun around. "You should get back to the village edge. These things are too..." I trailed off, distracted.

I'd heard everything she told me about her village's magic and her skills in it, but now, I actually witnessed it.

She held her two axes up and touched the flat heads against each other just as a scorpiron jumped down from a roof towards her. A second before the scorpiron landed,

Bayla scraped the axes and ripped a sound of metallic friction into the air. As she scratched and separated the axes, a blue ripple of energy pulsed out from where they had been touching. The blue flash splashed across the scorpiron and held him in mid-air as it seemed to absorb the energy of his fall, and instead threw him down the path away from her and the village woman. When it crashed into the corner of a home, nearby villagers leapt onto the scorpiron and finished the fatal work with spears.

"Your friend is back," Bayla notified me calmly.

My hissing enemy had returned. He jabbed at me with an open pincer. I dodged it with a swerve which was immediately followed by an attempted slice with his other pincer. I ducked under the creature's follow-up and jumped up with a sideways blow to one of its legs. It screeched a high-pitched yelp and buckled down to a knee. As it did, I spun back with another slap to the side of its head this time. It let loose another squeal, but after I swung and made contact with another bash to the other side of its head, it fell quiet before pitching diagonally to the ground. Before it slapped flat into the dirt, a tall, narrow tower of shadow behind me and to the side caught my eye. Bayla stirred into action again.

Before I could look to see what the source of the shadow was doing, I watched Bayla bring an axe to her chest and thrust it out in my direction with her arm's full reach. Another pulse of faint light shot out, smaller in size this time, and as I thought it was going to strike me it shot past me instead. I spun where I stood and followed it as it passed, catching the brunt of a different scorpiron's stinger on its way down. I darted around Bayla's barrier and cracked the scorp's tail, splitting it apart in the middle. The stinger remained lodged in Bayla's pulse of energy, suspended in mid-air.

With no other immediate scorp threat, I took stock of the street. I couldn't look at Bayla. It's not that I didn't want to, I was just bewildered and impressed. I waved over my shoulder for her to follow.

"I honestly didn't believe any of that magic talk," I said. As we alternated between quick walking and jogging down the village path, I scrutinized every doorway, window, and roof edge.

"I know," she said dryly. "You're welcome."

My eyes stayed on the path ahead, but she got a smile out of me.

"So, if we run into a group like that again," I wondered. "Can you do more of that kind of stuff?"

"Stuff?" She asked.

"The light thing you did. The protective... magic."

"Yes," she said, "but not indefini—wait. Why? What are you getting at?"

I must have still been smiling. I stopped and slithered over to a corner to look around an adjoining path.

"I'm just wondering," I said. "I need to know everything you're capable of so I know how best to fight with you."

"No," she said, lowering her voice from a shout to a whisper as the city's noise decreased for a time. "You're not going to use me to shield you from every fight. I'm not your bodyguard!"

"Shh," I said, wanting to listen for anything meaningful going on nearby. "I know, I know. I just need to know."

"I don't have to kill any of these things," Bayla added. "This isn't my fight."

I turned back to Bayla and looked her in the eyes.

"I know," I said to her. "Hold on. Let me listen."

"Let's just keep making straight for the other side of town," I said, not hearing anything new. Bayla nodded.

We dipped out from a row of covered stalls and into the path, starting out softly and slowly, whipping our heads back and forth to confirm the path was clear.

"Looks good," Bayla said.

"Yep," I agreed. "Okay, let's go."

We quickly returned to our jogging speed and as I was about to ask Bayla a question about her magic, we came up on an intersection. Before either of us could think of altering our approach to make sure it was clear, a half dozen scorpirons emerged from the adjoining street, popping and knocking. We all stared at each other for a second, but the scorps fanned out and surrounded us. As I was about to grab Bayla by the shoulder and shout at her to run, another three scorps shot out from the other adjoining street and slid to a stop. Their noisy fuss combined with the original six. I had never faced such odds before and had no idea what to do.

"It's going to take forever," Bayla raced to say, "but start with the one directly across from you. I'll keep the others busy. When you're ready for the next one, tell me."

"What? What are—" I tried to clarify.

"Start with the one across from you! Go!"

The scorps that I could see—but probably the whole group of them—lurched in towards us. As I pulled my club back, I saw the other scorps in my periphery get thrown dozens of feet back and up into the air, suspended helplessly. Various pops, hums, and slaps came from behind me as Bayla was working some kind of magic. I was completely free to focus on the foe in front of me.

It came at me with both of its arms spread wide, both pincers poised to dart in and snap my head off, but I took advantage of its exposed chest. I launched forward, decreasing the amount of time until we clashed and surprised it with a kick straight into its chest—one of its weaker spots. It looked as if it imploded slightly, its head and arms curving inward from the force of the impact. With a sweeping whip of my club, I knelt down and swooped it back up with all the energy I could muster and slammed the scorpiron in the meatiest part of one of its pincers. The scorp's arm flew back from the hit, close to a wall. I spun around and hit it again, splattering pincer parts all over it. The scorp screeched and fell to the ground. I followed with similar smashes onto its head.

Still alive. Gotta get another, I thought. *Gotta get Bayla to release one.* I turned to see what she was up to.

When I turned to check on Bayla, I froze. I didn't know what to think or how to react. If anything, I was a little intimidated.

Off to my left, I saw two scorps still floating in Bayla's cocoons or whatever they were. To my front were two different scorps trapped behind some kind of endless wall, repeatedly slamming their arms into it—when they weren't trying to outright ram through unsuccessfully. The remaining four were struggling against sticky traps of energy under them or in front of them, or were struggling against moving waves of energy slowly pushing them backwards. In the middle of all the controlled chaos, was Bayla. Between her violent slams of energy from her axes, flinging and thrusting her arms about, she looked over her shoulder.

"You ready for another one, or what?" She yelled.

I heard her but my mind got sidetracked before I could respond. I hadn't thought anything similar up to that point, but at that moment I was completely disarmed by her. My attention was pounded into unsuspecting submission by so many ingredients coming together at the most surreal of moments. The pose of her body as she was turned towards me. Her extended arms and tightened grips around the axes used to harness multiple occurrences of magic, which in turn restrained half a dozen beasts as if they were delicate blades of grass caught in an overbearing wind. Her hair, spread across her upper back and draped over her shoulder from where she whipped her head around. She was confident. In control. Powerful.

"Briz!"

I wiggled my head and laughed in astonished disbelief.

"Uh, sure!" I said. "Send 'em over!"

She looked over to one of the scorps being restrained by the blowing waves of energy. With a gesture of her axe as if curling it to her chin, she pulled the energy wave back towards her before absorbing it, releasing a scorpiron. It was furious, if a bit tired from fighting against its restraint, and darted for Bayla. I shot off to intercept him.

The scorp was fast. I was closer to Bayla, but it was faster than me. I dug in, leaned forward and sliced the air with my whipping arms, trying to make up just enough time to land a blow or deflect whatever it might try to do to Bayla.

"Bayla! On the right!" I warned.

Both Bayla and the scorp turned towards me, and instead of going for Bayla, the scorp spun in place twice, and on the second spin, timed its tail perfectly to bash me in the guts. But I leaned back and slid under its tail instead. As I slid, I reached out and grabbed the ground to help myself turn. Just as I passed the scorp, I rotated and kicked the scorp's legs out from under it. I rolled over and pushed myself up when I came to a stop and unleashed a half-dozen slams of my club into the scorp's chest.

Another one down.

When Bayla released another scorp, I dispatched it as I had the previous few. One by one, our orchestrated fight came to an end as the captured scorpirons were set free, and destroyed. Both Bayla and I turned in the yard, confirming we were the last ones standing.

"Wow," I said. "I had no idea you could do that kind of thing. That was amazing. I've never seen anything like that before."

Bayla stretched her neck and pinched at one of her shoulders.

"Like what?" She wondered.

I rolled my fingers around on themselves as I held my hand up in the direction of where she had previously held most of the scorps in mid-air.

"*That*," I repeated. "The magic and all those variations."

She jogged a few steps back onto the main path and stomped away waving me over to follow, never looking up at me.

"What?" I started. "You're not going to say anything?"

"I tried to explain all of this before," she said, dismissing me with a flick of her wrist. "You didn't listen," she bit, playfully.

"Well, I want to know, *now*," I admitted.

"It isn't exactly a good time," she said, stopping to turn. "I'll tell you more when we get done here. Speaking of which, what's next?"

There were no other immediate threats that I could tell. And all of the villagers were probably hiding or part of the chase after most of the scorps exited the city.

"Let's just see if we can finally break out of the village and meet up with the group that's chasing after the rest," I said.

"Okay. And as long as that last fight was, it's probably a good sign that more of those things didn't find us and join in," Bayla observed.

I grunted in agreement.

"Mmm, good point. The village must be about empty. All right. This way."

We darted down the path but had to weave in and out of a row of homes and join up with another route. A grouping of wagons had been set on fire.

"I guess they were trying to steer the scorps in a particular direction," I suggested as we ran.

"Maybe to dedicated defenses?" Bayla asked.

"Or they wanted to keep them away from the families," I added.

"Or both," my partner said.

We raced through the new path without interruption or challenge and soon reached the city's edge. Bayla jogged ahead and climbed up on the top rail of a fence, leaning against the wall of a goat shed. I scanned the other path exits and nearby windows to confirm our surroundings, and ran over to Bayla while keeping an eye on the village.

"What do you see?" I asked.

"There's definitely a chase going on," she said. "It looks like they're all moving towards that canyon over there."

I continued peering to the paths in and out of the city, watching for any movement or straggling scorps.

"Well, let's get down there and finish this up. I need that double stinger," I said, mostly to myself.

"And help the village," Bayla replied immediately, shaking me out of my greedy trance. I looked up and waved her down so I could look.

"Yes, you know I meant that, too," I said, squinting out towards the mob chasing the nest.

"Mmm," Bayla grunted. "You did?"

Before I could respond, she smiled a smirk of condescension and darted out towards the fight.

I let her comment slide and followed. As we ran, I

needed more info.

"So, before more fighting..." I said as we ran. "How does it work? Can you do that... enemy handling stuff... any time? All the time? Is there a limit to how many—"

Bayla interrupted.

"It depends on how much I can focus," she said. "That last fight was good... because I could focus on... a set number of them without interruption... or without more of them jumping in."

I tried to resume my last question.

"Is there a limit to how many you can... manage? Like you did back there?"

"Again...focus," she said through pulsing breath as we ran. "I need to be able to maintain a mental focus... on each thing being impacted by my magic... I don't know what my personal limit is... but I'm sure I have one."

I took a bit of our sprint to catch my breath.

"When we get into this next fight... are we going to do something similar... to what we did in the village? There will be more people fighting the scorps... don't think you'd need to control so many at once... this time."

"Good point," she said. "I think I'll focus more this time... at protecting you and the other fighters... more than restraining the beasts."

"Okay," I huffed as we ran. "Protecting me. I like the sound of that."

"And the others," she said through her own huff.

We raced to the other side of the valley and up a moderate dune before falling to our knees to rest and gasping for air. The light was perfect. We could see everything. Down below, the valley we were following terminated in a large basin surrounded by high cliffs. All throughout the rocky floor were eroded towers and outcroppings of rock. Between us and the pillars of stone were a large grouping of villagers huddled together. There were a few small isolated fights between the large group of villagers and the rock pillars.

"It looks like the villagers have the upper hand now. They seem to be planning something, or waiting," I said.

"Doesn't look like the scorpirons have anywhere to go," Bayla suggested.

"But these villagers shouldn't wait too long. Every minute they wait is a minute the scorps have to plan their defense in that canyon."

"That's true," she said. "Wanna go down?"

I slapped my club onto my back. "Might want to put those axes away for a minute."

Bayla nodded.

"Good idea."

We jumped up and ran down the other side of the dune and back into a valley when we were spotted by some of the villagers along the perimeter of the group. I held up both of my hands in a relaxed greeting. A few ran over to intercept us. Their faces were stern and concerned, but they didn't appear to be hostile towards us.

"Who are you?" A villager interrogated.

Bayla replied first. Some cold anxiety shot through my veins, unsure of what she was going to say, but as soon as she started speaking, I was relieved.

"Hello. We've been hunting a specific scorpiron and traced their nest to your village. We were caught up in a few fights back there or we would have helped sooner."

As we announced ourselves, more of the large gathering approached. A man weaved through the group and barked at us.

"We do not need your help," the suspicious villager said. "This is the business of my village and my people."

I stepped forward, causing some of the villagers to

take an extra step towards me.

"We have a bounty for one of these scorps," I said. "One with a double-stinger. Please allow us to join the fight and look for him. We were intending to help you with the others as well."

"I do not need some blood money man and silly woman endangering my men with their antics," the man said. "No."

"Hey!" I shouted back, offended. "We just killed some two dozen of those things back in your village for you. The village that you all had left undefended. We have already saved some of your people!"

Without registering it, I stepped closer to the villager as I spoke, getting louder and more animated as I approached. Some of the villagers near him lunged for me. By the time I realized what was happening, and before I could reach for my club, both Bayla and I were enveloped in a translucent dome of blue light.

Some of the villager's men slammed into it and bounced off. Others stopped in time to shoot an arrow or hack at it with a sword or axe. But like the arrows, each attempted hit from a blade bounced off. The thwarted villagers stopped and stared.

As I looked up and around at the interior of our protective dome, somewhat humored by the escalation in tension, Bayla stepped forward.

"I don't think it's unreasonable to ask to join your fight. We have our own objective, yes, but as you can see, we can help in more ways than one."

The primary village captain, or whatever he was, let his head roll around slowly as he considered Bayla's words. Without so much as a single tense muscle in his face, and without blinking, he stood there, silently.

But with no indication he was about to do so, the man

erupted in laughter. The villagers around him soon joined in. Everyone around us found humor in something. Bayla and I were not in on the joke. She looked at me in confusion. I flung my hand up towards the villagers in exasperation.

"Group laughter is never a good thing," I said.

Up and above the surrounding laughter of his men, the leader bellowed and howled loudest. After doubling over and standing back up, he took a step towards our protective dome and touched his palm to it. His laughing dwindled down to nothing as he focused. He then stepped backwards, held his outstretched palm out towards us, and curled his fingers into a fist. As he squeezed, Bayla's dome of protection cracked, split, and shattered away with a silent, magical poof.

Bayla and I froze. She stared ahead at the man.

As all hints of Bayla's magic floated away into nothing, we could only stand in place, dumbfounded. The man's surrounding comrades finally quit laughing.

"You know some magic!" The man said with a healthy pinch of condescension. A few extra chuckles rippled through the group. "But as you see," he continued, "we know a fair amount as well."

The man inched closer to Bayla. I stepped closer to her as well, to defend her if need-be, but was blocked by two villagers that stepped into my path.

"But I can assure you, young woman, that our skills are stronger, and older."

The man leaned in and over, staring a stab of enigmatic intimidation into Bayla. Without even looking in my direction, his implication humbled me a bit as well. Unexpectedly, the man hopped backwards and held his arms up in a welcoming hug to the sky. A hefty grin stretched across his face.

"But I can see that your hearts are good," he said.

"And anyone who practices the Arts of Ariadne are welcome here!"

I had no idea what he was talking about, or how he knew of Ariadne, but the villagers cheered and flooded in around us to slap me and Bayla on the back. Others started conducting magic, flashing bits of light into the air in and around Bayla as enthusiastic demonstrations. Some leaned into my ear and began discussing strategy while pointing at particular areas of the canyon down below. Bayla slowly turned towards me with an expression of shock that slowly melted into one of relief and joy. I could only shrug as our new friends explained their plan for the scorps.

As Bayla and I were brought in on their plan, I heard some of the villagers discussing their magic with Bayla. I understood very little. Whether they were talking about Ariadne, whoever that was, some of the Egyptian gods, energy, focus, whatever, all I really caught from the jumble of conversation was that their magic was similar in ability and execution to Bayla's. They were mostly a village of physical combatants with the ability to protect themselves and others. I didn't know how it all worked, but I had seen Bayla's magic in action, so I was excited to know we'd be in a group of people with similar skills.

What made more sense to me were the chats I had involving tactics, approaches, terrain descriptions, and weapons. The ways of efficiently getting to a place, getting there unseen, finding your enemy, and taking care of them. That's what made sense to me. Find. Get there. Kill. Leave. The concrete stuff. The physical part. I understand that there are a lot of mysterious, powerful things out there people can use, but I've just been left high and dry too many times waiting for someone to do something that I had to get done in a hurry with nothing but my blood, sweat, and force.

The plan wasn't too elaborate. It didn't need to be. The villagers took a few minutes to catch me and Bayla up, and besides, the scorps didn't seem to have anywhere to go. But like I told Bayla, each moment spent not fighting was a moment an enemy had to think, and little good rarely resulted from giving someone time to plan. Within about five or ten minutes of joining up with the villagers, we set out for the canyon.

We split into two groups. A smaller portion hung back at the canyon exit to make sure the scorps couldn't leave while the largest portion of us fanned out into the canyon. As we worked our way back to the rear of the canyon, we methodically began flushing out pockets of scorps hiding in ravines or in eroded holes in the rock pillars.

I was impressed by the villagers as we fought. They were coordinated and confident. They were swift and lethal. And their magic obviously added to how impressive they were. I still hadn't quite gotten over Bayla's magic. The streams of energy and defensive implements and structures that popped into place as we fought were almost a distracting hindrance. I was out of my element to some degree, and for the longest time at the top of the fight, I felt out of place to the point that I felt superfluous, if not completely removed from danger. But as Bayla and I continued to fight side by side with these villagers, I settled into a sense of respect fueled by an increasing fascination. As my fascination increased, my concerns dissipated, and I was able to focus more and more on what I was good at.

We scared group after group of scorps out from cracks, crevasses, and pits. And though they provided every bit of a legitimate fight, the sheer number of villagers along with their powers proved too overwhelming. The beasts never stood a chance. Group by group, one by one, we engaged them. We unleashed relentless violence upon them, all the while flying in and out of protective cocoons conjured up by Bayla and any number of villagers.

Bayla and I paused between encounters. The rest of the villagers shifted to the right towards an unexplored portion of the canyon.

"I haven't seen a double stinger yet," Bayla said as she wiped her brow.

"Nope," I added. "Not sure where he's at. He's one of their more senior scorps, so he's probably protecting one of their elders or something, or maybe *he's* being protected. I just hope he's around here or dead back in the village."

"Briz," Bayla said, her eyes widening. "Look!"

As the group of attacking villagers raced for one of the last few unexplored areas of the canyon, I spun to see a huge stream of scorps rush out from a cave and make for a narrow pass we hadn't seen before.

"Hey!" I shouted, turning back to the villages. "Hey! Over here!"

They were too far away and couldn't hear me. I turned back around to see Bayla waving wildly at the small group at the entrance to the canyon.

"Nah, they won't leave that exit undefended," I said. "They probably can't see this stream of scorps from their vantage point anyway."

"We have to go after them, Briz," Bayla said, her voice rushing along with urgency. "We can't let them get back to the village."

I looked to the small group guarding the canyon exit, over to the larger group headed to the opposite end, and then back to Bayla.

"I don't think they're headed back to the village. Probably just trying to get out. But my guy is probably in there," I said. "Come on."

We shot off in pursuit of the escaping scorps.

"Can you tell how many there are?" Bayla asked.

"No, but I'm hoping you can uh, well, work some of your magic again," I said.

"Just don't rush in before we can estimate what we're dealing with," Bayla said with a bite of frustration.

"I won't!" I replied in playful defense. "We just can't let them get away."

By the time we reached a full sprint, the trail of scorps had disappeared around the turn into the narrow pass. I was worried they had gotten enough of a head start to lose us, especially since we had to run flat out for a good sixty seconds before we caught up to the slice in the canyon wall. As we neared the cutout, we slowed down and crept over to minimize our noise.

"Let's see what we can see," I whispered.

I hugged the rocks and peeked around. Bayla knelt down and shuffled to my side to look around as well. The trail in the rock twisted numerous times, but there was a good line of sight for a while before the trail turned sharply up and to the left.

"I don't see anything," she said.

"I saw the last few of the group take that turn down there just as I looked around," I told her. "We need to catch up with them before they think to set a trap or leave some behind to hold us up."

"Okay," Bayla whispered. "I'm ready."

"All right."

After a last check to see if any of the villagers were following or nearby and seeing none, Bayla and I jumped into the narrow path and sprinted after our prey. Or, my prey, at least.

At first, Bayla and I had to run single file before the path widened just ahead of the sharp incline. The slope was slick with thin and frequent layers of gravel. We constantly grabbed onto boulders sticking out of the path's edges, or allowed ourselves to slide down some when we lost our footing just so we could wait until there was something else to grab onto. After spending more time than I wanted to making it up the path, we finally crested the top of the trail.

We had writhed our way not just up and out of the canyon to ground level, but due to natural blockages, barriers, or wall heights, had worked our way up to a small plateau.

"They have to be up here," I whispered to Bayla. "I didn't see anywhere for them to branch off to on our way up."

"Mmm, and there's nowhere up here for them, or us, to go," she said.

"Right..." I agreed.

"I don't like that. We don't know how many are up here, and there's very little room to fight."

"True..." I agreed again. "Come on, let's just go slow. If anything, since it's just us again, let's do something similar to what we did back in the village with that last big group we fought."

Bayla, holding her axes, nodded, stretched her neck, and rolled her shoulders.

I had only known Bayla for a few days. I didn't remember the name of her village and would have been hard-pressed to recall the names of the magic lessons she had studied, but I've already fought alongside her, protected her, and been protected *by* her, more than anyone else in my life. I lived alone. Traveled alone. Sought out bounties alone, and fought alone. Until now. For a little while at least. Until I could get her back on the path of whoever killed her family. But until that time came, and as we sprung around a towering outcropping, fighting next to her was starting to feel good. And feeling good when you're trying to kill stuff makes everything so much easier.

We darted around the boulder and came face to face with a scorp. Bayla smacked her axes together and immediately blasted that one into an opposing rock column with a wall of energy, stunning it and knocking it out. As it collapsed into a sleepy pile another scorpiron emerged from around the nearest tower of rock whipping its tail around its sides and across its front, keeping us at a distance. I pulled my club and lunged for it.

I jumped over another lash of its tail, but it wasn't needed. Bayla fell to her knees and slapped the ends of her axes on the ground, sending a wave of energy along the ground and knocking the scorp onto its back. I jumped over, next to the prone scorp and slammed it in the side of its head with my bronzed bone. As I looked up, I saw four pulses of energy fly past me and latch on to four scorps that had emerged.

"It looks like they're doubling back, Bayla. Be careful!"

She didn't answer. She was too busy launching another blast of energy towards a new target. I looked back to where the scorps were coming from and saw him. The hissing and popping scorp with a double stinger walked out from behind a boulder. It emerged and lurched forward, dodging Bayla's magical snare. After evading Bayla, the scorp spun and sprinted for me.

I took a few steps back and squared my stance. Behind my approaching bounty I saw a few other scorps emerge, which Bayla ensnared. As those two were caught up in Bayla's energy, two more emerged. One got caught up, and the other didn't as it weaved in and out of its frozen friends towards Bayla. As I prepared to engage my bounty, I looked over and saw Bayla having to back up towards the plateau edge. They were doing exactly what Bayla told me gave her the most trouble—being rushed in waves, and having her attention divided.

My bounty closed in. As it did, I saw most of the other scorps being scooped up in Bayla's magic, but too many made it through. I had to try and kill this guy as quickly as I could.

Once it got within a few tail lengths, the scorp jumped up and lunged at me from about twice my height. As it sailed down at me, the scorp pulled a pincer back in preparation. I raised up my club, ready to smack its arm away, but just before I swung my defending strike, I side-stepped to let it land next to me and slammed it as hard as I could in the back instead.

It let loose a screeching hiss as it landed and spun around to face me again. The hateful sound gave away that my blow had hurt, but it wasn't nearly as deterred as I hoped it would be. Not wanting to give it a chance for a fresh counter, I took off for him.

He lashed his tail at me again, which I hopped over. I came down at its face with a swing of my club, but the scorp's claw caught it. The scorp worked to snap it in half, but its bronze protection put up a fight. Before it wore it down and got through to the actual bone, I bent a leg up and kicked it in the chest, dislodging my club. I jerked it behind me to completely free it and brought it back around, crushing the scorp in its face.

It wobbled back, hissing, clicking, and flailing its arms around its head, wailing at its pain.

I groaned in relief.

Wanting to follow up immediately with as devastating a hit as I could muster, I squeezed my club. I brought it up to my side.

But before I could take a step towards my bounty, I was slammed in the back with a crunching slam, throwing me face-first onto the ground. The initial impact stung so sharply that I couldn't register I was going down until my arms and face dug into rock. I had no chance to protect myself as I fell.

I scraped along and skidded to a stop. My first thought was of the cold stone digging against my bleeding cuts and scrapes. My next was of seeing my bounty's tail flying at me.

The tail bashed into me—feeling as though it had crashed into the entire length of my body—and sent me rolling and tumbling back towards Bayla. When I came to a stop I blinked and fought to place her. She was completely surrounded. Though she herself was in a protective dome and was still shooting out traps of energy at the occasional scorp, too many were coming back. She couldn't keep up. The amount of returning scorps increased too quickly. While struggling to get my bruised legs under my busted body, they kept forcing her to walk backwards. She reached the edge of the plateau's cliff.

"Bayla!" I screamed. "There's no more time for defense! Fight! You have to fight!"

One of the scorps kicked me in the ribs. I reflexively curled up around the pain, but gritted my teeth and forced a thought through my mind. *Check for Bayla!*

I looked back up.

She was gone.

"Bayla!" I roared. "Bayla!"

Maybe she's holding on. Maybe she's on a ledge.

"Bayla!"

Before I could think or say anything next, I felt my feet being grabbed, and then my arms. The two scorps that had picked me up rushed towards the same plateau edge and threw me off.

All I saw was the sky. Closer to it just moments before, I registered the fact that I was falling away from it.

And just before I could begin to fear death, I slammed into something not too far down. Bayla sat next to me, as if she had stumbled backwards clumsily onto her rear. Looking back up to the cliff ledge, I saw my club being thrown over as well. The scorps hadn't looked over the edge yet.

I caught my club and looked over at Bayla, panting like crazy, holding her axes. I smiled by virtue of just being alive.

But how were we alive? I thought.

I looked below us and saw that we were being supported by some kind of magical platform. Changing the focus of my eyes, I looked even farther below, and saw a group of villagers gesturing up towards the energy that held us up.

"Keep them busy!" Shouted the village leader. "We'll be right there!"

I fell back to my elbows, smiling wider. As we rose back up to the plateau, I sucked in a few deep breaths and turned to Bayla.

"Yes," she said, with a cold finality. "No more defense."

Chapter Eleven - Mysteries

Bayla

I had no idea how long it would take the villagers to get up to us, and Briz was already hurt fairly bad, so I knew I had to fight. It was never a question of whether or not I *could*, but I could no longer refuse by claiming it wasn't my fight.

When I went stumbling over that cliff, I had a change of heart. As we reached the top of the plateau once more, some of the scorps who had approached the edge to confirm our deaths, stood, hissing in soft confusion at our almost-translucent voyage through the air on our friends' magical support. After helping Briz to his feet, I readied my axes and pulsed a wide arc of magic at the waiting scorps to clear a path for us to step onto. Once we were back on the plateau, I interspersed both my and Briz's fighting with frequent pulses of snaring or repulsing energy. Between our efforts and the reinforcements of the villagers, we cleared them out, and scored Briz's double stinger.

The villagers were an entirely different group of

people than they were before the fight. After only barely allowing us to fight alongside them, they congratulated us with hugs and cheers afterward, similar to the embraces and sentiments they shared with their own kin. More than once, Briz and I were thanked for our help in destroying the troublesome nest, and keeping the village and families safe.

"We heard the fighting from down below," the previously belligerent village leader told us. "We were trying to spot you when you made it easy for us by getting thrown off the edge."

The group of villagers erupted in robust blasts of hysterical laughter.

"Come," he said to us. "You must come back to our village and let us feed you. You must rest before you do anything else. I will not take any reply other than an acceptance!"

After rubbing my tired eyes, I looked to check in with Briz, panting on one knee and holding his side. He smiled and waved his arm, suggesting the man lead the way. The group roared in approval.

We returned to the village the way we came. After taking the steep path down from the plateau, weaving through the narrow ravine in the rock, back out through the canyon basin, and across the small valley, we crested a dune and caught site of our destination. Children, women, and elders streamed out from the village, catching site of our return. Many of the various men and women raced toward them to hasten the return, and jumped into each other's arms as they reunited. As we walked back, often times with me having to give Briz an arm of support, the village leader enthusiastically introduced us to members of his family, extended kin, or appreciative neighbors.

Many of the village's largest fires that blotted the sky

when we first arrived had been extinguished. As we crossed the village's perimeter, it appeared that a few remaining fires towards the center smoked only slightly and were mostly contained.

The residents that had met up and returned with us—and many that had just started to emerge—trickled through the street to greet us and receive word of how the fight had gone. Others surveyed damage to their homes or nearby buildings while others started to pick up debris or straighten strewn items like clothes and flower pots. Some wrangled livestock that had broken free through panic and force, or from destroyed fences and pens. And while our attention was occasionally drawn to news or glimpses of the dead, there were surprisingly few villager casualties. Most of the dead were scorpirons, who were being carted or carried out of the village by two or three men, each, to be piled up and burned outside the village perimeter.

Indeed, much of the mood was jovial and excited throughout the village as the relief of being freed from the constant harassment of the scorpirons began to sink in. And for many hours after we returned to the village, there was no shortage of citizens telling me and Briz how thankful they were for our assistance.

For many hours after the end of the fight, well into the early evening, we helped the village tend to their wounded, bury the dead, and extinguish the remaining fires. After that, Briz and I were taken to a small building with steps leading down immediately from the entryway. Inside the cool, damp room were their stores of water where we were each given a full bowl to freshen up with. When we discovered that their reserves were down to a few pots, Briz and I both tried to deny the water, but the village leader quickly grew offended at our denial. After a bit of diplomacy and reassurance that we were just worried their people would go without, we took their generous gift and retired to a nearby home to wash up and change into temporary clothes. We were assured that the well refilled quickly and had done so for years.

Once we freshened up, we emerged into their village square into a scene of comfort and peace I hadn't seen since the most beautiful of nights back in my own village. Tall torches and interspersed fire pits burned bright. Couples sat close together on blankets on the sand with children running around chasing dogs. Wine was passed around. Meat was seared and carved, and the air was filled with laughter and innocent recollections of memories, history, and love being shared between the villagers. A breeze blew through, dancing about looking for a comfortable place to land, free of sand, and filled the air with hints of meat, spice, wine, and mystery—the kind of mystery that heightened our appreciation for life and appreciation for the moment. Briz and I had helped defeat the menace that threatened their people and their food, and instead of a victory of territory or valuable ore and stones, the village celebrated their victory of survival and sustenance.

This is why I helped Briz.

Not to help him claim his bounty, but to help these people live. The village leader's wife strolled through the crowd, drink in hand, hugging and kissing as she approached us. She eventually spotted an available space next to me, pointed at it, and after a bit more weaving and socializing, reached it, and claimed it.

"It's such a joy to have you here and experience this feast with us," she said. "Thank you for your help, and for your skill."

"Oh, please," I said, almost embarrassed to silence. "There is no need to thank me. It was the right thing to do. I wanted to help. With those scorpirons preying on you like they were, hurting your people, stealing your food and resources. No. It was the right thing to do.”

The woman nodded repeatedly as she looked over the gathering of her happy kin and neighbors.

“We truly thought our arrangement with the zarafteryx clan would result in fewer scorps by the time they arrived, but that unfortunately wasn't the case. We hadn't considered needing help, and it was a blessing to have you all come along when you did!”

“You can communicate with the zarafteryx?” I asked in amazement.

“Oh yes!” She replied. “Well, not easily,” she continued, laughing. “It takes a great deal of time to confirm we understand each other through marking things in the sand, and making gestures with our hands.”

I tilted back with a smile.

“It was especially gratifying to have your help, being a fellow practitioner,” she added. “And one not of our village, or even this area,” she said. “How did you come to learn the magic you used today?”

I shifted awkwardly where I sat, only from not having answers to my own questions.

“That's something I was hoping to ask about before we traveled on,” I said. “Your husband somehow recognized my magic and referenced Ariadne.”

I turned to the leader's wife, hoping to prompt her for some additional information.

“I don't understand how someone so far away from my island would know about our magic and our goddess.”

The woman leaned back slightly, closed her eyes, and smiled.

“Surely your people told you that magic is an art as old as the world, no?”

I didn't know what she was implying and could only

wait for her to elaborate.

"The magic you have been taught shares roots with our magic. Much of the magic the priests in our desert know has spread throughout neighboring cities like Memphis and Thebes, up to Syria, over to Libya, north across the sea to Crete, Anatolia, down to Aswan and beyond, it is all derived from the same source, young one. It all comes from the same place, the same sacred ones. Just as we share this world, so too do we share magic, and the gods, if only by different names."

I couldn't take my eyes off the woman's mouth as she spoke. Something about the speed and smoothness of her words enchanted me. Together with the fire light and raw smell of the rich night air, her words combined with them to not only remove the potential for confusion, but led me to a sense of spiritual awareness and extrapolation. Her words made sense to me though I could have asked her to expand on her comments dozens of ways. But in her simple suggestion that the magic of the varied peoples of the world were connected, I found a peace that had eluded me ever since I lost my and Cilana's papyri—since my family was taken from me. In addition to losing a predictable but content future, and losing the presence of my family in my life for the rest of their natural lives, I'd had the possibility of any manner of consistency removed from my world. Her implication shored up the loose stones from my hope's foundation and shone light on the fading possibility that I would not only be able to resume my studies of magic, but advance it.

As I looked away from her to swallow and anchor my emotions, I stared at the village's massive bonfire near the square where Briz and I had fought earlier.

"You are incredibly gifted with the skills you have already studied," she said softly. "I would think you would want to continue those studies, no?"

Of course, I thought, but I did know how to provide the more detailed answer that she seemed to be wanting. Before the silence made me feel too uncomfortable, we watched as Briz walked through the crowd and sat next to a group of warriors we had fought with.

"What's your friend's name again?" The woman asked as she motioned at an attendant behind her. The young man brought over a slim and short bottle.

I laughed at the idea of him being my friend—not because he wasn't, but only because we had only known each other for a few days.

"Well, we just met a few—" I began before realizing it didn't matter. I didn't mind calling him my friend. Whether it's been a day or a decade, a friend is a friend.

"His name's Briz," I finished, as the leader's wife smiled at me. She then held up her hand and waved it gently.

"Briz!" She yelled warmly. "Briz!"

He looked around to place the voice and smiled back at her. She waved him over.

He stepped gently through the various groups sitting and relaxing, getting interrupted frequently with handshakes, cheers, and offers of drinks.

"What a strapping, sturdy man," she said as he neared us. I could only grin at her mild infatuation. But it was too late. Her suggestion set my mind on a path of evaluating her thoughts, and I quickly came to the same conclusion.

His skin was firm, and though the darkness of night obscured his ebony skin, the abundant fire light lit him in shifting shades of sparkling obsidian and amber flame. He walked with the confidence of a veteran warrior and as he stepped closer, I was overcome with an unexpected rush of anticipation. He nodded at me.

After all that earlier, and I only get a nod?

"Thank you, so much for this beautiful night," he said to the leader's wife. "The food, the generosity, the conversation, all of it. It's been one of the best nights I've had in some time," he added.

She dipped her head as she smiled broadly. "Of course. It was the least we could do for you both after all that you did for us, and keeping the scorpirons from getting away until our warriors could meet back up with you. It was the least we could do."

Briz returned her warm smile and turned towards me before stepping closer and squeezing my shoulder.

"Are you having fun?" He asked. "Have you had some of this delicious food?"

Ah, good, I said to myself. *I guess he was just being polite and greeting the leader's wife first.*

"I am, and I have!" I boomed. "I really needed this. It's been a perfect evening. Thank you."

"Well, I think," the woman said, as she reached to her side for the small bottle the attendant had brought her, "that we should mark this night with a special drink!"

"Oh, I couldn't," Briz said, tapping his stomach, even though we were talking about drinks. "I've already had a good bit of wine out there with your generous family and friends. "I don't want to spoil the evening."

I hadn't had any wine and was ready to take her up on her offer before she replied to Briz.

"Oh, this isn't wine," she said. Her voice hopped up into a playful lilt before sliding down to an enigmatic low note with the last syllable.

Briz and I looked at each other.

"Is it some kind of potion or elixir?" I asked.

"Some kind of magic?" Briz added. His question was monotone, but higher than he normally spoke, as if humorously paranoid that magic was more prevalent in the world than he previously realized.

The woman turned the bottle slowly with her fingertips, grinning at it oddly as if a playful friend whispered a secret into her ear.

"It's all of those and none of those," she said, still staring at the bottle. "It is all together, unique."

Briz and I didn't have to look at each other again to know we were both confused by what she was saying and lost for what was actually in the bottle. As our eyes remained locked on it, still being spun by his wife, the village leader walked up and sat by his wife. He said nothing and started to grin as well.

"Does it make you feel like wine does?" I asked innocently, truly curious as to what was in it.

Out of the corner of my eye, Briz rubbed his jaw.

"Is it something that helps you commune with the dead?" He wondered. "Or help you see visions of the future?"

The leader leaned over and plucked the bottle out from his wife's hands, who, upon finally having her stare of fascination disrupted, looked up to her husband and smiled even wider.

He walked up to me first, holding the bottle up with his fingertips like his wife had done, and presented it to me.

"It helps you *become* the future," he said to us. His voice drifted along as if whispered only by the energy of the nearby firelight.

Briz stepped towards me. I saw him approach but kept my eyes on the bottle. I reached up slowly, took it, and held it in my own fingertips for the first time.

"Bayla, I don't know if we—"

"I assure you," the village leader said sternly, "that this is the greatest reward we can give you for your help today, and will likely be the most profound gift you will ever receive."

Briz started to say something again, but paused when the leader whipped a look of burning objection at him—undoubtedly remembering his offense at our attempted refusal of their water earlier.

But I remained trained on the bottle. As the length of silence increased, I grew more obsessed with tasting whatever was in it, as my assurance of what it was seemingly drifted farther and farther out of reach. I untied the piece of leather wrapped around the bottle mouth and chugged a gulp.

Briz stepped forward again as I rushed to take a drink.

After swallowing, I brought the bottle away from my mouth and waited for whatever romantic imaginings my naive mind and its limited experiences could fathom. But as I registered a boring, and virtually absent aftertaste, I felt no change in sensation, and saw nothing. I looked down to my fingers as the leader pulled the bottle away from me this time, and handed it to Briz.

At first, Briz glanced back and forth between the bottle, now resting in his substantial fingers, and me. I imagine he was waiting to see if I transformed, died, started speaking gibberish, or exhibited any other demented or frightening behavior. But as the look of lucidity remained in my eyes, mixed with a healthy dose of disappointment, he too slung the bottle back and gulped the liquid down.

"Ah!" The wife exclaimed as she clapped her hands and held them. "What an absolute joy!" She said.

Briz wiped his lips with his forearm and handed the bottle back to her.

"What's a joy?" I asked.

"Watching people drink, partake, and join in our journey with us!" She said.

Briz and I looked at each other, and after inspecting him as he had me, I saw no hint of anything odd affecting his awareness or disposition. I had countless other questions about what we had drank. Maybe it was just a symbolic gesture. A flat wine or simple water for victors to share and salute each other with. I wanted to ask. I wanted to confirm. But a lingering peculiarity of the conversation we had been having, and how it shifted so abruptly, made me refrain. The fact that we had gone from talking about magic having commonalities with cultures across the world, to a discussion over abstract suggestions of the future and of drinks that they couldn't, or refused to describe, was odd enough. But the cryptic interaction passed, with Briz and I quickly returning to lighter conversation with the leader, his wife, and those nearby. In fact, I found a way to get back to our previous discussion regarding similarities of magic around the world.

"So, how did your people come to learn the magic that you have?" I asked. "Did it begin in your village here? Have you always known it?"

The village leader shook his head vigorously.

"Oh, no, not at all," he said. "By tradition, our people are nomadic. Always traveling to where the food is, the water is, where they could be safe, and survive. Our first generations encountered other travelers and traders and exchanged their knowledge with them over a period of many years."

"And everyone had their own magic?" Briz asked to confirm.

The leader's wife dipped and rocked her head from side to side. A grimace of uncertainty wrinkled her face.

"Well, in a few instances, yes," she said, "but a lot of it was similar. It's kind of like a recipe. One of us here can make a loaf of bread, but if we go ten days to the west, over to another village, they'll have bread, too, but it probably won't taste exactly the same."

"So, where did the original recipes come from, then?" I asked, smiling before I even finished the question. The wife looked over with a smile that seemed to approve of my flippant question.

"That honestly is a great question," she said. I asked another question before she could answer.

"You mentioned Ariadne earlier," I said, looking to the leader. "That surprised me. It was wonderful to hear her name, but somewhat startling that someone knew of her so far away from my home. How do you know of her? What are the gods like in Egypt?"

The leader took a moment to finish chewing the rapid bites of food he had been tossing into his mouth.

"Well, like my wife was saying... We were nomads. We traveled and traded. Others in any particular area traded and traveled as well. Our ancestors learned things and passed them down. We are as familiar with your Ariadne as we are of Minos in your neighboring Crete, or with the blessed Amun, Isis, Osiris, Ptah, and Ra. Countless others."

I took a moment to reflect on their words, still unsure if she was suggesting they were the same, separate, or equal, but before I asked her to explain further, I felt the beginnings of agitation stir within me.

Why didn't father ever tell me of these other gods? Did he not know? If he didn't, what else did he not know? Maybe what he knew was wrong! No, that's stupid. I used virtually everything he taught me to protect not only myself, but countless others today. Maybe he was going to tell me about the gods of the world, but just never had time.

"What made you all settle down?" Briz asked. "You say you were nomads, but you have quite a permanent town built up here. It's a great place to call home."

"Well, thank you for your kind words," the leader said through more chewing. "Our tribe has swelled greatly in recent generations. It started to take a great deal of work to move so many people. Sometimes our more recent ancestors would move just to find that available water had dried up, or hunting became scarce soon after settling. It just became too difficult to continue being so mobile. So, our people settled here. We began to raise animals, farm crops, and build a permanent home. This area also serves to keep us fairly safe from those who would do us harm."

The leader's wife shot her husband an alarmed glance. I wasn't expecting that.

"You mean, the scorps?" I asked.

"Right, yes," he raced to say.

My mind meandered away from the conversation surrounding their village's history to focus on the prospect of returning to that which was familiar to me—something I thought was lost. I looked over at the leader's wife and waited for a break in conversation to hopefully catch her eye. She quickly saw me and greeted me with a new, warm smile, as if she knew what I was going to ask.

"Forgive me," I started meekly, struggling with what I wanted to ask and how to ask it. "But I was wondering... You mentioned something earlier... suggesting I may want to resume my studies. How might I go about that?"

The wife nodded while I asked the questions she seemed to be expecting. Briz slid closer to us after finishing his separate conversation and his rugged but exhilarating musk caught my attention.

"There are plenty of people to help and ways to

continue on your path," she said, tapping me gently on the knee. "You must only seek them out. In fact," she continued after looking to her husband quickly, "you are more than welcome to stay with us for a time if you like."

I turned my head quickly to Briz, but not long enough to gauge his reaction.

"Oh, that is an even greater generosity on top of a night full of generosities," I gushed. "But…"

I stopped myself. I looked back and forth between Briz, taking enough time to weigh his reaction to her proposal, and back to the leader's wife. I wanted to stay and start studying more magic *immediately*. I wanted to get back to recreating my papyrus. I wanted to learn, and document, and advance, and make my family proud, wherever they may be.

But as I looked back to Briz again, I felt a different urge. Before I could make my family proud, they needed to be able to rest peacefully. And in order for them to rest peacefully, I needed to avenge them. And Briz was going to help me find those I needed to hold responsible.

I twisted a final turn back to the leader's wife.

"You say there are many ways to learn and continue on my path?" I confirmed.

She smiled and laughed softly.

"Yes," she replied softly. As I said. You only need seek them out. Don't let this world make you fear magic, or those who practice it, as it so often tries to do. Most people in the world rely on magic in more than one way or form, and are afraid of the same things simply called different names and used by different people."

I swallowed and let my eyes shift to the flickering fire while I confirmed what I wanted to do.

"Then I will do that," I said. "I will seek those out who

can help me resume my studies, but I'm afraid I must not accept your incredible offer just yet."

Turning to Briz, I continued.

"Briz and I have business together that I must see done. If I am welcome," I continued, "I may return another day once I have finished my other tasks."

She patted my knee again.

"Of course," she said. "Of course. Please come visit us again, even just to visit, if not to study with us."

"Thank you, so very much," I replied. The wife stood up and stepped towards the fire in the middle of the square before reaching out for me.

"Please travel safely," she said while squeezing my hand. "Remember that you will always have friends here. And remember that you will always have friends wherever you go. You need only find them."

She squeezed my hand a final time before smiling at me, and then turned to Briz with the same warmth and sincerity. After holding her regular wine cup up to us, she stepped down into the crowd and was quickly smothered by a sea of embraces and kisses to the cheek. The fire roared and soared, rising and falling with a rhythm that seemed to echo that of the drums played by nearby villagers. Together with the pulsing beats and matching dance of the flame, the ebb and flow of the light basked the area in a synchronized symphony from another time. Another place. I felt as if the entire scene dripped over me and everyone in the square, taking us not just to another time and place, but an experience out of what I knew as place, or what I knew as time.

Briz leaned closer and with his comment, injected an added note of mystery.

"I don't know what that was about earlier," Briz

whispered. "But I didn't like drinking whatever it was that we drank."

I nodded to reciprocate his concern.

"I'm with you," I said, holding my stare on the fire. "That was odd. The whole conversation was odd, but the bit with the bottle seemed like we were talking with completely different people."

"Okay, good," Briz said. "It wasn't just me then."

My eyes unfocused as I asked myself a question internally before posing it to Briz.

"So," I started. "Why did we drink it?"

Briz scratched his face and sat silently for a few moments.

"I really don't know," he finally said. "I was a little curious, but mostly… It almost felt like they were threatening us."

"Mmm," I hummed, considering his thoughts. "So, none of that made any sense to you?"

"No," he blurted, befuddled. "I was hoping you knew what she was talking about."

I shook my head.

"No, I haven't studied anything involving liquids or potions or anything like that yet."

"I guess it was something symbolic, maybe, I don't know," Briz suggested.

"I thought something similar."

"Well, whatever," he added. "We don't seem to be any worse for it. I'm going to try and sleep soon."

"I need to do the same," I said, turning to him. "What's next? What happens next?"

"Well," he said, before being distracted by a pair of girls dancing nearby.

"Briz," I prodded.

"All right," he snipped, while slapping the air at me. "We'll go collect payment on the bounty tomorrow, I guess. And then we'll start looking into your, uh, situation."

I swallowed, nodded, and after turning to face it again, dared the fire to miss a beat.

Chapter Twelve - The Pyramids

Briz

My bed of straw and blankets held up fairly well through the night. I remember waking up only once to roll over, and smiled myself back to sleep when I saw the silhouette of a donkey sticking its head through the window above me. Other than that, I slept like the dead and stirred awake slowly despite the hints of early sun tapping on my eyelids.

Gotta go get paid for this double stinger guy.

I gave in and peeled my eyes open.

Sand.

I saw nothing but sand. Inches from my face and lit golden, openly exposed to the sun, was nothing but sand.

Past the sand that was immediately in front of my nose, was only more sand. And then beyond that—cracked and caked sand, being whipped and kissed by even more, gently blowing sand.

Nothing but *more* sand stretched to the horizon, growing fainter in the heat-blurred distance.

I shot up to my feet and spun around, once, twice,

three, five times until I started to get dizzy. There was *nothing* around me. No homes. No buildings. No walls. No structures. But Bayla was there. Still asleep.

"Bayla!" I shouted, still wobbling around like a drunkard, drunk with fear.

"Bayla!" I barked again, followed by rapid repetitions growing in volume with each iteration.

"Bayla, Bayla, Bayla, Bayla! Wake up!"

She rolled onto her belly and hid her head in the insides of her elbows.

"Why," she started, with an elongated groan, "are you yelling?"

"Look! Get up, get up. Look!" I shouted.

She stirred again and as she did, a snort from behind me tried to scare my skin off. I jumped-spun around. In my panic I hadn't seen them, but there were two camels standing only feet from us.

As Bayla registered her own panic, I felt my head twist, turn, and shift forward and backward at the odd appearance of these two camels.

"What is..." Bayla started to yell. "What's happened? What's going on?"

I couldn't break off from the camels just yet. Looking them up and down, I silently begged for some kind of clue from them as to what had happened. While not necessarily expecting them to speak—though I wouldn't have been surprised if they had—I walked over and reluctantly put my hand up on one of the creature's neck.

Hair. Feels normal.

"Where is everyone, Briz? What happened?" Bayla shrieked. I barely registered her confused shadow wandering aimlessly off to my side.

The reins and blankets on each camel seemed plain and normal. As I gave up on the camels providing any clues, I turned around to face Bayla, but one of the camels shifted. When it did, I saw the double stinger tied off to a strap on the camel. Not only had I never seen these camels before, but I definitely did not tie the stinger to one of them. I stepped backwards. My skin tingled with wave after wave of increasing paranoia as if I were being watched by every person in the world, without being able to see them. I stumbled back and finally turned to Bayla, ready to shout out in hysteria, but her beautiful, sullen face stunned my fear into enough submission to be worried for her instead. She looked as though she were crying, but I didn't yet see any tears.

Bayla was so small and tiny against the backdrop of the desert, and I supposed I must have looked the same way to her. That's all there was. Just the shattered ground, sand, and dunes, with the cliffs and canyon far in the distance.

"Where did they go?" She whined.

"I don't know," I said, surprising myself at how short of breath I apparently was. "I don't know. I woke up and it was like this. Just like this. No homes. Nothing. No people. *Nothing.*"

"What is happening?" Bayla asked again, mostly to herself. She held her hands up in exasperation as she stared at the ground, searching for some kind of clue in the weather-worn ground.

I continued panting while looking to the horizon. Perhaps there was a caravan. Wagons. People. Other structures than the ones we expected to see when we woke up. No. Nothing.

"That... liquid we drank," Bayla started. "We must have been drugged or something?"

I didn't understand.

"You think that stuff just made us fall asleep?" I asked.

Bayla stammered. "Or... maybe it's... maybe it's

making us see this."

I turned around and around again, slowly.

"I don't think that's it," I said, not really having any kind of clue. "I... Would we both be seeing the same thing?"

Bayla stepped backwards and spun to examine the area again for herself.

"Maybe they took us somewhere?" She said. "Carried us off somewhere and left us?"

"That's... that's a very good—" I began, poking the air with my finger in agreement. But before I finished, I realized the distant landmarks were familiar.

"Wait, no," I said. "See that tower of rock over there? That's the same formation we could see from the village yesterday. And the plateau that connects to it is below it, just above the horizon and spans out to the right."

I continued to pant as the questions only mounted.

"And the cliffs over there... No," I said as I noticed a tinge of worry returning to my voice. "No. The... The village should be... Right. Here," I said, flinging my open hands in the direction of the ground below us.

Bayla turned towards me and we looked at each other for the first time since waking up. She shook her head as she swallowed, appearing to struggle to hold her anxiety back.

"And then there's these camels," I said, gesturing behind me.

Bayla walked past me towards the animals.

"They must have been left for us," I said.

I watched as Bayla patted the camels and curled her fingertips to absentmindedly itch at the blankets draped over them.

"And you're not going to believe this, but on the other side of that one... My bounty's stinger is tied to it."

She shot her head around at me in disbelief, almost

as if she were frozen mid-scream. While sliding her hand along the side of the camel, she went to look. I heard her muffled voice creep out from the other side of the camel.

"Briz, I don't know what this is. I don't know what's happened," she said.

I didn't either, and I didn't know what to say to her.

"Let's just..." I forced myself to say. "I just want to get out of here. Let's just get to Memphis and get paid for this bounty. And then we can start looking for the people you need to find."

She shook her head, emerging from the other side of the camel. "Right. Let's go."

* * *

We spoke very little as we rode on our magical camels. Well, they may not have been magical. They still needed food, water, and rest. We just didn't know where they came from. I couldn't speak for Bayla, but I was somewhat afraid of speaking too much and possibly saying something that angered these special mounts, or angering whoever gave them to us—whether it was whoever these apparent ghost villagers were, or whatever. I didn't know what was going on. I was just eager to get back to something and surroundings that made sense. Even when we stopped to camp and sleep the few times we had to, there was very little said. Bayla and I stuck to simple conversation of food, fatigue, water, and rest as we traveled. We had already discussed plenty about our lives and past—even before encountering the village— and as far as I was concerned, we could come back to those topics after we confirmed we were back in civilization. Back in a city, surrounded by other people. Back in reality.

Our last overnight camp was just outside Faiyum. We stopped to catch some fish from Lake Moeris, which was a successful endeavor, and after eating in silence, we went to sleep, hoping—as we had each time we slept since leaving the location of the village—that we wouldn't wake up to any new alterations to our world. Luckily, we ate and slept well, and woke up at dawn to what we expected to see, and rode northeast into Memphis.

As signs of life other than our own crept into view, I immediately felt my nerves relax. Caravans and wagons dotted the horizon as they approached the city. Goats and donkeys could be heard singing from the city outskirts, and men and women strolled to and fro along the roads. And then there were the children. Seeing children running about always lifted my heart. Children were life. They were innocence. They were good to see. Girls chased boys to steal kisses, and boys chased girls with frogs spilling out of their hands. Giggles and screams. It all made me smile.

Bayla was smiling, too. I frequently looked over at her as we rode, taking in all of her reactions to the sprawling city and its thick layers of life. With each foot we grew closer to the city center, I felt safer in my desire to resume more involved conversation.

"You've never been here before, right?" I asked.

With a mouth hanging partially open in wonder, she flicked her head to and fro, soaking in as much as she could as she responded.

"No," she said. "I hadn't been anywhere in Egypt before the shipwreck."

"Mmm," I said. "I didn't think so."

"I can't believe it, Briz. I had heard stories from my parents, but even then, those were just stories relayed to them by traders or gypsies in the village square. It's so... grand. So extensive. I've never seen—"

She interrupted herself with perhaps the harshest gasp of air I'd ever heard.

"Oh, Briz!" She shouted. "Is that a—"

"Pyramid?" I said, smiling. "It is."

She stopped her camel.

"Wait, there are more! Well, I knew there were more, or I had heard there were, but there they are! In front of my eyes!"

She looked back and forth to them, and to me, her jaw dropped down as low as I think it could go. She covered her mouth as she looked back and forth.

"I can't believe..." she started, taking her hands away. She sniffed two or three times and shook her head. "I can't believe I'm seeing this, Briz."

As she continued, her volume dropped down to a whisper.

"What I'm seeing right now has only ever been dreams in a legend told by mysterious wanderers."

An indescribable warmth swelled in my chest as she spoke. I was in awe of her awe.

"Oh, how I wish my family could see this," she added. After what felt like an eternity of joyful wonder, she finally looked back over at me. I hadn't quit smiling since she stopped her camel. I waved my head towards the city and continued on.

As we approached, children raced up to us wanting a ride. Merchants ran up holding fabric, holding it loosely and letting it ripple in the breeze. Fishermen yelled at us from their stalls, pointing at their fish strung up by the dozens. Another man with a massive khopesh approached. That was what I noticed about him first. I guess it comes with my line of business. And the massive hilt of the sword made it that much easier to spot. The thought that first entered my head was that he may be a guard of some kind coming to be nosy, but then he held his hands up with a few dozen amulets hanging from them. He had ankhs, knots of Isis, nefer amulets, serpents, Horus eyes, among others.

Once most of the political business of the region

shifted to Thebes, there was much more freedom to live and enjoy Memphis. And while there were still some stationed garrisons and guards wandering around, they were far fewer than there had been in previous years. People could move about with less arbitrary harassment. They could practice their crafts, trade their goods, and take part in some of the less refined aspects of society. Overall, Memphis was the best of all worlds. All the art, all the goods, all of the food, temples, and structures, but with much less bureaucracy.

"How does someone live in such a place, Briz?" Bayla asked, in-between trying to greet each and every child and merchant that ran up to her. "I wouldn't know where to start, what to do, or who to talk to first!"

"It definitely is a much busier life than living out in the desert, or," I said, changing mindset, "living on an island. There's always something going on here. Always something being said. Always someone needing or wanting something. People being hurt. People getting lost to the ages."

Bayla spoke up again, quicker than I expected.

"Well, I'm sure there is also love," she said. "Art, and beauty. Great complexes where people can commune with their gods. Temples. Temples!"

"Yes, there are those things, too," I said. "I only meant that the bad things seem to be more pronounced in such a large place as this. Just saying to be careful."

Bayla didn't listen.

"I would love to visit the priests while we're here," she said, excited. "Can I do that? Will they let me do that even though I'm not from here?"

I rolled my eyes.

"Yes, you can talk to whoever you wish, for the most part. Didn't you want to, uh, tend to your business first, after I turn in this bounty?"

She reluctantly pulled her head away from all the sights and sounds she was caught up with.

"I was thinking I could do both," she said, ending her statement with the sound of a question.

I snickered and just closed my eyes as I nodded.

"Okay," Bayla said, tightening the reins of her camel. "Where do you go to turn that stinger in?"

* * *

The main market of Memphis was a vast grid of stalls and booths offering all degrees of goods, ranging in function from finely woven garments, to rat traps. Items meticulously carved and decorated with expert craftsmanship hung from shelves next to items of lesser quality like rotten food and oils of questionable effect. There was furniture, jewelry, *good* food, pottery, and everything in-between. In addition to physical goods to buy and barter, there were also those who offered their services, or in addition to services, sold byproducts of their services. For example, one might find a pest hunter selling pelts made from boar hide, or a hunter selling fresh meat, as well as the treated hides from his kills. And though their work was rarely discussed or referred to publicly, there were also those who offered their services to hunt the types of beasts that I do, and even still, those who provided services of hunting men.

As we strolled through the market, I had to frequently tap Bayla on the shoulder or tug on her sleeve as she often stopped to admire a necklace, ask about a dress, answer a child's silly question, or somehow get distracted another way.

"We're looking for a very talented carpenter," I told Bayla when I finally had her attention. "He makes these gilded chairs. You'll know them when you see them. They're kind of like the ones you only see in palaces and temples. Much simpler, but beautiful, and expensive."

"I.. I've never been into an Egyptian palace or temple, Briz," Bayla said, doing her best not to stop at another stall. "What's 'gilded' mean?"

"Oh, yes," I said as I laughed at myself. "It's when you cover something in gold, or silver, or another type of metal."

"Covering something in gold?" She repeated, astonished. "I don't even know how that's possible. I've already lost count of things I've never seen before. But this carpenter hired you?"

"Yes," I shouted over the crowd. "He and his brother were hunting when they came across a group of scorps that were hunting in their usual spot next to their village. They both tried to get away, but my double stinger guy caught up to and killed his brother."

Bayla said something, but I couldn't hear her. A fast-moving cart filled with musicians strumming sistrums and harps, and bashing clotals and drums wheeled by. The music and singing took over command of the path's noise for a moment as another man held up filled wine skins off the back of the cart.

After they passed between me and Bayla, I caught Bayla with a face completely overtaken with excitement and happiness. She watched as the wagon rolled down the crowded path until we lost sight of it.

"He's just up there," I said, pointing further up her side of the street. I crossed over to Bayla and slapped her on the back.

As we approached, I could already see Menna's arms pointing and sticking out from his stall as he discussed something with what looked to be a customer. Hanging from his stall supports were his beautiful frames, and when I got in range to see the gorgeous reliquaries, boxes, and candlesticks on shelves behind him, Menna noticed me and smiled. His eyes collapsed a little. He blinked rapidly as his chin bounced in numerous, quick nods. He leaned over to his customer and held up a finger before darting around his counter.

"Briz!" Menna greeted warmly, squeezing my shoulders. "It is good to see you my friend, and it's especially good knowing what your appearance here must mean. Please... tell me..."

"I have it Menna," I said softly. I patted him on the shoulder and smiled as I swung a sack from around my side. "Look my friend."

I pulled and stretched the top of the bag open and tipped it over so Menna could see in. He grabbed my arm and nodded many times. After staring into the bag for a long time, he finally looked back up to me with watering eyes.

"Thank you, my friend. Thank you, Briz."

Menna let go of my arm and looked up to the sky.

"Praise be to Petbe! Thank you Petbe! Thank you for making Briz the instrument of my revenge. Thank you for giving my brother peace."

Menna snapped rigid as his eyes shot open wide.

"I..." he started, stuttering nervously. "I don... I don't have your payment here with me. Please, let me go get it, or come with me to my home."

"I would prefer to settle this as quick—" I attempted, but a cough from Bayla caused me to hesitate. I looked over to see her leaning in towards me with patronizing eyes.

"That will be fine," I said instead. "I can go home with you when you're done here for the day."

Menna bowed slowly and grabbed my hand, tapping it warmly with the other.

"I'm so glad you did this without any harm coming to you," Menna whispered graciously. "Was it difficult?"

I looked to Bayla, immediately flooded with a wealth of lengthy answers. I shrugged and smiled as Menna took notice of her as well.

"And who is this beautiful young woman?" He asked. "Wait. Do not tell me," he said, stepping back and holding a contemplating finger to his lips. "She took care of all the others while you focused on this one!" Menna held up the bag with the double stinger in it, smiling as wide as the Nile. His expression got to me. I busted into laughter that took all of my breath.

"That isn't far from the truth!" I said sincerely. "Bayla here is a friend. Quite capable of taking care of herself and others. We actually only met recently and are helping each other tend to some of our individual business."

Menna curled his lips down as his eyebrows rose with intrigue.

"Is that so?" He asked, glancing back and forth playfully between me and Bayla. But his face soon sank into one of dark reality.

"Well, I have to say that I pity whatever *business* you have, Bayla, that Briz here is helping you with. He has quite the reputation for unparalleled... carnage, and unlimited persistence until his job is done."

Bayla started to reply but Menna bounced on the balls of his feet with a sparkle in his eye.

"Speaking of reputation, Briz," Menna said. "Someone came through recently and asked everyone—at least up and down my row—about you. Asking us about the types of work you usually do. How good you are. If anyone had experience working with you. The types of payment you've accepted in the past. All kinds of things. From what I heard talking with some of the others, you were spoken of very highly, but no one owned up to having hired you in the past."

"Ah, I see. That's kind of funny considering I've done work for half of you," I said. "What did you say to this stranger?"

Menna shook his head.

"Well, I didn't talk about this job," he said, holding up the bag with the stinger, "but I did repeat some of the things others were saying. We just assumed it was someone wanting to hire you."

"Was that it?" I asked. "Did anyone recognize him or did he say anything specific about work needing done?"

"No, I don't think any of us knew him. He looked too well off to have a quarrel with you, or to need your services. I don't know. He gave no info. Just asked questions."

Bayla, listening intently, jumped into the mystery.

"But it is possible that he was wanting to hire you?" She posed to both me and Menna. "I don't know how this works. Is this type of hunting spoken about in public? Do the people that do what you do Briz, discuss it openly?"

I shrugged and waffled.

"It's a tricky situation. Like I've said before, I don't hunt other people or other humans because of the drama it brings. The trouble. Too much risk for too little reward. But there are those," I said, weighing the invisible sides of my statement with my hands, "that *do* hunt humans. There all types of bounty hunters, and because there are a good number of human targets, the whole profession has those possibilities associated with it, so traditionally, the whole spectrum of work just isn't discussed openly."

"And the people that commission bounty work," Menna added, "usually want their needs kept confidential."

"Was this person like that?" Bayla asked.

"Well, other than asking such broad questions about Briz, yes, he was," Menna answered.

"And you said that he was dressed really well, or

that he didn't look like he needed anything? What did that mean?"

"Hmm, it doesn't really mean much, come to think of it. There are so many healers, priests, and military officers, it could have been anyone asking about Briz for any reason."

A neighboring merchant startled us all as he exited his stall, slamming a stack of wood to the ground. We watched as he approached a wagon that had just pulled up.

"Couldn't you bring it closer, boy?" The man said to the young man. "These things are heavy."

"I'm sorry papa!" The boy said with a shaky voice. "Should I move the wag—"

"No, no," the father interrupted. "There's no point now."

The merchant slid the back piece of wood up from grooves in the wagon's walls and slung it forward. He then grasped one of the two boars in the back by its rear hooves and pulled it out of the cart.

"You talking about that man that came through the other day?" The merchant asked, grunting as he bent under the boar, catching it on his shoulder before it fell off the wagon.

"Yes," Menna replied. "What was that all about?"

"I don't know why he was here," the merchant replied, slamming the dead boar down on the counter of his stall. "But his name's Neferhotep. He's a scribe for a lot of the palace types and priests. Whatever his reason for being here, I wouldn't want any part of it."

"Why do you say that?" Bayla wondered.

The merchant grabbed the other boar off the wagon and carried it over before slapping it down next to the first one. He turned and wiped his brow.

"When people like him come into the market," the merchant started. "You're either in trouble, or they want people like us to do the things they wouldn't dare do."

"That sounds terribly ominous," Bayla said.

"It sounds incredibly lucrative to me," Menna said, winking at me. He tapped my shoulder and returned behind the counter of his stall.

"You say his name was Neferhotep?" I asked the merchant. He nodded.

"Well, thank you very much for the information," my friend.

I turned away from the hunter and started back down the street aimlessly picking at my lip. Bayla was off to my side with her hands on her hips, but after a slight huff, she joined back up.

"We'll come back soon," I said to Menna before he was out of earshot, and before I got too distracted by my thoughts.

"Okay, my friend. Thank you again!" He said, sending us off with a wave.

The merchants and booths were lost to me as I walked, head down. People of all types had sought me out before, and delivered or relayed their requests in all manners of ways. But something about this scribe didn't feel right. If what Menna and the other merchant said was true, he would definitely be the most elevated person to ever offer me a job. I didn't know what job, and I was fairly sure I didn't want to know, but I at least wanted to find out how much it paid.

"Briz?" Bayla asked gently.

"Hmm?"

"Does that sound all right with you?" She asked.

My scalp itched too much to allow me to respond immediately. I closed my eyes and raked my fingernails across my head. Side to side. Up and down.

"Does what?" I asked.

Bayla huffed and let the weight of one side of her body bend a knee some.

"What I just asked..."

She sighed and looked about.

"After you collect the payment from Menna," she continued. "Can we start looking into... my issue?"

There would be plenty of time for that, but I didn't want to have to explicitly say it. Helping her and maybe even helping her track and attack these raiders was never a doubt in my mind. It just wasn't all that pressing. I couldn't *not* try to check on what was going on with the scribe.

"Well of course," I said. "We won't leave here until you have some good information to act on."

She turned to look me straight on, one eye squinting from the sun.

"It isn't just about information, Briz," she said. "It's about timing. Getting that information and looking into it."

"Yes, Bayla," I said quickly. "We will get information and act on it. Before we leave the city, though, I want to find out what this scribe wanted. Your family will get their justice. They're not going anywhere."

Somehow, before the last pinch of breath left my mouth, as I said the last word of my last statement, I had a premonition of the future and knew that Bayla would slap me. By the time I knew what was coming, it was too late. The moment I said it, I knew her hand was on its way, and came it did. Between speaking the last syllable and actually getting slapped, I knew I shouldn't have uttered those words.

Her slap was punitive. It hurt, and I deserved it. My face flew sideways with the impact, and as the dense sting settled and stayed on my face, I turned back to her slowly, completely at a loss for how stupid I felt for what I said. Lost for words, I was simultaneously impressed by the strength of her punishment for my cruel statement. As I finished turning back towards her, I looked up to see an axe raised high above, poised, ready, held by her taut arm. She stood there, shaking with what I assumed was pure fury ready to kill me. She could have. But instead of fearing for my life, I only felt my regret grow as I looked at her. Glimpses of her lethal combat and powerful magic as she helped me fight the scorpirons flashed through my mind.

She finally began to shake less. Her eyes, previously wild with passionate hate, relaxed. She brought her axe down to her side before taking off down the path. She stepped slowly first, but then faster, stomping away and almost out of sight.

"Bayla! Wait! Bayla!"

As I jogged after her, my guilt compounded and spilled out of my head, onto my shoulders, down my back and sucker punched my heart. The confidence I had in my justification for delaying Bayla's vengeance crumbled behind my pride as if I were running down the street naked. She had helped me when I needed her help, and this dismissal of her urgency was an insult. I caught up and reached for her arm.

"Do not!" She shouted, spinning around and hopping out of my grasp.

Bayla pointed at me with her arm fully extended. She then swallowed, shifted her feet, and scanned the market without actually looking at anything before settling back on me.

"I freed you from a cage. Saved you from an agonizing death. Helped you fight an army of those, scorpiron things... just so you could kill only one of them and then get paid for it!"

"And I told you I would give you some of that payment!" I shot back.

"That was never what I negotiated for, Briz, and you know it! I asked for your help! Not your money. Your help!"

As the crowd in the market slowed to look at us, I had a growing piece of my conscience that made me feel like they were on her side. But, right or wrong, I still didn't see the problem with taking a little extra time.

"And you'll get it, Bayla! I've never said I wouldn't help you!"

"Briz?" Bayla started, as her hands and arms stabbed and slapped the air. "Every minute that goes by. Every day... That's a minute or day those people have to distance themselves from me, and from justice. More and more minutes and days that add up make it less probable that I'll find them. Menna back there? You saw the relief and peace in his face when he saw that his brother had been avenged. Imagine the blackness that ate at his heart between the time his brother was killed and today. A blackness that itched, chewed, and festered on his heart for each and every minute until today. Now look at me. Look at me and know that a similar blackness eats away at me."

As she pointed and waved her hands, her voice grew louder, and her eyes grew wetter.

"Look at me when I say that blackness, times *three* is destroying me. So, go do whatever it is you need to do and come get me whenever you have time to help me. I'll be here."

When she finished speaking, she dropped her arms and focused on me, unblinking, absolutely unwavering, giving me a moment to reply, and daring me to at the same time. I didn't say anything. She turned and tore off into the crowd.

I wanted to run after her. I wanted to run after her, grab her, apologize, and start asking everyone in the city what they may know about the raids. As she walked away, I wanted to give up everything I knew and did for a living to help her get her justice.

But I didn't.

I watched her until I could no longer see her fine, dark hair bouncing up and down above the crowd any longer. And when the massive throng of the market swallowed her, I looked around, working to place Menna again. I needed to find out where Neferhotep lived.

* * *

I knew when Menna told me his name, it wouldn't be a problem finding Neferhotep. All I needed was a name. All anyone would need is a name. With a little sense, charm, a proclivity for lying sometimes, or the ability to formulate meaningful questions, anyone can get answers to anything. And then, after some practice, you can go from taking weeks or days to get information, to hours or minutes.

I went back to Menna and asked his neighbor if he knew where Neferhotep lived.

"Nope," he said. "But the jeweler at the end of the next row over delivered some necklaces to him recently, I believe. He went on and on about how long they took to make. How he had to spend most of his savings…"

I quit paying attention after "jeweler at the end of the next row," and headed that way after Menna's friend finished yammering.

The jeweler the next row over was mostly useless.

"Menna's friend needs me to bring a few boars to Neferhotep," I lied. "Apparently a pretty prominent scribe. Told me you might know where to find him?"

"Oh, right," he said, never even looking at me. His head and arm were halfway down a basket of beads as he spoke. "He had to change plans and told me to give them to his tailor. He runs a shop towards the opposite end of the row."

Tailor. Opposite end of the row.

I headed back the way I came but pressed on towards the end of the row until I came upon a booth with fabric and clothes flapping about invitingly from a taut piece of rope.

The tailor, I thought. *Has to be him.*

I strolled up to his stall quickly, but with my best, fake smile.

"Hello there," I began. "Beautiful work," I said, fondling the bottom of a shirt with my fingertips.

"Please don't touch unless you're going to buy it," he uttered while unrolling cloth. His chin was almost touching his chest as he looked at me from under his brow.

"Ah, right, of course," I said.

The tailor flapped and slapped the fabric, apparently uninterested in my presence.

"I was hoping you might be able to tell me how to locate the scribe called Neferhotep. I have a few boars I need to—"

"No, no," he interrupted. "I am not going to tell you how to find my employer. Either buy something or be gone."

"Okay," I muttered to the dirt at my feet. I then slapped a piece of wood out from between the two separated counters it connected, and ran at the tailor, pinning him in the corner.

"Listen," I said, whispering. "You probably already know this, but he was looking for me. My name is Briz."

The tailor quit squirming and looked me dead in the eye.

"Mm hmm. Now do you want him to eventually find out that you're the one that delayed my finding him? Or did you just want to go ahead and tell me?"

The tailor's fear seemed to make his mouth do something almost resembling a smile.

"Walk straight back through three streets after exiting the main temple's center exit. Take a right. It's next door to a large plot of pastureland on the corner."

"Ah!" I said smoothly. "You've been so helpful!" I said with a gigantically fabricated smile which I allowed to fall immediately. After stepping out of the booth and back into the street, I set out in the direction of the temple. But after only a few steps, I stopped and looked behind me. I took a moment and scanned the market.

I didn't see her.

* * *

As I walked through the streets of Memphis, I remembered why I loved the city. I actually remembered that I loved the desert, city, everything equally, but I just relished wherever I was at a particular moment the most. I often end up playing a game with myself. I list reasons why I love a place as if trying to convince, or rather, remind myself. Maybe it's part of immersing myself in an environment as much as possible to fit in, blend in, disappear. Or maybe I just love being alive.

Memphis had a limitless supply of fascinating characteristics. The animated but customary arguments between merchant and customer as they quarreled over payments and items to barter were some of my favorites. Their voices rose and fell as they carried out their ingrained traditions of offer and counter offer, each encounter a minor battle with no casualties, only respect.

As I approached the sun-laden primary temple, I looked up from the shadows of surrounding structures, in awe, at least at the majesty of the towering front entrance. I had very little use for the gods of Egypt—from this part of the country or elsewhere—though I would someday be interested in learning which of them I might need to thank for letting me live to the age I have.

After my eyes traced up the massive blocks of the temple's front entrance, they jumped up to the massive banners flying above. Just simple fabric, they rippled and whipped about, beckoning with their magic of majesty to all around to come in, pray, and of course, leave offerings. Once my focus hopped from the banners to the massive, obsidian obelisks flanking the approaching path, I followed them down to the ground to see children running around their bases, weaving and chasing each other through long rows of sphinxes that lined the path to the temple entrance. I smiled at the children and continued around.

The streets behind the temple weren't as busy as the ones closer to the market. They became narrower and less populated. Many of the merchants selling wares in the market did their primary work in this area with artisans and apprentices minding the businesses while they were away. Conversations between craftsmen and women as they baked or hammered on anvils floated between the stalls, most frequently ending in laughter as they made fun of the day's politics or silliness perpetrated by their families. Afterward, a few sections of fenced livestock pens opened up to a wide street. Up and to the right was a large piece of open pastureland. Directly in front of me was a large building, second only to the massive temple behind me, at least in the surrounding area. It looked far too ostentatious to be a scribe's residence, but according to the last bit of direction I received, this was Neferhotep's home.

I waited for a garrison wagon to pass and crossed the street. The residence was surrounded by a stone wall that came up to my chest, with a marvelously verdant and ornate garden inside between the wall and the main entrance. There was a tall entryway that beckoned at me to enter much like the massive banners atop the temple. But I hadn't considered entering yet as I draped my arms over the wall and stared inward like a child waiting to be tossed a piece of candy. I had no idea what the names were of any of the variety of flowers and plants inside the garden, but I slowly examined each one as if it would come to me.

Much like the imagined enchantment I projected onto the temple, the residence was equally as enigmatic. After sliding my arms back over the wall, I stepped sideways slowly, inspecting the wonder of each feature of the home as I walked to just in front of the entryway. I still hadn't even considered crossing the threshold into the garden yet, something in me just couldn't have the wall between me and the home anymore.

Leading from the entryway to the front steps of the residence was a long path of creamy paving stones, set out perfectly flat, each one appearing to be smoothed by hand. At the opposite end of the path were a dozen steps leading up to the home's portico, each step wide and deep with symbols etched into their shallow rise. They matched the surrounding pomp of the home perfectly as if giving a visitor a triumphant ascent into the afterlife. On each side of the steps were two sphinxes made of gold, obsidian, and stones colored turquoise and rose.

The home itself stretched into the sky with four stories worth of walls, each topped with a terrace. Lattice sprawled out from each exit, peppered with ivy and flowers reaching out to corner posts, with additional lattice stretching out and down to the balcony ledges. More sphinxes rested atop numerous columns for each level of terrace, in addition to numerous griffins. In contrast to many of the neighboring buildings, the home was orderly and tended to, with all of its decorative vegetation meticulously manicured and embellished with ornate pottery of impressive size and design.

I hadn't yet completed my visual inventory of the

spectacle in front of me before I was startled by a voice that seemed to emanate from the house itself.

"Sir, can I help you?" A man shouted from the top of the steps. His voice spanned the gorgeous garden with volume, but without aggression. With one hand on his hip, he stood at such an angle that I couldn't tell if it was an arbitrary stance or one of preparatory defense, potentially grasping a weapon I couldn't see from my vantage point. Though I was being politely challenged, there was no immediate threat of conflict due to our distance.

"Hello!" I replied quickly, tossing my hand into the air. I backed away from the wall a few steps. "Is this the home of Neferhotep?" I asked, pretending not to be as keen and suspicious as I was. "I was told he was asking for me."

"And who exactly are you?" The man asked.

"My name is Briz," I yelled, only loud enough to be heard.

The man twisted into a more relaxed pose. As his torso straightened out, the full length of a blade swung out from behind his leg.

"Ah, yes, Briz! You are most welcome. My master Neferhotep has indeed been seeking you out," the man said.

I gestured at the entry way, from me to it, to confirm I had permission to enter. The man waved me in. I took a step forward, crossing the threshold into the garden, and began to traverse the beautiful path toward the home.

The guard—or whatever he was—interlocked his fingers and held them at his waist as I approached.

"If you will follow me," he said, "I will see if Neferhotep is at liberty to see you right now."

The fronds of a massive tree in the garden stole my attention. Though I continued walking towards the steps, my pace slowed. The flowers and trees seemed to flaunt themselves in this garden that was full of more life than even some of the most elaborate gardens in and around the temples. But as the steps neared, I focused forward once more and looked up to the guard.

"This way," he insisted.

The wide steps welcomed me though I felt uncomfortable stepping on them. As I ascended the intricately-designed steps I felt my shoulders bow in if just a bit. Once I reached the landing, the shadow of the portico cooled me and transformed my impression of the world around me. Feeling as though I had been picked up and placed in an entirely different existence, I felt my confidence crumble to uneasiness as I was escorted inside.

My eyes kept wanting to return to the floor whenever I would start to look around the impressive home. Never before had I seen such extravagance. Luxury on such a scale was previously unfathomable to me. Massive stone columns lining the home's main corridor climbed up to the ceiling four stories up and were engraved with countless varieties of the same types of symbols on the most sacred and intimidating of Egyptian sculptures. Other embellishments and carvings covered the columns and were filled with gold, silver, or with the richest of blues, creams, reds, and greens.

While being led to Neferhotep, the guard's heavy steps reverberated off the massive stone planters and statues that lined the corridor between the columns. Though the guard and I were the only ones in the corridor, the gilded and painted faces of gods and past pharaohs provided us with abundant company as we walked deeper into the residence. And when I finally found myself at ease enough to look past the statues and columns, I discovered there were in fact additional guards silently watching from the shadows, ready I'm sure, to respond to any need.

The corridor stretched on with the countless statues and columns obscuring whatever end to the corridor there may be. The corridor and most of the rooms branching off to both sides were covered, though we passed many areas with open ceilings streaming light onto courtyards, each one with their own garden, rivaling the largest and most lush of desert oases.

As we walked deeper and longer, the exact scope and size of the complex was lost to me while being overloaded with the colors, life, and energy of the building. But a wall at the end of the walkway finally presented itself and as the guard turned into a room, the sounds of birds rang out.

Still following the guard, I turned into the room and was immediately pummeled with disbelief. The room ahead was a gigantic, cavernous space, roughly half the size of the entire residence that I had already seen. Numerous ponds were scattered throughout the middle of the room with groves of vegetation and thick clusters of trees. Dozens upon dozens of aviaries sprung out from the walls, with a few smaller aviaries resting on stands throughout the room. Baboons raced through the contained tree canopy, and leapt from branches, or off the tops of columns as they played. More cats than I could count perched on the branches of smaller trees and groomed themselves in constructed meadows.

I didn't know if the guard I had been following had left, disappeared into the room, or if this interior wilderness had swallowed him up. Whatever his fate, I wasn't expecting to hear from the person I hadn't yet noticed.

"You'll have to forgive my hippo," the man said, startling me enough to whip my head and place him instantly. "She's usually much more personable than this. I was really hoping to show everyone off to you at once," he added. "But she's being shy."

The man was a good distance away from me, and despite the echoes of his voice bouncing throughout the room, I could hear him fairly well. He hadn't yet looked at me, and instead, began to traverse a path made of river rock to a small island in one of the ponds. He then reached into a bag tied at his waist and produced what must have been something edible before tossing it at a pair of baboons in the tree ahead of him. They caught it and instantly started rolling it around in their hands as they ate it.

I felt my face contort at the man's reference to having a hippo.

"This room is big," I said, "but if there was a hippo, I'd see it."

The man laughed and tossed another bit of food at the baboons before turning toward me. He crossed back over the rock path in the pond and approached.

"No," he said before laughing again. "Back in the corner over there…" he continued. "There's an exit dug into the floor that leads to a path which in turn leads to a series of natural tunnels. She likes to go down there when she's not feeling particularly sociable."

The man untied the bag of food from his waist and tossed it onto a nearby table. He then walked within a few feet of me and snapped his fingers. A servant that I hadn't yet seen flickered into my periphery, carrying a tray with fruit and a decanter.

I knew the man must have been Neferhotep, but I worked to keep any mannerisms in check and kept all outward appearances as calm and unassuming as possible. This huge home crushed my confidence. The wealth and adornments worried me. The accompanying power scared me. But I knew he wanted me there. Regardless of the reason, I knew I was needed for something. I had never taken any work for humans, so unless I had taken a bounty on one of his hippos or something, I was sure I had nothing to worry about. I was suspicious of everything, and open to possibilities. I had the advantage.

"So, are you Neferhotep?" I finally questioned.

The man took a wad of grapes off the servant's tray and nodded as he popped some in his mouth and chewed.

"I am," he said between bites.

"Neferhotep the scribe? A scribe?" I asked in clarification.

"Yes," he said dismissively while reaching for the wine decanter.

I accidentally allowed a small laugh to find its way through a sniff and a scoff.

Neferhotep stopped halfway from the tray to his mouth with the wine and looked at me.

"Well, you have to know that I'm going to ask what it is that you find funny," he said.

I quickly held up a hand with my palm out.

"Do you honestly think that I would believe this is the home of a scribe?" I asked, chuckling again.

"What do you know of the lives or resources of a scribe?" He asked, with noticeable agitation.

In feigned impatience, I let my eyes and head roll.

"Listen, I know the types of work scribes do and the types of people they do it for, and none of it would ever pay for something as grand as this."

Neferhotep slammed the decanter back on the tray. The servant holding it shot their free arm up to catch and balance it before everything fell off.

"Don't presume to know what work I do, who I do it for, or lump me in with any group of forgettable commoners. If you do, I will see that you regret it. Do you understand me?"

I rolled my head back to him and stared at him, visibly unflinching, but internally, I was wanting to scramble backwards, turn, and flee.

"It is true that I am a scribe," he added, calmly. "And it is true that I do the work of a scribe. And while I have no interest in discussing or revealing my employers, rest assured that I work for many of the most powerful in Egypt. I have documented laws set forth by kings, marriages of royalty, trade agreements between kingdoms, prayers of our most illustrious of priests, and declarations of war that resulted in the deaths of thousands. So, let me ask you a final time... *Do you understand me?*"

I swallowed my facade. I gulped my apathy and did all I could to stomp down the dark fear his last question instilled in me, and replied with a single nod.

Neferhotep walked towards me, holding his hands behind him.

"Good," he said, smiling slowly. "I'm glad to know that you understand me."

He stared at me for a time, holding his smile before finally releasing it. When his smile crumbled, he whipped around and snatched the bag of food off the table before marching back towards his baboons.

"Now that I'm reasonably assured that you're paying the proper amount of attention, and respect, I'm anxious to get to the reason for why I was looking for you."

I said nothing, trying to help my nerves get back to a semblance of calm and confidence. If he thought my silence was obedience, I was fine with him thinking that for now.

"As you can imagine, Briz," he said, grinding on my nerves with his use of my name so casually, "that in my line of work, I am exposed to matters of great distinction... wide-reaching impact, and immense horror. I am constantly being dictated to, and yes, sometimes I am at the mercy of some of the most important people to walk this earth. And occasionally, I bear the terrible burden of having to turn a blind eye to monsters. Miscreants of such depravity, masquerading around as good people, taking advantage… abusing… using… our fellow man and woman. But there are times, rare they may be, that I sometimes am in a position or am empowered to be in such a position, to have certain matters addressed. This is one of those times."

"Mmm, no," I said immediately as I turned to leave. "I thought for a minute after seeing all these animals that you might want me to catch something for you," I continued with my back to Neferhotep. "But now I know where this is going."

Before I could cross the threshold back into the main corridor, I heard Neferhotep clap. A stream of guards spilled out to block my exit. As they drew their swords, I pulled my club off my back. I stopped and prepared for the impending fight. But they stayed where they stood, poised and ready.

"I thought we had an understanding," Neferhotep said, his voice gently gliding across the room. "Part of that understanding includes your listening to everything I have to say… that you will remain until you are dismissed."

The guards didn't even look at me. With my back still to Neferhotep, I smiled and huffed. I pulled the strap away from my back and stowed my club behind me. I turned around.

"Yes, I'm proposing a bounty. A bounty for a human," he said. "And the very next thing I want you to hear, Briz, is that this man is vile. He is corrupt, grotesque, and uses his power to prey upon the weak and helpless to further his own needs. One of the most prominent priests in Memphis, this man uses the gods to steal, persuade, harm, and violate. He brings nothing to the people of Egypt, but pain."

I took a long, deep breath and let it spill slowly back out through my nose.

"I really don't understand why you want me to do

this," I said. "I'm a hunter of beasts, creatures, scorps. Not people."

"Oh, enough!" Neferhotep screamed quickly. "You and I both know that's a lie! You are a renowned hunter throughout the region of beasts, *and* other things. I know this for a fact!"

My heart began to pound an erratic rhythm as his demeanor violently shifted from arrogant aristocrat to a mysterious man with more knowledge of my past than he had initially let on. I tried to move past it.

"See, this right here. This situation right here is exactly the kind of stuff I stay clear of humans for. I hate the politics. The intrigue. I can't stand it. I only hunt things that can't drag me into their drama."

"Did you not hear me?" Neferhotep boomed. "I know better than that, Briz. I know where you're from, and what happened there! I would suggest that you cease your charade!"

I didn't know exactly what he may or may not have known, and I had no intention of confirming anything, but the fact that he would even allude to my past in the way he did stabbed me with a cold finality that I could no longer avoid or deny. I hung my head and scratched it while struggling to figure out what to say next.

"Of all the people who could do this," I asked, "all the experience out there. The people actively doing such work. All the power and riches at your disposal. Why do you want me to do this?"

Neferhotep seemed to genuinely consider my question as he rubbed his lips.

"Everyone in any position of power in this city is attached to another in some way. And then that person is attached to another. Any one person can be traced back to another. Any act can be attributed to another. Every trail in Egypt leads somewhere. You are a new trail, with no origination, and no destination. You cannot be traced back to anyone."

"Yet, you knew of me," I said. "You claim to know of my past. You... traced me."

"Yes, well," Neferhotep muttered through a new grin. He looked around the room as he spoke as if trying to contain laughter that would burst out at any moment. "I am the only one with your map, so to speak," he said. "Your past is safe with me."

"And if I refuse?" I asked.

"Well, you would be missing out on riches that you don't have the capacity to measure or understand!" Neferhotep exclaimed, bringing his arms up presenting his home as an example.

"What?" I asked. "You'd give me a home like this or something?"

"Mmm," Neferhotep replied, wagging his finger. "I wouldn't give you a home, but you would be paid more than enough to get started on such a comparable structure."

Something in me had to press him for the real implications of a refusal.

"That's it? I'd just miss out on getting rich?"

He turned to look at me. His body deflated with a forced exhaustion. But he immediately stood rigid once again and leaned over as if to whisper though we were dozens of feet apart.

"Do I really need to say it?"

"No," I said, smiling at the silent threat. "No, I guess you don't."

"Ah!" Neferhotep shouted, easily shifting conversation. "She's emerged! Come, Briz! Look!"

I looked up and walked slowly around the nearest clump of brush to match Neferhotep's line of sight. The hippopotamus had climbed up from the caves. Neferhotep ran over, reaching into his bag for some kind of food. I turned and marched for the line of guards. I'd had enough.

As I approached the guards, not one flinched or hinted that they would make way for me to leave. I flexed my fist and reached over my back. But before I could grab my club, Neferhotep shouted out from behind me.

"Briz!" He yelled.

I stopped and looked partially over my shoulder.

"You have until tomorrow night to prepare and accept. Next time I see you, I will either be giving you further instructions, or... well... something else."

Neferhotep ended the conversation with a clap.

The line of guards broke and allowed me to pass.

Chapter Thirteen - A Moving Target

Briz

As soon as I passed between Neferhotep's guards I took off in a sprint down the corridor, at least I did in my mind. Despite the panic induced by Neferhotep presumably knowing about my past, I bit down and concentrated on one step at a time. *Stomp. Stomp. Easy pace. Take it easy.* The smiles I flashed at the subsequent guards on my way out had to rival the performances of the world's best entertainers. And though I felt small, powerless, and exposed, more than I ever had in my life, I didn't notice how much I had been sweating until I crossed back out onto the portico and felt a hardy breeze smack my forehead.

I had no desire to help Neferhotep and just wanted to find Bayla and get out of the city. I didn't know what would happen after that, or if I would be able to continue my profession of the past many years. I just knew I couldn't and didn't want to kill the priest. And like I had told Bayla, I only wanted to check into why he was looking for me. *Now I know, and now I'm done with it.*

Once out of the residence, my pace was fairly

measured. But, as I passed through the streets on my return trip to the market, my steps quickened, and by the time I had reached the primary temple, I was jogging. I dipped back into the market and started scanning for Bayla.

Being deep in the crowd again helped me relax, but also allowed my pent-up adrenaline and emotion start to work me over. As my impatience mounted while searching the stalls, tables, and booths for Bayla, my throat started to hurt. I was waiting for everyone in the congested market to turn and start laughing at Briz, the silly beast hunter. Briz, the lovable creature hunter. And after they finished laughing, they would start a new round of humiliation, laughing at my past that wasn't as anonymous as I had thought all these years. They would laugh at me, my past, and the time where I lost all control. But if they too had seen my slaughtered daughter or heard my wife's weak voice as she perished in my arms, they wouldn't laugh.

I stomped and weaved around in odd patterns. Something in me knew I wasn't searching efficiently but I didn't adjust my behavior. I just kept stumbling around aimlessly snapping quick glimpses of the market as my neck craned, my head whipped to and fro, but eventually, with the greatest of luck, I spotted her. She was sitting on the ground leaning up against a stall. As if I had been wandering the desert for months, I carelessly grabbed people and shoved them out of the way so I could get to a drink of water. And so I could get to Bayla.

"Bayla!" I blurted as I cut through the throng. "Bayla."

She looked up and saw me, but then let her chin fall back to her chest. One hand was draped on a knee, and the other played with the dirt around her. When I reached her, I stood next to her and peered around suspiciously as I spoke.

"We need to get out of here," I said.

I kept looking around but shot her a quick glimpse as she looked up.

"What?" She asked.

"I checked it out and it's no good. Let's get out of here."

"What's wrong?" Her voice took on more of a worried tone than one of pure concern.

I looked down and back up. I turned and examined the crowd before completing a spin and sitting down next to her.

"I was right. He wants me to kill somebody... a crooked priest," I said. "But that's not the scary part. He knows me. He knows my past."

Bayla flung her hands into the air.

"And what exactly *is* your past? I don't know what you're talking about," she said.

"Right—I know. We can get into that later, but he more or less said he'd kill me if I refused. Let's go."

"Wait a minute, Briz," Bayla said, rekindling her agitation from when I first set out to find Neferhotep. "You do what you need to do, but I need to spend some time here to rule out the Egyptians."

I continued looking around with a jumpy-eyed paranoia.

"I'll help, but we need to be gone no later than tomorrow night. That's the deadline for giving him a decision or not."

"Why don't you just go," Bayla asked, perturbed. "Just tell me where you're going and I'll catch up, okay?"

"Maybe, we'll see," I whispered back. "Can we just get out of the market? He's probably got people watching me. Come on."

Bayla grunted a growl of annoyance.

"Hey!" She shouted in my face, waving her hand in

my face. "Don't you see that what I need to take care of keeps getting pushed farther and farther back? Oh, let me just help you kill a nest of scorpirons. Oh, you'll be right back after you check on another job after saying you'll help me, *before* you take any other work. Now we have to leave the city that's potentially rife with information just because you got scared. Do what you need to do, Briz. I'm obviously on my own."

She pushed off the side of the booth and jumped to her feet before getting swallowed up with the flowing crowd. I shot up to follow.

"Bayla!" I said, jogging to catch up while banging into people. "Bayla. Listen to me. I'm not taking the job."

She somehow seemed to be navigating the crowd better than I was. With each of her steps, I felt like I had to stop and let a cart pass, apologize to a man carrying a sack of flour that I ran into, or dip out of the way of children running past. Each time I would catch up to Bayla, I'd do all I could to reassure her.

"I'm not going to do it, Bayla. I'm here. I'm ready to help. Let's just get out of this market so we can come up with a plan. Okay?"

She wouldn't stop. She argued with me over her shoulder.

"You'll just find a way to avoid helping me again. Some old friend you'll see. Some kind of pressing business you'll need to tend to. I'm done. Do you hear me? I'm done!"

"Bayla! I'm asking you to just wait a minute. I want to help. Nothing new. No more delays. I just want to get out of the mark—"

She suddenly came to a dead stop in the middle of the busy market path. Frozen in place, she stared ahead and to the right. I finally had the opportunity to catch up and stand behind her. I tried to follow her line of sight to whatever had caught her eye.

"Bayla?" I asked. "What's wrong?"

She wouldn't say. I peered ahead trying to get a clue as to what she was looking at. *Was it a person?* No. No one else was stopped, and her head wasn't tracking anyone as they walked past. Was it one of the merchants ahead of us? While squinting to examine the items in the various booths, I saw nothing that stuck out. Nothing that seemed important. Not to me anyway.

Bayla inched closer to the row of booths, simultaneously aware of and oblivious to the crowd around her. I took the opportunity of the distraction to calm myself down. We had about a day to get out of the city, so I had time to calm myself. I had time to relax.

"What's the matter, Bayla? What is it?"

After getting within a few arm lengths of the nearest booths, I scrambled to place what the object of her attention was. My eyes darted uneasily back and forth between Bayla, the merchants, and their wares. And just before reaching out to grab her shoulder, I saw what must have caught her attention.

As if trying not to disturb the eternal rest of her sister and parents, Bayla stepped softly over to the merchant's table which looked as though it were constructed recently. Its wood was clean and bright. On the table were all manners of hand tools, cups, dolls, figurines of pets, bread, clothing, and jewelry. It wasn't the booth of an artisan. This was something else. Bayla leaned over the table and placed her hands on the edge as she looked down on the odd assortment of items.

"Ah! Hands off the table, please," the merchant said. "Is there something you'd like to see?"

With absolutely no indication of what was about to happen, Bayla blasted out in wild violence, swiping two dolls and a figurine of a serpent off the table. She raked her other arm across, sending everything else flying into the street. She then slammed her knee under the table and sent it flipping back into the lap of the merchant. His eyes were stung wide in fear, and before he could shift to anger, Bayla loomed over him, shoving her fists clenched around the dolls and wooden snake into his face.

"Where did you get these?" She screamed. Her voice grated with raw hate. "Where?"

"Bayla!" I snapped quickly, not wanting to add too much to the volume. "What are you doing?"

The merchant tried to push her away, but Bayla parted his arms with hers, flinging them back out to his side.

"Where did these come from?" She screamed.

The surrounding citizens and merchants had stopped to watch the scene unfold.

"Bayla!" I tried again as I reached for her. "Come on. What is it? Everyone is—"

As I brushed my fingertips on her shoulder, she spun around and shoved me in the chest, knocking me back into the crowd. My vision throbbed from the surge of surprise as my adrenaline temporarily spiked. I froze, gasping for air and watched Bayla's primal interrogation unfold.

"Get away from me, you crazy woman!" The merchant snapped bitterly.

Bayla shook the items wildly in front of his face again.

"These are mine!" She said. Her voice tearing into the sky. As he continued, she looked down at her fist. "This one is mine. This one is my sister's, and Lady Ariadne's serpent here—our father carved this for me! How did you get these?"

The man hesitated as his face twitched and strained under the shadow of Bayla and her fury.

In just seconds and with no answer, Bayla grabbed the man by a clump of shirt and shook him out of his seat, throwing him to the ground. With one hand still clutching the dolls and snake, she reached back and slid an axe out from behind her.

"Tell me how you came to have these. Tell me!" She screamed. Her voice had morphed. It was deeper and ripped confidently throughout the market as if she were a woman twice her age, with three times the amount of misery she had known in her life so far—which was already more than a soul should have to endure.

My mind raced with different thoughts sprinting in varying directions. *This is going to get back to Neferhotep. They'll associate her with me. What would that mean? Would it make getting out of Memphis harder? Should I let her do this and be done with her? Should I just try to grab her and drag her away?*

The merchant's face had shriveled from taut and defiant to wrinkled and worried. His arms and legs were drawn up, confusedly preparing to defend against whatever Bayla was about to do.

"This man clearly wants to die," Bayla shouted. She spun slowly pointing her axe out in front of her. "My village was destroyed. All of its people killed, and these toys are from my home!"

"If you will not tell me how you got them," she said, completing her rotation, "then you will have to pay for the lives of my people with your own blood."

She lifted her arm quickly, uninterested in giving the man any additional opportunity to speak. The crowd began to mumble various sentiments of "Don't! Wait, wait!" And, "Someone grab her!"

I had to stop her. The situation just didn't feel right, and I doubted the aging man on the ground perpetrated the attack. I lunged forward for her again, but just before getting my hand under her arm, the old man erupted with fearful ramblings.

"His name's Ahmose!" The merchant shouted. "Ahmose! Ahmose! A spear captain. He only recently returned home and sold me many things. That's it! I just bought these things from him!"

The man's eyes were wide as he awaited Bayla's reaction. His hands shook nervously as they rested on his chest while his legs remained bent up to his waist.

"Bayla," I whispered while eying the crowd. "Ahmose. He said he got them from Ahmose."

Hoping she would break out of her rage so we could get out of there, I repeated the merchant's information so she might focus on the next course of action.

With a mixture of urgency and slight melody, I spoke again.

"A spear captain. Ahmose. Let's go find him."

Though we were still in the massive market with thousands of people, the deafening silence was all I heard. We were exposed, and had the attention of hundreds around us.

"Bayla, come on," I said, moving around to look her in the face. I reached up for the side of her arm. "He gave you what you needed," I added. "Come, let's get out of here."

Bayla's eyes had long since relaxed. She was rigid and poised, ready to kill. But she couldn't quite disarm herself.

"Bayla," I tried again, speaking up a bit. "Let's go."

She looked at me. She stared into my eyes as if replaying the altercation in her mind, and listening back to all I had said, reassuring her that we had information to act on—waiting to confirm she could believe the merchant... that she could believe me. I nodded. She turned her eyes back to the merchant and lowered her axe, slipping it behind her back. As the axe fell and the blade caught the loop around her waist, she shot out into the crowd. After catching eyes with the merchant quickly, I jumped away and caught up.

We darted away from the scene so quickly that we found ourselves once again lost in the sea of the surrounding market crowd. And as I chased after Bayla yet again, I found my agitation growing despite our return to relative anonymity. While collecting my thoughts, I let her weave and delve farther away from where we had stopped. When I felt good about the spot, in an especially congested intersection of market paths, I jogged ahead of Bayla and spun in front of her.

"If you're really serious about avenging your family..." I began, before she tried to weave around me. I threw my arms out and corralled her. "You'll stop and listen to me."

She tried to dash around to the other side.

"Do you even know where you're going?" I asked with a flippant bite.

"To find Ahmose," she said, glaring through me. She then tried to duck under my arm, but I lowered it, caught her in the waist and shoved her back gently.

"And where is Ahmose?" I asked, turning and pointing in the direction she had been marching. "Is he over there? How did you find that out?"

She gave up on trying to evade me and stared up at the sky.

"Or maybe that's him over there!" I suggested. "Oh, wait, no, that's him over there!"

"Bayla!" I continued, stepping closer to her and shoving my face into hers. "We don't even know what he looks like! You need to stop. You need to calm down. Think. Plan."

"Well, thank you so much for finally showing an

interest," she blasted back. "Finally starting to do what you agreed to do. We're only having this conversation right now because I got the first bit of information!"

"All right! Yes, I know!" I squeezed through gritted teeth. "I'm sorry that I wanted to check on that other job. I just wanted to find out what it was about. I just wanted to see what the pay was."

"Because, getting paid is all you care about, right?" She said with eyes squinting a ray of contempt at me.

"It's all I've ever known, damn it!" I shouted back with full volume. "It's just been me, for years, surviving, barely existing, wanting to give up. Do you think you're the only one to have everything you've ever known ripped away from you? Do you?"

Bayla had nothing to say as her eyes relaxed.

"See?" I said, fueled by the everlasting coals of my painful past. I inched back towards her, coating my next comments in a smooth plea.

"If you'll just give me a minute and stop tearing through the city, we can figure out how to get this done, and maybe even survive it. I'll do right by you. I'll make good on my promise to you. But Neferhotep wanted me to give him an answer about the priest by tomorrow night, and if we're still here, well, that scene back there won't exactly help us blend in."

Bayla's shoulders fell. I watched as she twirled her tongue around in her closed mouth. I backed away from her, giving us both a bit of space. After swallowing, her lips finally parted.

"I thought you were going to back out," she said through an exhausted sigh. "I thought I was in this alone."

"I know," I acknowledged. "I'm sorry. I didn't handle this right at all. Like I said, I've just always been on the lookout for the next job for years. It's habit."

I walked around to her side, removing myself as an obstacle from her path forward and leaned in from the side to whisper.

"But listen," I started. "We have a name. And we know he's in Egypt. Let's find him and take care of this."

* * *

Some of the best meals I've ever had are the ones I've enjoyed while thinking about how to kill something. As Bayla and I sat outside a butcher's hut on the edge of the city, eating, my epiphany—sprinkled with savory memories of past meals—struck me in a concrete and morbid way. For the first time since I started taking bounties and hunting professionally, I realized that there's just something about planning a hunt that seems to go hand in hand with ripping bread, slugging wine, pinching at figs, and slicing goat meat. Chewing and chomping food seemed to help the keep wheel of ideas on how to kill spinning in my head. But this meal was different.

"I'm closing up for the night," the butcher said, leaning out over the ledge of his shop's window. "Need anything else?"

Bayla and I shook our heads as we chewed. Two men across from us grunted in the negative. A third man by himself waved the offer away. The butcher swiped at the stick holding up a bank of boards that fell into place, sealing the window shut.

Bayla and I ate in silence for the longest time and at first, it seemed neither of us could east fast enough. We each tore into a few bites of bread first, followed by some of our cheese, with varying orders and combinations of olives, garlic, dates, and cucumber after that. I don't think Bayla noticed that I was paying attention, but I love watching people eat. It doesn't have anything to do with their mouths or anything like that. I'm fascinated by the order they choose their foods. I finished just ahead of Bayla, and as our food ran out, we started to shape a plan.

"I would think this guy should be fairly easy to locate, given his rank," I said. "The biggest challenge will be to find out what garrison he commands... where in the city he may be. We might be able to find out tonight and if not take care of it tonight... first thing tomorrow."

Bayla continued chewing through a nod, but rushed to swallow.

"Why are we in such a rush again?" She asked. "I obviously don't want to wait, but, why the hurry?"

A breeze blew through the small yard where we sat, bringing with it the scent of smoke. It was probably just a fire from a nearby home, but I didn't like the smell. I never have. Fire and its accompanying smoke were old elements. Old wonders. And though it moved around the world, created in countless ways and taking just as many forms throughout the years, I hated it. It was always there. Always aware. Always watching me.

"Neferhotep wants an answer by tomorrow night," I said, flinching slightly at the smell in the air.

Bayla finished chewing and wiped her mouth. She leaned back and looked over to the other men, but sat back up and leaned closer.

"Why does he think he can... I don't know..." She said, struggling to find the words. "What's all this about your past you said he knew about?"

The smell of the fire lingered. As it settled over the area, small hints of light popped up around the city. More fires were lit as darkness consolidated its hold over the world and seemingly mocked me as the innumerable flames surrounded us.

The two men eating together erupted in laughter at what must have been a final joke between them. They got up and took off down the street. Only the man by himself remained with his back to us.

My vision throbbed out and back into focus. The memory of my past wrath and the human blood I spilled decades before flew past my mind's eye as grotesque and vivid as the day it happened.

"I have only ever been paid to kill beasts… creatures… pests," I began, loud enough only to pierce the smoke-stained air between me and Bayla. "But I have killed men—only because I wanted them dead. And I have never regretted ending one of those lives."

After my eyes drifted to a distant palace wall with so many of the small flames, I despised staring back at me, I turned back to Bayla, belatedly aware of what I had said. Her chest rose and fell quickly.

"I wasn't much older than you," I said, letting my eyes droop to the table. "As they have for centuries, the Egyptians sent armies into my country, raiding the villages and land. Some Egyptian infantry came across my home outside Kerma and murdered my wife and daughter."

Bayla gasped and covered her mouth as her eyes sprung wide.

I breathed in deeply to steady myself as the combined loss and hate resurfaced within me.

"I spent the next two days tracking them," I continued. "I watched them and followed them and made sure they were alone. I crept into their camp the second night and killed them and left them to rot and roast in the sun where they took their last breath."

Bayla whimpered behind her hands but stifled herself immediately.

"I know your lust for vengeance, Bayla," I said. I looked over at the man by himself out of suspicious habit and leaned in even closer to her.

"I have felt that same pain. That same need. And though it takes a chunk out of your very soul to see it through, I know what it is to need that. I swear to you that I will help you avenge your family."

She finally let a crunchy sob fall into her hands, still cupping her mouth. She closed her eyes and leaned into the hands that poorly shielded her from emotion. She eventually sat up, shaking her head.

"I would have told you sooner," I said, anticipating her pitiful remarks of empathy. "But, I don't know."

Still crying softly, she brought her hands up to wipe her eyes and scraped down the sides of her face. Her eyes shot up to the stars as if searching for what to say next. I was confident I knew what she was thinking and just wanted to move past it.

"You didn't know, Bayla. You just didn't," I said.

Whether it was appreciation for my empathy, a release of her sympathy, a combination, or something else, she replied with a cascade of heartfelt sobs that rippled out into our disgusting smoke-scented surroundings.

To try and wrap up the storm of emotion that was eating away at the peace of apathy I had created for myself over the past many years, I grabbed her hand and bent over to catch her eye.

"I'm with you. From now until you have the blood you justifiably crave, I'm with you."

Bayla replied with a tight squeeze of my hand in return with a poorly attempted restraint of her tear-laden smile.

"Thank you, Briz. Thank you," she rushed out through quivering lips.

I tapped her on her hand as it rested on mine.

"So, how do we find this Ahmose, hmm?" I asked.

Before Bayla could reply, the lone customer, who

had previously only hacked what must have been feigned, painful coughs, spun up and off the bench. As the man thrust forward, bringing the point of his spear within inches of my head, a dozen infantry drew their swords and flew out from the shadows, encircling us.

"You've found him," the spearman said.

Chapter Fourteen - A Proposal Reconsidered

Bayla

I reached back for my axes.

"Hey, hey!" One of the infantrymen barked. "Move those arms again and I'll cut 'em off!"

Instead of moving my arms, I turned my head just enough to look at Briz. He let out a gritty sigh as his head drooped.

He didn't need to say anything.

"I heard you were asking about me earlier," Ahmose said, still leaning forward, spear poised. His voice was amiable. Almost jovial. He pivoted and shifted the focus of his spear to me.

"Specifically, you," he said, beginning to smile, but the expression fell almost immediately. He tilted his head and strained his neck forward.

"Hannu," he said while continuing to stare. "Bring your torch closer to the girl. I want to see her better."

One of the surrounding swordsmen walked towards us and stuck the torch out at me. Its heat warmed my skin.

"Ah, you are very beautiful," Ahmose said. "Though young and fairer-skinned than most of our people. Where are you from?"

"You know *exactly* where I'm from!" I yelled, saying nothing else as my eyes fixated on a host of fleshy spots I wanted to dig an axe into.

"What?" Ahmose asked. "You don't really think you can make a scene like that and not be found, do you?"

I didn't care that I couldn't get to my axes, nor that Briz and I both were surrounded. Like looking across the top of a fire, my vision blurred with rage.

"Bayla..." Briz warned.

In the stillness that followed, only hints of a distant conversation could be heard—that and the crackling of the soldier's torch. Ahmose spun his spear out of its offensive position and stood up. Some of the swordsmen around us shifted their feet. They seemed to be relaxing some, and I only grew angrier.

"Don't insult me or the memory of my village by playing stupid, Ahmose. You know where I'm from. And you know what these are!"

As I reached down into my pouch to grab the dolls and snake, the soldier with the torch jumped back into his group's circle. As he rejoined them, each of the men around us extended their sword arms at us, pointed them at the sky, and as they brought them back down, snapped them to the left, then the right, clanging the flats of their blades against the blades of the men next to them. After the fast, synchronized movement was complete, each sword pulsed a brilliant gold flash ahead of it, revealing a ghostly clone of each weapon.

In the two seconds it took for the soldiers to magically extend their offensive reach, Ahmose stepped back, thrust his spear into the sky and followed its tip into the air with his eyes. When he brought it back down and assumed another offensive posture of his own, his spear had also been magically duplicated.

When we noticed the men were preparing to attack, I whipped my arms back and grabbed my axes instead of going for the toys. While Briz produced his massive club and dagger, I tapped my axes together and produced a protective dome over us.

Having surprised each other with our displays, we stared at each other awkwardly through, and over, our enchantments.

"We told you about going for those axes," Ahmose said calmly.

"I wasn't going for the axes," I snipped. "I was going for these!"

I took both axes in one hand, reached into my pouch and pulled out the dolls and snake.

"These are from my village! My home! You took them when you killed my family!"

Ahmose took longer to respond than I expected. After stepping backward, it was difficult to see his face behind the brightness of the conjured weapons.

"Did you hear me?" I screamed. "You're nothing but a murderer!"

Ahmose's conjured spear began to move. As it and the real spear retracted back to Ahmose, fear crushed the air out of my chest.

"Briz," I said in a panic. "He's going to—"

Before I could finish, Ahmose launched his spear at us. The conjured one hit our dome first, sending a weakening wave of sizzling cracks rippling over it. Almost immediately after, the real spear hit what was left of our protective dome, causing it to disintegrate into falling sand. With nothing left to get stuck in, Ahmose's spear plopped and bounced to the ground. I looked down at it in awe, in confusion, and in fear.

Ahmose stretched out his hand and willed the spear to fly back into it.

After catching his spear, he stomped towards us while his men took a few steps in and constricted their circle around us. A few others came closer and shoved me and Briz back down onto the benches.

"I will not allow some foreigner," he began, flinging his hand dismissively at me, "to accuse me—"

"Come on," Briz shouted in rapid, hateful bursts. "The man in the market said you sold them to him!"

Ahmose raised a hand, summoning some of the other swordsmen to his side. He then shifted his feet and looked at Briz with a face tense with confusion.

"And who are you, exactly?" He asked Briz.

"I'm her friend," he replied.

"Her friend," Ahmose repeated. "And where are you from?"

Briz sniffed.

"South," he said.

"South," Ahmose echoed before laughing through his own sniffs and hums. "South is great," he said, mocking Briz. Ahmose turned to his men. "Have any of you been to South? Great place, South."

A wave of mumbled laughs rippled around the circle of Egyptians. After the laughter amongst them had died down, Ahmose turned back to Briz.

"Anywhere in particular, South?"

"No," Briz replied immediately.

Ahmose rolled his eyes, and before stepping back

towards me, reached back and slapped Briz. Ahmose leaned over and caught Briz in the eye and held his gaze.

"So, as I was saying," Ahmose continued, turning back to me. "I will not allow you to accuse me, of anything really. Especially of something I did not do."

I looked over at Briz as Ahmose spoke. He seethed through gritted teeth as he wiped his bleeding lip. His eyes peered out from under his brow, compressed with fury.

"I have killed, yes," Ahmose added while strolling around in front of us. "I have destroyed and ruined. I have cleansed regions and wiped cities off the face of the world."

He completed his final circle and stopped in front of me. His solid baritone voice dragged along the depths of its range.

"I have done and will do anything required of me by my king, for the glory of Egypt, and for the eternal pleasure of Ptah."

He reached down and ripped the dolls out of my hand, with the serpent falling to the ground.

"But I did not take these. I didn't steal these," he said as he glanced at them. "They were part of a collection of items sold to me by another. I picked through them and had the rest sold at the market."

I wanted to scream in frustration. My heart raced and I had to look down as my mind peppered me with thoughts.

Who then? Who sold them to you? I wanted to ask. *But he's not going to tell us. We're stuck here at the mercy of him and his men. Too many steps backward to count, for a single step forward.*

"So who was it?" Briz growled.

Ahmose pulled away and wiped his face while looking around at his men and exchanging laughter. He grinned with eyebrows dipped inward with confusion.

"Now why would I tell you that?" Ahmose said, through continued chuckling. "You were obviously out to kill me, which I could, and probably will kill you for here, and now. If for some reason I allow you to live, why would I tell you? Just so you can go and kill this other poor person?"

He clicked his tongue rapidly while shaking his head. "No, no, no. I don't think so."

Ahmose's eyes glided back and forth between me and Briz. When they eventually sprung wide, giving up on a reply from either of us, he tapped the butt of his spear on the ground and shot it up into the sky, once again following the point upwards with his eyes. The spear pulsed with golden light. After reaching up to grab the spear's shaft with both hands, the spear flashed again as he pulled a second spear out from his original. He brought them both down, pointing one each at me and Briz.

I started to shake. I didn't want to die.

I looked over at Briz, swallowing and holding my face as neutral as I could while hoping he had an idea on what to do next. But my desperation spawned an option of my own. I blurted it out as quickly but coherently as I could.

"I'll teach you my magic," I said.

Ahmose's spears remained trained on us. The original, glowing with its stores of magical energy, and the other, semi-translucent, glowing fainter in his other hand.

I had no idea if he was the least bit interested in my skills, or if he knew similar skills already. But his silence gave me hope as he lorded over us with frightful ferocity. Though the light from his spear and the swords of the men around us basked us in pulsating swaths of light, I felt extremely cold, surrounded by the darkness of doubt. As the delay grew, however, I began to consider that he and his men only knew offensive magic and if so, a wise military tactician might see the benefit to my defensive arts.

"You'll teach us your skills, in return for what, exactly?" He finally replied.

He's considering it!

"...for the name of the person that sold you those items from my village," I said, finding more strength in my voice than I realized I had. I wanted to keep the conversation moving past our potential deaths.

Ahmose's eyes danced quickly.

"But that's not all, though, is it?"

Briz and I exchanged confused glances.

"You're also expecting me to turn a blind eye to what you plan to do with this person once you have their name!" Ahmose said.

"You've said yourself, Ahmose," Briz began. "You've killed. Destroyed. Cleansed."

Briz slung his chin out at me as he continued.

"This girl's family was murdered. Her village destroyed. You can understand vengeance, right? What's one man's death to you in the name of avenging family, especially if you are given new skills for your men to protect themselves?"

Ahmose's stance remained unchanged as we negotiated.

"I'll give you the name and let you act on it as you wish, after you teach me and my men," he dictated.

"No, no," Briz responded with surprising politeness. He seemed calm and confident as if bartering for fruit.

"You know this is our only way of staying alive, and trying to get justice for her family," Briz said.

"I will teach you what I know," I said. "I will. Track me. Have us followed as we take care of this person. Do whatever you need to do, but after I kill the person that destroyed my family, I will teach you."

Ahmose remained rigid; his spears ready to puncture our throats any second. But up and through the light of his weapons, I saw his eyes. They scanned the area, seemingly weighing the disposition of his men. But he quickly settled his sight back on me. And with a movement of his spear that shocked and startled me, causing me to flinch, he brought his physical spear up to his side, and with an underhanded fling, tossed its magical clone into the air, right in-between my and Briz's heads.

"His name is Minmontu. High Priest of Heka."

As Ahmose revealed the man's name, he stepped back once again into a relaxed posture. His surrounding guard stepped back as well, but not before slapping the sides of their blades against those of the men next to them, dismissing their cloned extensions.

I felt my jaw drop in relief from anticipation for the answer. My eyes unfocused and spun on various spots on the ground as I worked to process what had just unfolded. But my insides felt as though they were quivering. Relief reverberated out from my jaw to the rest of my body. Tears bubbled up from the torrent of emotions ranging from an expectation of imminent death, to hope, to answers. I looked over at Briz, smiling.

He wasn't smiling. His vision was trained ahead at nothing. Something was wrong. Ahmose hadn't picked up on it yet and continued.

"We will release you, but as you yourself suggested," he warned, "we will have you followed. We will monitor your progress. You will not know where we are. You will not see us. But I assure you, when you have killed this man, we will make sure you find your way back to me."

As Ahmose motioned at some of his men, I took

advantage of our newly-bestowed freedom and slid over onto Briz's bench.

"Briz," I whispered, trying to minimize my concern. "What is it?"

He looked up at me and licked his lips, but he turned, shying at the proximity of Ahmose and his men. As some of the swordsmen approached Ahmose for directions before departing, Ahmose spun and shifted, gesturing at various elements of his group. It wasn't long before Ahmose caught Briz's suspicious posture. He held his hand up to his men and looked down at Briz.

"Well, what's the problem, South?" Ahmose jabbed.

Briz's face was taut, but calm. His eyes flicked back and forth between me, the ground, and Ahmose.

Ahmose whistled at his men to bring all commotion to a halt.

"Okay, South," Ahmose heaved through gritty breath. As he berated Briz, he stomped over to him, pointing with his free hand. His voice grew shorter and louder.

"This arrangement we just made can get canceled very quickly," Ahmose continued. "I do not have the patience for this mysterious reluctance and sudden silence, and I do not care to have any information withheld from me!"

Ahmose paused, waiting for Briz to speak up, but didn't wait long.

"All right," he said, vexed.

Ahmose shot up, spun his spear around and pivoted on his torso, bringing the spear around, preparing to strike.

"Briz!" I shouted, completely lost for what the issue was.

Ahmose stopped it inches from his nose. Briz's hands flew up, ready to try and grab the spear.

And then it hit me.

"Someone hired him to kill him!" I shouted, remembering Briz's bounty he said he was offered.

"What?" Ahmose snapped.

"Minmontu," I blurted. "Someone wants Briz to kill him."

Briz turned to me, fuming.

"*What* is she talking about, South?" Ahmose said with exhausted patience. "Who wants you to kill him?"

"He was going to kill you," I whispered to Briz.

"Come on, South!" Ahmose shouted. "Out with it!"

Briz sighed and shook his head.

"Neferhotep. Neferhotep tried to hire me," Briz answered.

With his spear still inches from Briz's face, Ahmose glanced around at his men.

"Which Nefer—" he began, interrupting himself. "The scribe?"

With a fresh blanket of confusion and panic strangling any sense of calm I had, my eyes darted between Ahmose, his spear tip, Briz, and the equally-confused swordsmen near us.

Briz nodded.

Ahmose remained still for moment, but abruptly flew up, twirling his staff once more to his side. He turned to leave and waved at his men.

"This is ridiculous," he said after a sharp sigh of annoyance. "Bring them. Let's go talk to Neferhotep."

* * *

I had started to understand what Briz alluded to previously about the drama that surrounds the hunting of people. Every revelation was a lead to a new revelation. Every truth was a lie. Every lie had some truth. The truth was merely an annoying prankster shifting, changing, and hopping from prairie to desert to city to sea—beholden only to the person with enough stamina, desire, or luck to find it. And ever since my village had been destroyed, truth had displayed numerous times how much of a master of evasion it was.

After being led through the empty market, streets, and corridors with no light save the carried torches, we arrived at what I assumed was some kind of military complex. *Maybe Ahmose and his men needed to tend to something on our way to see Neferhotep*, I thought.

"No, I don't believe it's too late," Ahmose whispered to a subordinate. "Run up and tell them Ahmose is here and needs to see Neferhotep on an urgent matter."

What? I asked myself in disbelief. *This is a home? One man's home?* When Briz went to check on the bounty, and I stayed behind in the market, I couldn't have imagined such grandiosity belonging to one man.

"He lives *here*?" I asked to anyone that would confirm.

"Yes," Ahmose said, not even looking at me. "Not all of us are born in the bush, or desire to stay there if we are."

"Well, that's a bit much, isn't it?" Briz asked of Ahmose, his voice crisp with disapproval. "We were making agreements just a little while ago."

Ahmose waved at us and our swordsmen escorts as he stepped under the arch that joined the outer walls.

"We'll see what good those agreements are after we find out what Neferhotep thinks about all of this."

Even in the moonlight, with assistance from nearby torchlight and flames from braziers, I could see the massive spectrum of beauty in Neferhotep's front garden. Lush petals of lavender and gold unfurled extravagantly amid soil-colored buds and bulbs, reminding me of the richness of home. There wasn't such color and life in most of the city that I could tell. Quite a bit of effort had been put into creating this private oasis. And while I was enthralled with the garden's foreign beauty that made me feel at home, I almost missed Ahmose's man jogging back down the path towards us.

"I was told he will see us, but he doesn't appreciate the hour of our visit," the swordsman said.

Ahmose whipped his arm, gesturing for the soldier to get out of his way as he continued marching up the path.

"Yes, yes," Ahmose grunted.

In front of us, one of Neferhotep's servants stepped out onto the landing at the top of the steps.

"Hurry up, Ahmose," the servant said. "He's only agreeing to see you at this hour because of your... guests."

"Do not rush me," Ahomse said, holding a shushing hand up to him as he strode up the walk. "I have urgent business for Neferhotep and am making every effort to respect his time. I need no comment from you."

As the two argued, I felt myself slow to a stop as my head slowly flipped backwards.

Neferhotep's home wasn't humbling or beautiful, as many of the temples or other structures in the city were. This very large, bulbous home was sharp and vast. There were no hints of intricacy or reservation. The walls soared up with fat slabs of stone, lacking in decoration and plain in design. Despite the balconies between the floors, the only defining characteristic of the building was its size, which it more than excelled at.

I followed the clean lines of the building up, down, and to the sides, and would frequently look behind me, puzzled at the contrasting consideration exhibited in the garden, the statues within it, and those that lined the path between the outer walls and the home's entryway, and the path itself. There had to have been unifying characteristics between the garden and the home, and I lost myself in trying to identify them.

"Bayla!" Ahmose barked. My mind twitched out of its inspection of the home. The majority of the guards, Ahmose, and Briz were waiting for me at the top of the stairs. I jogged up the steps to catch up.

After rejoining the others, we passed through the portico and walked by the noticeably irritated servant. At first, I felt like I needed to apologize, but I dismissed the notion after hearing Ahmose blurt, "Where is he?"

"Follow me," the servant said flatly.

As we started walking again, the interior of the home answered my curiosity about why the exterior of the home was so plain. Inside the house was every bit of luxury and beauty that I could fathom, and more that I previously didn't know how to fathom. Columns—taller than I knew could be erected—were etched, painted and decorated with images of gods, pharaohs, and scenes of Egypt. Statues of gold and silver stood on hulking tables of ornate ornamentation. Walls were constructed from colored blocks and draped with fabric. More fabric swam down from the ceiling and surrounding balconies in luscious bundles.

Sounds of animals from an indeterminate distance made me feel as if I were simultaneously inside and outside. My inability to decide if I should have felt endangered mixed with the surrounding opulence and created a sense of insecurity that I had never felt before. I was scared of it, and taken by it. I didn't know how to feel or how to think. All I could think while in my captivated trance of awe was that I wanted to see more as I followed the group deeper into the home. After hearing the sound of a splash to my right, I looked over to see a pool of water, but the group turned left into a different room. The servant jogged a few steps ahead of our group.

"Neferhotep, if I may," the servant began. "Here is Ahmose, and his men."

The servant turned to me and Briz. His eyebrows darted up quickly.

"...and his... guests," he added.

Neferhotep stood towards the other end of the room, looking at a papyrus, but upon hearing the servant, looked up and allowed the papyrus to roll closed. After poking the document back into a small open cabinet on the wall, he turned and marched towards us. As he approached, my chest pulsed with a wave of anxious cold at the sight of the entire room's walls being completely covered with cabinets and shelves, each filled with papyri.

"Ahmose," Neferhotep began, aggravated. "I hope there is an *actual* reason for needing to rush to my home at this hour."

"Yes, of course there is," Ahmose replied confidently.

"Not something that could have waited until the morning?" Neferhotep challenged.

Ahmose cut a perturbed glance back at him.

"No, I don't believe so," he said. "I'm here as a courtesy to you."

Neferhotep glanced quickly at Briz, then to me, lingering a bit while tilting his head, then back to Ahmose.

"Okay," Neferhotep barked. "Out with it then."

"I heard that these two caused a scene in the market with a merchant earlier. Asking about some dolls," Ahmose said, gesturing at whichever guard that had them to hold them up. Once they were displayed, he continued.

"They harassed the merchant to the point of forcing him to say who he bought them from. The merchant gave them my name at which point they began to seek me out."

"Who cares about dolls?" Neferhotep asked. "Had you even sold them to the merchant?" Neferhotep asked through a poorly-stifled laugh.

"I care about them!" I shouted, unabashed in my anger. Neferhotep turned to me with a grin mixed with condescension and intrigue, which made me chew into the conversation with a nastier bite.

"Those are mine and my family's!" I spit with raw disgust. "They were stolen after our village was attacked. I was looking for the murderers when I came across Briz and traveled with him here, where we were told about Ahmose, who then said Minmontu sold him many things that came from my village."

"Listen, girl," Ahmose shot in, pointing at me. "I can speak for myself. Neferhotep was speaking to me."

"I don't care what you can or can't say or who was talking to who. My family is dead, and I'm tired of all the annoying delays—such as yourself—getting in my way of finding their killers!"

Ahmose stood, seething, eyes wide and jaw tight, though he let his pointing arm fall to his side. I spun, ready to tear into Neferhotep when I heard him laugh, but after turning to look, I saw that he must have been laughing at Ahmose, entertained by my response to him.

"All right, everyone," Neferhotep said calmly, after reaching down to a table for a few rolls of papyri. He turned and inspected the shelves on the walls. After unrolling a papyrus partially to confirm its topic, he walked to the appropriate section of cabinets and placed it inside.

"Everyone just calm down for a moment," he added while sorting through more of his papyri. "We all apparently know that I have, shall we say, pressing business, with

Minmontu. Pressing business, I might add," as he turned to look at Ahmose, "that serves the interest of every Egyptian in this room, and stems from the insistence of those with greater authority than anyone in this room."

"Is that unclear for anyone?" Neferhotep asked the room, while still looking at Ahmose.

Ahmose shook his head.

Neferhotep held his gaze for a moment, before scanning around the room to catch the eyes of the other soldiers. But he ended his assessment of the room back on Ahmose.

"Perfect," Neferhotep exclaimed, returning to rolling, examining, and filing papyri.

"And it seems that Egypt, and our new friend here," he continued, glancing at me, "have a shared interest in seeing that the business concerning Minmontu is carried out successfully, which I would like to discuss with you and your friend, privately."

In an abrupt twitch of his head, Neferhotep looked back up to Ahmose.

"You and your men are dismissed."

Ahmose was taken aback, and started to laugh uncomfortably.

"What? I have private matters with these two as well," Ahmose said, stabbing a pointing finger in the air. "They're only here because I brought them here."

Neferhotep let him finish speaking but then roared a rumbling reprimand through the room.

"And was it ever your place to take them against their will to begin with? No!"

"I will do as I see fit, Neferhotep," Ahmose boomed back. "I do not answer to you! You're just a scribe!"

"You know who I work for," Neferhotep shouted, his

voice climbing up to and breaking upon the ceiling before spilling back down over the shelves, cabinets, and floor. "You know very well. I would strongly suggest you choose your next words with great care."

Ahmose's mouth twitched and his eyes stretched. Whether he was scratching around in his mind for what to say, or doing all he could to refrain from saying something already decided upon, I couldn't tell. Regardless, he remained frozen between intimidation and wrath. But one finally won out. A few moments after the tense exchange, he slowly brought his fingertips up, rubbing them slowly against each other, before finally snapping them together in a crisp crunch. Ahmose's accompanying swordsmen jumped to attention and took a step towards him before the group turned and surged out of the room.

Neferhotep kept his eyes on Ahmose and his men until the last man had turned the corner out of the room. And after that, he waited for a servant to signal that they had exited his home entirely.

"He's just another example," Neferhotep said, returning to his pile of papyri. "Another example of the corruption in this city. Men getting brazen beyond their position. Overstepping their bounds. Taking what doesn't belong to them. Abusing their power, and abusing the people."

"And you are without such corruption, Neferhotep?" Briz asked.

Neferhotep looked up in disbelief and slammed the papyri he was holding down on the table.

"Did you not just hear what I said about men getting brazen?"

Briz held his hand up in a silent and gentle apology.

Neferhotep sighed and leaned over onto the table

in front of him, trying to find some calm for the first time since we arrived.

"I'll accept that bounty," Briz said.

Neferhotep looked up.

"You mean, you both will, right?" He asked.

Briz nodded.

"Up until twenty minutes ago, I knew nothing of the girl," Neferhotep replied as if I weren't in the room. "What makes you think I'll extend my proposal to her?"

"Hey!" I shouted, having already grabbed my axes without thinking. The handles flashed as my energy surged through them, culminating in bright pops of light on the blades where it then subsided and pulsed gently.

"My name is Bayla. I'm helping with this bounty and the only payment I want is all of Minmontu's blood!"

As I helped Neferhotep understand the situation, and me specifically, he stared at me as he had earlier, but this time, with complete intrigue. No noticeable condescension. As he carefully considered my demeanor, due in no small part to my axes, I'm sure, he looked to Briz.

"You heard her," Briz said.

Neferhotep took a moment, but finally smiled. He then started to pace a slow circle while rubbing his chin.

"Mmm," he mumbled, likely from some conversation he was having with himself. As he took his stroll, Briz and I caught each other's eyes in fleeting glances of calm confidence.

"Two on the job, hmm?" He asked rhetorically. "Better than one. Usually."

He scratched his cheek and rubbed his face a final time before setting out the rest of his terms.

"If anything gets back to me," Neferhotep continued. "I've never seen you before Bayla."

I shrugged. I didn't care.

"Same goes for you, Briz. And the payment I initially offered is the same," he said.

Briz shrugged.

Neferhotep laughed and clapped his hands.

"It's settled then," Neferhotep said. "Stay as my guests tonight. Tomorrow we can discuss how you will proceed."

Chapter Fifteen - Plotting

Bayla

I slept horribly. With every toss and turn, each statue, rug, drape, piece of furniture, and engraving throughout the wooden and stone room kept me up all night as if whispering, *you don't belong here.* Golden figures of Ptah, Sekhmet, Heka, bulls, and pharaohs looked down at me from atop their perches, frowning through the shadow of the moonlight seeping into the room. The room was bigger than the entirety of my family's home and I expected it to swallow me up and spit me out of some underwater canyon in the Mediterranean. In a parting sentiment of hostility, it would tell me to get back to where I belonged. But no, I survived the night. Briz and I were originally escorted away from Neferhotep together but were quickly segregated. I don't know where he ended up, but I imagine he had his own room as well.

When I restlessly stirred the final time, I shuffled to the entryway and slowly crept out, only to be met with a female servant standing just outside. She backed up, making way for me to pass in front of her.

"Oh, I... was hoping to speak with Briz," I said, testing the situation.

"Yes, of course. If you will follow me," the servant said, "I will take you to him."

"Oh, um," I started, looking back into the room, trying to find a reason not to go with her.

Unable to fabricate something quick enough, I gave in.

"I... Well... Great. Thank you."

The servant led me out of the room into one of the many great corridors throughout Neferhotep's home. It was just me and the scantily-clad woman for the longest time, but after a few turns and catching sight of a few other servants, we turned another corner and were met by Briz and his own escort. I smiled briefly when I spotted him, but found it odd that we were being led around like we were. After a few more halls, we were brought into a towering room where Neferhotep sat at the center of one side of a gigantic, square table, eating.

"Please, sit, eat. We have much to discuss," Neferhotep said cheerfully through his chewing.

Neither Briz nor I moved. I didn't know about Briz, but I was confused by Neferhotep's hinted urgency. Looking up from his palm full of figs, he stopped chewing.

"Sit. Eat," he repeated sternly.

Briz and I swapped glances and approached the table.

"I'm sorry, Neferhotep. I don't understand. Is there a rush of some kind?" I asked.

Neferhotep held up a finger, finished chewing, and wiped his mouth before standing up and walking to the balcony behind him. The day's new sun washed across the tops of the palm trees, striking everything in its path with a beacon of revelation. The peaks of the pyramids floated in and out of focus as the morning heat and stirring sand worked together to confuse the world's sight. Fronds of green, sunbeams of orange, dunes of yellow, and obelisks of black enchanted me through Neferhotep's balcony, their beauty almost enough to make me forget my question.

"When Briz and I first spoke of my proposal surrounding Minmontu, I told him that I needed an answer by no later than today, so that he could take action tonight, or so that I could make other arrangements."

I looked to Briz for confirmation. With a slow blink of both eyes, he nodded. Neferhotep continued.

"I need Minmontu to be taken care of before the morning. He is, well… he's planning to set out tomorrow morning for another expedition. Similar, I would imagine," he said, turning to look at me straight on, "to the one he oversaw with your village. But this time, he is carrying out activities closer to home."

I started to take my first bite from the huge selection of food in front of me, but paused as my village was mentioned.

"You see," Neferhotep continued. There are significant efforts being made to reunite Upper and Lower Egypt once again, like in the days of Sneferu, Khufu, and Sahure. Some of us are working to realize that peace once more. Working to unite our blessed nation again and together, return to our previous glory, and not only return to it, but surpass it. Minmontu however, and people like him, are doing all they can to disrupt and prevent that. They conquer and pillage in an effort to bolster those who resist that union. They will do anything they can to keep the country divided, so that they may personally benefit from the strife caused by the ongoing segmentation. That's why I have hired you," Neferhotep said, looking at Briz, and then me. "And now, both of you. Tomorrow, Minmontu plans to oversee a group of clandestine resistance to attack and destroy a caravan of food that is meant for delivery to garrisons and barracks throughout the area."

"Why are they attacking food supplies?" Briz asked.

"Food supplies for the armies," Neferhotep reiterated. "If the army is fed, they can fight against the resistance. If the resistance falls, Egypt can be reunited. They don't want that to happen."

It made sense to me, and judging from Briz's silence, he was also on board.

"I have to say," Briz began. "I don't really care about the reason. I just want to get paid."

Briz's honesty, though hard to hear, stirred some honesty in me, and it didn't bother me to verbalize it.

"Like I said last night. I don't care about money, and I don't care about the reason. I just need him dead. I just need him to pay the debt my family's deaths demand."

As I clarified my position, I looked over at Briz and felt a fist of guilt tighten around my heart. Sitting there, having just proudly proclaimed my blood-lust, happy to hunt and kill for a reason that only I cared about, I realized that *my* reason—as much as I tried to convince myself and Briz previously—was no more honorable than his. Mine was no more justifiable than his. And not only did I originally turn my nose up at his hunting things for money, he initially *turned down* this job to kill Minmontu—until I agreed to get involved. And now, there we sat, discussing a plan to kill the man.

Over the next few hours Neferhotep prepared us for our task by marching in servants with arms full of papyri. The first few servants delivered recently created maps of the city to help us navigate intelligently, not only in the dark, but around the cramped paths and jumbles of buildings in the area immediately around the temple. The majority of the maps focused on the temple itself, with most of the time spent discussing our movements in the temple. Once Briz and I ran out of questions after pouring over maps, and when we thought we were done discussing the temple's layout, a fresh wave of servants brought in small, wooden replicas of the temple's outer and interior walls, and statues.

"The most challenging part of this will be not getting lost," Neferhotep said at one point, "which is why we're spending so much time on this. The goal is to get you in and out as quickly as possible."

"I think I'll be seeing this temple in my dreams for the next five years," Briz said. "But even with the layout memorized, how do we know where he'll be?"

"Mmm, yes," Neferhotep said. "I was getting to that next. You're dismissed," he said to the group in the room. "Send in the other group, but don't go too far."

As the group of servants left the room, a row of men and women appearing and dressed differently than the previous groups lined up side by side next to Neferhotep.

"Go on," Neferhotep urged, reaching for some olives. "Tell us what you know of life in the temple. You," Neferhotep said, slinging a hand at the first person in line, accidentally tossing an olive. "You start. What's your name?"

"Yes, of course," the first man in line said. "My name is Hapuseneb." The man, about thirty years of age wore clean linen and had a shaved head. His voice was soft as he looked at the ground.

"Every morning, we dress the blessed Heka. We remove his previous day's wardrobe and then drape him in clean clothes made by our best weavers. We please him with paints and oils and decorate him with our most precious metals and stones. We sing the most pleasing melodies, and pray until the great Heka desires his meal so that his Ka may be sustained. Close to mid-day, we prepare a vast meal of all tastes and textures so that he will know all flavors and sensations pleasing to him, and so that he will bless us for the day as we seek to do his work.”

“So, forgive me,” I said. “I’m not very familiar with… Well… Are you… a holy man?”

“Yes, miss—” he started.

Neferhotep stepped in.

“Yes, he’s one of the priests at the temple of Heka. We have asked him here to report on the daily happenings at the temple.”

“Erm,” I stammered, glancing with confusion at Briz, to the line, and then finally to Neferhotep. “Does he know for what reason his information…”

Before I could finish my question Neferhotep’s voice scraped a loud and violent rip from under his closed lips. He stretched his eyes wide and shook his head so subtly that I thought I might have mistaken him. He then started to approach me after rapidly shifting into a grin, followed by a polite chuckle directed at the people standing awkwardly. As he grew closer to me, the light from the beauty outside was clouded over by his silhouette.

“Bayla,” he said, whispering. “We have to be very careful about what we say. What we suggest, or possibly reveal when we ask certain questions. While we have secured certain resources to provide us with information as it pertains to the activities in the temple… No, we have not revealed to what end their assistance will be used.”

“I… understand,” I said.

Neferhotep continued looking at me for a moment, his grin sliding down into his cheeks. He then abruptly spun away from me with a raucous laugh, opening his arms at the citizens.

“Please, continue, Hapuseneb. Tell us, what happens after the meal ritual.”

"Uh, yes," the priest resumed. "A lot of our time between presenting Heka with his meal and the closing of the sanctuary is spent speaking with citizens who have come to pray and seek counsel."

Neferhotep turned, waiting for the priest to finish his sentence.

"Closing of the sanctuary?"

"Yes, Neferhotep," the priest answered. "At sunset, we close the sanctuary off from the general citizenry so we may clean, sweep, make preparations for the next day…"

"Ah, I understand," Neferhotep replied, nodding to himself. "And do you take part in this cleaning? These preparations?"

"I do, yes," replied the priest. "Well, I should say that I tend to the statues and cleanliness of the front causeway."

"Mm, I see," Neferhotep said. "Do you always have the same assignments each day?"

"No. We all decide who will do what at the time we close the sanctuary."

Neferhotep had no immediate reply or question, but the priest had an addendum, regardless.

"Except for the sanctuary. That's tended to every night by the same person, High Priest Minmontu."

Neferhotep turned around slowly towards the line of informants. The lightning-quick flash of his eyes to me was the only allusion to his excitement over the revelation. With the poise of the most veteran of actors, he contained his enthusiasm and maintained the calm of the conversation.

"Oh, that's interesting. Why does this same High Priest always tend to the sanctuary?"

The priest shrugged.

"The sanctuary is where the blessed Heka resides. Only the High Priest has the right, power, and discipline to care for him."

"Right, of course. I wonder... Do these tasks take everyone a long time to complete each night?" Neferhotep suggested through another polite laugh. "I can imagine it is quite the errand to tidy up after the city strolls through the temple each day!"

The priest reciprocated Neferhotep's laughter, out of respect, it seemed, more than finding Neferhotep's comment humorous.

"Ah, no," Hapuseneb replied cheerfully. "It is an honor to present our blessed Heka's temple in its best light each day to his people. As we finish our work for the night, we each report to the High Priest, and go to bed. Only after we all have reported our work finished will the High Priest say a final prayer to Heka so that the temple goes to sleep having praised him a final time for the day. After that, the High Priest will also retire for the night."

"Thank you Hapuseneb. It is a rare privilege to have such an amazing account of life in our temples! I have only caught bits and pieces in my various visits, but never before had I known all that transpires, or how much work is done after everyone leaves. You girl," Neferhotep continued casually. "The one next to Hapuseneb..."

As Neferhotep made his way down the line, additional lesser priests and priestesses shared their accounts of a day at the temple. They spoke about Heka's meal, and how it would be escorted throughout the temple and shared with the other statues, and once the gods had sustained themselves on the spiritual essence of the food, it would then be shared with the community or physically consumed by the priests.

"What a beautiful ritual," I couldn't help but say during the discussion. "This is done each day?"

"Yes," an older priestess confirmed. "We make sure the spirits of the gods are nourished each day so that they might nourish *our* spirits each day. That is our first and foremost concern. And once that has been seen to, we provide the physical food to the people."

Briz's questions were less romantic.

"Once the sanctuary is closed, does the general public completely disperse?" He asked the group. One of the plainly-clothed women answered. Based on her previous presentation, it seemed as though she had been hired to visit the temple frequently as a regular citizen.

"It appeared that way, yes," she said. "Once the sanctuary was closed, access to Heka was impossible for the rest of the day, so citizens had no real use to visit the temple until the next day when the sanctuary was reopened."

After rounds of my questions of intrigue—spawned from my fascination with the exquisite ceremonies—and rounds of Briz's practical questions of logistics and detail, Neferhotep had an additional question of his own.

"Can you share with us some of the magic performed at the temple?"

The line of priests and citizens shifted uncomfortably as they looked to each other with faces of hesitance.

"What is it?" Neferhotep questioned.

A priest towards the end of the line spoke up.

"Apologies, Neferhotep," he said, shyly. "It's just that our work is tremendously sacred. It would be an insult to Heka to go into such detail."

Neferhotep stuck his chin up and sniffed quickly, stifling what I thought was going to be an immediate response, before coming out with something more measured.

"Right, yes. I meant no offense," Neferhotep said— whether or not he was sincere, I wasn't sure. "I was just curious what types of things you do with your magic. What types of work you do. The help you provide... That sort of thing."

The priest quickly looked to the other priests and priestesses in the line.

"Um, ye.. Yes," the priest began. "Much of our work is centered around prayers for those that request them. We also prepare foods and medicines to assist those with ill health, or who are in need of potent, spiritual assistance."

"Oh! That's beautiful!" Neferhotep said with something akin to sincere regard. "Everyone in the temple performs this work of medicine and magical healing?"

"Yes," the priest replied.

"Even the High Priest?"

"Yes, well, at least until the sanctuary closes."

"Right," Neferhotep replied, confident in his understanding. "And that's when everyone turns to cleaning and preparing for the next day."

"That is correct," the lesser priest said. "But that is also when the High Priest also practices his own magic."

The other priests and priestesses in the line gasped in shock.

Neferhotep turned towards us with one eyebrow raised, and continued turning back to the group.

"His own magic?" Neferhotep repeated, curious. "What types of magic would that be?"

The poor young priest interlocked his fingers, wringing his hands nervously.

"I'm afraid I don't know that, Neferhotep. None of us do. That is a most private matter between the High Priest and Heka."

I watched as Neferhotep held the priest's gaze. I just knew he was wondering whether or not to press the priest. He finally replied with a gentle whisper conceived from the intimidation he knew he was causing.

"Yes, of course," Neferhotep said. "Of course."

After the tense interrogation of the group about the temple's magic, others in the group went on to speak about the size of the crowds throughout the day, and described the areas of the temple the priests congregated at most. There were also additional details provided on the god's meal, and how it was sent around to local funerary chapels so that the dead may gain what sustenance they required.

As the sun approached the horizon and the light took on dark shades of burnt gold and amber, the group of temple patrons, priests, and priestesses ran out of pertinent information to share. When Neferhotep finally released them and the last in the group filtered out of the room, I caught Neferhotep lifting his head awkwardly and making eye contact with a guard at the room's entryway. The guard bowed and soon exited the room. Before I could speak to the odd display, Briz let out a large sigh as if taking stock of how he felt.

"That was quite a lot of information to take in," he said.

Neferhotep waved in a set of servants we hadn't seen yet. They scurried in and lit lamps hanging off the sides of the stone columns and darted out.

"Yes," Neferhotep said. "I took great care to gather as much information as possible."

"There's just one thing that concerns me," Briz added.

Neferhotep turned, waiting.

"The magic," Briz said. "The unknowns surrounding the magic. Doesn't that bother you Bayla?"

I shifted in my chair as I confirmed how I felt about it.

"I'm honestly more concerned about getting to Minmontu without being caught than I am about the magic," I offered. "I can keep us safe."

Neferhotep let a quick laugh escape.

"No," Briz said, politely challenging Neferhotep's doubt. "She has some amazing abilities. Passed down from her people. I've fought alongside her. I know she can keep us safe."

Neferhotep looked at me and bowed his head.

"I just didn't like what they said about Minmontu having magic to himself, practicing it alone with the gods," Briz said.

"Well, like I said," I reiterated. "I'm more worried about getting to him than the magic. If we can find him, we will kill him."

Leaning backward slightly, Neferhotep stared at the ceiling and reflected on the earlier discussion.

"It sounds like he'll be in the sanctuary," he said.

"We'll need to time it so that most of the other priests have gone to bed, but before Minmontu does," I suggested to Briz.

"Come with me," Neferhotep requested. "Re has nearly completed his journey across the day's sky, and night is not far off. You must make your final preparations."

* * *

The next few hours felt like minutes as I ran as much of what we had just learned back through my mind. The area surrounding the temple. The approach. The layout. The chores of the priests. All of it. Briz and I also had something to eat, but both of us seemed to pay just enough attention to chew in-between discussing our plan. After eating, we separated temporarily as we were escorted to different rooms to change clothes, but soon reunited wearing dark linens tinted some shade of blue or purple—I couldn't tell for sure. We were covered head to toe beginning with sheer but multiple wraps of cloth across our foreheads and mouths, topped by a hood attached to a shirt with flowing sleeves. Though all the clothing was extremely comfortable, both

Briz and I wore heavy pants, secured by a belt over the low-hanging shirt. Once we had dressed and reunited, we were surprisingly left alone for a time. We quietly discussed our route, our speed, and the timing we were hoping to achieve, as well as discuss various methods of communication for when we needed to be silent. But as we made our way to a balcony, we also found time to veer away from strategy while hints and bits of the vast city struggled against the night by way of fires dotting the streets.

"I've been wanting to ask you," Briz said. "What are you wanting to do after we... take care of this?"

I strained to see the pyramids, but it was too dark.

"I don't know," I said. "I've thought about it a million times, but after all the chasing, the shipwreck, the delays, and a few wrong targets..."

Briz sniffed a huff of amusement.

"Waiting to decide until after it's actually taken are of?" He said.

While staring out across the city, I saw him look at me.

I nodded. My smile that had formed crumbled away.

"What about you?" I asked.

Briz took in a huge breath and let it out as he looked back into the flame-speckled darkness.

"Oh, I have a few ideas," he said. "But..."

As he trailed off, I couldn't help but look over. His chin and cheeks twitched but his face quickly settled into a stare that seemed to peer into a darkness beyond that of the city.

"But," he repeated. "I suspect I'll feel differently once this is done."

His words floated out into the nothingness as if accompanying his stare. I tilted my head and squinted, unsure of what he meant. But then it struck me, or at least an idea of what he meant struck me. Hints of regret tingled in my skin, itching at an urge of doubt. But before the doubt could grow into anything meaningful, he turned to me. He blinked and grinned with just enough muscle movement to let me know he was grinning.

"Ask me later," he said as his delicate grin shattered. "Are you ready?"

With a huge breath, I turned and scanned the top of the city, my eyes settling on where I knew the pyramids were.

"Yes," I said, reapplying my wrap to my face. Let's go."

After a few words of reassurance and encouragement from Neferhotep, with a healthy dose of the implications if we failed, we set out from his home. Initially, we wore an added layer of regular clothing, with a second hood, to cover our clandestine attire. Though the streets were dark and the hour was late, we wanted to draw as little attention as possible at all times.

The extra clothing mixed with the warm and humid air and made breathing a chore. There was little wind, and as we jogged through the city, my head started to grow dense with nagging pain. My clothes clung against my damp skin. It wasn't long before I was pinching and readjusting my clothes and wiping my sweaty forehead. And then my stomach began to turn.

I couldn't get comfortable. While Briz and I took turns leading our sprints from the darkest shadows to physical cover, my anxiety rippled out from my core. The discomfort compounded. Not only was I getting hot and nauseous, but doubt scratched at our plan, our path, and our goal. With each step, I waited for someone to yell at us, question us, or challenge us.

One missed glance, one missed check around a

corner, I thought, *and that's all it would take.*

We'll be discovered.

I feel like I'm going to vomit.

Briz came to a dead stop in front of me and flung out an arm before slowly inching us backwards. Being careful not to make a sound, we both flattened our backs against a wall. Just as I started to whisper and ask what the cause for alarm was, I heard the faintest hint of a conversation. The volume of the voices grew quickly as they approached. My heart beat angrily, rapping on the inside of my chest as if displeased with how close we had allowed ourselves to come to being discovered. When I considered that my heart was beating so forcefully that it might attract attention, two men with massive spears passed into view. Adrenaline stung me, shooting an extra beat into my heart's rhythm. My sticky skin itched. My head throbbed even harder. But the two guards walked on.

As we ducked away from exposed streets, ran, hid, and avoided the brightness of torches and braziers, complete confidence in our actions eluded me. But not enough to make me stop. I wanted Minmontu dead. I wanted justice for my family.

When the temple came into view, I was in the lead. I stopped and pointed at it, and then patted my sleeve softly. Briz looked around me and nodded. We both pulled off and stepped out of our extra clothes, and stuffed them into a nearby pot before dashing over to a cluster of buildings surrounding the temple.

No longer suffocated by the extra fabric, I instantly cooled down. My skin grew less sticky and the pressure in my head began to dissipate. The rolling waves of constant nausea drifted away as well. As I found relief from my physical pain and sickness, my mind was able to make room for focus, determination, and confidence.

The area immediately surrounding the temple was the darkest and least-populated portion of the city that we would be running through. The darkness, combined with my improved physical and mental state increased my efficiency. Briz and I weaved in and out of the tight corridors, whisking from one corner to another, through empty stalls, down alleys, and around massive stacks of crates. With my nerves finally feeling stabilized, we shot across a street and crept along the length of a wall, stopping just short of an opening leading to the temple's main approach.

Before passing into the temple grounds, Briz turned and grabbed my shoulder. I reached out and tapped his. After glancing back to confirm the area was clear, he looked back to me and held a finger up to his lips. Per our earlier planning, there would be no more talking until we had finished our task and made it to safety.

We whipped around the opening in the wall and scurried along the inside of it, tracing the edge of the interior courtyard. The rows of sphinxes and towering pylon at the center of the yard seemed more intimidating than just a day before. My anticipation for getting inside caused my emotions to rock back and forth between excitement and dread, but as we finished our sprint along the inside of the wall and came upon the entrance to the main causeway, I found a mental base of calm that I was able to settle into.

I peeked around Briz and down the length of the causeway. Seeing no one, I leapt over to the other side of the entrance.

Briz and I had decided that we would not under any circumstances harm anyone but Minmontu unless attacked. After having the nightly events relayed to us at Neferhotep's home, we knew we would just have to wait the lesser priests and priestesses out. Once we had confirmed they all had checked in with Minmontu for the rest of the night, we would attack.

With one of us on each side of the main causeway entrance, we took turns periodically looking around the corner, and down into the darkened hall. There was very little light, but enough to make anyone out if they were present. After confirming there was no one to be seen, and that there was no noise of someone possibly working or cleaning just out of sight, we slipped into the causeway.

We stepped quickly—as quickly as we could without making noise. We passed by statue after statue, and while being sure to keep an eye on each other, we would stop and sneak behind one of the mammoth likenesses of the gods whenever either of us suspected movement or thought we heard a sound. But we each only paused once. After easily traversing the substantial length of the causeway, we stopped and visually checked in with each other again.

I held up one finger at Briz and then mimed a slash to my neck.

I guess the priest responsible for the causeway has already gone to bed, I thought.

Briz shrugged and nodded.

The next area of the temple was an expansive, enclosed courtyard that Briz and I sat and studied for many minutes. I hated to just sit there, but we had no choice. While we were able to cut down on some of the time needed by looking in at cross directions, we had to wait in case there was a patrolling priest walking the courtyard's perimeter. Our diligence and patience eventually paid off.

As I peered in from my side, watching the left side of the courtyard, I saw Briz across from me wave his hand gently while he looked to the right of the courtyard.

He held up a single finger and then pointed it in the priest's direction. After indicating to me where the priest was, Briz then brought one hand's fingertips together in a point before cupping them with his other hand.

Ah, the priest is snuffing out the torches, I said to myself. Initially, having the flames put out and the light decreased worried me, but I found quick relief in the realization that once the priest from the courtyard had retired, the light of the moon would be plenty to pass through the courtyard.

We waited for the priest to snuff out all of the torches and watched as he exited the courtyard and made his way, we presumed, to check in with Minmontu for the night. We had waited longer than I would have liked to identify whoever may have been in the courtyard, but luckily, the priest didn't take too long to finish snuffing the torches. Once the priest had disappeared through the passage on the other side of the courtyard, we inched in and followed the peristyle around, avoiding the bits of light streaming in through the columns as if they were pools of lava.

Methodically, we pressed deeper into the temple and as we stole glimpses of the moon through windows in corridors or openings in subsequent courtyards, we watched the white orb climb higher in the sky, but then start to slide down.

After waiting out one of the priests in a subsequent section of the temple, I tapped Briz on the shoulder. When he swung around to see what I wanted, I pointed up at the moon, poked at the air a few times, before shoving my palms forward and back. We needed to move faster. Briz nodded, but then brought his open hands up and lowered them, as if telling me to relax. We didn't have time to relax. Once again, I pointed at the moon and poked at it a few more times.

When I began to feel as if we'd never get to the main sanctuary in time, and after crawling through courtyards, halls, and secondary rooms, we finally had the entryway to the sanctuary in sight. We alternated between slowly sliding our feet along, and tiptoeing as we approached the sanctuary. As we had throughout the night, we took turns watching behind us while the other looked forward. Creeping along almost shoulder to shoulder in case we needed to grab an arm or tap a shoulder, we closed in on completing our incursion.

The end of the corridor approaching the sanctuary neared. I felt my heart begin to race for the first time in what felt like hours. Up until that moment, it all only felt like a plan. A hypothetical. Justice for my family was that ever-elusive trickster. But with my prey hopefully being on the other side of the entryway ahead, the trickster seemed to be running out of games.

As we had with the rest of the temple, we inched along with the goal of coming to the end of this particular section and scouting the next area. Just before we reached the end of the wide passage, a priestess emerged ahead of us from between two columns.

Briz and I froze, but only for a moment. In a fraction of an instant, we saw that she hadn't noticed us. Not only had she come out ahead of us in the passage, but she was already facing and heading for the sanctuary. Briz and I leapt to the side and hid behind a massive column. As we both sneaked around it, clinging as closely to it as possible, I saw the slightly-obscured alcove she had entered the hall from. I rolled my eyes at the close call and watched the priestess enter the sanctuary as I caught my shortened breath. Briz slid back next to me, closed his eyes and let his head fall back against the column. After countless glances and sneaking peeks from behind the column over the course of about twenty minutes, we finally heard footsteps and watched as the priestess left the sanctuary. Briz and I flattened ourselves against the column once again, and listened to the priestess leave through the passage she had surprised us from.

Chapter Sixteen - The Nile

Briz

Even though our plan involved sitting outside the sanctuary for a while to confirm no one else would be visiting Minmontu, Bayla kept tapping me. Every few minutes came a *tap, tap*, and an impatient gesture at the moon.

Yes, yes, I know, I'd think to myself. *But you know the plan. Calm down! We have to wait to make sure Minmontu is alone!*

But of course I couldn't say all that to her, so I had to settle with flicking fingers at her to represent the other priests, and then swiping my hands out from my center to the side—reminding her of our need to confirm all priests have visited. After that, I pressed my hands down in the air, asking her to relax. Despite a few more pokes towards the moon and a few whirls of her impatient hands, she waited quietly.

We had decided that after we saw a priest leave the sanctuary, we would start counting, and once we had counted to 1,800 seconds, we would enter the sanctuary.

But, if another priest visited before we reached thirty minutes, we would start the count over when that priest left. After the priestess that surprised us, there were two more priests that visited. A priest came through about eight minutes after her, and then another about twenty minutes after him. I'd say we were standing there hiding behind that column for close to an hour. Once we finally counted up to thirty minutes, we grabbed each other by the shoulders and stared into each other's eyes to confirm each other's disposition. After some nodding and pointing at weapons, we struck out for the sanctuary, only a few dozen paces away. I looked up to the sky as we emerged from behind the column and could no longer see the moon above the roof.

Bayla jogged over to the sanctuary's threshold, leaping slightly between footsteps to give herself small bounces with which to cushion her landings. I ran behind her, spinning and running backwards to watch behind us. After turning to face forward again, I saw Bayla slow and hold up her arms as she looked to the left and right of the sanctuary's entryway. I slowed down while she confirmed there wasn't anyone to the side, and joined her for a quick pause at the wall before stepping in. I slipped my club off my back and after scanning the area a final time, Bayla pulled her axes from under her belt and slowly touched them together. They slowly pulsed with light, and then dimmed. She looked up and nodded at me.

We stepped through the threshold and entered a small passage that immediately split to the left and right before meeting back up on the other side—according to the information we had been given at Neferhotep's home. The passage was lit with more torches than I would have liked and revealed life-sized reliefs and carvings of pharaohs and gods that seemed to whisper warnings against our murderous intentions. But their attempted guilt didn't distract me long. After walking around to the other side of the split passage, there was a small set of unlit, shallow steps up into the sanctuary proper. Bayla and I slowed, moving forward at a crawl only until we could get the first line of sight into the sanctuary. As our heads slowly slid out from around the preceding corner, my vision floated across the most extravagant images of figures splashed with vibrant colors, as well as a shrine and statue of gold, before finally settling upon a man's back.

There he is, I thought. *Minmontu.*

Towards the back of the robust sanctuary, Minmontu knelt, holding his hands up to the alter, humming and singing. Though there were steps leading up, they were few, with the inner sanctuary's floor being no more than a foot higher than where we stood. With Minmontu's back to us, I took the opportunity to stick my head out further and inspect the entire room. There was nothing that impeded my view of all four walls and I could see that he was alone. After ducking away from the corner, I saw Bayla scanning the room as well. As she came to the same conclusion as I did, she lowered her axes, one to each side. As I mentally checked off our final preparations, I caught Bayla's eyes and bent my head in Minmontu's direction.

He's alone. It doesn't look like anyone else is coming. It's time.

We both stepped out. With tenderness similar to stroking the cheeks of a sleeping baby, we feathered our feet up and crested the top of the steps. After entering the sanctuary, Minmontu remained kneeling across from us, unaware of our presence.

Step by step and crouching slightly, we crept up behind Minmontu. His chanting became more decipherable the closer we came. The volume of his voice ironically helped shield our approach from his senses. I only slightly repositioned my fingertips and secured my grasp of my club as I prepared to strike.

I slowly turned my head to Bayla to confirm our readiness. She extended an axe out to her side and one over her head.

Minmontu's chant grew ragged and sharp. His voice climbed in volume as his hands raised higher in the air as if trying to touch the face of the Heka statue in the shrine ahead of him.

Bayla took an extra, quick step to close the distance. She wanted to make the first strike. Her axe raised up just a bit more to the top of her arm's extension.

Minmontu's chanting stopped. His arms dropped.

"You are not one of my priests," he said.

After uttering his dark observation, he spun around to face us and stretched his arms back out to his side.

"Heka, protect me as I protect you!" He yelled.

Before Bayla or I could make our next move, Minmontu began to emit a golden energy. Beginning at his fingertips and feet, the energy raced along his arms, up his legs, to his torso and head. Once the energy had encompassed him totally, faint images of extravagant jewelry and clothing made of gold thread flashed across him. As the wardrobe from what seemed to be from another world superimposed itself onto him and then dissipated, his face took on the slight hint of Atum, then the ram-headed Khnum, followed by the face of Khnum's wife, Neith, and finally taking on the likeness of their son, Heka. The face of Heka, god of magic, remained in place the longest, though quickly gave way to Minmontu's sinister grin.

I shot towards Minmontu. Bayla sprang towards him and slapped her axes together as she bounded. After smacking her axes, she pointed one in my direction and shot a dome of protection onto me, and at the same time, thrust her other axe in the air to conjure a dome for herself.

After closing to within feet of Minmontu, he shot his arms into the air and grasped onto something invisible. As he pulled his clutched fists back towards him, the carved and painted reliefs of gods and pharaohs popped off the wall and shot down to the floor. Before we could strike, the room filled with countless, two-dimensional figures of kings, gods, viziers, officials, as well as massive representations of other symbols from the walls such as bread, birds, boats, and plants.

"Bayla!" I shouted, after losing sight of Minmontu amid the sea of lifeless obstacles.

A room-filling boom of laughter erupted throughout the sanctuary.

"I was expecting assassins," Minmontu's voice bellowed. "But I had hoped my skills more well thought of than to be challenged by a common brawler and novice practitioner from across the sea!"

As Minmontu spoke, I beat and slashed at the maze of fake obstructions, striking them down as if they were nothing more than palm fronds. I could hear Bayla working her way through the jungle of diversions as well. But as Minmontu finished speaking, he erupted in laughter once again and shocked the room from wall to wall with a wave of energy, obliterating his conjured figures.

After shielding my eyes from his magic's blinding flash, I readied myself for a counter-attack. But when my eyes opened, only the shrine to Heka stood before me. Bayla and I spun around. Minmontu had reappeared close to the room's entrance behind us.

"Quit your games, Minmontu," Bayla screamed, slashing angrily at the air. "Fight me!"

We took off for Minmontu once more and as we sprinted along, he antagonized us again.

"What do you think I'm doing, child?" He said, standing calmly as we raced towards him. "Here," he continued, unconcerned. "Why don't you wait for a moment," he added, gesturing at Bayla. "Have a taste of your own powers."

After a roll of his wrist he stuck his palm out at Bayla and shoved forward, catching her in a barely-noticeable ripple of wind that froze her mid-stride when it struck her. He then turned to me.

"Let's test your friend's abilities first," he said.

As Minmontu prepared to engage me, he bent slightly at the knees and stretched out his arms. After rapidly flexing both hands, a massive sickle sword appeared in each of his palms, emerging from a quick blaze of flame. He held one at an angle to his front and brought one up behind his shoulders. While running at a full sprint, I readied my club, grabbed my long dagger in my other hand, and looked over at Bayla. Though her body was frozen, her eyes weren't. She followed me as I ran.

I leapt into the air and brought my club down on the flat of the intimidating sword's massive hook shape before Minmontu brought his second sword over his head. But I blocked it high above with my dagger before he could get too much weight behind it. After blocking both initial attacks, his chest was left open. I bent my leg back and crashed my foot into him, sending him stumbling back. Though the strike wasn't too jarring, it gave me time.

I swung at his chin before he had completely secured his footing, but he pulled himself out of the way in time. As he dodged, he brought a sword around in a mighty swing and chopped my dagger out of my hand. As he followed through with the blow, I took the available blink of time to grab my club with both hands, and after swinging it over my head, brought it down into a violent crunch into

Minmontu's shoulder. He couldn't help but let go of a sword, and as he recovered from the blow, I continued with my own follow through, spinning around and striking him again. This time, I clipped the back of his head. It was just enough to finally send him tumbling, and rolling to the ground, but not from pain—only disorientation. When he came to a stop, he reached up and grabbed at the air, freezing me like he had Bayla.

He slowly scrambled to his feet, giggling with condescending chuckles and exaggerated gasps for air while patting the back of his head, checking for blood.

"Hah!" He said, tapping his head. Looking back and forth between me and Bayla.

"Impressive bout, my friend!" He said to me. "But of course, I couldn't let you continue. The killing blow would have come next."

He amused himself with a few more laughs and glances to his palm.

"Yes, that last hit could have been much worse," he said, holding his slightly-reddened palm up at me. "But not too bad."

"But then again," he said, turning to Bayla. "I was never all that interested in such physical displays."

"Come, young one," he said to Bayla. He stretched and swiped some composure back into his clothes. "Let's see how little you know of magic."

Minmontu began to smile, but his face was once again overtaken by the image of Heka's semblance before returning to his own. Though Minmontu made no gesture or noticeable effort to release her, Bayla stumbled forward before quickly catching herself. Slowly, she stood straight, and crossed her axes in front of her.

Minmontu stood across from her, motionless. Waiting.

Other than her steadying breath making her chest rise and fall, Bayla made no movement.

I yelled at her, but my frozen body prevented my thought from leaving my mind.

Bayla! You don't know any offensive magic!

Minmontu's face of anticipation and readiness fell into one of impatience as he scoffed with haughty aggravation. With a swirling whoosh of his arms he conjured two horizontal cones of spinning sand and shot them at Bayla.

Get out of here! I wanted to scream. *Get out...*

I interrupted my own thoughts. *She knows defensive magic! She can use his against him!* I couldn't scream a reminder at her. But I didn't need to.

Bayla stood her ground as Minmontu shot the sand at her. Just before it struck her, she jerked her axes away from each other and unleashed a violent wave of magical deflection. Her defensive maneuver struck the sand and slammed it back at Minmontu with the sound of a metallic rip. Minmontu jumped out of the way of Bayla's counterattack and took off running. As Minmontu circled around towards her side, Bayla turned slowly to track him and brought her axes back to her front. While running around the room, he started to recite a spell while waving his hands at the towering statues throughout the room. One by one the statues came to life and marched towards Bayla.

She backed up slowly as the two dozen living statues approached her. Her face was wrinkled with worry and when she took a pinch of time to look at me, I saw nothing but panic in her eyes.

Bayla started to speak, though I couldn't hear her over the pounding marching of the statues. She beat her axes together once in a flash of light, but the statues continued marching. She slapped them together a second time as her voice grew louder. Still, there was no change from the statues. After a third and fourth strike of her axes, each with their own accompanying spell, the huge statues of gold and vibrant colors continued closing in. She only had time for another attempt.

Bayla's voice soared to the tops of the sanctuary and filled the entire chamber with words from another attempted spell. She held her axes up as high as she could while reciting the spell and rotated the axes in her hands so that they were backwards, the sharpened edges facing behind her. She then crashed her arms down furiously, sending a ripple of energy through the room. As each statue was struck by Bayla's magic, it stopped, and turned around to face Minmontu. Within seconds, the army of possessed statues was on the march for their previous master.

Once again, Minmontu's face twisted from one of being entertained, to one of boredom and annoyance.

"Is this all you're going to keep doing?" He screamed through snarling lips. After waving his hand and freezing Bayla in place once again, he recited a spell and commanded the statues back to their place.

"Let me show you real power," Minmontu said, boasting. "Let me show you what it means to harness the power of the Nile!"

His arms stretched out once more, grasping at another unseen force. As if pulling on invisible ropes, Minmontu strained and struggled against the magical resistance. He pulled and pulled and grunted, sinking a little at a time before crumbling to his knees. Just as it looked as though he were about to succumb and release his magical hold, something stirred along the walls and grabbed my attention.

Water streamed into the room. Through hundreds of holes and passages incorporated into symbols, pictures, etchings, and reliefs, water raced along, filling connected channels in the walls. Like an ornate web creating repetitive outlines throughout the room's perimeter, the water filled the entirety of what appeared to be a pattern carved into the walls especially for this magical purpose.

But as soon as the water filled the channels, the water continued to move, consolidating into a single, seamless line connected across all for walls. When all the water had flattened itself into the single line's channel, it shot out from the wall in a thin sheet only a few feet off the ground.

Minmontu had fallen prone in anticipation of the event. Bayla and I, stunned still by Minmontu's magic, were unable to dodge his harnessed water. It flew across the room as if dissecting it and sliced its way through both me and Bayla.

It happened so quickly, I almost didn't have enough time to register that I had been sliced in half. I almost didn't have time to fear death.

But I did.

My chest lashed out with a cold sting as I registered what had happened, which was partially influenced by the metallic slice I felt through my waist. But it didn't stop there. The water sliced into me at the waist and severed me completely. I felt my body tear and rip as the water diced me. Initially there was cold stinging, internal pain, and then a loss of feeling to my legs.

But as soon as I felt the water pass through me, I stumbled forward. I reached for my stomach, my sides, my back. The last few seconds of pain dissipated. There was no lasting wound.

I looked up to Bayla, my eyes flickering all over as my brain raced to understand what had happened. Finally, I fixed my eyes on Bayla. She too was no longer bound by Minmontu's magic, and though she was also sliced by the sheet of water, she was also feeling around and discovering she had healed almost as soon as she had been sliced in half. She looked up at me with an expression that bordered on one of fear.

We stared at each other, lost, and at a loss for words.

"What?" Minmontu whispered up from the ground.

"No," he added. "It's not possible. It isn't possible!"

Minmontu frantically whipped his head back and forth to me and Bayla, seemingly as confused as we were.

"Not just one… but both of you?" He posed rhetorically. "I saw it! I saw the water cut into you both. I saw the Nile kill you!"

My mind felt thickened by thoughts made of varying sizes of sand that shifted and rattled around inside my head. I didn't know if I should still be in fear of Minmontu or if I should be afraid of myself. Afraid of what had happened to me, to Bayla, to us. Fear didn't even register in my mind. Fear, hostility, strategy, all evacuated from my mind. All I could keep repeating to myself as I stared ahead to Bayla was, *we should be dead*. I tried to say it out loud.

"We should be dead," I uttered, surprising myself at having regained my ability to speak.

Minmontu swallowed and measured his next words carefully.

"You should be!" Minmontu gasped, slowly crawling up from his hands and knees. "You both just weathered the full wrath of the Nile and laughed at her will. This is not possible!"

"Don't take another step, Minmontu," I threatened as reality slowly worked itself back into my thoughts. We could figure out what happened to us later. For now, Bayla and I still had a job to do. Bayla spun her axes and crashed them together in a fantastic display of rippling light as I flipped my club end over end. After reaching down and reclaiming my nearby dagger, we marched towards Minmontu at the speed of a funeral dirge.

"For my parents. For my sister," Bayla began with a raspy hate. "For my entire village. For all those you've slaughtered and stolen magic from..."

Though Minmontu previously outmatched us in every way, he cowered like a weakling before us after surviving his lethal barrage.

"For the conflict you seek to perpetuate. For the peace of a united Egypt you seek to prevent," I added, "you must die."

Minmontu's eyes grew wider and wetter as we approached. His hands shook with increasing violence as his end neared. But as we finished our statements, the fear on his face drooped and mixed with twitches of confusion.

"Wait! Slaughtered village? Stealing magic? Preventing unification? I have slaughtered no one! And I am loyal to Mentuhotep, and to a united Egypt! Please, stop!"

I stopped walking, but Bayla continued. As I raced to process Minmontu's comments, I almost didn't notice her. One of Bayla's axes rose into the air and stole my focus.

"Please!" Minmontu shouted. "You are being lied to! I am not—"

"Bayla!" I screamed. With her back to me, I saw her flinch and slide down off the balls of her feet. I ran over to her, grabbed her shoulders and squeezed them gently.

"Hold on," I whispered to her, before pointing my club at Minmontu's chin.

"What are you talking about?" I growled.

"I'm not..." he started, voice quivering.

"Come on!" Bayla roared. "You were just commanding the Nile a minute ago. Speak up!"

"And you survived that!" He said, gasping for air. "How?"

Bayla slowly looked back at me as if asking me the

same question. I could only shake my head.

"We..." Bayla began after swallowing and licking her lips. "We were given a gift," she said, looking to me again, struggling with how to continue.

"We helped protect a village," I added, clumsily recalling the events that Bayla and I hadn't spoken of since they happened.

"They invited us to stay and eat with them," I continued. "While we were there, we were given a drink, and were told that it would... preserve... extend our lives."

Minmontu's face changed little as I spoke, but the shock in his face shifted just enough to notice, from anxiety to wonder.

"I can't believe what I'm hearing..." Minmontu said. As if knowing what I was going to say next, he rolled and bent his legs up, holding his head and hands in his lap.

"When we woke the next morning, the entire village had disappeared," I said.

"Nomads?" Minmontu asked with a whisper.

"What?" I whispered back.

"Have you... not heard of the Nomads?" Minmontu asked, carefully pulling his head out of his hands.

Neither Bayla nor I spoke.

"The Nomads. The fabled keepers of the world's magic? They have no known origin, and no known destination. They are said to roam the world and bestow their gift of immortality upon those who they deem worthy. Those who they believe will protect the world's magic and respect it as the most powerful force in the world. Those who will forever guard the grace of magic against the arrogance of the Vikarans."

As Minmontu described this struggle, and relayed the story in which these groups exist, Bayla and I found ourselves locked in a blurry stare of disbelief.

"Do you expect me to believe that?" I asked with a scoff. "You're saying that I'm immortal?"

"How?" Bayla asked. "How can we... know for sure?"

"I would say surviving being cut in two is a fairly good way," Minmontu said.

Bayla's eyes glossed over as she seemed to stare through me in some distant disbelief.

"I have never knowingly encountered anyone," Minmontu said, his voice falling to a softer and steadier, more reverent tone, "much less two people, that were granted the gift. But in my studies, I have learned that those who are given immortality by the Nomads, are adorned with a scar. A marking of sorts. On their backs, apparently."

As Minmontu finished speaking, he looked up at us slowly in poorly-veiled anticipation.

Bayla wobbled where she stood, but quickly steadied herself and focused a refreshed look into my eyes. Neither of us made any additional movements, but when Bayla nodded at me, my impatience finally won over. With a massive step, I slid over behind Bayla and pulled her hood and collar away from her neck. I didn't have to pull far, and made a final attempt to stall yet another confirmation of what I was increasingly coming to believe.

"What does the mark look like?" I asked Minmontu while holding my eyes to Bayla's back.

"I, uh," Minmontu started, his voice shaking again. "I don't, um, remember the exact numbers, but I believe it's a ring made of numerous, separate circles, seemingly connected to each other with multiple lines."

I couldn't take my eyes off of the darkened and raised symbols on Bayla's back. They matched his description perfectly. My eyes stayed on them as if trying to contrive something different.

"Well?" Bayla snapped, more anxious than angry.

"What do you see?"

I let go of her clothes and stepped around to face her. Having no words, I could only nod with a face drooping in perplexity. My own vision blurred this time as I slowly turned my back to Bayla. I clawed at the bottom of my own shirt and jerked it up to my neck.

As Bayla gently glided her fingers across the middle of my upper back, a surprising and soothing shiver rippled over me, which almost counteracted the growing beat of alarm in my heart.

"Circles," Bayla uttered with a softness that matched her touch. "And lines."

After letting my shirt fall, I turned back to Bayla where we locked eyes in the most beautiful fear.

"I can't believe it," Minmontu said. "Surviving my harshest assault, and now, the mark of the Nomads? I've spent my whole life studying, believing, and practicing such things. Having my own experiences is one thing, but this is, something... new, for me."

"Why is it new?" Bayla asked, breaking out of her trance of astonishment. "What is the connection between these Nomads and your country's magic? Heka?"

"My dear, Bayla," Minmontu said. "Heka is Egypt's bastion of magic in this world. In this life. Just as Ariadne is a cornerstone of magic in the region of the world your people are from. In the magical teachings I have studied I have learned that the Nomads trusted their most sacred principles and powers to those purest of spirit and truest in intention. They graced the most powerful, able, and influential with their gifts and gave to each being a relic that is not only a symbol of that gift of knowledge, but a physical link between the god and the Nomads. As they traveled through creation, they knew that to uphold the foundations of life and of nature, they must impart their wisdom upon those who can uphold life's grace to all those within a realm. And as they bestowed their knowledge upon select representatives, so too did they create a mechanism for others to learn of this path, of this awareness. They created a way to bond with and share the burdens of these powerful beings. Only then can these select few challenge the Vikarans who live to seize these powers for their own gain."

Bayla's eyes were locked on Minmontu. Her lips were parted as if trying to ask a question she didn't know how to form.

"Minmontu," I began, on Bayla's behalf. "What are you talking about?"

Minmontu huffed, as if frustrated with my question despite what he had been trying to explain. He squared his sight on me and shot out an answer.

"The Nomads shared their magic with those who came to be known as the gods of the world and created a mechanism for a select few to interact with that magic and to protect it."

Bayla scoured the ground as she contemplated her own question.

"So, Heka and Ariadne are all guardians or protectors of the same magic? They understand and protect the same ideals?"

Minmontu's eyes floated throughout the sanctuary while considering the answer.

"Yes," he finally answered. "I believe so. Just as the Vikarans, who hail from a similar time and place, work to steal it and circumvent the will of the Nomads. They will stop at nothing to gain these powers. They will kill, steal, and lie to get these powers illegitimately."

Bayla knelt down to a knee and did her best to stare through him.

"Speaking of lies... Tell us what you meant earlier. What are these lies have we been told?" She asked, her lips and tongue sharply annunciating the impatience in each syllable.

"I have not killed anyone," he said. "And I do not resist reunification. I am the High Priest of Heka and I serve Mentuhotep II. I suspect it is our enemies who have lied to you, and have hired you to kill me."

"See?" I said to Bayla, disgusted. "Humans. Constant deception. Nothing but diversion and lies... all the time."

"I frankly don't care if you're not what they say you are," I said, looking back down to Minmontu. "I was paid to kill you, and..."

"Briz!" Bayla shouted as she grabbed my arm. "First, this is *our* job. And what makes you think we would get paid if this job was constructed from lies? They probably arranged it to look like he had something to do with my family just so I would go along with your lust for money!"

"I didn't want to take this job, Bayla, remember?"

I took advantage of her silence to press Minmontu.

"Who are these enemies of yours that you mentioned, hmm?"

Minmontu's eyes flickered back and forth between me and Bayla.

"In this world, my enemies are those loyal to Merikare, and those obedient to him. Those who would benefit from perpetual struggle and a divided Egypt."

Bayla looked away and shot out a huff of air.

"And what are their names?" She asked.

"Neferhotep," he blurted immediately. "Neferhotep, the charming scribe with many masters. He sees to the work dictated to him by Khety, Merikare's most formidable governor. They pursue riches, knowledge, and magic from around the world in an effort to maintain their ability to resist unification. It is they who destroy villages. They are the ones who slaughter."

Bayla's face was stiff and still.

"How do you know this?" She asked.

"I have been approached many times by Neferhotep and others, threatening me with increasing violence upon the people of Egypt if I refused to assist them. I have been trying to beseech Heka to reveal a way to defeat them and remove their plague upon our people before it comes to that."

"Perhaps..." Minmontu continued before his thought was fully formed. His head whipped up and locked onto us with wide eyes.

"Perhaps both of you are that revelation!"

"How can we—" Bayla attempted.

"As Khety and Neferhotep have sought to increase their influence, the priests, priestesses and I have sought numerous times to gain access to Heka's relic to secure it, relocate it, and keep it safe. Twice our priests have performed what we have learned to be the ritual needed to gain access to Heka's relic. But each attempt has been a failure. Each priest has been killed during the attempt. We had previously concluded that harnessing the relic is impossible because it can only achieved by surviving death!"

Bayla and I looked at each other with heads weighted with dread.

"I don't think we—" I started.

"You're immortal!" Minmontu began. He raced over and grappled at my sleeve with eyes strained in desperation. He let go and slid over to Bayla as he continued his plea.

"Please! You've seen that you can survive death! You can perform the ritual and keep the magic of Heka safe!"

"Bayla," I said calmly while turning to face her straight

on. "This is not a good idea," I said, leaning in. "We've gone from taking a bounty for a priest—sorry Minmontu—to not killing him, to wanting to take on powerful aristocrats, governors, would-be kings, and now the lethal magic of a god?"

I rapidly shook my head while searching for what to say next in case my point hadn't been made.

"We can't do this. This is beyond us," I added.

"Please," Minmontu begged. "If we are to try, we must try before the day's first ray of sun!"

"What?" I said, aggravated. "Why?"

"Because he can only be summoned during dawn's glow," Minmontu explained.

I spun to Bayla, preparing to blurt another objection, but only saw her back as she marched to the alter.

"We survived Minmontu's attack, Bayla," I admonished. "But you might not survive whatever a god can do!"

"Briz, if I can keep these people from raiding any other villages, I'm going to."

With a whirl of my arms, I shrugged impatiently at Minmontu, pleading for him to do or say something to keep Bayla from going through with it. But with a growing smile, he instead only watched her approach Heka's shrine.

"What do I need to do, Minmontu? Something with the shrine?" Bayla shouted over her shoulder.

"Yes!" He yelled. He finally looked at me with a face elongated with elation, turned, and ran up behind her.

"Wait!" I said as Minmontu sprinted over. "What happens? How does this work?"

"She must recite a prayer to summon Heka and demand the relic!" He rushed to say as he ran.

As Minmontu slid into place behind Bayla, he lightly latched onto her and craned his head over her shoulder while approaching the shrine.

With an undefined worry itching at me, I kept a steady eye on the shrine and inched over to Bayla. Minmontu whipped a pointing finger about to various symbols on the shrine while instructing Bayla where to stand and what to say.

"You must kneel here, on one of these depictions in front of the shrine," I heard him say while pointing. "As long as you are on one of these symbols for Heka, his grandfather Atum, his father Khnum, or his mother Neith."

Bayla jumped over to one of the depictions on the floor and fell to her knees. Minmontu knelt behind her.

"Say the words after me," Minmontu commanded. "Heka will only attack you since you are the only ones on the symbols."

"Bayla!" I shouted. "We can take care of them without having to do this! Don't summon him! We don't know what will happen!"

"We don't know what powers they have!" She yelled back, leaning away and then back to Minmontu. "We need Heka's help!"

Minmontu continued leaning in, hovering over Bayla's shoulders as he shared his instructions. I could only hear the words when Bayla repeated them.

"Great Heka, Great Son of Khnum and Neith, stir upon the Nun and wake Atum's pristine power. Reveal to me your glory. Reveal to me your terror. Test me how you will and determine if I am worthy."

As Bayla recited the prayer, the shrine to Heka started to glow. Appearing as though the sun was contained inside, the shrine began to split and crack along superficial seams, spilling and shooting a light much darker than where it originated from at the shrine. Though the light source raced along the shrine erratically, there was no damage being done. Before I could even surmise that the prayer had been completed, Minmontu shoved himself backwards, up to his feet and away from Bayla.

I noticed the prayer was complete not only when Minmontu had flung himself back, but also when the shrine began to glow. Inside the shrine's cavity where the statue of Heka resided, a nebulous ball of smoky light grew and pulsed about. After looking to Minmontu, wringing his hands, he nodded at me. I turned back to the shrine and looked at Bayla, kneeling, by herself, waiting.

Without knowing what to do, what to say, or what would happen, I shot off towards the shrine, and slid down to my knees next to her.

"You don't need to be here!" She yelled. The increasing scrapes of wind and rock coming from the shrine made us strain to hear each other. "I *need* to do this!" She added. "I have to make sure they're defeated!"

The statue of Heka had been enveloped by the nebulous mass of energy. A primordial groan crept out from the shrine and clawed at my attention. But not enough to silence my response.

"I told you," I said with a composure formed from my dense dread. "I'm in this with you."

While staring at the shrine, I saw Bayla turn to me, but then joined me in looking ahead. The otherworldly veins of light raced along both new and existing paths in the sacred structure. The crunching and tearing of sound roared while the gaseous void filled the final inch of its interior. As I registered the thought that I wanted to cover my ears, the sound stopped. The light receded and the smoke in the shrine condensed into nothing, revealing the previous statue of Heka. Everything appeared as it had moments before.

I turned my head to ask Minmontu what had

happened, but new activity in the shrine stopped me.

"Briz..." Bayla said with a fraction of a breath.

My eyes focused back on the shrine and after squinting and inspecting it, I watched as the eyes of the Heka statue blinked. The statue blinked again and took a step forward. With its next step, the statue of Heka stepped down and out of the shrine. By the time it had brought its other foot down to the floor, it had grown dozens of feet in height and shed its outward, golden appearance for what I could only assume was that of the flesh and bone of the deity, Heka.

He finished growing in seconds. His skin, features, and clothes took their colors and forms just as quickly. Standing only a few feet from us, Heka's gigantic form loomed over us as he examined the room. Upon recognizing his location, he slowly looked down, and along with his enormous shadow, cast his menacing gaze down onto us.

Chapter Seventeen - Relics

Briz and Bayla

Briz and Bayla each took turns shuffling on their knees and cut glances of panic back to Minmontu.

"What now?" Bayla shouted at the priest.

Briz leaned over and grabbed for Bayla, but fell back onto his hands. With his eyes locked on Heka, he tried again.

"Minmontu?" He barked, successfully taking hold of Bayla's arms the second time. Together, they scampered up to their feet and crept away from Heka. "What happens now?"

"This is when…" Minmontu began, his voice shaking. "This is when he… strikes you down. May Osiris spare you!"

The towering deity peered down onto them, rolling his head slowly from Bayla, and then to Briz.

"Three times have I recently been beckoned to this world," Heka said. Though the god spoke softly, the resonance of his incredible bass and expansive sound crashed along the walls and thumped their ears.

"And this," Heka added, forming a sickening smile, "will be the third time I dispatch those who summoned me!"

Heka launched out his arms, one towards each side of the chamber and grasped at figures drawn into the walls. As he reached, the figures resembling Heka rippled with the energy that had previously encompassed the shrine. After a flash of sparks monetarily blanketed the figures, each one ruptured out of the wall and jumped down to the floor. As the smaller versions of the god marched towards Briz and Bayla, Heka announced their mission.

"Just as I have devoured my siblings of lesser dominion, and those who summoned me, so too will I devour you."

Briz and Bayla shuffled aimlessly on their feet and looked back to Minmontu. The priest could only offer helpless stares of wide eyes and swallows of fear as the two bounty hunters crept closer to each other and grabbed on to each other.

"Oh, Bayla..." Briz said with a small laugh rooted in fear. "I really hope we can't die."

"Mmm, me too," Bayla replied with no reciprocation of humor. "I'd prefer not to know what it is to be eaten by a god."

"Quiet!" Heka roared. "Be still! Be silent, and prepare to meet your end however you will. But your end has come!"

As Heka screamed at his impending meal, his two identical minions marched at Briz and Bayla, quickening their pace with each step before tearing off at a full sprint and launching into the air at the two. The minions' mouths stretched open to a grotesque size, threatening with each inch to tear apart at their contorted mouths' seams.

The two beasts flew through the air, poised and ready

to fall onto Briz and Bayla and consume them. As they reached their apex, Heka erupted into laughter.

"Feast!" He bellowed. "Feast upon them!"

The entities fell onto Briz and Bayla, sinking the abyss of their massive mouths upon them. But when they should have disappeared into the mouths and bellies of the abominations, the entities sank into the floor instead, revealing Briz and Bayla still standing, alive and unharmed.

Heka seethed and flexed as his body swelled in size and closed the remaining gap between himself and the ceiling. As Heka's body grew his eyes rolled back and were supplanted by orbs of similar shades of dull light as before. His skin cracked with small rivers of energy as the shrine had when he was summoned.

"What?" He erupted angrily. "You cannot survive my will! Nothing can withstand my wrath!"

"It... It is true, L-Lord Heka," Minmontu stuttered. Through nervous panting and swallows, Minmontu exchanged glances between the anxious Briz and Bayla, and Heka.

"They have survived your onslaught," Minmontu continued. He shuffled nearer to Briz and Bayla though held his eyes up to Heka as he walked. "They have survived. But it was not out of disrespect, or due to a superior power, for none is more powerful than yours."

Heka's furious chest heaved. As Minmontu continued his plea, Heka's eyes and cracked skin pulsed with the heartbeat of his primordial fury.

"They have been blessed, Great Heka. They have been granted an eternal life. The gift of the Nomads. They have been charged to protect the great magic of the world. They have come here to help your humble priest protect you, and protect your relic."

Briz and Bayla nervously danced their eyes between each other, Minmontu, and Heka. In the awkward silence, Bayla slowly spun and turned her back to Heka. As she did, she wriggled out of her outer shirt, allowing her dipping undershirt to reveal her marking of the Nomads. Briz followed, pulling his shirt up around his neck.

Heka inhaled a massive breath as the two revealed their markings and let it out slowly as if silently shifting his mood.

"Yes. Only those acknowledged by the Nomads can survive summoning me," Heka said. His voice rolled through the room with an ominous authority. "Only those chosen by my kindred will I spare. Only those who seek to serve the roots of this world will I grant access to my relic."

As Heka finished speaking, he turned slightly, holding a hand out towards his shrine. It flashed with another wave of light and as the amber energy subsided, Heka's relic rested in place of his statue.

"There it is!" Minmontu whispered in delighted exasperation. "Heka's relic! The idea that I would ever see it had long left me!"

Though momentarily caught in a trance of awe, he finally turned his attention to Briz and Bayla. As he did, Heka's form slowly gave way from its massive physical presence to a translucent shade of itself as it constricted and reduced into a twirling cone of light, receding finally into the relic."

"Go!" Minmontu directed. "Heka has revealed his relic! It is yours to claim!"

Briz and Bayla turned to one another, still in reverent shock, but before either made a move a new voice thundered from behind them.

"No, I'm afraid. It is not!" Khety boomed.

As Minmontu, Briz, and Bayla turned to face the startling speaker, they were met by Khety, adorned in a headdress, necklaces, and clothes colored by most of the rainbow which fell atop extravagant leather armor. His hand was outstretched, palm open and aflame with the bright blue glow of another relic. Next to him stood Neferhotep dressed in less flamboyant clothing, but wearing the most garish of grins.

Behind Khety and Neferhotep—only partially visible in the shadow of the tall entryway—was the beautiful horror of the imposing Ariadne.

"No!" Bayla shrieked. Her voice ripped through the chamber with the combined power of ultimate mourning and maximum hate.

Khety laughed through ripples of condescension.

"Yes, actually," he said. "We discovered Ariadne's relic only a few days after we searched your village. It was unfortunate that your village could not be spared, but it was necessary. We knew it was somewhere in the Aegean."

"Searched?" Bayla screamed, salivating with murderous intent. "Searched? You call devastating an entire village and its population a search? How dare you! How dare you destroy my people and use our Ariadne. How dare you use her like this! We will not allow it. You will not leave here with Ariadne's relic, and you will not have Heka's!"

Neferhotep and Khety cut each other quick glances of contempt.

"We shall see," Neferhotep said.

In the pinch of silence that followed, one might have heard the bristling flow of the Nile, even from deep within the confines of the temple's inner sanctuary. But it passed quickly, giving way to a flurry of action.

"Get the relic!" Bayla shouted at Briz.

Bayla launched out towards Khety and smacked her axes together three times, pouring a dome of protection over Minmontu, Briz, and herself. As the domes unfurled over them, Briz dug his heels in and sprinted for the shrine and Heka's relic. Minmontu slowly walked backwards, bringing himself closer to a side wall and scanned the room.

Before Briz or Bayla could race more than five steps in any direction, Ariadne stepped over Khety and Neferhotep and into the chamber. With a face weighted in despair and concentration as those wielding her relic controlled her, Ariadne shoved one of her hands at Bayla and summoned a line of identical copies of Bayla ahead of her. With her path to Khety blocked, she slid to a stop and took in the group of her cloned opponents ahead of her. Each copy stood slightly taller than Bayla and with an exaggerated face stretched in twisted wrath, they squared their stance. Through eyes bloodshot with conjured rage, they stared at Bayla and prepared to take on their natural counterpart. But the sinister specters took only a moment and flew across the room before pouring upon Bayla's defensive barrier.

Immediately after Ariadne whipped her hand and created Bayla's diversion, she scooped her other arm up in Briz' direction. As her arm dipped and curved upwards it began to grow dark brown in color and quickly took on the semblance of bark. Ivy, moss, branches and leaves rapidly sprouted from it, and as her arm transformed, a structure began to take shape up and around Briz.

Reaching up through the floor of the temple, confusing walls of vines and thorns lurched towards the ceiling and encompassed Briz in an overgrown labyrinth. Though no one else in the room saw the maddening complex spring to life, it was very real to Briz's eyes and mind. He instantly began swinging at the vegetation with his club and dagger.

"Bayla!" He shouted. "She's trapping me! Bayla!"

Bayla couldn't immediately respond. Though her dome was protecting her, it wouldn't hold up indefinitely. One by one she tapped her axes allowing a portion of the dome to weaken enough to let one of her cloned attackers sink through. If she didn't take care of them fast enough, individually, the dome would fall under the prolonged strain on her focus and allow the entire mob to attack.

After letting loose a guffaw dripping in delight, Khety shouted to Minmontu.

"Oh, and don't think we've forgotten about you, priest!" He shouted, before curling his fingers up around the relic hovering above his palm. "Ariadne! Surely you have something for him as well?"

Without saying a word, Ariadne turned towards Minmontu and reached up, plucking a strand of her hair. As she pulled it away, it grew exponentially, with one end falling to the floor in a jumble of lengthy coils. Ariadne then threw the other end at Minmontu to bind him.

With all of Khety's potential resistance occupied, he leaned to Neferhotep with a demented observation.

"Ah!" He said, laughing. "How ironic."

"Hmm?" Neferhotep asked casually.

"The High Priest of Heka being mummified alive... by Ariadne's thread."

As the two conspiring men laughed at their mutual entertainment, Ariadne's thread viciously encircled Minmontu, trapping his legs and arms tightly to his body before he could move or make gestures to invoke any magic. But Ariadne's thread had not yet reached his mouth. Before it did, Minmontu looked up and back to the floor, searching frantically. Just as he spotted what he was looking for, his constricted limbs caused him to lose his balance. Though his wrap was accumulating rapidly, he struggled against it to roll slowly to his intended destination between matching symbols on the ceiling and the floor.

The Eye of Ra.

While he still could, he rushed through a prayer.

"Blessed Hathor, wrath of Ra, ignite me but protect me. Spread through me a fire. Burn that which confines your allies. Free us to protect Heka from those who desecrate this temple."

As Minmontu uttered the last syllable of his prayer, a column of fire exploded down from the ceiling to the floor between the two symbols, engulfing him. His wrappings were instantly incinerated, and though enveloped from head to toe in flames, Minmontu calmly came to his feet.

Ariadne spun to react, but Minmontu—imbued with the power of Ra—pulled down with his fists and shot out his arms unleashing an ocean of flame that washed across Briz's labyrinth and Bayla's clones, reducing them all to ash.

"Run! Take it!" Minmontu screamed at Briz.

Freshly released from his prison of vegetation, Briz took only enough time to blink and tore off once more for the shrine. Bayla resumed her slow, plotting plod towards Khety and Neferhotep who in turn had Ariadne focus on the priest who had undone her work.

The Cretan goddess took a step towards Minmontu who was still temporarily endowed with the power of the Eye of Ra and planted her feet. She stared at him still rumbling in flame and searched the room. After spotting the symbols for grape arbors and wine along the walls, a grin crept onto her face.

She walked over to Minmontu and picked him up,

squeezing the priest and his borrowed flame tightly in her hand. She then leaned over and from deep within her, began to pour from her mouth a massive river of wine onto him. The priest's flame of the Eye of Ra was extinguished by the goddess of wine. And as the wine poured down upon Minmontu, so too were his breath and life extinguished. Ariadne closed her mouth and stared down to Minmontu's lifeless husk to confirm her prey was dead before tossing him to the ground.

"Bayla!" Briz shouted.

Minmontu's fiery assault and freeing of Briz and Bayla had distracted Ariadne. As Ariadne focused on killing Minmontu, Briz had leapt to the shrine and snatched the relic before running back to engage Khety.

"Here!" Briz yelled as he ran by, tossing Heka's relic to her.

Bayla stopped her march towards Neferhotep and Khety to lunge at the relic. She caught it and looked up in fright as Ariadne turned her focus to her.

"Get Heka out here to deal with Ariadne!"

Briz finished yelling just as he met Neferhotep's sword. While Khety continued his focus on controlling Ariadne, Briz exchanged glancing scrapes and devastating smacks of club and dagger upon sword.

Bayla's vision blurred as she waded through her mind's scrambled panic. With wild disorientation she looked up to Ariadne, over to Minmontu's corpse, and then to Briz, Khety, and Neferhotep. She had no thoughts, at least nothing she could focus on. Her eyes fixated on the relic in Khety's hand as he controlled Ariadne, but together with the desire not to do harm to the goddess of her people's own region, she couldn't concentrate enough to conceive an idea on how to summon Heka.

But an unexpected jolt of clarity finally punctured its way into her thoughts. Her region's magic, rooted in providing for and protecting others first, set her thoughts on a path of realization that surged through her in a rolling wave of relief. She clutched onto Heka's relic and closed her eyes.

Her father floated into her mind's eye as he sat across from her at their dinner table. The salted breeze from the Aegean blew in and curled a corner up of her papyrus.

Never forget, Bayla, the memory of her father said. *Your greatest powers will only ever be realized when you act for others.*

Her eyes shot open in epiphany as Ariadne's shadow grew closer.

"Heka, great master of magic,
With your relic in hand, I ask that you appear.
Help me free your sister in magic,
And protect your people from Khety."

Bayla opened her eyes and flinched at the sight of Ariadne looming over her. The goddess reached back and prepared to strike.

"Ariadne, please!" Bayla implored.

Just as Ariadne prepared to swing her arm down in a lethal swipe at Bayla, a massive ball of fire slammed into Ariadne's face. She angrily brushed away the ash and bits of ember and turned to see Heka—successfully summoned by Bayla.

As Ariadne pivoted and turned her attention to Heka, Bayla huffed out a teary gasp and choked down the rush of relief before confirming her grip on her axes. Her face tightened with hateful anticipation as she finished stomping her bloodthirsty march. Just as she prepared to launch an axe at Neferhotep, Briz beat her to a killing blow and slammed his club into the side of his head. Instead of flinging the axe at Neferhotep, she instead threw it at Khety's hand. Her axe struck his wrist, disrupting his hold over Ariadne's relic and sent it spinning across the floor. Khety could only stand sheepishly like an impotent dotard, clutching at his wounded wrist as Briz and Bayla closed in. Briz paused, letting Bayla approach first.

"He's all yours," Briz said as he looked back to confirm Neferhotep's demise.

"My family is here with me, Khety," she said darkly. "They will know that they have been avenged, and that you will not kill again."

Khety trembled, still holding his wounded arm, but looked up at Bayla with the intensity of an eternity. His eyes cycled between squinting and stretching as if documenting the moment for all time. With an eerie determination, his breathing relaxed, and his arms slowly fell to his side.

"I might be ended today," Khety said in tranquil darkness. "But the Vikarans will persist. They will outlast the Nomads."

Bayla's mind spun into a frantic tempest, confused by his statement, and horrified by the implication. But before she could question him further, Khety jerked his good arm up to the sleeve of the wounded arm and produced a dagger of his own before plunging it into his stomach. He pitched forward, gasping in choppy breaths as he twisted the blade. Bayla lunged at him in desperation for more information, but it was too late. He smiled through quivering lips, but his satisfaction faded with his life as he slumped to the ground. Bayla looked up helplessly to Briz.

"Did you hear him?" She asked. "What did he mean?"

At a loss for understanding, Briz could only shake his head. Bayla grew short of breath as she stared down at the governor's corpse, growing cold and hollow in the burgeoning fear of the unknown. But once again, her focus was stolen.

In a metallic rip of sound, a cascading series of painful hisses filled the chamber. Briz and Bayla turned to see Ariadne holding two monstrous serpents—each the size of the tallest statues in Memphis—one in each hand. With a violent spin Ariadne used her momentum to hurl the snakes at Heka. As he caught them and squeezed their gargantuan necks while they coiled around his, Briz whipped around to locate Ariadne's relic before diving for it. He slid over to it and swiped it up.

"Bayla!"

She turned as he shouted and caught the thrown relic. Together with Heka's relic, and now Ariadne's, Bayla looked to the two combating gods and commanded them with a shout that seemed embellished from powers beyond her own.

"Stop!"

Both Ariadne and Heka ceased their last movements and settled into a quiet posture of repose. The flames and light about Heka's skin snuffed themselves out. The orbs of light in his head rolled forward, returning to the appearance of human eyes. Ariadne's enormous serpents, wrapped around Heka's neck as they tried to suffocate him, slowly faded into nothingness.

The chamber was quiet. The two gods were still. Bayla turned to Briz as both relics roared with power in her hands.

* * *

The aftermath of the events in the temple brought more questions than answers. Though they had defeated Khety and Neferhotep, and secured the relics for Heka and

Ariadne, their contemplations of what else may be in peril created in Briz and Bayla a nagging pang of urgency they didn't know how to immediately satiate.

In the days following the fight, they worked to recede into the dark and disappear from the public eye until they could determine how Khety's, Neferhotep's, and Minmontu's deaths would be received. Luckily, the losses of Khety and Neferhotep were celebrated, while Minmontu was mourned. Though it took time, Briz and Bayla eventually secured meetings with the surviving priests and priestesses from the temple of Heka to reveal their experiences, but also gleaned additional information from the servants of the temple on the enigmatic statements made by Khety about the Vikarans.

A unification feast was prepared in the subsequent months and the priests of Heka made sure to invite Briz and Bayla. They reluctantly agreed to attend, though they kept their distance. Just before leaving, a priest spotted them.

"I don't believe anyone here knows how much of this they owe to you," the priest said.

Bayla smiled and tilted her head innocently.

"And that's fine with us," Briz said.

The three gazed out quietly across the crowd.

"Is it true?" The priest asked.

Briz and Bayla shared a neutral glance.

"Hmm?" Bayla hummed. "Is what true?" She asked the priest.

He cleared his throat and rolled his tongue across his lips.

"Your, um, condition," he clarified.

"Oh, that," she said.

The priest waited for her to elaborate, but nothing

else was said. He turned and considered Bayla's face, but looked over the crowd as everyone roared with applause. Mentuhotep II had arrived.

With his detractors severely weakened due to Briz's and Bayla's anonymous involvement, Mentuhotep II finished consolidating his authority over the remaining seats of resistance, as well as the pools of forces loyal to Merikare and his successor. Despite Briz and Bayla helping to bring peace to generations of families in a unified Egypt, the singular nation would still suffer from cyclic rises and falls. And there would be some, who would witness them all.

Epilogue

Rome's streets were empty.

Briz and Bayla had lingered and allowed too much time to pass. The triumph had already ascended up to Capitoline Hill and neared the Temple of Jupiter Optimus Maximus. Their original intention was to approach it while mixed in with the city's thick throng who were ravished by wine and celebration—when they were too ravished to pay attention.

It was too late for that, but it didn't matter. They planned ahead.

The two bounty hunters jogged along the edges of the streets, ducking behind carts and sneaking into doorways. Pausing to look and listen, they ran along silently, anticipating each other's hesitance or confidence. Their combined movements were innate. They were instilled. They had been ingrained after some two thousand years together.

After a slow but steady climb up the hill, the two ancient friends caught up with the outermost bands of the crowd.

Bayla dashed across the street and together with Briz,

slipped into a bakery just off the cobblestone path.

They swept the room, looking behind counters and cupboards to confirm the shop was empty. Once they knew they were alone, Briz shot over to the only untied sack. He stabbed his hand into the exposed flour and after sifting and squirming his hand about, came up with a palm sized stone. On it was a word scribbled in Latin.

Clibanus.

Oven, Briz said to himself.

Briz snapped and pointed to the oven, beckoning Bayla away from the window she was guarding. As she ran over, Briz stuck his arm in the cold bread oven and rummaged around before quickly coming out with a helmet. In his arm went again and again, interspersed with Bayla reaching in. Within minutes, they retrieved and changed into two official sets of armor of the Praetorian Guard.

From then on, their plan was to hide in plain sight. They would hide in plain sight in disguises that should not gather any challenge from anyone, including the consuls.

With perfectly matched steps and properly positioned lances and shields, Briz and Bayla marched along and eventually crested the Capitoline Hill. Having reached the rear of the thickest part of the crowd, their plan had changed from infiltrating the crowd, to avoiding it as long as possible. Still maintaining their form, they walked along the perimeter of the crowd, and made the final march up to the Temple of Jupiter.

While walking past groupings of loitering infantry, drunken centurions, and legitimate praetorian guards laughing between themselves, the two bounty hunters maintained their disposition and marched straight through to the temple. After reaching the front of the mob, they breached the crowd and weaved through to the front.

Briz forced a cough to clear his throat. Bayla shifted

her helmet and confirmed her sights on the gathered senators ahead.

One of them bellowed to the crowd.

"All hail the saviors of Rome! All hail the Vikarans!"

Acknowledgments

We often hear about those who spark initial inspiration, those who drive us to do something. Create something. The people who first send us off on that adventure or quest to improve ourselves are the people that get thanked frequently. But rarely are those who *sustain* that passion called out and appreciated. They're sometimes different people entirely from those who first put that sparkle of an idea in our eye. The people who sustain me, refresh my motivation, and drive me to keep going when most other inclinations say otherwise, are the ones I want to acknowledge.

The TT. Your endless wisdom, camaraderie, motivation, and experience are priceless. I learn something from you daily.

The Self-Published Fantasy Blog Off community. From Mark Lawrence, to every blogger, fellow author, reader, follower, and podcast producer, the community I've been exposed to because of the contest is one of the most fulfilling and rewarding communities I've ever been a part of. You help add a bit of excitement and passion to everything I write.

Thank you for reading *Briz and Bayla: The Bronze Age Bounty Hunters*!

I hope you enjoyed it!

Stay tuned for book two!

Visit jeramygoble.com to sign up for my newsletter and receive free short stories and news on upcoming projects.